BY THE SAME AUTHOR
ALL PUBLISHED BY HOUSE OF STRATUS

JOHN HARRIS

THE UNFORGIVING WIND

HOUSE OF
STRATUS

This edition published in 2001 by House of Stratus, an imprint of
Stratus Holdings plc, 24c Old Burlington Street, London, W1X 1RL, UK.

www.houseofstratus.com

Typeset, printed and bound by House of Stratus.

A catalogue record for this book is available from the British Library.

ISBN 0-7551-0227-4

Katabatic winds...may have no relation to the distribution of atmospheric pressure... these winds can be violent...and up to storm force locally.

Meteorology for Mariners.

Author's Note

While I have drawn on expedition diaries for facts, *The Unforgiving Wind* remains a work of fiction and all the people and the scientific organisations in it are fictional.

J H

PART ONE

Disaster

There were eight of them, standing in a loose semicircle on the turned rocky earth that fringed the grave – eight men in ill-fitting clothes, their bodies leaning against the keening wind that came down through the snow-covered peaks round Prins Haakon Sø. Behind them, the high ridges of black volcanic rock, capped with their everlasting mantle of ice, screened the watery sun from the sullen valley in which they stood.

'Man that is born of woman hath but a short time to live and is full of misery – ' The words came in a muttered monotone from the tall spectacled man standing in the centre of the group, slightly hurried, and mumbled in a faintly embarrassed fashion, as though he were unused to prayer. 'He cometh up and is cut down, like a flower – '

As he intoned the sombre phrases, reading from a battered prayer book that he held in a bandaged right hand, the worried gaze of the men around him absorbed the majestic Greenland peaks beyond the valley, patchy on the lower slopes in red and grey where they had been swept bare by the everlasting winds that fretted the east coast. Beyond them was the fringe of the ice cap, a vast frozen carapace that covered the entire continent, two thousand miles long and a thousand miles wide, devoid of life or vegetation; an endless icy plain stretching from the Arctic Ocean to the North Atlantic and unrelenting even in the summer except in coastal valleys such as this.

To one side, in a fold of ground beyond the grave, there was a restless flicker of movement from where the dog teams squatted near the splash of yellow that marked the cab of a Weasel. Behind them, three small tents had been erected, dark and lost-looking against the sombre background, their outlines broken by a pile of equipment, some of it charred, that seemed insignificantly small against the vastness of the landscape.

Beyond, forgotten, like the blackened bones of a dead monster, were the charred timbers which had been their hut until the merciless winds always pouring like vast invisible waterfalls off the ice cap down to the sea had built up the night before into a screaming gale that had whipped a small spark into a roaring conflagration and left them devoid of shelter and dangerously short of food; mere flyspecks of humanity in the gloomy grandeur that surrounded the frozen lake which stretched away into the distance in a wilderness of new ice, grey-white in the gloom.

'Forasmuch as it hath pleased the Almighty God of His great mercy' – Legge-Jenkins' voice rose a little, as though he were summoning their wandering thoughts back to the task in hand – 'to take unto Himself the soul of our brother here departed, we therefore commit his body to the ground, earth to earth, ashes to ashes, dust to dust – '

One of the group bent abruptly and, picking up a handful of the stony soil, threw it into the grave between them; then, self-consciously, as Legge-Jenkins went on reading, the others stooped and did the same, stepping forward one by one until the blanket-wrapped bundle in the shallow hole scooped from the stony ground was sprinkled with dirt. Then Legge-Jenkins paused and tucked the prayer book under his injured arm, and taking off his glasses, he polished them clumsily and stared round him at the others with pale uncertain eyes.

'I don't propose going through the whole service,' he said. 'I don't think he'd have wished it and somehow, without all the trappings, it doesn't seem quite right. I think we'll just say the Lord's Prayer together now and leave it at that. Don't you agree?'

Someone nodded and he paused again, then the others joined in with him, and the prayer they spoke came in a mumble, lost on the rising wind which whipped the scattered patches of snow on the broken ground into little feathers of white that blew with irritating persistence into their faces.

When they had finished, two of the men picked up shovels and began to scrape the piled earth and stones into the shallow grave, and a third began to erect at the head of it a cross made out of the charred plankings of the burnt-out hut.

He looked round at Legge-Jenkins who was still standing a little alone, his face sombre.

'What shall I put on it?'

'Just his name and rank. That'll do. Then we'll put up a cairn so it can be seen.'

The man with the cross nodded and with a pencil scratched a few words on the planking before sticking it in the ground.

'Edward Hyams Adams,' he said, reading what he had written. 'Lieutenant-Commander, Royal Navy.'

'Better put the date and his age on it,' Legge-Jenkins suggested nervously.

'And RIP or something?'

'I suppose so.'

When the cross was in position, they began collecting stones and piling them round the upright until the heap rose almost to the cross-member, then Legge-Jenkins nodded and they all stood back, straightening their shoulders as though they ached.

'That ought to do.'

They stood for a moment longer, staring at the grave with thoughtful faces, then almost as though someone had given a command, they turned away together and began to walk down the sloping ground to where the tents flapped dismally in the rising wind.

In the valley below the grave, they gathered together again, all of them still thoughtful, their movements slow, as though their minds were full of foreboding, and stood gazing back uneasily towards the cross that rose starkly on its little ridge of ground, sombre and lonely looking against the empty sky.

Above their heads, the low clouds were ragged wisps driving before the wind that brought the freezing air down from the north, bouncing it off the slopes of Mount Priam which stood in the way of their view to the south, black and forbidding, and obscuring the distance as though it were an obstacle in the way of help.

After a while, as though the sight of the new grave depressed them, they began to turn their backs on it and stood in a ragged line near the tents, staring at the collapsed piles of charred timbers. Among them they could see the metal frame of the petrol generator that had supplied their light and power and the teetering chimney of the stove which had given them warmth, the remains of the electricity panel with its hanging wires and the melted front of the radio transmitter. On the rocky ground in a wide circle round them were charred and useless blankets, fragments of clothing, scorched books and crumpled letters, and scraps of equipment that had been flung anyhow among the ruined cases of food as they had scrambled to safety from the blaze.

The scattered articles stretched in a long line down the valley, with here and there a fragment of clothing plastered wetly against a rock or a torn tent flung like a discarded dishrag among the smooth, weather-worn boulders that littered the ground boxes, planks, cooking utensils, all flung aside by the violence of the gale that had swept the blaze through the hut and snatched up everything they had tried to save.

One of the men, a tall thin individual, with pale eyes that were still red-rimmed with the smoke, kicked at a charred board on the ground with a bitter gesture and it skidded away from him clumsily.

'*International Geophysical Year*', it proclaimed in amateurish letters. '*British East-West Greenland Expedition.*'

Legge-Jenkins had painted it when they had first erected the hut, on their arrival, and had secured it enthusiastically over the doorway like an inn sign. For a moment, the tall man stared at it heavily, then he turned and gazed up at the radio mast that jabbed at the sky in a long antenna, curiously lost-looking without the hut alongside it to give it importance, his mind occupied with the problems which, overnight, had been flung at them, insoluble it seemed, but nevertheless demanding a solution, and an immediate one at that if they were to survive.

He was still staring up at the mast, a silver rod scraping at the underneath of the cheerless sky, when Legge-Jenkins appeared alongside him, holding a log book and a sheaf of notes, his glasses gleaming in the stormy light that came between the mountains, his thin scholar's face troubled, his bandaged hand held awkwardly against his body, as though he didn't know what to do with it.

'Where's Doctor Piercey?' he asked.

'Still in the tent. Fixing Ivey's burns.'

Legge-Jenkins nodded and glanced at the radio mast.

'Well?' he asked. 'What do you make of it, O'Day?'

The thin man shrugged. 'I thought I might get the spare Nineteen working,' he said, 'but' – he stopped and shrugged again – 'it's as bad as the other.'

'Can't *anything* be done, Sergeant? If we could only get off a message – '

Legge-Jenkins left the sentence unfinished and Sergeant O'Day shrugged again.

'The panel's cracked,' he said. 'The veins of the condensers are shot to hell. Twisted up like an old woman's guts.' He shrugged once more in a wild expansive gesture which flung his long arms outwards from his body and allowed them to slap back to his sides. There was something hopeless in the gesture that annoyed Legge-Jenkins.

'What about the set in the Seismic Weasel?' he asked sharply.

'It was out for maintenance,' O'Day said. 'It was in the hut with all the spares. '*Everything* was in the bloody hut!'

Legge-Jenkins stared at him for a second, his face stricken. 'Can't you put *something* together?' he asked.

'Not here. We've got no spares here. All the spares we've got now are in the dump Adams dropped near the Søster Nunataks when he was testing for dead areas.'

Legge-Jenkins frowned. 'I'd planned to move south at once,' he said uncertainly. 'We've got to get to Cape Alexandra. Those were the instructions in case of emergency. The barometer's falling and Pink says there are gales coming. And snow – '

'Already?'

Legge-Jenkins gestured with his bandaged hand at the frozen surface of the lake. 'Look,' he said, 'you can see for yourself. The temperature went down to 12 degrees last night.'

'I can't do anything on the move,' O'Day insisted.

Legge-Jenkins drew a deep breath, then he seemed to pull his parka closer about him, as though he felt the sudden onset of the cold.

'Haven't we any means *at all* of telling anybody what's happened?' he asked desperately.

'I might eventually make something out of the two Nineteens,' O'Day said. 'But it'll take time and I need spares. The Fifty-Three's had it. It wouldn't work even if we had a jenny.'

He shrugged again and Legge-Jenkins' voice became edgy with anxiety.

'For God's sake,' he said, his eyes flashing behind his glasses, 'stop shrugging and tell me something.'

O'Day sketched the beginning of another shrug then changed his mind.

'We haven't a set that works,' he said with the formality of a serviceman on his dignity.

'Not one?'

'Not one.'

'And you didn't get through?'

'I never got near the set.'

O'Day's blunt negatives seemed to shake Legge-Jenkins. 'We can't go to Cape Alexandra without radio,' he said in a low uneven voice. 'Aren't there any other spares *anywhere*?'

'Only at the Søsters. There's nothing here.'

Legge-Jenkins swallowed and his eyes flickered nervously about him.

'We'll have to go by the Søsters then,' he said quietly.

O'Day looked surprised. 'It's a long way,' he said. 'A hell of a long way.'

Legge-Jenkins turned on him angrily. 'There's no alternative,' he said sharply. 'We can't stay here. That's obvious.'

'But, Christ, the Søsters! That'll double the journey to Cape Alexandra.'

Legge-Jenkins stared at him.

'Can you suggest any other way of picking up your damned spares?' he asked irritably.

O'Day studied him for a moment with eyes that seemed suddenly cold and unfriendly, then he moved away without speaking to a windbreak he had erected out of a charred canvas sheet and squatted heavily underneath it among the ruins of his radios. Legge-Jenkins saw him flash another angry glance in his direction, then, as he dragged one of the damaged Nineteens towards him, Legge-Jenkins turned away, snubbed, and stared uneasily towards the north where the mountains seemed so ominously dark. O'Day watched him for a while, his long limbs twisted under him like a spider's, then he began to fiddle with the ruined transmitter, his face gaunt in the grey-green shadow.

Legge-Jenkins sighed and, squaring his shoulders, walked to the edge of the bluff where they had buried Adams. Pink, the meteorologist, slight and spectacled and terrier-like under his bulky clothes, had started to dismantle his instruments and was packing them into one of the few wooden containers that had escaped the blaze.

'How long have we got?' Legge-Jenkins asked, stopping alongside him.

Pink indicated the darkening sky on the flank of the mountains to the north. 'Not long,' he said laconically.

'What about inland?'

'Inland?' Pink's eyebrows shot up.

'We may have to go inland,' Legge-Jenkins explained. 'What's it going to be like there?'

Pink frowned. 'Same as always,' he said. 'Cold and windy. Why are we going inland?'

'Because we've no option,' Legge-Jenkins said angrily. 'We haven't a single damned radio spare left here.'

Pink gave him a sharp inquisitive glance, trying to assess his mood, then he bent abruptly over his packing cases again as though he had suddenly lost patience. Legge-Jenkins stared at his back for a second, his mouth working, before moving on to where the other men were gathering the few scraps of equipment they had managed to rescue and were placing them in piles near the sledges, watched with bright-eyed interest by the restless dogs. By the black and blistered framework of a burned-out Weasel, a blunt-faced youngster was poking among a small pile of spares he had salvaged, and he lifted his angry face as Legge-Jenkins stopped alongside him, his eyes snapping with rage, his cheeks and the backs of his hands puffy red where the flames had scorched his flesh.

'Can you make it go?' Legge-Jenkins asked.

'Go?' The blunt-faced man's voice was sharp and resentful as he gestured at the Weasel. 'Go?' he repeated. 'This?'

Legge-Jenkins stiffened at the implied rebuke. 'Come on, Hellyer,' he said with a sharpness that managed, somehow, still to sound uncertain. 'Don't beat about the bush.'

Hellyer stared at him for a second before he spoke. 'It was at the wrong end of the hut,' he said in a flat voice after a pause. 'Everything on it that would burn has burned.'

'Isn't it possible to do *anything*?' Legge-Jenkins' voice was growing thin and irritated with frustration.

Hellyer shook his head. 'The bearings have melted,' he said. 'They don't fit any more. It *would* have to be *this* one,' he ended bitterly, 'instead of Number Three. That bastard's been developing a knock for days.'

His face twisted suddenly with a bitter expression. 'We ought to have got it out before the blaze got to it,' he said loudly. 'And we might have done if it hadn't been for all that damn equipment he insisted on stacking in there. The arrangements were bad. If they hadn't been, Ivey wouldn't have been burned. *Or* Doree. *Or* you and me. But he wouldn't listen.'

'Commander Adams was in a hurry, Hellyer,' Legge-Jenkins said stiffly.

'He was always in a bloody hurry.'

'He had a job to do. So have I. So have you.'

'When I joined this show,' Hellyer said sharply, 'it was a geophysical affair, not a half-baked quasi-military outfit. That wasn't what I expected.'

'We all know your pacifist feelings, Hellyer.'

'I never agreed with those bloody secret weapons of Doree's.'

'They're *not* weapons,' Legge-Jenkins snapped furiously. 'They're meteorological rockets.'

'They're military equipment.'

Legge-Jenkins' face grew taut, almost like a schoolmaster dealing with a defiant pupil. 'So are the radios,' he said. 'So are the Weasels. So are the clothes on your back. Your argument doesn't carry much weight.'

Hellyer stared at him resentfully, then he seemed to get control of himself and he spoke more normally. 'I'll cannibalize it for spare parts,' he said. 'Tracks and suspension and so on.' He indicated the other two Weasels standing apart from the wreckage. 'They'll never stand up to a long journey without spares,' he said. 'They were too old when we got 'em, and they've never been strong enough for the job he expected them to do. He should have given me the chance to overhaul 'em before we left.'

He seemed on the point of bursting into anger again, then he stopped himself.

'We'll need the spare radiators,' he went on. 'They're always leaking. I think they must have been corroded to hell and gone before he even bought 'em. And we'll need the spare tracks, the welding equipment, and the oxygen. And as much antifreeze as we can carry.'

'There's the food and fuel, too,' Legge-Jenkins reminded him coldly. 'We'll need enough to get to the Søsters.'

Hellyer's face went red again at once. 'The Søsters?' he said. 'Why the hell are we going *there?*'

Legge-Jenkins' eyes glittered behind his spectacles, almost as though with tears of irritation.

'There's a food dump at the Søsters,' he said. 'Adams dropped it there. You know he did.'

'We could manage without it.'

'The dump contains other things besides food. There are spare parts there for O'Day and we've got to have them.

We've got to raise Base or West Camp and let them know what's happened – or even Tom Fife with the *Brancard* – '

'Tom Fife ought to have been *here*,' Hellyer said bitterly. 'Not left behind with the bloody ship.'

Legge-Jenkins became angry again at once. 'There's nothing we can do about that now,' he said. 'And, under the circumstances, perhaps it's as well we've got someone like Tom Fife in a position where he can help us.'

Hellyer seemed more subdued, as though he saw the sense in what Legge-Jenkins said. 'It'll double the journey going out there,' he said.

'There's plenty of fuel at the Søsters.'

'Yes, I know but – '

'Can we do it?' Legge-Jenkins demanded furiously.

Hellyer glared at him. 'Yes,' he said.

Legge-Jenkins half-turned away satisfied, but Hellyer's voice, hard and bitter, pursued him.

'Providing Number Three's big end doesn't go first,' he said.

t w o

Legge-Jenkins moved away from Hellyer thankfully. There were times when he found Hellyer's aggressive ability a little too much for him. His own background was a university lecture room and the mechanic's was the London engineering shop where he had learned his profession. Hellyer had spent all his life fighting and didn't seem to know how to stop. He had jeered at them all at some time or other – at Clark, the geologist, for his habit of telling long-winded stories, at Pink for his weather reports, at O'Day, for his wireless operator's absorption with his sets, at Doree, the RAF officer, for his secret rockets and his affectation of dropping the 'g's at the end of his words, even at Legge-Jenkins himself, he knew, merely for the hyphen in his name. Hellyer, he decided, was a class-conscious troublemaker with whom he would never normally have chosen to spend an arctic winter and who, but for Adams' stubbornness, would never even have left the base camp.

His face was still pink with irritation when he saw Doctor Piercey emerge from one of the tents and he quickened his pace, looking forward with relief to the doctor's sanity. At least, he thought, he ought to get some sense from Piercey, who had had previous experience of the Arctic and the emergencies it could throw up, and was the last man in the world to be panicked by their situation.

He was a stocky, square man with alert eyes that never showed much anger or depression, and he was standing now, his feet apart, staring calmly across the bleak valley at the new ice that was forming rapidly on the surface of Prins Haakon Sø, as though the disaster that had destroyed their base had not even touched him.

Legge-Jenkins stopped in front of him, looking eagerly for encouragement.

'Well?' he said immediately. 'How's Ivey?'

Piercey turned slowly. 'Second degree burns. Hands, face and feet. He's fit to travel, though, of course, he'll have to be helped.'

'What about Doree? How's he?'

Piercey considered. 'Doree has a curious quality of endurance,' he said slowly, 'that doesn't seem to go with that languid air of his. He's not as bad as Ivey, of course. Hands and face again. He'd better ride in one of the Weasels with Ivey.' He glanced up at Legge-Jenkins with the ghost of a smile. 'That means, of course,' he added, 'that we can carry that much less equipment, but as we seem to have damn little to take with us, anyway, it doesn't seem to present much of a problem, does it?'

His optimism annoyed Legge-Jenkins. 'How are the medical supplies?' he asked quickly, as though he were eager to learn the worst details of their plight.

Piercey shrugged. 'Short,' he said bluntly. 'They went up with the rest of the things, but at least we don't have to worry about germs up here.'

He glanced at the austere scholar's face in front of him. 'What about you?'

Legge-Jenkins held up his bandaged hand and stared at it as though he were startled to find it existed at all, as though injury weren't a part of his ordered life. 'It's nothing,' he said uncertainly.

'This is no time for heroics,' Piercey pointed out quietly with the air of a man who had seen every kind of horror in the course of his profession and was no longer moved either by courage or fear. 'The expedition's finished – here, anyway. We've nothing to do but make sure we get taken off by Fife.'

'My hand won't make any difference.'

'It might,' Piercey pointed out, 'if things don't go right for us.'

Legge-Jenkins seemed to thrust the thought aside with an irritable gesture and Piercey got the impression that the urgency of their situation, the need for clear thought and swift action, worried him, as though it were alien to his scholar's nature.

'How did it happen?' he asked. 'East and I were ten miles away on the glacier, and all I know of it was seeing the wreckage when we got back and Adams dead.'

Legge-Jenkins moved angrily inside his clothes. 'You should thank God you *were* on the glacier,' he said. 'If you'd been in your bunk, you'd have got those damned chemical bottles full in your face. They went up straight away and almost asphyxiated O'Day.'

'They shouldn't have been in the living quarters,' Piercey said shortly, his calm eyes narrow.

'It wasn't my fault.' Legge-Jenkins was on the defensive at once. 'The hut was badly planned. He wouldn't listen. It might have been easier if it hadn't happened in the middle of the night. The current failed and we couldn't see a thing in the smoke. And the extinguishers were hopeless in that damned gale. As you fought it back a foot in one place it went forward three feet in another. We hadn't a chance.'

He paused and went on heavily. 'I don't suppose we'll ever find out now what caused it.'

He halted again, as though trying to get control of his emotions, then went on more calmly. 'How are we for food? How much have we?'

The doctor eyed him squarely. 'Not enough,' he said quietly. 'A lot of the dried and powdered stuff's gone. Most of the tinned food's spoiled too. It should have been stacked away from the hut. So should the petrol.'

'We hardly had the time,' Legge-Jenkins said with a nervous gesture.

'It was the first job,' Piercey pointed out, his face showing anger for the first time. 'It's always the first job to store spare food and fuel and spare kits and tents out of reach. There've been fires in the Arctic before. Adams knew what might happen.'

'You know what he was like,' Legge-Jenkins said quickly. 'He always behaved a bit as though he were still on the bridge of a destroyer.'

'He said he'd tackle it. He told me he'd tackle it before East and I left.'

'Well, he didn't. I tried to tell him but he wouldn't listen – '

Piercey interrupted, sensing that Legge-Jenkins was troubled by the enormous responsibility that had suddenly been thrust on him.

'I'd better let you have a list,' he said quickly. 'I'll give you a scale of maximum and minimum rations. It might be useful.'

Legge-Jenkins nodded and began to fiddle with the papers in his hand. 'Ought we to start cutting down straight away?'

'I wouldn't,' Piercey said. 'But it depends on how much we have to do. I assume you're going to move south to Cape Alexandra as arranged.'

'Yes.' Legge-Jenkins answered stiffly, as though he guessed his words would result in an argument eventually. 'Those were the instructions. I'm recommending that we go via the Søsters.'

Piercey lifted his head quickly. 'What on earth for?'

'There's a food dump at the Søsters.' The irritation was creeping into Legge-Jenkins' voice again. 'With what Adams left there, we can get to Cape Alexandra easily and Fife can get the ship to us as arranged.'

'If we get there in time,' Piercey pointed out. 'It's a devil of a distance the way you're planning to go. We'd be far wiser to go direct along the coast and rely on the rifle for food.'

'We've plenty of time. Besides, there are radio spares at the Søsters. We must have them. Our instructions were to inform Fife if anything went wrong.'

'Even without a wireless?' Piercey asked sarcastically.

Legge-Jenkins looked at him nervously out of the corner of his eye, as though he were slightly afraid of Piercey's knowledge of the Arctic and his down-to-earth bluntness.

'It's those damned rockets of Doree's, of course,' he said defensively. 'They were worried about them. What we had to do about the rockets were the only clear instructions that were ever made out.'

'It's a pity they were made out by people who couldn't possibly have had any knowledge of what might go wrong,' Piercey commented acidly.

'Doree's raised no objection,' Legge-Jenkins said in a thin voice. 'He agrees that the rockets must come first under the circumstances.'

'Doree's a serviceman,' Piercey pointed out. 'The rockets were his responsibility. He had his orders about them and naturally there's no question in his mind what he must do about them. But what about the others? Hellyer, for example.'

'Hellyer's the original anti-everything.'

'What about you?'

'I've got my instructions,' Legge-Jenkins said stiffly. 'They were Adams'. I'm supposed to follow them.'

Piercey stared at his feet for a moment. He disagreed with Legge-Jenkins but, being a kind man, he hesitated to be too blunt about his disagreement.

'I wouldn't have thought it necessary to inform anyone as experienced as Fife,' he said slowly. 'He'll know what to do now we've gone off the air, and going on to the Søsters only increases the difficulties.'

There was a note of defiance in Legge-Jenkins' voice as he replied, as though he'd known Piercey would disagree.

'Instructions are set out to be followed,' he said.

Piercey glanced at him, knowing very well that he was insisting so firmly on trying to make wireless contact because he was uncertain of himself in the new responsibility which had been thrust so unexpectedly on to his shoulders. He was reaching blindly for directions from a higher authority.

'I don't agree,' he said. 'In fact, if there were the slightest chance of there being any game here for food, I'd go so far as to recommend staying here.'

'It's not a question of game.' Legge-Jenkins was frowning now, with the blank stubbornness that had reminded them again and again that he was deputy leader of the party and in charge now that Adams was dead. 'The instructions were rigid.'

Piercey frowned. The whole expedition had been plagued by pig-headedness, he thought – first Adams' and now Legge-Jenkins'.

'You know what the Air Ministry was like over those damned IRMAS of Doree's,' Legge-Jenkins was saying now. 'You know what a fuss they made – the insistence they made about loading them, the demand that Doree and Green join the party. They even overrode the Port Authorities' ruling about explosives being loaded in midstream. They've got something new there and, as far as *they* were concerned, the expedition existed only to try it out.'

He paused, watching Piercey's face, as though he desperately needed an ally. 'In case things go wrong,' he said more amicably – 'just in case – we can head for Fraser Bay. There's a stone hut there that Rollo Fraser built during the 1923 expedition. I've seen it. Fife may be able to get Captain Schak to bring the *Brancard* up as far as that if he's quick.'

He seemed cheerful and optimistic for a moment, then he sighed and broke the spell again.

'I wish to God I could contact Fife. We'll have to leave a message in case they come up looking for us.'

'It won't be much use when the snow comes,' Piercey pointed out.

'Well, we can leave it, just the same. We've got to tell him our intentions.'

Piercey nodded. 'Have you told the others?' he asked. 'Do they know what's in your mind?'

Legge-Jenkins gestured. 'I haven't told them all,' he admitted. 'But I shall. They know enough about this place to know we can't stay here.'

Piercey took out a pipe and began to fill it calmly. 'Where will Fife be now?'

'Somewhere on the West Coast on the way to Sampson's Camp. It'll take him some time to get back to Cape Alexandra. We must be prepared to wait. We might even have to hold on till spring.'

'My God, I hope not,' Piercey said.

Legge-Jenkins' face tautened again and a muscle twitched along the line of his jaw. 'If only there were fewer of us.' he said, half to himself. 'Just six, for instance, instead of ten. That's how Scott failed. *He'd* have pulled it off with four men instead of five.'

There was an awkward pause, then Legge-Jenkins nodded towards the dogs, his expression eager.

'I've been wondering,' he said, 'if we ought not to construct another sledge. There's wood and iron we could use. We could man-haul it.'

'I'd recommend saving as much of our energy as we can,' Piercey said bluntly. 'We may need it if we're going to the Søsters.'

Legge-Jenkins gave him a sharp, irritated look, then he got control of his temper with an effort. 'Yes,' he agreed. 'Yes, I suppose you're right.' He glanced at the book in his hand and looked at Piercey again. 'By the way,' he went on, 'if anything happens to me, you're to take over. That was Adams' wish.'

Piercey nodded. It didn't seem very important just then, but Legge-Jenkins seemed anxious to discuss it and held out the book towards him.

'This is Adams' log,' he said. 'Under the circumstances, you'd better have a glance at what I've written. You may conceivably be making the entries yourself eventually, so you might as well.'

Piercey felt he was making a great deal of it, but he took the book from him and glanced at the pages entered in Adams' sprawling handwriting, the record of the little they had managed to do before the blaze had occurred. Then, opposite the date of the previous day the writing changed to Legge-Jenkins' neat nervous hand, the precise writing of a man of exact and scholarly habits, and Piercey began to read the details of what was already forming in his mind with alarming clarity.

The page was smudged with soot marks and the writing was uneven.

Commander Adams was buried near Camp Adams, he read. *A burial service was held over the grave. Lieutenant Ivey is still in pain from his burns but the injuries of the others are less. My own hand is difficult to use. O'Day has reported that we have no serviceable radio and much of our food supplies have been destroyed. So far we have found two primuses and a butagas stove but, of course, most of our fuel has gone. Our situation seems very grave.*

'That about fits the bill, I think, don't you?' Legge-Jenkins said.

'I imagine so,' Piercey said without much interest. He handed the book back and turned away, as though he felt the need to get on with something instead of merely talking and making gestures of heroism.

Legge-Jenkins stared after him, his spectacles gleaming, his face wearing a hurt expression, as though he felt that Piercey hadn't come up to expectations. Then he glanced at the book in his hand and slowly turned over the last page.

He had set down the day's date there and his last entry, and he read it now with a morbid feeling of self-satisfaction, as though he liked the sombre phrases.

We must now make our move from Prins Haakon Sø, he had written, *in an attempt to get to Cape Alexandra before the weather shuts down. God grant that we shall succeed. Our party now consists of the following:*
Dr Thomas Piercey, deputy leader, physiologist,
Frank Pink, meteorologist,
Sergeant Clement O'Day, signals,
Lieutenant A H P Ivey, navigator, surveyor,
Henry William Hellyer, mechanic,
George Rawdin East, physicist,
Simon Clark, geologist,
Flying Officer James St John Doree, i/c experimental met. apparatus,
Sergeant Wilfrid H Greeno, assistant to F/O Doree,
and self, Newby Evelyn Legge-Jenkins, physicist, leader.

three

By the following morning, the blizzard that Pink had predicted had moved round to the east, a menacing cloud in a dirty grey-yellow sky on the flank of the mountains, and they stood by the Weasels watching it, waiting for Legge-Jenkins to give the word to go, their faces sombre and expressionless.

It had been a restless night, full of too much thinking for them all, and now in the early light the mountains looked somehow bleaker than ever and the stony surface of the valley with its patches of snow more barren.

The two big yellow Weasels, with their trailers, stood alongside each other, sturdy-looking and beetle-like, and it seemed odd to think that, under the conditions they might have to face, they could be so frail. Just behind them, the dog teams squatted, their tails moving restlessly, their tongues hanging out, their bright eyes watching the men as they moved about.

They had finished their tasks now and were merely waiting, impatient to be away from the valley that seemed so remindful of disaster. Hellyer had already stripped the burned-out Weasel of everything that could conceivably be used and they had lashed the last canvas cover into place. Touched by irritation, they were fidgeting restlessly now as Legge-Jenkins stood among the wreckage of the camp, taking a last uncertain look round to make sure they'd forgotten nothing that might make all the difference between life and death to them.

Alongside him was the cairn they had built containing their planned route and a suggested rendezvous and the names of the party, copied from the logbook. None of them set much store by it being found, for when the snow that Pink forecast arrived, it would blot out every landmark in the valley, even Adams' grave on the slope of the ridge and the stark charred poles that had been their hut, obscuring them until the thaw the following spring. Even supposing anyone were mad enough at that time of the year to attempt to break through to Camp Adams, the chances of their finding the instructions they'd left were slender to the point of impossibility.

Occupied with the problems of their departure and the greater difficulties that beset their journey south, Piercey was watching the faces of the men around him, their eyes glinting in the stormy light as they were lifted nervously to watch the progress of the ominous grey shape of the blizzard moving swiftly down across their path. Inland, he could see the grim shadow along their intended route, but where they stood, by a trick of the atmosphere, the air was still and brooding. There was an eerie glow in the sky, though, turbulent and full of foreboding, that came through the driven clouds and seemed to etch the outlines of the mountains sharply, picking out the muted colours in the valley in a way he had never noticed before.

Ahead of them, once they had climbed away from the lake on to the surface of the ice cap, the frozen desert stretched for hundreds of miles to west and north and south, devoid of life, scentless, silent and still, a freezing, ice-swept continent, cloaked in calm aeons of white. There was no living soul up there, and the temperatures could fall to God alone knew what fantastic depths in vast frozen regions that men couldn't endure. There was no vegetation and no life. Only occasional precipitous cliffs showing through the everlasting whiteness in mottled patches of red and grey, and bottomless chasms that could swallow up men, dogs and sledges without hope of recovery.

He could hear the men behind him muttering, and Pink's references to the weather. Ivey was sitting in the leading trailer, waiting quietly, his face expressionless, staring round him with wondering, boyish eyes. He was the youngest of the party but now, with the flame that had whipped across his face, singeing his brows and hair-roots and leaving his eyelids curiously bare-looking, like a chameleon's without their lashes, he looked curiously aged.

·'How does it feel?' Piercey asked, looking up at him. 'I don't want you in pain but I don't want to dope you more than necessary.'

Ivey turned towards him, still shocked a little and puzzled by what had happened to him, then the skin crinkled at the corner of his mouth as he tried to smile.

'Hurts a bit,' he admitted, lifting his hands. 'It's these chiefly. And my feet.'

Piercey nodded, remembering the ruckled flesh under the bandages, the ghastly blistered lacerations that looked like sticks cruelly peeled.

'That's the worst of fire-fighting in pyjamas and without shoes,' he said mildly, trying to avoid any show of sympathy. He knew Ivey wasn't very far from tears with pain and misery and he had no wish to encourage him.

Ivey nodded. 'How long will it be, Doc?' he asked. 'Before I'm all right, I mean.'

Piercey studied him for a moment, and Ivey's face twisted.

'Come on, Doc,' he urged. 'Let's have it.'

Piercey took a deep breath. 'Months probably.'

Ivey's scorched eyelids fluttered and he was quiet for a moment.

'I think we might just as well be honest with each other from the start,' Piercey said. 'Does it shock you?'

Ivey lifted his gaze to Piercey's. 'A bit,' he admitted.

'Of course' – Piercey tried to be encouraging – 'that's all the way – until they're properly healed. You'll be active long before then.'

For a moment Ivey was silent, then he glanced at Piercey again. 'How'll I look?' he demanded. 'I mean, when it's better.'

'Thinking of a girlfriend or something?'

Ivey nodded. 'Well, you know how it is, Doc. You're married. You've been through it all yourself.'

Piercey nodded and Ivey managed a smile.

'That's the worst of being so bloody old, isn't it?' he said apologetically. 'Everybody comes to you for advice.'

'According to some views,' Piercey said, 'I'm quite young really. Fuchs was fifty when he crossed Antarctica.'

'You've got a family.'

'One daughter.'

'I don't suppose I'd have been here,' Ivey said, 'if I'd been married and had a family. At least I don't think I would. I just thought of it as a bit of a lark.' He sat staring at the bandages on his hands for a second, then he glanced down at Piercey again. 'Why *did* you come, Doc?' he asked.

Piercey paused for a moment, wondering why himself. 'Perhaps because an out-of-work explorer's never happy,' he said. 'That must be it. He's born with an eternal unrest in his body and when he tries to suppress it he becomes difficult to live with.'

Ivey managed another stiff smile. 'Tom Fife in a nutshell,' he said.

Piercey nodded thoughtfully. 'I'm glad Tom Fife'll be in charge of picking us up,' he said. '*He*'ll not let us down.'

Ivey paused. 'How did your wife feel about you bunking off like this?'

Piercey smiled. 'I try to persuade her that it's fieldwork essential to my research,' he said. 'And she tries to pretend that she believes me, and that suits us both. She's used to it, of course. She always has been. Her father was Talbot Forbes, who was with Shackleton on *Quest*.'

Ivey's eyes widened. 'You never told us.'

'Nobody ever asked me.'

'She must be a pretty nice person, Doc.'

'She is.'

'What's your daughter like, Doc?'

Piercey smiled. 'She's a doctor too. Helps me with research.'

Ivey smiled again, young and naïve. 'Hellyer said Tom Fife fell like a ton of bricks,' he said.

Piercey thought for a moment. 'Hellyer always did have too much to say,' he pointed out mildly.

Ivey managed the ghost of a laugh. 'I bet Tom Fife'll take some getting to the starting post,' he said. 'I just can't imagine him settled down.'

'He was once. His wife died.'

'Wonder what she was like. I bet he took some holding. He always looks to me like a big black bull looking round for a china shop to wreck.'

'Tom Fife,' Piercey said slowly, 'has more qualifications and energy than anybody else on this expedition, and on an affair like this, there's nobody to beat him.' He paused, his eyes distant. 'Yet curiously,' he went on thoughtfully, 'on the only occasion I ever saw him with his wife he seemed very quiet and well content with his lot.'

Ivey smiled. 'It's amazing how it affects a chap.'

Piercey nodded. 'What's *your* girl like?' he asked.

'Oh, like any other girl.' Ivey seemed to be stricken suddenly with the embarrassment of the young. 'She's all right. She'll be there waiting, I suppose. I don't think a burn or two will put her off. Not really. Not unless I look like

Frankenstein when the bandages come off. No girl relishes being the Bride of a Monster from Outer Space, does she?'

'Do you know,' Piercey said seriously, 'I don't really think it matters all that much to them what a man looks like. Most of them don't marry you for your looks anyway.'

Ivey seemed satisfied. 'I suppose you're right,' he said. 'Only needs a bit of hospital to put it right, doesn't it?' He paused, looking down at Piercey in a stiff-necked way that came from the bandaging. 'Only things are a bit different now, aren't they?' he pointed out slowly. 'With the hut gone and no radio and having to move and so on.'

They were still talking when Hellyer appeared and climbed into the Weasel, energetic, hostile, and aggressive as ever as he settled himself with a fidgety restless movement, like a fussy terrier squatting in its basket. He had been standing by Sergeant Greeno's Weasel, with his head cocked as he listened to the throbbing engine, and Piercey had seen him shake his head once or twice and say 'Christ' as though something were paining him. He looked now as though he were looking for someone to quarrel with.

He glanced round him at the sky and the first drifting flakes of snow that were coming down from the muddiness to the east, small and dry and dusty in the still air, powdering the roofs of the Weasel cabins and filling the folds in the tarpaulins stretched over the sledges and the trailers.

'He's taking his time, isn't he?' he said, nodding to where Legge-Jenkins was still standing among the abandoned stores, making notes in his book. 'Tempus bloody fugits and it's getting a bit late in the season for hanging about meditating.'

Piercey nodded. Hellyer was quite right, of course. The time factor *was* becoming acute. There had been another fantastic drop in temperature during the night and the ice on the lake was thickening. The pack along the coast would be spreading south already and cutting off their hopes of relief, and the shadow in the sky was moving with incredible swiftness across their route.

Hellyer glanced again at Legge-Jenkins and frowned. 'He might be all right at setting up a lab,' he said, 'but he's no bloody Hillary. Why doesn't he have the guts to do what he thinks best instead of behaving as though this show were being run from London?'

He glanced again at the sky, then squinted disgustedly again in Legge-Jenkins' direction. 'I heard he was earmarked for the coastal survey originally,' he said. 'And Adams only brought him up here because he knew that with Tom Fife there'd be fur flying.'

'You seem to have a remarkably active source of information,' Piercey commented mildly.

Hellyer's face was expressionless. 'I took one of the girls from the office out,' he said. 'It's surprising what they picked up. She told me the committee was even divided on Adams. She said Admiral Lutyens wasn't keen on him and that it was Mortimer who swung it.'

Piercey shrugged. 'You should never listen to gossip.'

'It sounds sense all the same, doesn't it?' Hellyer insisted. 'Mortimer was Adams' father-in-law.' The thought seemed to remind him of his anger and he went on fiercely, 'I volunteered for something I thought was being organised. Not a slapdash affair full of secret weapons that ends up being led by a bloke who wears the hyphen in his name like a badge of office. It's a sort of status symbol to people like him – like a Jaguar.'

He stared bitterly at Legge-Jenkins, then he leaned out of the window. 'The whole bloody affair was rushed,' he went on in aggrieved tones. 'Nobody ever got onto skis and the dogs never got exercised. And look at the clothing and those damned stoves. Clark's still not got over having to go short of food on that trip to the Søsters.'

He gestured angrily in the middle of his harangue and Piercey was suddenly and curiously reminded of one of the orators at Hyde Park corner.

'Tom Fife ought never to have been left behind,' Hellyer said. '*Or* Jessup and Hannen. Or that bloke from the Danish Geodetic Institute. He always said he wasn't being properly employed.'

'If Fife and Jessup and Hannen and the others had been here,' Piercey pointed out, 'doubtless *you* wouldn't have been.'

Hellyer shrugged. 'I expect they'd have got by without me,' he said unemotionally. 'I'm no hero, anyway.'

'You might be surprised,' Piercey observed. 'Courage comes in different shaped packages.' He patted the throbbing side of the Weasel and looked up at Hellyer, determined to change the conversation. 'Will they make it?' he asked.

Hellyer nodded. 'This one will,' he said. 'It's Greeno's that worries me – Number Three. I think the big end's going and we've got no spare – naturally.'

Hellyer was still complaining when Piercey moved away to where Doree was leaning languidly against the trailer of the second Weasel, in which they had packed his apparatus. He was a big blond young man with a deceptively languid air, and he was staring round him with an expressionless face at the few scattered remnants of abandoned equipment near the charred hut. Alongside him, a scrap of canvas which had once been a trailer cover had caught on a fragment of twisted, blackened iron and hung limp and damp and strangely dead-looking in the dull light from the leaden sky.

'How're the hands?' Piercey asked.

Doree didn't answer immediately. He lifted his gaze towards the sky, and a few dry flakes of snow fell on his face, dusting the incipient beard on his chin, then he seemed to become aware of Piercey and he glanced down at his bandages with mild blue eyes.

'Mendin',' he said slowly, with the easy-going affected manner that always annoyed Hellyer so much.

'No trouble?' Piercey asked.

'Should they be causin' me trouble?'

'A bit, perhaps.'

Doree shrugged. 'Hard luck, Doc,' he said. 'I've been too busy to have trouble.'

Piercey nodded at the crates.

'How's the family?' he asked, and Doree shrugged again.

'I expect they're all right. I've done all I can.'

'I have a feeling,' Piercey smiled, 'that the civilians with this party aren't very enamoured of your rocket gun, Doree.'

Doree gave him a long, innocent look. 'It isn't a gun, Doc,' he said. 'It's a launcher for ionospheric rockets, meteorological (arctic). IRMA. That's how they're classified. They're secret and they're important and with the information they could give us, bad-weather flying could be revolutionised, but they're still only met rockets, whichever way you look at 'em.'

For a while, they stood in silence, watching the slow dusting of the fine snow, then Doree spoke again, his voice faintly cynical.

'Doc,' he said. 'Why *did* Adams accept these babies of mine? They had no place in his blasted expedition.'

Piercey shrugged. 'Money,' he said simply. 'He needed money. Funds weren't coming in as fast as he'd expected and when he got a chance of picking up Treasury help, he jumped at the chance.'

Doree's gaze didn't flicker. 'With the reputation he had,' he said, 'he didn't have to have anything he didn't want. He could have raised the money all right without taking IRMA on. He was just in an almighty bloody hurry, that's all. Why was he in a hurry, Doc? Why didn't he wait?'

Piercey didn't answer for a moment. Ambition? The hope of reward? Fear of being forgotten after his earlier successes?

There were a thousand reasons that Piercey might have suggested for Adams' disastrous decisions but he guessed they were all of them probably not correct.

'I don't think he could have done it,' he said frankly. 'He *had* to go ahead. It became a sort of touchstone for him. Besides,' he added, feeling he was probably coming nearer to the truth, 'he married Sir Willard Mortimer's daughter. He was eager to live up to her background.'

'Pity she never tried to live up to his,' Doree commented. 'They say she *always* marries commanders in the Navy.'

Piercey frowned. He'd heard stories about Adams' wife more than once – everybody who went in for polar exploration always knew everything about everyone else who did – and somehow, thinking about it, she seemed to go with Adams. She seemed to˙be part of the picture he'd formed of the man. At a distance, Piercey's impression had been one of an expert polar traveller and an efficient if not a loveable man; working alongside him, he had begun to see a much smaller man, envious of his father-in-law's wealth and influence and anxious to emulate it, a man of monstrous ego and drive without the clear-sightedness either to pick a good wife or to direct his tremendous capacity for work.

Suddenly, as he considered all the things that had contributed towards the disaster that had overcome them, the expedition seemed to Piercey to have been conceived in confusion and haste, and there had been too much of Adams and too much of his father-in-law, Sir Willard Mortimer. They both belonged to the same class of society, both were ambitious and opportunist and ruthless, and both were over-hasty and careless.

Doree seemed to divine what he was thinking and he gestured round him at the group of men and dogs huddled against the sinister bleakness of the dark mountains and the scattered patches of grey-white snow that showed starkly through the mist against the bare rock. The look of bland cynicism was still on his face.

'Heroic lot, aren't we?' he said. 'To be representin' the International Geophysical Year. No home, no food, no hope, and not a scrap of bloody equipment between the lot of us. Sir Willard Mortimer won't get that barony he was after now.'

Piercey affected a look of blank innocence. '*Was* he after a barony?'

Doree gestured. 'You forget, Doc,' he said. 'My old man has a handle, too. I belong to the privileged upper class and the upper class has an instinct for these things. You'd be surprised at the things I got to know.'

Piercey nodded mildly. 'Yes,' he said. 'I might.'

Doree's face was expressionless. 'My old man told me,' he went on, 'that Admiral Lutyens said he thought from the beginnin' that this expedition would go off at half cock. I didn't think much of it at the time, I must admit, but I've thought about it a lot this morning. It's still goin' off at half cock, isn't it? L-J's helpin' it to.'

He glanced towards the north, his eyes roving round their bleak surroundings and squinting up into the muddy sky at the snow that was falling more rapidly now. The grey woolliness hung near the fringe of the mountains to the south now, and though the air was still motionless about them, there was suddenly a difference, a suggestion of unseen movement and a hint of deeper cold that seemed to make Doree shudder.

'Afraid?' Piercey asked.

Doree shrugged.

'I never fancied bein' one of these vast heroic men like Shackleton or Oates or Scott,' he said frankly, 'but by the look of that lot up there I'm goin' to have the chance to be. I think it's goin' to be quite a party before we've finished.'

As he stopped speaking, Legge-Jenkins closed his book and turned towards them, the weird light that was streaming between the mountains gleaming on his spectacles; and even as he approached, the first real flurry of snow fell on them like a handful of scattered confetti, and with it came the first of the wind.

'Pink's weather,' Doree commented as they went to their places.

At first it was just a cold breath of air out of the north, just strong enough to flap the scrap of charred canvas hanging on the remains of the hut; but the sudden smacking noise, remarkably loud and clear in the silent valley, was enough to turn their heads. Then the first gust hit them, whipping and plucking at the tarpaulins over the sledges and the Weasel trailers, and Piercey saw the expression of self-confidence on Hellyer's face change abruptly to a look of angry despair that was reflected in the faces of the others as they were brought face to face with a fact that Piercey had learned years before. An Arctic journey wasn't merely a matter of preparation and equipment.

The wind was coming down on them now like an unexpected demon, snatching at their clothing as they staggered away from it into the lee of the Weasels, making them turn their backs and sending the dogs creeping into the shelter of the sledges. At once the air was full of flying particles of ice and the thickening cloud of snow was a smothering blanket that filled their mouths whenever they drew breath. What they were going to have to face was brought home abruptly to all of them – coming, it seemed, like the whiplash cut of the wind itself.

It had suddenly become bitterly cold, too, and the wind was steadily increasing, snatching at the trailers in a muffled roar, twisting and tearing out of the mountains and banging at the sides of the Weasels like a solid object in terrible, blustering gusts, and driving the pea-sized particles of ice at them in clouds.

Doree, his head bent against it, was looking strangely at Piercey and, at that moment, the doctor noticed that, with the exception of Legge-Jenkins, the eyes of every other man there were following him, too. There was a second of tension in which he realised they were looking to *him* to give them a lead, not to the austere scholar who was nominally in command. Then Legge-Jenkins, staggering under the buffeting of the wind, raised his hand and indicated the route towards Mount Priam.

Piercey saw his mouth open as he shouted something but his voice was lost on the booming of the wind, then he was carried sideways, almost as though from a physical blow, as a gust almost lifted him off his feet.

Legge-Jenkins is wrong, Piercey thought with a sudden fierce intensity, caught before the other's determination to move by the same sense of futility and frustration that Legge-Jenkins himself had doubtless felt earlier, in the face of Adams' insistence on leaving things to chance. We shouldn't be going to the Søsters, he felt angrily. The stubbornness of one man had brought them to this condition and the stubbornness of another would complete the fiasco. In the flash of revelation, he recalled Doree's words and seemed to sense a worse disaster than they had already experienced.

Then he saw Pink, with the leading dog team, looking at him, as though for confirmation of Legge-Jenkins' instructions, and heard the sudden roar of the Weasel engines. Against his will, he found himself nodding, and as Pink grabbed the handlebars of the sledge for the initial heave that would set the unwilling dogs moving, East gave a violent wrench at the traces. The sledge shot off with a jerk and an empty jerrican rolled away as it was knocked flying, then the dogs were off, their tails up, yelping with excitement, vanishing into the grey-white murk as the Weasels made their first uncertain jolt forward.

four

The remains of the old whaling station at Stakness lay in the bleak Helberg Bay of North Western Iceland in a scattering of disused hutments and deserted cooking sheds. Across the dark water, where the ship was turning, the silver tanks and girders of the new station crowded round the town of Helbergfjördur, a huddle of bleak concrete slabs built alongside the docks. Above the trawlers hugging the black stone wall, and the warehouses and jetties and the tall chimney of the fish manure factory, Helberg Hjelmen, a high peak of chocolate-coloured rock, rose to a jutting pinnacle on which the white pencil of the lighthouse stood among its scattered outhouses.

From among the paintless buildings of the old station, on the spit of land that held the rusting tanks, a decaying jetty ran out into the water. The growling wind set up the clang of loose corrugated-iron sheets and slapped the lead-coloured waves among the ribs of ancient boats that sagged on a gravelly beach swarming with oystercatchers, purple sandpipers and dunlins. Beneath the mountains that rose naked and black as slag heaps behind the half-empty village, a few crude crosses in the shadow of the ancient fuel tanks showed where the people of Stakness had buried their dead; and round the lopsided stones bearing names like the battle cries of Viking warriors – Guthmundur Thorleiffson, Eihar Gustavsson, Nils Hermansson – the zing and twang of

36

whipped wire fencing added its arpeggios to the low hum of the weather.

On the old slipway there were crates and packing cases marked with the sign of the British East-West Greenland Expedition and three Weasels parked in a row like squat yellow bugs. As the ship approached, a line of men in heavy weather shirts, who had appeared from among the huts where they had made their base, waited in the wind with hunched shoulders among the baulks of timber and rusted ringbolts and the coils of ancient hawser on the concrete apron. They had been waiting there from the minute when the ship had first made her appearance between the two bleak headlands that circled the bay, watching in a silence that was broken only by the echoing sound of the gulls against the hills as she edged gently towards the ancient jetty.

She was a German-built Canadian-registered sealer, not much bigger than a trawler but with the rounded reinforced hull and raised stern of an ice-strengthened ship. On her grey painted stern as she swung in the wind, the name BRANCARD showed clearly in the gloomy weather.

There were a few calls back and forth as she drew closer, but they were subdued by the brooding day and the news that was beginning to spread round the camp.

Someone flung a heaving line ashore and a stern rope was passed across the oily surface of the water, then there was the sharp metallic clatter of a winch and the ship bumped gently against the jetty with a shove that was felt through every one of the rotten timbers.

One or two crew members scrambled ashore, then the stocky man who had been waiting on the jetty jumped aboard and headed towards the bridge, one hand clasping a file of papers and books against his side.

By the bridge ladder, Captain Schak was waiting, a big German-Canadian sealing skipper, dark-haired and thickset, and chewing the wet butt of a cigar as he stared up at a tern battling against the sharp Arctic wind, its wings piercingly white against the dark rock of the hills.

'Made it,' he grinned, turning towards the newcomer. 'We made it, Hannen. Nobody arrested us.'

Hannen nodded, 'Did they try?' he asked.

'That goddam gunboat was waiting off Latrapjarg for the trawlers,' Schak said. 'They'd have picked us up, sure as hell, if anybody'd lowered so much as a bent pin on a string.' He nodded towards Helbergfjördur. 'Trust us to pick Iceland for a base just when the Icelanders decide to start a fish war with the UK. What's it like here?'

Hannen gave him a fleeting smile. 'Difficult,' he said.

'Difficult?'

'Mail's late. Jessup's spares haven't arrived. That sort of thing.'

'Well, if your goddam government *will* start shoving its nose in. I've been coming in here years and never had any trouble before.'

Hannen made a move to push past him but Schak, with garrulous friendliness, laid a hand on his arm.

'It's their sea,' he said. 'If they want to shove their fishing limit out to twelve miles, why can't they?'

'Because if you draw a line from headland to headland,' Hannen smiled, 'the limit's sometimes *twenty-five* miles out in the middle of the bay. Perhaps that's part of the problem.'

'Yeah.' Schak nodded. 'Yeah, I guess so.' He thought for a moment. 'South Georgia and Graham Land are nice safe places for exploration,' he said ruefully. 'Why didn't we go there?'

'Because Fuchs and Hillary got there first,' Hannen said. 'When they'd finished, there was nothing left for Adams to find.'

Schak nodded heavily. 'Talking about Adams – ' he began, and Hannen interrupted quickly.

'There's nothing more,' he said. 'Nothing's turned up.'

'Nothing? Hell, it's a long time now.'

'It's probably nothing. Where's Tom Fife?'

Schak nodded towards the companionway. 'Watch it,' he warned.

Hannen smiled. 'I've been watching Tom Fife for years,' he said warmly. 'I'm used to it now.'

At the end of the companionway, Fife was standing inside his cabin, a bulky man with a dark sensitive face that looked brooding and angry. He jerked his hand.

'Come in,' he said. 'Let's keep it quiet as long as we can.'

Hannen followed him inside and Fife pulled forward a chair and slammed the door to, then he threw a tobacco pouch across as though he were making certain they were comfortable before they started business.

'OK,' he said finally. 'Let's have it. Who knows, up to now?'

Hannen stared at him for a moment, then he began to stuff his pipe with tobacco. 'Me. Jessup, of course. One or two more. I've told them to keep quiet about it, but it's getting around.'

'What happened?'

'I don't know. They just disappeared off the air. We stopped receiving because they stopped transmitting.'

'Know why?'

Hannen shrugged.

'At first we thought it must be the jenny or some accident to the Fifty-three,' he said. 'It's happened before. We just assumed it was technical trouble and didn't get alarmed. O'Day's as sound as they come and we just waited for him to put it right. When they didn't come up again, I set a continual watch. After a fortnight, I got worried.'

'Did their last message give any indication of trouble?'

Hannen shook his head.

'No, nothing. They signed off in a perfectly ordinary way at the end of the sked. A bit of chit-chat from O'Day. Then later Jessup heard him fiddling about with the Morse key. He was in touch with some amateur in Canada. He wasn't listening for him but he knew it was O'Day. He's got a peculiar touch on a key. It's easily recognisable. Then nothing.'

'What about Sampson? Has he picked up anything on the West Coast?'

'No. He was in touch just before we were, it seems. That was his last contact. Since then neither of us have had a peep out of them. What about you?'

Fife shook his head. 'Think the weather's caused them to shut down or something?' he asked.

Hannen shrugged. 'Why should it? It never has before. Besides, surely to God if they were still working a sked we'd have raised *something* whatever the conditions up there. God knows, Jessup's been trying hard enough.' His face became grave. 'But there's nothing, Tom,' he said. 'There's been nothing because there's nothing there.'

Fife looked up quickly but he didn't speak, allowing Hannen to continue with his story.

'It was only when Sampson said the snow had started and we'd still heard nothing that I began to get anxious,' he said. 'I asked the Americans to lay on a flight. They sent an Arctic rescue DC54 across.'

'What did they see?'

'Nothing. There was nothing there.'

'But, good God, man' – Fife spoke in a low voice without changing his position – 'the place couldn't just disappear. Not even if all the snow in the Arctic had come down. Something would show. They couldn't have made a mistake, could they?'

'There was no mistake, Tom,' Hannen said. 'They identified the place all right. The wireless mast was still there, sticking through the snow.'

'Is that all? Nothing else?'

'No.' Hannen shook his head. 'No sign of life. No footprints. No Weasels. No sledge tracks. Nothing.'

Fife stared at the charts on his bunk, frowning. 'Eleven men can't just vanish off the face of the earth,' he said. 'If there was a wireless mast, why didn't they transmit?'

'There wasn't even any sign of the hut, Tom. The Americans have been over there three times altogether. They gave it all they'd got. You know what they're like. They even had a jet-assisted take-off job standing by in case they had to land on the lake. But there was nothing to see. Nothing. Then one of their Grummans crashed on take-off and naturally they lost interest a bit. Besides' – Hannen gestured – 'I was getting a bit worried by this time about how the committee in London was going to react to a bill for dollars. We're supposed to be self-supporting and, let's face it, we may be worrying for nothing. In spite of everything, there may still not be anything to get alarmed about. It was just that I felt so helpless here without an aircraft and without the ship. This bloody base is too far away,' he ended angrily, as though his patience had suddenly run out.

Fife showed no emotion. 'I know that,' he said. 'Go on.'

'There ought to have been a base on the mainland,' Hannen continued. 'This place's hopeless – especially since this damn fishing dispute began to get in the way.'

'For God's sake' – Fife came to life suddenly with an angry gesture – 'don't keep on saying that. I know it. You know it. We all knew the things that were wrong. Even without this blasted fishing dispute, the whole expedition was badly planned. There wasn't enough thought behind it. Adams was just anxious to get in on what Fuchs and Hillary had started. That's all. For God's sake, go on and don't waste time finding excuses. What else is there?'

Hannen waited until Fife's anger had burned itself out then he spoke slowly, without rancour.

'There's nothing else,' he said. 'That's all there is.' He tossed his pile of papers, folders and books onto the table. 'There's the wireless logbook. I impounded it. It occurred to me that if anything was wrong – seriously wrong – it'd be as well to have everything we could. I thought there might be an inquiry.'

'You're damn right there'll be an inquiry,' Fife said slowly. 'There'll be an inquiry whatever happens. Without Adams in the east camp, Sampson's camp in the west might just as well not exist. The expedition's finished and every damn bit of cash that's been spent has been wasted. And, my God, there *was* some cash behind us. They'll want to know where it's gone.' He indicated the logbook. 'Doesn't that tell us *anything*?'

Hannen shook his head. 'No' he said. 'Nothing. Daily routine reports and weather for transmission to London. A bit of back and forth with Sampson's camp. And that's all.'

Fife stared at the charts for a moment. 'This was a damned badly planned affair,' he said slowly.

Hannen managed a smile. 'Now *you*'re at it,' he pointed out.

Fife sighed. 'Yes,' he said. 'I'm at it. But if something's gone wrong, I'll be dogsbody.'

'It wasn't your fault, Tom.'

'No.' Fife paused. 'No,' he said. 'I don't think it was. God knows, I put my threepenn'orth in often enough. Especially about this place. I could see this damn fishing dispute coming a mile off and I knew there'd be trouble. In fact, I think I got Adams' back up about it in the end.'

'That's why you were here instead of up at Camp Adams where you ought to have been,' Hannen pointed out. 'You ought not to have been in charge of the coastal survey, Tom. Legge-Jenkins could have done that.'

Fife ignored him. 'He could have had so much more time if he'd wanted it,' he said slowly. 'Perhaps he even knew he could have had more time and felt a bit guilty about not taking it. But he'd set himself a date and he wouldn't back down.'

'Adams would never have backed down, Tom,' Hannen pointed out. 'It wasn't in his nature. Besides, because he'd stuck his neck out a few times – look at the way he pulled Hubert Wilkins out of South Georgia – he thought he could stick it out again. All he wanted was a share in the Geophysical Year. He was scared of being left out. He wanted a bit of the kudos that was flying around Fuchs and Hillary.'

Fife nodded.

Hannen began to search among the papers he'd brought. 'There's another cable from Sir Willard Mortimer, by the way,' he said quietly.

'Another?'

Hannen shrugged and Fife hunched his shoulders.

'There are too many damned cables from Mortimer telling us what to do,' he growled. 'You can't run an affair like this with someone like Mortimer's hand on the wheel. He was always too involved elsewhere, being a politician or a businessman, making money or watching votes. His secretary has instructions to send one of those damn cables every month. He dictates 'em between business lunches at the Savoy. They're just to indicate that he's showing his usual keen interest in what we're doing.'

'This one isn't.' Hannen moved a bundle of newspapers across to Fife. 'It's this,' he said, jabbing a finger at the headlines. 'That Russian base on Novaya Zemlya up near North Cape. They're using it for atom-testing. The last one was a forty-megaton job and the fallout area touches the Norwegian coast. The Americans have joined in the protest and we've followed 'em, and Mortimer's offering in the Commons to have their wireless transmissions watched from here.'

'What in God's name does he think we can do here better than they can do in London?' Fife exploded in disgust.

Hannen shrugged again. 'It's just the usual nonsense. Keeping himself in the public eye.'

Fife frowned. His impression of Adams' father-in-law had been one of an ambitious man seeking whatever honours he could get, a ruthless businessman hamstrung all the time by all the things that were pulling him different ways at once – politics, ambition, personal publicity – a man whose every decision was influenced by other decisions he had made in the past or might have to make in the future.

'It's a pity,' he said, 'that Mortimer ever came into this affair. He was only trying to impress his friends. He was the man who could get things done, the man who knew the short cuts through all our difficulties. All that damn nonsense about "Call on me in the House any time" and his references to the FO and the PM's interest.'

'He had some money to put down, too,' Hannen reminded him, cutting through his bitterness. 'And, besides, Adams was married to his daughter.'

Fife nodded. 'Yes, I suppose so.' He sighed. 'It was a good idea, this survey of Prins Haakon Land,' he admitted slowly. 'I'll hand it to Adams. He has the ideas, if he'd only use 'em properly.'

'Polar Research blew a bit cool, all the same. They thought he was biting off more than he could chew. And Admiral Lutyens couldn't stomach Mortimer. Adams had raised no funds from the Cozzens Trust till the Air Ministry came in with those gadgets of Doree's.'

Fife didn't disagree. He sat motionless for a moment, his big body giving the impression of immense controlled strength. Then he shifted uneasily.

'There should have been more thought,' he said slowly. 'More organisation. More reliance on air. More Weasels. There were never enough for what Adams was planning, especially with three here all the time. If he'd waited another year, we could have been well-equipped. People would have given him all he wanted. God, after Fuchs and Hillary, everybody's polar crazy.'

He rose, his bulk filling the cheerless little cabin that smelled of damp steel and brine and fuel, and reached for the tobacco pouch. Hannen watched him silently as he began to fish in his pockets, his eyes brooding and reflective.

'Adams and Mortimer,' he said. 'One after glory. The other after publicity. I ought not to have let them get away with it. I ought to have resigned or something. Only I was sick to the back teeth of that bloody laboratory, Pat, and I wanted to come and it didn't seem fair to you and Jessup and the others to back out then. I thought I could do more if I stayed.' He paused and looked at Hannen. 'I think he damn near asked me to withdraw once or twice,' he concluded.

He slammed the logbook shut with a bang and stared at it for a moment. 'Well, he didn't in the end,' he said heavily. 'And if anything's gone wrong, I'm carrying the can.'

He dragged a pipe from his pocket and stuffed it with tobacco, his eyes on the charts.

'Anything else?' he asked.

'Well, you know about Ted Gibb here breaking his leg. I've arranged for him to be flown home. Otherwise – just messages from headquarters, telling us not to get involved in the fishing dispute.'

'What do they think we're trying to do?' Fife growled. '*Everybody's* involved in the fishing dispute up here. You're involved the minute you set foot on the soil. It comes up out of the ground at you. Is that all?'

'Not quite.' Hannen pulled another slip from among the papers in his hands and skated it down on top of the charts.

'There's another happy thought there for us,' he said quietly, nodding at it. 'Doc Piercey's wife died.'

Fife lifted his head slowly. 'Oh, God, no,' he said. 'When?'

'It came some days ago. Car accident.'

Fife was stock-still for a moment. 'That's what happened to me,' he said. 'Five years ago. They cabled to South Georgia that my wife was ill. By the time they flew me home it was too late.'

His face was sombre with old sorrow. 'I know what he's bound to feel when he gets to know,' he said slowly. 'The only thing I could ever think of, I remember, was what a rotten husband I'd been and how much time I'd spent away from home.'

Hannen said nothing and after a while Fife lifted his head.

'Did Rachel Piercey send the message?' he asked.

'Yes. Cable. For Piercey. I acknowledged it for him and said I'd inform him. Then another one arrived for him. It asks if he could possibly get himself replaced and go home. It seems there's a lot of family business to attend to.'

Fife sucked at his pipe. 'I got to know Piercey's wife well, you know,' he said. 'It was me Adams sent to persuade him to join the show when Gardiner backed out. I spent a day or two down there. She was Talbot Forbes' daughter, did you know?'

Hannen nodded. 'What are you going to do, Tom?' he asked. 'About Adams, I mean.'

Fife looked up slowly, his eyes steady.

'Find 'em if I can,' he said. 'It's my pigeon, Pat, whichever way I look at it. They'll be waiting at Cape Alexandra, I expect, and whatever I thought of Adams and his planning, it's still my job to fetch 'em out.'

He struck a match and puffed at his pipe for a moment, as though the action helped him to think.

'What happens if we don't find 'em?' Hannen asked.

'We've got to. If we don't pull it off now, nothing on God's earth will get through till spring. Better get the Yanks to watch the route down to Cape Alexandra. They're bound to be along it somewhere. We'd better ask their radio stations to listen out, too.'

'And the weather stations?'

Fife nodded. '*And* every amateur in the northern hemisphere. In the meantime, contact Sampson and tell him to sit tight and take no risks. If everything's all right with Adams, we might be able to carry on. If it isn't – '

He shrugged and stared again at the charts.

'For the time being,' he said, 'I think we ought to keep it to ourselves. We don't want it plastered all over the papers until we're certain that there really is trouble. We don't want Mortimer blundering about in it just yet. I want to be able, if necessary, to go to Lutyens for advice without that old fool accusing me of going over his head.'

Hannen smiled. 'I hope you're lucky. You'll never keep it dark if you're bringing the hams in. They chat to each other all the time.'

Fife's shoulders hunched stubbornly. 'We'll just have to chance it for the time being. I'm taking the *Brancard* up to Cape Alexandra as arranged. I'll need someone to lead the Weasels in case I have to put 'em ashore. I'd be glad if you'd do it, Pat.'

Hannen smiled and rose. 'I shan't be sorry to hand over this place for a while,' he said, turning at the cabin door. 'They sent someone over from Helbergfjördur last week to see me. There's talk of asking us to leave.'

Fife's face darkened. 'They *lent* it to us.'

Hannen shrugged. 'They're just being difficult. It's this trawler trouble, of course. They feel a bit like a small boy being pushed around by a big one. They send a gunboat to chase our trawlers outside the new limits, and we send a frigate to chase away their gunboat, and because they can't go bigger than that, they feel humiliated. They're just hitting back anywhere they can land a blow. They don't like our trawlers fishing in their waters.'

'They're international waters.'

'They say they're not. They say we've fished out their grounds.'

'You don't have to give me a history,' Fife said. 'You can hear all this lot any day – every day – all day – on the radio. These trawler skippers are like a lot of old ladies at a tea party with their gossip. They're more nuisance than the static. You'd think the Icelanders had horns and tails.'

He paused. 'Adams didn't help much with that damned high-handed manner of his when we were negotiating for the place,' he said. 'It took him long enough to fix it, though I thought he'd fixed it good and proper.'

'Circumstances have changed a bit since then,' Hannen pointed out. 'They're not merely unco-operative now. They're obstructive. Things we want urgently don't turn up. Mail's late. Cables are delayed. The only things that seem to get through without difficulty are the messages from Mortimer. It's unsettling. Everybody's on edge. They know what it would mean if this place were closed down – to Sampson, and to Adams.'

Fife looked at him, then he turned towards the charts and brooded over them again for a moment, his eyes flinty. 'And to Adams,' he repeated. 'And to Adams.'

He drew a deep breath and straightened up as Hannen stepped into the alleyway outside.

'Tell Schak,' he said. 'We'll shove off immediately. There's no time to lose. There are eleven men up there, Pat, and it seems they've no hut now. And without shelter in winter, my God, that's an awful place to be.'

f i v e

The sun's light had paled so that it had become a thing of chill rather than of warmth, its glow long since vanished in the misty greyness of the sky as it hung like a dull red orange over the southern horizon, sinking with horrifying speed towards total winter darkness so that they could see the difference with every day that came.

Low torn clouds were pouring across the sky like a beaten enemy, pursued by a storm that was howling somewhere in the north and sent flurries of snow over the *Brancard*. The ice was forming fast and the migrant birds had already begun to move south to where they might find food away from the ice-covered sea. A damp chill had gripped the ship and the colour had drained out of everything so that the landscape had become like a black-and-white photograph of itself, as sharp as an etching and just as cold.

Fife stood on the bridge, his big shoulders hunched, his hands deep in his pockets, listening to the swish of the water alongside. The lookout was huddled in the bows, his head down against the wind, staring forward silently, and Fife watched him for a moment, shifting restlessly in his corner. Inside the wheelhouse, Schak chatted quietly with Hannen, watching the compass card revolve slowly as the ship's head swung.

Fife's thoughts were dark as he watched the growlers drift past them, half-submerged lumps of ice with fretted edges, and the loose floes that stretched ahead like an unending plain away from the sun.

There had been no sign of Adams' party at Cape Alexandra – nothing in the cheerless landscape to indicate they had ever been there. They had searched to the north, hoping against hope they'd see the Weasels bouncing and bumping towards them, just a little late perhaps but well on their way, but there had been nothing and no reports from the American Douglases flying along the coast farther north towards Camp Adams. They had waited for several days, with the dog teams forming outposts along the route, hourly expecting messages that they were on their way at last, still trying to convince themselves that they were only over the brow on the next slope, but nothing had come and reluctantly the dog teams had been withdrawn and re-embarked and they had moved north once more, half-formed plans taking shape in Fife's head.

All the doubts and fears that had been in his mind ever since the start of the expedition, all the certainty of mismanagement and confusion that had sprung from an awareness of too much haste and too little preparation, came crowding round him once more, nagging at him now with the insistence of a blistered heel.

He had joined the expedition at the outset on Adams' suggestion, going willingly because there was something in his nature that took him back again and again to the loneliness of the last frontiers of the earth. Perhaps, now his wife was dead, there was nothing to hold him at home. Perhaps it was a desire to get away from the hurry of modern life. And perhaps it was something else – something that got into all of them, or they wouldn't have been there, and without which the life they had to live would have been worse than that of a prisoner in a labour camp.

He'd heard of Adams' idea to mark the International Geophysical Year by making a survey of the vast basin of

Prins Haakon Land at the base of Mount Priam – news of these things always got around to the people who were interested in them – and he'd followed the development even from the day when Adams had first submitted his plan. The rumours had spread that volunteers were to be asked for and he'd seen a copy of Adams' pamphlet proposing the expedition. When he'd been invited to join, he'd jumped at the chance.

He'd never met Adams, though he'd heard of him, heard of his courage and endurance and, in a backhand way, of his reputation for slapdash planning. But he'd been surprised, nevertheless, to find just how little planning had been done when he'd walked into the office in London which bore the expedition sign on the door. Inside, there'd been a group of bewildered young university graduates who, on their first venture into polar regions, were finding themselves baffled by the boxes of rations, tents, sledges and other equipment that filled the place. Nearby, as though their experience set them apart, was a group of old hands, noticeably less vociferous, examining the equipment with a critical eye and being none too complimentary about its usefulness.

In spite of the outward appearance of industry, there had been a tremendous amount to do and a remarkably short time to do it in, and Fife had been angered at Adams' insistence on what had seemed immediately an impossible date for leaving. He'd seemed to be occupied chiefly with what was to be done when they arrived at Prins Haakon Sø and not at all with what had to be done before they left London.

There'd been a move to get a patron of some standing but none had come forward – none, that was, except Sir Willard Mortimer, Adams' father-in-law, and Fife had wondered more than once if he'd come into the project on his daughter's persuasion because no one else would. Help up to that point had been surprisingly sparse and reluctant, and all the societies that normally assisted had managed to find excuses not to be too deeply involved, and Fife had heard whispers that they'd considered the expedition too ambitious. Then, with Mortimer's arrival, the British Geodetic Trust had offered a measure of help and eventually industry had joined in, too. Finally, the Ministry of Science had given a little cautious assistance, but Adams was still short of funds until Mortimer's influence had brought the Air Ministry into the expedition and they had attached Doree and Sergeant Greeno and sent along their apparatus for testing in sub-zero conditions. No one was very certain even now what Doree had brought with him, and the fact that Doree wouldn't tell them and nobody else could had antagonised the civilian members of the party who had found that their plans had suddenly changed direction.

Nevertheless, Doree's three or four secret crates had managed to rescue the expedition from the hesitancy that seemed to have beset it and, from then on, they had made progress. In retrospect, however, it still seemed not surprising that so many things had gone wrong, for Adams, in his aloof, cold-eyed, imperious county-background way, had always pooh-poohed Fife's appeals for care.

' "Plan courageously but execute cautiously," Gino Watkins said,' he had told him. 'That's what I'm doing.'

Fife had retorted in a blunt fashion that was devoid of any of Adams' finesse and all the work in the office had stopped for the stand-up row that had ensued. He had been on the point then and there of withdrawing, but Adams' request that he resign had been suddenly pulled back – at Admiral Lutyen's request, Fife had heard, and because Adams had been persuaded that they couldn't manage without him.

So he had stayed, fuming at the smallness of the Weasel fleet that Mortimer had acquired through an East End scrap dealer and the rushed overhauls and the unsuitable equipment Adams had obtained and had never tested or changed. He had still not recovered his equanimity when the *Brancard* was ready to weigh anchor at Deptford, where there had seemed to be too many pressmen and photographers – particularly, he had noticed, from the glossy magazines that Adams' wife liked to read – and a little too much of Sir Willard Mortimer on the quayside with a plummy farewell speech, and too much of Adams' wife, with her chattering friends and the cold-eyed naval captain whom they'd heard was giving Adams so much to worry about. Fife had kept rigidly in the background, surrounded by bewildered young experts from universities all over England who had expected the departure of an expedition to the Arctic to be less of a society occasion.

And now what he had feared had happened. Confusion, diffused effort and uncertainty had resulted in disaster and eleven men were missing.

Fife stirred restlessly in his corner of the bridge. Death wasn't unknown to expeditions. It had happened before and to the greatest of explorers – the Poles were always claiming their victims – but it was rare that a disaster of the possible magnitude of this one overtook an expedition these days. Eleven men. Half the men involved. Adams. Hellyer – aggressive, capable, difficult Hellyer. Doree, with the bland innocence he always affected when they questioned him about his rockets. Ivey, with a girl waiting back in Devon to marry him. Legge-Jenkins, a capable physicist but a doubtful quantity in an emergency. Pink. O'Day. East. Greeno. Piercey. Fife dug savagely into his pocket for his pipe as he thought of Piercey. He had a more-than-official interest in finding Piercey.

Fife had been the one who had gone to see him at his home in Buckinghamshire to persuade him to join the expedition. Adams had wanted another man originally, but he'd turned out to be one of Adams' bad guesses and it had stuck out a mile that he'd have been no good, and Fife had gone to isolated Orford in the end and had arrived at Piercey's house smouldering with annoyance and impatience.

The girl in Piercey's laboratory had been so absorbed, he'd assumed at first she was just an assistant. She'd been in a corner working with a test tube underneath an angled light, her face bent over a book in which she was making notes, and her face, pale and tired-looking, as if she'd been concentrating too long, had seemed attractive to him at once. She hadn't looked up and Fife had found himself to his surprise trying to find a suitable pretext to speak to her, but he was a shy man and he'd been at a loss, and the moment had passed and they'd remained silent. Then Piercey had come in and introduced her as his daughter, and she'd looked up and the absorbed frown had been replaced by a smile, automatic, friendly, but given with solemn beautiful eyes that were still far away, as though she resented the interruption. He'd talked to her for a few moments but her thoughts had still seemed to be elsewhere and Piercey had dragged him away quickly, and he'd followed reluctantly, imagining that he was missing something, and that she hadn't really noticed him at all, though he'd still had the feeling, in spite of nothing coming from within to meet him, of some secret inward tribunal summing him up.

Then, a month later, while he'd been stalking up and down the corridor in the office Adams had set up near London docks, waiting for Sir Willard Mortimer to come out of Adams' room so that he could go in with another of the interminable complaints about poor organisation that had been getting him such a bad name, he'd seen her again. She'd come in, carrying some folders, and asked for Piercey. She appeared not to have seen Fife and he'd assumed she'd simply forgotten him. But as she turned towards the door again, Fife had found himself face to face with her, and she'd looked at him keenly, her scrutiny brief and embarrassing, her face impassive, and she'd smiled suddenly, in a whole-hearted way that lit up her features.

'You look as angry now as you did then,' she'd said, and he'd realised at once that she *did* remember him after all and, in spite of her faraway look, had noticed far more of him than he'd guessed that day in her father's laboratory.

He moved again inside his clothes, shifting his shoulders restlessly as though he were easing off an uncomfortable thought, then he noticed Hannen behind him, smoking.

'You remember that batch of mail that came in just before we left?' he said in a flat voice after a while.

'Yes,' Hannen nodded. 'My wife wrote to say the dog had pupped. We all thought she was past it. The dog, of course. Not my wife.'

Fife didn't smile. 'There was a letter from Rachel Piercey,' he said. 'I think she knows.'

'How? Nobody told her anything.'

Fife shrugged. 'Mental telepathy. Something like that. I expect the experts have a name for it. She was very close to Piercey, you know, and she wouldn't have written to me, would she, if she'd thought she could get in touch with Piercey himself?'

They were silent for a while and the gusting wind drifted sleet across the ship, blurring the horizon in grey swirling squalls. Hannen rubbed his hands together but Fife seemed not to notice the cold.

He shifted his position again, staring over the bow of the ship. The northern arch of the heavens was sombre and dark towards the horizon, a black vault that grew deeper daily as the sun receded. Very soon the sea would be frozen, and the scene immobilised and silent. The icebergs, moving south from where they had calved off the glaciers, would be frozen in, to become part of the landscape until the following spring. Soon there would be no movement, except the movement of the sky, and no sound except the whine of the wind. No water would move; there would be no plants, no birds, no, animals. Very soon they would have seen the last of the sun.

He wondered uneasily how the men with Adams would react to the polar night. It had different effects on different men, but whatever their nature, it always accentuated whatever qualities or faults a man had; and men without spiritual resources could find it frightening. And Fife wasn't sure of the qualities of the men with Adams. Apart from Legge-Jenkins and Piercey they were without experience, and that sharp feeling of responsibility for them all persisted, particularly whenever he thought of Piercey.

Hannen was watching him as his eyes roamed over the ice towards the north, a big, dark man with restless movements, his whole figure showing the turbulent impatience inside him.

'I'm taking the *Brancard* up as far as I can get her,' he said. 'Then I'll put the dogs ashore. Four men with two teams to go to Cape Fraser. They may be held up there, using Rollo Fraser's old hut. If they're not, we'll press on as fast as possible to Camp Adams and radio back what we find.'

Hannen looked startled. 'That's a hell of a journey at this time of the year,' he said. 'The weather's changing.'

Fife frowned. 'I'm not asking anybody to do what I can't do myself,' he said. 'I'll take Erskine, Smeed and Jessup. They're the best we've got with the dogs and they'll be faster than the Weasels along the coast from here. The Weasels can back 'em up for the return journey.'

Hannen nodded. 'It's going to take you all your time to get there and back before it's too late, Tom. It'll be harder than you think.'

'It's always harder than you think,' Fife said, unmoved. 'But we can't go home and tell them we didn't try just because time was short.'

'No.' Hannen moved uneasily. 'Perhaps there's some explanation for it all,' he said. 'The Americans *could* have made a mistake, I suppose. You know how difficult it is, with the lights and shadows on the coast. A hut or a tent's invisible unless you're directly over it. I suppose *we* couldn't have made a mistake, could we? We'd look fine fools if we turned up, up there, and there was nothing wrong at all.'

Fife stared over the ice for a moment before answering, his face expressionless as he was touched by foreboding. Somehow, there was always a feeling of living, breathing actuality about rumours. Even in their infancy, they seemed to impart a chill, if there were gravity and truth in them.

He shook his head. 'No,' he said. 'We haven't made a mistake. I think there's something wrong all right.'

For two more days, the *Brancard* manoeuvred northwards, passing easily through the zone of ice-free water off Cape Alexandra then on again into the pack once more towards Skjolborgsund, moving round the zones of hummock ice where the tides and winds had forced the floes into collision, so that they had ridden over each other into a broken chaotic mass like a vast and frozen ploughed field. Then the weather deteriorated again, with the sleet turning to snow and squalls blotting out the view, and Fife became more and more morose.

'For Christ's sake,' he said to Hannen. 'How much longer?'

'Hold it. Tom,' Hannen cautioned. 'You could do nothing on this stuff.'

Finally the clouds dispersed and, as the pack ice became looser, navigation became easier and for two days they moved northwards without trouble until the ice floes began to crowd in on them again, binding together in a falling temperature. Then finally the leads of dark water that stretched away to the north stopped and the ship came up against the immovable bulk of the pack, solid, endless and impassable, stretching as far as the eye could see towards the distant line of cliffs.

Fife turned slowly on the bridge, assessing their situation, watched silently by Hannen. Out at sea, a line of grampuses moved southwards, and towards the coast where they could see the white-capped black mountains at the entrance to Skjoldborgsund, seals were resting on the ice. A few giant petrels had found them now, soaring overhead with rigid wings and filling the air with banshee cries while smaller birds like swallows circled the ship,

Fife thrust himself away from the bridge rail with an impulsive energetic gesture. 'This'll do,' he said abruptly. 'I'm going to put the dogs ashore here. Tell Schak to put her alongside, Pat, and get me a met. report.'

Hannen went into the wheelhouse, and Fife saw him talking to the captain, and the quick glances in his direction, then he heard the engine-room telegraph ring for slow ahead, and the ship's bow swung round and she was driven hard against a big floe. As the ice anchors were put out, he saw the sudden eager movement of the dogs in the stern, then Hannen came out of the wireless cabin with a slip of paper in his hand.

'Temperature's dropping fast,' he said. 'It's going to go well down. Daneborg confirmed it. They predict wind and snow, too, Tom. It's going to be a rough journey. Autumn's started. We were just too late.'

Hannen was right. The journey north to Camp Adams, with the onset of winter and the worsening weather, and the constant winds that poured down off the ice cap on to them, was far worse than any of them had ever expected; and by the time Fife's little party reached the flank of Mount Priam they were all already exhausted.

The wind that had troubled them throughout the journey, driving the hissing particles of frozen snow into their faces, had subsided at last as they looked down into the vast frozen basin that contained Prins Haakon Lake, and the silence was so absolute as to be shattering. It was as though the earth and all its elements were stilled, to allow the tiny innumerable noises that still existed to underline the profundity of the greater silence. In the distance, they could hear dull rumbling sounds behind them that came from the movement of the ice twenty or thirty miles away. The air was crystal clear for a brief moment and the solid glistening sides of the glacier acted as a resonance board, lifting the sound like a bouncing ball.

To the north the atmosphere had deepened to the hue of navy blue now, as though they were advancing into a sea of ink, the colour stretching upwards until it gradually faded, so that behind them the horizon was pale rose and the sky an enormous canopy over a white carpet. The two sledges and the four men in the middle of it made the scene one of fantastic unreality as they paused, staring down into the valley towards Prins Haakon Sø; the dogs flopped in the traces, their tongues lolling, their breath hanging round their heads in clouds.

Fife jammed his ski sticks into the snow and drew a deep breath, conscious of a tightness across his chest that was part relief and part dread. All through the journey the feeling that some unknown catastrophe would overwhelm them before they reached Adams' camp had been growing on him. There had been no need for it – they had taken all the precautions of experienced polar travellers – but it was a state of mind that wasn't abnormal. It was brought on by a lowering of the resistance after a sustained physical effort and a continued forced steadying of the nerves and, above all, by exhaustion.

They had driven the dogs until they no longer had the strength to whine or snarl or fight, and as the conditions had grown worse the nearer they had drawn to Prins Haakon Sø, they had begun to suffer in the driving snow which had frozen in lumps to their fur and forced them into the lee of the sledge every time they stopped, shoving and biting to get the best places until the traces became tangled, and glassy with frozen saliva.

Within a day of leaving the ship, they had seen a belt of what looked like fog forming across the northern horizon and, shortly afterwards, a grey wall of drift had swept down on them on the katabatic winds that poured from the ice sheet, and in a few minutes they had been blinded by snow and bent low before the tearing gale, battling grimly into the teeth of the blizzard until, after half an hour, they had had to give up and pitch camp while the dogs huddled wretchedly behind the sledge.

For three days, they had been forced to crouch in the tents, with the cobwebs of hoar frost hanging like lace on the inside of the canvas, uneasily counting the hours and knowing that every one that passed made their position more dangerous and their chances of success less.

Their fears of disaster had been heightened by the absence of any sign of life at Cape Fraser, where they had searched with a flattened sense of failure the vicinity of the old half-collapsed hut that had been built there forty years before. Silently, all of them occupied with their own thoughts, they had pressed on again, struggling grimly northwards by day and camping by night in whistling gales that flung lumps of snow against the sagging canvas of their tents, until they had begun to stumble with exhaustion and grew fretful and bad-tempered at the conditions under which they were living.

Now, at last however, they were in sight of Camp Adams, standing on the flank of Mount Priam and staring towards Prins Haakon Sø, their minds obsessed by the delays that had made them late and by the desperate need to hurry so that Captain Schak could take away the *Brancard* before the ice closed up around him.

The cold numbed their throats as they gazed into the valley. The dog smell of sweaty harness and seal oil, tarred rope and leather, surrounded them, hanging on the frozen atmosphere that put icicles round the dogs' eyes and stiffened their clothes as it bit at the exposed flesh of their cheeks.

The menacing grey cloud still hung along the northern horizon and Fife guessed that the present stillness couldn't last long. Trying to assess just how long they had before the weather shut down on them and sealed the valley up for the winter, he stared towards the frozen grey sheet of the lake in the lee of the mountains where Adams' camp had been situated. When he had last seen the base two months before, it had been a thriving little community built round the large wooden hut which was being erected for living quarters. There had been bunches of saxifrage then and clumps of white flowers among the rocks behind the scattered tents where everyone was sleeping until the permanent living quarters were finished. Now, all that he remembered about it had vanished. Even the scattered boulders, black with age and worn round or ovoid by their passage through the glacier, had disappeared under the mantle of snow, and the whole valley was nothing but a vast ice-bound bowl. To the north and west, the land was white and featureless, a bare unrelieved frozen desert stretching for hundreds of miles.

'We've got to make this quick,' he said slowly. 'We can't stay long.'

He gestured at the grey cloud that was edging round to the east, filling the northern horizon like fog.

'That's more of Hannen's snow,' he said. 'It'll be with us soon.'

Even as they turned down the slope to the frozen surface of the lake, they felt the first hint of a breeze on their cheeks again and they glanced over their shoulders towards the grey cloud, hoping they could get into the shelter of the valley before it caught them. On the spurs of the mountain, little spirals were already rising, standing on their ends like small waterspouts as the wind lifted the snow.

Then Jessup, the wireless operator, with the leading team, flung out an arm and pointed.

'There's the wireless mast!'

They came to a halt, the dogs sinking to the snow again as they stared, their breath coming in gasps, their eyes straining into the unrelieved whiteness for the slender stick of metal.

'There, Skipper! See it?'

For some time, it was difficult to distinguish the silver rod against the snow, then a gleam of light through the hurrying clouds caught it and threw it into prominence, a long antenna clawing upwards against the mountains.

'Let's get down there,' Fife said quickly, glancing up at the sky.

The wind descended on them like a mortal enemy as they set off again, striking them obliquely so that on the bare ice of the mountain the sledges began to slide sideways before it, rattling over the polished surface and slewing round on top of the startled dogs. Then it seemed to call up its reserves in the form of snow, and the flakes whirled down among them in vast white flurries that made it impossible to see more than a few yards ahead. Crouching lower, they struggled into the wind, still descending the slope, until Fife threw up his arm.

'The hut should be over there,' he said.

Jessup glanced at him, wincing against the bitter cold that frosted his breath on the furred hood of his parka.

'There may not *be* any hut,' he shouted against the howl of the wind that plucked up the loose snow and drove it in clouds across the ice, plastering their clothes and the dogs' fur, numbing their hands and faces and crusting their beards.

The others seemed sceptical, too, but Fife gestured peremptorily, and they moved further into the valley. Reaching the wireless mast, they turned and faced away from the lake, their backs to the wind, peering through the driving snow, then Jessup stopped and shouted.

'Here's the chimney!'

They crowded round the top of the teetering cast-iron column, kicking the snow away from it and throwing it aside with their hands.

'Shovels,' Fife ordered. 'Let's have the shovels.'

For a while, they dug in silence, their morale low, their tempers quick, all of them caught by an air of foreboding. Then Jessup brought up a fragment of charred wood.

He straightened up, holding it in his hand, his face expressionless, while they all stared at him, leaning against the wind, their heads held awkwardly to enable them to see round the protecting angle of their hoods.

'Fire,' he said. 'They had a fire.'

He tossed the piece of wood towards Fife and, pushing clumsily at the snow, produced the charred remains of the base library, all the standard copies of the classics that had been given to them by well-wishers to while away the winter nights – Jane Austen, Thackeray, Dickens, Trollope.

'Bet they never read 'em,' he said shortly. 'I never did. I never did at school and on these shows I always took the opportunity of never reading 'em again.'

He bent and picked up another book, a solid wad of glassy paper, the sheets ice-bound together into a block, turning it over in his mittened hands before showing it to the others.

'*Scott's Last Journey*,' he said slowly.

He stared sombrely at Fife and slowly dropped it into the snow again by his feet.

After a while, they found the remains of Hellyer's workshop. It was snowed up and collapsing and the floor was covered with ice. All one side of it was charred and there were scraps of wire and pieces of sheet metal and a couple of screwdrivers with their handles burned off frozen into the floor.

'Too near the base hut,' Fife growled.

The snow was coming down thicker now, filling the air with millions of wind-driven particles that forced their way into their hoods and coated their eyebrows with icicles.

'Keep shovelling,' Fife ordered. 'We might find something.'

Jessup gave him a glare. 'Christ, Skip – ' he begged.

The snow had formed drifts behind every pile of wreckage but, after a while, they unearthed the yellow sides of a Weasel. It was choked with snow, which had got into the carburettors and ventilators, and Jessup began to scratch away at the engine with a knife.

'Can you get it going?' Fife asked.

Jessup shook his head. 'Not a chance,' he said. 'Everything's burned away. Ignition. Piping. Injectors. Batteries. The lot.'

There were the remains of an inflatable pontoon, a mere melted fragment of yellow rubber, a boat, blown over by the wind and full of frozen snow, the icicles hanging down over the charred side like harp strings, and a few food cases, looking like small icebegs. They had to use ice axes to get at them, but they were all either charred or broken open, and the stakes which had been set up for identification purposes were all twisted and broken and layered with ice.

'They've obviously taken all that wasn't destroyed,' Fife said.

The main hut had been gutted and had collapsed, and they could see the twisted wiring of the bunks half-hidden among the trampled snow. The seismograph was undamaged but the electricity panel was hanging grotesquely askew and its disconnected wires looked like disordered hair alongside the remains of the transmitter, the cooking stove, the wind gauge and the diesels.

While they worked, Jessup had cleared Hellyer's workshop. He had shovelled away the snow, though the ice remained on the floor, and had erected a shelter where they could eat. They were all cold and wet by now and Erskine and Smeed were suffering a little from frostbite, but when they got the stove going the ice on the floor melted so that they were sitting in slush. They were all too exhausted to do anything about it, however, and dumbly waited to thaw out, baffled and depressed by the organ-booming of the blizzard. The stove kept losing pressure for some reason and the little shelter creaked and groaned and threatened to collapse with every violent gust of wind, but they were all too tired to care and fell into a restless sleep, instinctively huddling together for warmth.

The wind died a little during the night but when they left the hut in the morning, fighting their way to the surface through a drift that had built up, the snow had hidden everything they had unearthed, and was still falling. It was possible to work, however, and they all started digging again, uncovering the motor that had provided light, two dynamo rectifiers, and a variety of ruined wireless equipment, a theodolite, the geophones, a damaged compass, and a rifle with the stock burned away.

'Where've they gone to, Skipper?' Jessup said. 'They've obviously gone somewhere because they've sorted out all the things they'd need.'

Fife said nothing, straightening up and staring round him, his eyes narrow. He could hear Jessup swearing quietly as he dug and Smeed grumbling to Erskine.

Several times he caught the name, 'Adams – Adams – ', and he knew they were all laying the blame for the disaster and for whatever had happened to him and the men with him where it belonged. There was a sense of doom over the little camp with its scattered cases and trampled snow, and the forlorn twist of canvas that Jessup had erected over the end of the collapsing workshop. Somewhere near them was the answer to where Adams and his party were, but they had arrived too late and finding any messages under the depth of snow there was now only a matter of luck.

'Skip!'

Jessup had wandered off a little way and his voice as he called was urgent and sharp with excitement.

'Quick! Here!'

They struggled through the deep snow towards him. He was on his knees in a drift and was scooping a hollow by what appeared to be a piece of wood standing erect in the ground. He was plastered with snow, and ice was sticking in frozen globules to his half-grown beard and moustache.

As they drew closer, Fife saw there was a crosspiece on the wood and that Jessup, waist-deep now in the drift, had unearthed what appeared to be a pile of stones.

'It's a cairn,' he said. 'They must have left a message or something. No – ' the excitement went out of his words immediately and his voice became flat and empty-sounding – 'No,' he went on, 'there'll be no message here.'

He looked up quickly at Fife, his eyes alarmed, then he began to dig again.

'Edward Hyams Adams – ' he was saying aloud, his face close to the wood – 'Lieutenant-Commander Royal Navy. Died – '

Fife dropped on his knees alongside him and brushed the snow away from the date.

'Aged 41,' Jessup finished solemnly. 'RIP.'

He turned slowly and stared at Fife.

'Adams,' he said softly. 'It's Adams' grave. He's buried here.'

They stayed three days altogether, on the site of Camp Adams, digging away the snow, trying to find some clue to what had happened to the rest of Adams' party, collecting what salvageable equipment they could carry. By Adams' grave they left a message saying that they'd been there, in case Adams' party returned, hoping all the time, in fact, now that the snow had stopped that they'd emerge from some shelter they'd made for themselves. Then on the fourth day, with the weather reports relayed from Hannen's party growing more ominous, they turned their faces to the south again.

The sledges were loaded and Smeed and Jessup were bending over the restless dogs, checking the harness, as Fife moved among the trampled snow and the uncovered remnants of the charred hut, deflated with a sense of failure.

He glanced at the others and saw they were still busy with the dogs, then he stared again at the silent camp, the few charred beams they had uncovered, the useless Weasel, the lopsided electricity panel with its ends of wire like the hair of a drowned man, and the scrap of burned canvas Jessup had fastened over the half-collapsed lean-to.

Surrounded by the evidence of the disaster that had come upon Adams' party, the little cairn of stones that marked the solitary grave, the charred timbers and the burned-out Weasel, and the two or three punctured weather balloons

Jessup had found, they were all depressed by a chill inexplicable fear.

Fife shivered inside his clothes, his mind roving backwards over the events of the past few months, the things he had experienced which even then had set him worrying.

The dispute between him and Adams had simmered all the way up towards Iceland and flared up again over Adams' choice of a base at Axel Helberg Bay and the disagreement had soured the whole journey north, spreading through the entire ship until everyone on the expedition had found themselves taking sides.

Adams had talked no more of Fife's resignation, but he had made it clear what he felt by leaving his name off the list of men for the advanced camps and putting him in charge of the ship and the coastal survey and the useless camp at Stakness. It had been obvious that he had regarded both Fife and Hannen as troublemakers and he had treated all their former comrades similarly, leaving the hardened Jessup, Erskine and Smeed behind too, and taking north with him men without experience.

'Conceived in confusion and operated in chaos,' was Fife's favourite description of the expedition. While Mortimer in London tried to run it from his office in Park Lane between business lunches and political conferences, Adams seemed to have lost interest in everything except getting up to Prins Haakon Sø as fast as possible and leaving the rest to Fife.

There had been another row at Camp Adams when the *Brancard* had landed the advance party on the coast and Fife had denounced Adams' plan for his hutments as dangerous and hurried, but Adams' eyes were clearly on the interior and the planning of the base had been only a nuisance to him. He had promised to attend to the matter later and Fife, troubled by the shortness of the time at his disposal, had had to leave it at that and take the *Brancard* round to the West Coast camp.

Almost immediately, he had been inundated with radioed complaints about unsuitable equipment, about the troublesome cookers the advanced parties were using, about the high unserviceability rate of the Weasels, and the unfortunate choice of sledges. The stores had not been properly loaded and had thus been unloaded in the wrong order, and there was a shortage of milk powder and tea, and the Hodde-Graz boots they were using allowed the feet to grow cold. All the ravens of dissatisfaction had come home to roost, and now Adams had effectively killed himself and probably all his party. Bad planning had destroyed his base and if there were any survivors they were without help somewhere with inefficient equipment.

Fife drew a deep breath and turned round. Jessup and Smeed had finished what they were doing and Jessup was walking towards him, his face grim, his eyes uneasy. Then, unexpectedly, one of the dogs started to howl, and in a moment for no reason at all, the whole lot of them were at it, heads back, filling the air with their mourning, in a way that made the flesh creep.

Smeed and Erskine began to cuff at them with their mittened hands, but they merely shifted their positions, squatted down again and started once more. In the silence, the howling sounded like a dirge and Fife stared round at his companions, trying to assess from their haggard faces and hollow eyes just how much the journey had taken out of them in exhaustion and effort. They were all tired enough now to be irritable with each other; and sleeping, eating, washing in the confined spaces of the tents and struggling with their inefficient stoves and unsatisfactory sledges had left them full of a sort of numb exhaustion that was made worse by what they'd found. The duties that would normally have aroused cheerful cursing were now performed with a monotonous chorus of muttered viciousness.

Jessup appeared alongside him, a stocky figure in ugly, ill-fitting clothing, his red face wind-whipped and already bearing the marks of frostbite. He straightened up, his breath hanging in the air, and stared at Fife, his blue eyes uneasy.

'We're ready, Skipper,' he announced sombrely.

Fife nodded. There was nothing else to do now, nothing left to them but the hope that the rest of Adams' party were still safe somewhere, biding their time until the weather improved or the damage to their transmitter, that was implicit in their long silence, could be put right. It was a slender hope at the best but they had to hang on to it if they weren't to give up trying.

'Right,' he said. 'Let's go.'

Jessup glanced round him for a moment, then he seemed to shudder. 'Thank God,' he said. 'I'll be glad to get away from this damned place. It was always unlucky. I think it's haunted.'

seven

The *Brancard* was waiting for them at the entrance to Skjolborgsund when they returned. A snow-chaser was unwinding phantom waves off the surface of the ice, moving them ceaselessly, stretching them away out of sight and lifting them occasionally like clouds of spindrift so that the horizon was blotted out by fleeing white vapour.

The floes were drawing nearer now and there were anxious looks on the faces of the men on the bridge as they stared towards the south. All day, they had been backing and turning the ship, leaving a clear patch of water round it, so that they could manoeuvre into the lead that opened away from the land, and head for the ice-free waters as soon as possible.

The Weasels came first out of the hummock ice towards the ship, their yellow paint startlingly bright against the blue whiteness of the background, and immediately there was a cheer and the men working alongside the ship dropped what they were doing and stood waiting. For a moment, the vehicles were hidden again by the rolling waves of vapour that made the ice itself seem to move as it disappeared under the undulating waves, then they re-emerged and behind them this time the restless tails of the dog teams were visible.

The little cavalcade drew nearer, rolling and swinging in and out of the uneven floes, appearing and disappearing among the nature-made gulleys and mounds, then someone saw Fife's face staring out of the leading Weasel and the expression on his face told them all they wanted to know and the questions they had started died away to silence.

Fife jumped down as the engines spluttered into stillness, and Erskine and Jessup brought their dog teams up alongside him.

There were one or two enquiries as Fife strode through the waiting men, but he merely shook his head and went straight towards the ship, moving slowly, stiff-legged with weariness.

'What did you find?' Jessup was asked.

'Nowt,' he said in the broad north-country accent that always became more noticeable when he was tired or angry. 'Nowt at all!'

'Hannen radioed you'd found Adams' grave.'

'Yes. Adams' grave.' Jessup's broad face was drawn with weariness. 'And that's all.'

'For God's sake,' someone said, 'they couldn't just disappear.'

Jessup's face grew hot and aggressive under his beard and he rounded on the speaker. 'If you don't believe me,' he snapped, 'you can take these bloody dogs up there and go and look for yourself.'

The group around him backed away before his anger, splitting up as he shoved his way through and started to unload the sledge with a bitter unspeaking fury.

'Take it easy, Archie,' he was told softly. 'No offence intended, old boy.'

Jessup gestured angrily, the movement laboured and full of weary irritation, then the spirit seemed to go out of him abruptly and he bent over the dogs, his head down. 'Come and give us a hand with these blasted dogs,' he ended heavily.

As he fought to keep the restless animals under control, several men moved forward to help him, their faces concerned, their voices low, as though respecting his exhaustion.

'What was it like?' he was asked, and he straightened up slowly.

'Bloody awful,' he said, without any attempt to impress them. 'It's not a journey for this time of the year. Tom Fife's the only one who could have done it.'

'What about the dogs?'

'Usual useless set of bastards!' Jessup grunted, and relented. 'They're all right,' he admitted grudgingly. 'Pulled their hearts out. We lost three of them. Just lay down and died. And twice we had half the team hanging in a crevasse by the traces.'

He moved around the sledge slowly, his footsteps dragging, as though the last ounce of energy had been drained from his body, the last fragment of resistance softened.

'Those bloody winds were enough to drive you bonkers,' he said harshly, his face bitter with the disappointment that showed in every word he spoke. 'Just built up and kept on going. They shifted all the snow off the slopes and there we were, edging round the mountain like men with no legs, and the sledges crabbing all the time on top of the dogs. The teeth broke off the brake claws and we had to wind ropes round the runners to act as drags. And all the time that bloody lead dog of mine was deciding it was his responsibility to navigate, not mine. I'll have to get rid of him. He starts too may fights.'

He straightened up, as though his back ached, and stared across the ice towards the leads that opened like black lanes, towards the sea.

'When are we moving?' he demanded with the irritability of someone who had lived too long in a confined space under conditions which made even the simplest operation difficult.

'Straight away,' he was told. 'Schak says he can't remember when the ice was so far south at this time of the year. Winter's coming early.'

Fife's face was blank and exhausted when Hannen joined him in his cabin, and the bitter winds had put the brown marks of frostbite on his cheeks.

Outside, they were lifting the Weasels to the deck already and the clatter of the winches echoed through the iron plates of the ship.

'Schak's got the wind up,' Hannen said, reaching for the whisky bottle that stood on the charts on the table. 'He's been getting reports of ice at Cape Alexandra.'

Fife looked up, heavy-eyed with weariness.

'It's damned early for ice round there,' he said.

'That's the report. He says he can't risk waiting any longer.'

Fife nodded and, taking the whisky bottle as Hannen put it down, sloshed some of the liquid into a tooth glass.

'What are you going to do, Tom?'

Fife lifted heavy eyelids. 'I'm not just going back to Stakness for the winter,' he said grimly. 'I'm going to put the Weasels ashore in Scoresby Sund. There's still time and Schak can get us in. I wanted it that way all along but Adams insisted on Stakness. We can be on hand then if there's any sign of them and they need help. We can establish a base of sorts somewhere round Clavering Island. We might even get up to Cape Alexandra from there. If not, we could get aircraft flown in to pick them up.'

'We haven't much time.'

'We've enough. At least, then, if they land on my neck from London, to ask what we're doing, we'll be doing *something*.' He paused and looked up at Hannen, his face haggard with tiredness. 'Because they *will* be on our necks soon, Pat, asking how we came to let it happen.'

He stuffed his hands into his pockets and stared at the charts.

'The Sledge Patrol'll keep a lookout,' Hannen said. 'And the Americans have promised to fly whenever possible.'

'This damned continent's two thousand miles long and a thousand miles wide,' Fife reminded him. 'It's no good hoping for much. In another month, they'll all be tied to their bases. For weeks at a time. Unless we pick 'em up soon, Adams' party's on its own.'

Hannen said nothing and Fife gestured wearily. 'And you know what that makes me, don't you?' he said. 'The man who abandoned Adams.'

'Good God, man,' Hannen burst out. 'It wasn't your fault.'

Fife lifted his head slowly. '*You* know that. *I* know it. I hope all the rest of 'em know it. But Mortimer's back in England waiting to shove his nose in. *He doesn't know it*, and he's soon going to notice the absence of all messages from Adams, the absence of any references to him or his party or his camp, the absence of all met. reports from up there. He'll soon be asking questions, if he isn't already asking them.'

'It wasn't your doing,' Hannen insisted.

Fife shrugged. 'Things might look different back in England,' he said. 'These people who gave us funds – businessmen for the most part. They don't know what it's like up here and they've sunk money into this affair and now it looks as though they're not going to get anything out of it.'

'They weren't seeking profits.'

Fife shook his head. 'Maybe not,' he said. 'But they were seeking results. The *Record*, for instance. Look how much Kinglake sank into the expedition for the chance of a story. Now there isn't any story, unless they call it a story that the expedition's gone wrong and killed its leader and, for all I know, all the rest of his party. They're going to ask why wasn't I there to prevent them being lost. Why didn't I take action before I did? Why didn't I get up here as soon as it happened? Meet Tom Fife, Pat, former explorer.'

The wind died away to a whisper as the *Brancard* cleared the ice and headed south. The thermometer was falling steadily and there was no wind at all now to ruffle the slow swell.

A grey mist rose from the sea in a writhing curtain that lifted higher than the masthead, drifting in ghostly wraiths through the rigging as the ship drove through the black sea on its southerly course, obscuring the bow from time to time as it thickened abruptly, and blurring the yellow shapes of the Weasels on the foredeck that glowed momentarily from time to time as someone opened a door and a shaft of light sped between the derricks towards them.

The bridge was silent except for the static on the wireless set that they could hear through the half-opened porthole of the wireless cabin.

The radio operator was amusing himself listening on the ship-to-ship receiver – to the chatting of two British trawler skippers who were complaining about the new Icelandic twelve-mile limit for fishing. Even through the interference the indignation and the anger in their voices was obvious.

'They'll be waiting off the Humber Light for us soon,' one of them was saying bitterly. 'They'll pinch us as soon as we cast off.'

'Where do we go now when we want to run from a gale?' the other said. 'Shove your nose inside the limit and they'll nab you and it'll be up to you then to prove you hadn't got your trawl down.'

The operator, his headset on, fiddled idly with the knobs, listening to the normal traffic with one ear and the trawler traffic with the other, while he read a paper-backed novel bearing a frontispiece of an anatomically impossible blonde.

'I'll stem him if he comes near me.' The broad Yorkshire vowels filled the cabin over the static. 'Those damned gunboats are only timber-built, and I bet he'd clear out smartly if he saw me coming round on him.'

The voice boomed for a moment and grew thin again as the operator moved his fingers idly, growing tired of the dispute, and Fife joined Hannen on the bridge with Captain Schak.

'Can't we go any faster?' he asked.

The Canadian shrugged. 'Maybe you've not seen the fog,' he said gently.

Fife was silent and Schak stared at him sympathetically. 'I know what's on your mind,' he said. 'But I've been sailing in these waters a long time now and I know what I'm doing.'

Fife nodded dumbly and Schak looked at him, his heavy Germanic face concerned. 'I guess it's more important to get you to Scoresby Sund an hour or two late than not at all,' he said.

Fife nodded again and Schak, as though the argument were dismissed, offered his tobacco pouch.

'Trawler war's hotting up,' he said shortly, cocking a thumb in the direction of the radio cabin.

Nobody said anything and he went on, half to himself. 'I'm going to say I'm on their side when we get back to Stakness,' he said. 'It's easier.'

'We shan't be going back to Stakness,' Fife pointed out. 'Except to clear the rest of the gear. I'm shifting base to Scoresby.'

'Who says?'

'I do.'

'There'll be hell to pay when London hears.'

'I'll chance it. It's my decision.'

Schak grunted. 'Well, it's not before time,' he said. 'It should have been there long since.'

He paused, staring into the fog. 'Let's hope they haven't impounded everything,' he said.

'They'd better not,' Fife growled.

'You can't fight the whole goddam Icelandic police force if they have,' Schak pointed out. 'And they *might* have. This damned fishing situation's getting nasty. First it was threats, then it was blanks, but now, bejesus, it's shells across the bow.'

'They'd never dare aim for a hit,' Hannen interrupted.

'No,' Schak agreed. 'Maybe not. But one of these days some guy's going to wake up hung-over and his calibrations are going to be wrong and then somebody's going to get hurt. Did you know the Navy's moved in with destroyers as well as frigates now? The trawler owners have been yowling to their MPs, and they're going to create two boxes inside the fishing grounds and patrol 'em as long as the trawlers are there.'

'Maybe it's as well we're not going back to Stakness,' Hannen commented.

'You're telling me, brother. This is nothing. Just wait until some bloody-minded skipper decides not to conform. I've met plenty of 'em who wouldn't. Some of 'em would board a goddam battle-wagon if they thought it had cut their trawls. I've had 'em throwing coal at me often.'

They were silent for a while as the ship drove through the night, quiet except for the thump of engines and the swish of icy water alongside. Then, from the saloon, they heard the thin strains of radio music and the sound of voices, and abruptly, the loud metallic chatter of trawler skippers filling the radio shack again.

'That sounded goddam close,' Schak commented sharply, his head up, listening.

As he spoke, the radio operator's door opened and he stuck his head out.

'Trouble,' he said laconically.

'What sort of trouble?'

'A couple of trawlers. They're right across our course and not far away.'

'What the hell are they doing up here?' Schak demanded. 'They're miles away from where they should be.'

'Where they should be?' The radio operator grinned. 'Where's that these days? You never know now where the hell the s.o.b.s are going to turn up. There's been a bit of a shindig with some Icelanders, it seems, and they decided to move north. I've just been listening to the gabble.'

'Where are they now?'

'Due south of us, I reckon. You can hear 'em if you want to.'

'I don't want to hear 'em,' Schak said shortly. 'I just want to know where they are. I don't want 'em across my bows in this stuff. Can you get a bearing on 'em?'

'I guess so.'

The captain nodded and went into the wheelhouse and Fife pulled his scarf tighter round his neck. He was silent for a moment before he spoke.

'I've been writing a report for London, Pat,' he said at last to Hannen. 'I didn't find much to say that was helpful.'

Hannen didn't reply and Fife lit his pipe.

'It'll have to go off sooner or later,' he said.

'To Mortimer?'

'To the committee. Same thing.'

Fife thrust his hands in his pockets and stared over the bow into the darkness. Hannen watched him for a moment, listening to the sound of the water and the thump of the engines and the noisy chatter from the radio cabin. It wasn't just what might be said in London, he knew, that was worrying Fife. Fife had never worried much what people said about him when he felt he was right.

He was on the point of questioning him, guessing that in his taciturn way he was wanting to unburden himself, when he decided to wait, knowing that sooner or later Fife would find the weight of his worries too much for him.

After a while, Fife sighed and turned, and Hannen was glad he'd said nothing.

'With Adams dead,' Fife said slowly, 'Legge-Jenkins is in charge of the party.' He paused while Hannen waited for him to continue, then he hunched his shoulders as though his thoughts were difficult to bear. 'I like L-J,' he said. 'But he's no man to get them out of a hole, Pat.'

'He's been up there before,' Hannen pointed out.

Fife shrugged. 'All the same, I can't see him looking after nine others – if there *are* nine others. Some people lead, and some follow. L-J wasn't a leader. Tell him what to do and he'd do it, and damned well, too, but there's something missing that stops him having the ability to run a show on his own. I wish Adams hadn't picked him for his Number Two. He could have had Piercey. Piercey was much better.'

Hannen managed a smile. 'Perhaps he was tired of deputies who had strong views on things,' he said. 'Piercey was never afraid to say what he thought.'

Fife gestured. 'He could have taken Sampson and put you in charge of the West Camp. He could have left L-J at Stakness with me.'

'He could have taken *you* up to Camp Adams and left L-J in charge of the Stakness base and the shore survey party. I'd have been happy enough with that arrangement.'

'We all make mistakes,' Fife said. 'Personnel problems crop up from time to time on these affairs. Bad guesses. Misfits. It's one of those things.'

'Adams ought to have had someone stronger than L-J to deal with young Hellyer,' Hannen insisted. 'I bet that damned hyphen of his got Hellyer's back up more than anything.'

Fife turned round and stood facing the stern, his brows down, his face brooding, then Schak came out of the wheelhouse, his face angry.

'Here you are,' he said immediately. 'This is your bloody-minded skipper already. Two of 'em smack across our course. Keep your ears open, for God's sake!'

He shouted a warning down to the lookout on the bow and disappeared again, his face worried.

'I wish to God the fog would lift,' he said as he vanished.

Fife struck another match for his pipe. 'This lot won't lift for a bit,' he commented. 'Look.' He held up the match and they watched the flame burn straight and steady. 'Not enough wind to blow it out,' he said.

For a while they stood in silence, shivering in the frosty atmosphere, then something made Fife lift his head, certain that the air around them was full of sound.

'Listen,' he said sharply. 'What's that?'

For a second, all they could hear was the flat slap of the water along the side of the ship and the thin strains of music in the saloon coming over the gabble of static from the radio cabin, then Fife swung round and stared to starboard.

'There,' he said, 'I heard it again.'

Hannen strained his ears and eyes into the swirling mist, then abruptly, as the clatter in the radio cabin grew to a shout, he heard the distinct boom of a siren coming to them over the black water. Even as they saw Captain Schak cock his head inside the wheelhouse, the siren came again, this time by some trick of the atmosphere deafeningly loud and close.

'There's a ship there,' Fife said.

Captain Schak had heard the sound too and had leapt out of the wheelhouse, the door swinging back with a crash and a jingle as he leaned across the windcheater to stare into the fog.

'Where is it?' he snapped.

'Over there,' Fife said. 'Starboard. There's something on the starboard bow.'

'It's a trawler –!' Even as Schak leapt for the whistle toggle, they saw the vague shadow through the fog, scarcely more than a thickening of the mist, then the *Brancard's* siren howled.

There was a shout from the foredeck lookout that rose to a high-pitched yell. 'Trawler on the starboard bow!' – then Fife's mind was full of momentary impressions – the sudden hardening of the outline of the approaching ship, the high ungainly stem, the white bow wave in front of her as she drove at the *Brancard*.

'Hard a starboard,' Schak was shouting at the helmsman. 'Get your bows round, man, so that the son-of-a-bitch doesn't hit us broadside on. Get her round, for Christ's sake!'

The helmsman spun the wheel desperately, his eyes on the ship ahead, and the converging trawler, approaching at a wide angle, seemed to slide sideways across the swinging bows. But the *Brancard* wasn't fast enough and the trawler's knife-edged bow drove deeply into her side and Fife found himself stumbling to the deck on top of Hannen.

As he staggered to his feet, he felt the ship roll over on her starboard side, then, as she slowly recovered, the trawler ground along her side, and his ears were full of the scream of tortured metal, his eyes full of the showers of sparks that leapt from the twisted plates. He saw a rope twang tight and snap, and rust and flakes of paint come down on the Weasels as the two ships swung together with a shattering metallic bang. Then the trawler reeled off drunkenly into the grey-blackness of the fog and they were alone again.

For a moment, as the trawler vanished, there was absolute silence, then the noise of trampling feet burst out all over the ship, along alleyways and up ladders, and confused voices came as everybody tried at once to find out what had happened and how bad the damage was.

The feet and the voices reached their climax at the foot of the bridge ladder, where the Second Engineer was scrambling up to report to the Captain. The radio operator's door opened and a harsh voice called out in the darkness. 'Set's dead, skipper,' it said. 'I'm switching to emergency.'

The ship-to-ship receiver on which the operator had been listening to the remarks of the trawlermen was suddenly loud with a nasal Grimsby voice.

'Mayday. Mayday. This is *Lady Harding*. This is *Lady Harding*. Have been in collision with unknown ship.'

'I expect the goddam fool was asleep on watch,' Schak snorted. 'Or probably at the bottle.'

The air, which had been full of chatter, was cleared at once as a thousand ears listened intently.

'Starboard bow holed.' The voice from the *Lady Harding* was calmer now, as though the first emergency had passed. 'I am taking water. Stand by me. Am going to head due south –'

'Shut that goddam thing off,' Schak snapped, 'and send out our own.' He swung round to the Second Engineer. 'What's the damage?'

'It's a shambles below. Chief says the engines are all right, though they were nearly jolted off their beds. We're taking water and half the lights are out but we can hold it. There's one of the greasers trapped but we'll get him out all right, I guess. He's not hurt. Who was it hit us?'

'Never mind who hit us,' Schak snapped. 'We can worry about that later. Get back to the Chief and ask him what he wants me to do. Can we carry on?'

'In a minute. He'll let you have a full report as soon as he can.'

'Right. Get going.'

There was a crowd of men on the deck below the bridge, some in their shirts, some still dressing.

'What happened, Skipper?' Jessup, his red, bearded face still heavy with sleep, appeared alongside Fife.

'Collision. Trawler. Everybody all right?'

'I think so. Smeed had a narrow squeak. The side of his cabin fell in on him, but he's all right except for being wet.

Benediktsson was trapped for a bit but he's out now and he's not hurt.'

It was bitterly cold suddenly and the iron trampling of racing feet on ladders seemed to ring twice as loud, and the ship felt sluggish and helpless. Forward, the ship's electrician was already dragging batteries of lights towards the shrouds for them to work by.

Fife moved between the Weasels on the decks, looking for damage with a torch, then Hannen joined him and they climbed over the big yellow vehicles, checking the moorings.

'I think they're all right, thank God,' Fife said.

He indicated the deck plating of the forecastle alongside, buckled and bent as though it had received a blow from an immense axe. From aft somewhere heavy fume-laden air came up at them in waves.

'If you need us, call on us,' he told Schak who had left the bridge to the Mate and had come to inspect the damage himself.

Schak nodded, absorbed as he watched one of the seamen lash a rope across the twisted deck, and Fife had the feeling that for a moment he resented the expedition and the extra men who got in the way of his crew.

'I'll check that everybody's safe,' Hannen said. 'I'll send Smeed up to look over the Weasels.'

As he vanished the sound of hammering began and a Canadian voice in the darkness saying, 'Take a turn there. Take a turn there,' over the endless surge and thump of the swell alongside that had started a new noise forward, a mixture between a thud and a clang like the tolling of a bell, as though something had broken loose and was swinging as the ship rolled.

Groups of men, some of them in arctic clothing and clutching lifebelts, appeared on the deck now and one of them began to sing.

'The bravest man was Captain Brown.
Who played his ukelele as the ship went down.'

'Cut that out,' Hannen's sharp voice stopped the singer at once. 'If you've nothing to do, get into the saloon out of the way.'

There was a little muttering and the shuffle of feet and a shaft of yellow light as a door opened. Smeed, his shirt black with oily water, joined Fife by the Weasels and climbed into the cabin of the one nearest the side of the ship, scrambling over the tumbled hawser that was draped across the track and brushing at the flakes of rust that filled the cabin.

'She looks all right, Skipper,' he said. 'She's full of paint but I don't think she's been touched.'

Fife nodded and, as he turned away, Hannen approached, pushing purposefully through the men who were moving about in the bitter air clearing the rubbish from the decks.

The ship was quieter now, as though her head had come round and she wasn't suffering from the cumbersome roll any more. The clanging forward had stopped too.

'Number Two Hold's flooded,' Hannen said. 'That's where all our gear's stowed.'

'We can pick up more at Scoresby,' Fife said quickly. 'We can buy if necessary. The insurance will cover it. The Weasels are all right. We've nothing to worry about.'

'There's just one thing –' Hannen's face was troubled and Fife swung round on him.

'I heard the Chief Engineer telling Schak there was a lot of water below. He said the bulkhead was damaged. He said it would mean Iceland for dry-docking.'

They were still standing about when dawn came, grey-faced men shivering and staring at the buckled deck and the hole where the oily scum leaked out into the sea as the ship limped south.

Fife's anger was frustrated and weary now. 'God damn that trawler,' he kept saying bitterly. 'God damn her!'

'We're still heading for Scoresby,' Hannen pointed out.

Fife moved restlessly, as though he didn't believe him, then the Chief Engineer, wearing a pair of oily gauntlets, pushed past them, tired eyelids drooping in a lined face.

He paused at the starboard rail by the gaping wound in the ship's side and thrust his head outboard, listening for sounds of distress over the thin ripples of the bow wave. Then he turned and called up to the bridge.

'Steering all right?'

'Seems all right.'

'OK, then. You can come round now.'

The ship's head began to swing and the wind that had been kept from them by the high forecastle began to blow across the deck. Fife's brows came down as he felt its cold touch on his cheek, and he looked up at the masts swinging across the sky.

'We've changed course,' he said bitterly. 'We've turned east.'

Hannen looked sick under the half-grown beard that covered his face.

'Iceland,' he said. 'That's what the Chief told me. I'll go and check.'

As he moved towards the bridge, Fife stared aft where the pale light glittered and spread in the grey sunless morning, throwing varying shades of colour across the sea. He was cold and stiff and his eyes felt crusted with tiredness, and he was obsessed now with a new feeling of failure, almost as though the responsibility for the collision were his, too.

After a while, Hannen came back through the groups of men clearing the deck of the ropes and tackles and crowbars they'd been using during the night.

'It's Iceland all right,' he said shortly. 'For dry-docking.'

Fife drew a deep breath.

'Schak says he's sorry but he's no alternative,' Hannen went on. 'He says he daren't stay in these waters with a hole like that in his side.'

Fife nodded, his face expressionless. 'There'll be no Weasels in Scoresby Sund now,' he said. 'Not unless we can scrape up another ship from somewhere and the weather's kind to us.'

'The forecast's milder now,' Hannen said, trying to be cheerful. 'And the wind's coming round to the opposite quarter. Daneborg seems to think the ice might hold off a bit longer after all.'

'If it does,' Fife murmured, 'if only it would, we might just make it.' He drew a deep breath. 'There's only one drawback,' he said. 'We can't keep it from Mortimer now. And once it gets to Mortimer, there'll be no keeping it from the Press.'

Hannen held out a slip of paper. 'You're behind the times, Tom,' he said flatly. 'Mortimer knows already. This came from him. Schak just passed it over. Shall I read it?'

Fife stared at him then nodded.

Hannen glanced at the paper and spoke almost as though he knew the words on it off by heart. '*From Mortimer, HQ Greenice, London. To Fife*, MV Brancard.'

'Go on,' Fife said quickly. 'Never mind the formalities. What's he say?'

'Not much,' Hannen pointed out. '*What has happened to Adams? Request news immediately. Cable facts at once and forward detailed report as soon as possible. Committee concerned at rumours.*'

'That all?'

'It's enough, isn't it?'

Fife nodded. 'He makes it sound like a memo for a board meeting,' he said.

He was silent for a second then he shrugged. 'Well, he's heard,' he said. 'That's it, Pat. My head's well and truly in the noose now.'

'They can't touch you,' Hannen reassured him. 'There are plenty of people here to vouch for what you've done.'

Fife swung round on him. 'I don't give a damn what they do to me,' he said. Then he paused, his hands thrust into his pockets. 'It's not that, Pat,' he went on. 'It's just the thought of the damage Mortimer can do now with his interference. Memos and votes of confidence and committee meetings aren't much good in a business like this, and that's the only system Mortimer comprehends. God knows, I'm sorry about Adams and for his wife and for Mortimer, too, I suppose, but if there are any of Adams' people still left alive up there, Pat, they aren't going to be helped much by Mortimer making this into a boardroom affair.'

Part Two

The Final Straw

one

The streaming drift had whitened out the horizon now so that it was impossible to see more than a few yards. It was everywhere, coating every cavity with snow as fine as dust; penetrating every cranny, clinging to outer garments and defying every clumsy effort to brush it off; filling the air with millions of needle-pointed fragments that swept out of the blankness, stinging the exposed areas of the face; hissing against the sides of the tents and driving the wretched dogs into the lee of the sledges, biting and snapping to get the best positions out of the wind. The visibility was no more than a few yards now and the Weasels, already half-drifted over, were mere hazy shapes in the white dimness.

Doctor Piercey, struggling from the tents, angry and deflated as the odds mounted against them, found that the sense of guilt he felt at not resisting Legge-Jenkins' wild scheme to reach Cape Alexandra via the Søster Nunataks was growing with the news he carried.

The journey from Camp Adams had been dogged by ill luck from the start. A broken towing bar had stopped them even before they had got clear of Prins Haakon Sø, then the limping Number Three had developed a series of leaking radiators and broken bogey wheels that had forced them all to take their turn at lying flat under the vehicle on the snow, fumbling with numb fingers at nuts and bolts in a frozen purgatory of ice, with the temperature dropping all the time and the drift coming in incessant clouds into their faces.

Rubber had been like iron, and metal had been like knives cutting through their layers of mittens, until their hands had been clumsy and agonisingly painful and they had had to crawl into the tent or the cabin of the Weasel to thaw them out.

And now, in the worst possible conditions and after infuriating delays for repairs or for weather that had eaten into their rations and transformed what they had hoped would be a quick if difficult journey to the Søster Nunataks into a desperate struggle against time, the maddening Number Three had finally given up the ghost; and Hellyer, already exhausted by the extra work that had been put on his shoulders, had unwillingly pronounced sentence.

'She's had it,' he had said viciously. 'Big end's gone.'

There had been no alternative but to pitch the tents and Piercey had set off to find Legge-Jenkins with Hellyer's words hanging like a loaded pack on his shoulders.

In his self-dissecting manner he felt that, by allowing Legge-Jenkins to have his head against all the warnings of common sense, the blame for their position was laid squarely at his own door and that now the time had come to accept that responsibility and do something about it.

It was never easy beforehand to assess values on an expedition. Long ago a leaky paraffin tin had been the final straw which had crushed Scott, and it was only the scale of things which had altered nowadays. The decisions which, for good or ill, a leader had to make had increased in their complexity and more often than not were based on pure guesswork. But Legge-Jenkins' guesses had proved to be wildly unreal and his rapidly fading confidence was making the less experienced members of the party uneasy. There could no longer be any case for trying to avoid hurting anyone's feelings.

Piercey found him in Hellyer's Weasel, crouched over the expedition diary and trying to write, the pencil held in his bandaged hand, his feet in a puddle of melted snow, his face wearing a blank, defeated expression. He looked up with heavy eyes as Piercey entered, wincing, it seemed, at the cloud of fine drift that accompanied him.

'Number Three's finished,' Piercey said bluntly, fighting against the temptation to let his feelings show in his face. More and more in the past days, he had noticed the eyes of the others resting on him and he knew that the most important thing to them all just then was that he, the man with experience, should show no lack of confidence.

He saw Legge-Jenkins' expression change as he spoke but he went on quickly with bitter realism, not believing in beating about the bush with bad news.

'The big end's gone,' he said. 'And there's no spare. We'll have to abandon it, together with two of the trailers. It'll mean a reassessment of what we can take with us.'

Legge-Jenkins stared at him, his expression numb and stupefied. 'We can't manage with just one Weasel,' he said despairingly. 'Especially with one man unable to walk!'

'We'll cope,' Piercey said briskly. 'We've been expecting it for some time, after all. I've been trying to work out a list of what we can leave behind.'

'We've already left *two* lots behind! One at Camp Adams and one on the way.'

Piercey nodded. Certainly it hadn't taken them long to realise they had been trying to carry too much.

'We can still manage,' he said. 'We've got to manage. We'll just have to leave the instruments behind.'

Legge-Jenkins gave him a gloomy look, the empty stare of a sick man in his eyes. 'I suppose you know we're lost,' he said. 'The compass is useless. When Hellyer took the engine cover off to change that radiator, he altered the magnetic field.'

'We shall be all right,' Piercey said quickly, trying to sound more cheerful than he felt. 'It's probably the Søsters working on it. They're notorious for what they do to compasses and radios.'

Legge-Jenkins' expression was heavy with doubt. 'We should have seen them yesterday,' he pointed out.

'We shall see them all right when the drift stops.'

'You don't seem very perturbed,' Legge-Jenkins sounded like a worried old woman.

'I've been busy,' Piercey said. 'I've been helping Hellyer and I seem to have more invalids on my hands just now than I can cope with. You, Ivey, Hellyer, Doree. There's Pink too, now. He fell on the handlebars of the sledge. He's bruised his chest and it's growing worse. He might have broken a rib.'

Legge-Jenkins scratched at the half-grown beard that covered his face. 'You didn't tell me,' he said. 'I have to know these things. I have to log them.'

'It didn't seem important. He's not complaining.'

Legge-Jenkins stiffened under the implied rebuke. 'What about the others?' he asked.

'Greeno says he thinks he's twisted his ankle. But he'll be all right. I've strapped it up. They can rest when we reach the Søsters.'

'*If* we reach them.' Legge-Jenkins paused, shivered, and began in a lost way to pick at the ice on the inside of the windscreen, then he looked up as though he were trying a new line of thought. 'Why don't they send an aircraft looking for us?' he demanded.

'They obviously did,' Piercey said. 'We saw one.'

'Days ago and too far away even to make it worthwhile starting a smoke pot.'

Legge-Jenkins seemed to huddle inside his clothes, encased in his own despair. 'Think they'll send another?' he asked.

'I should think so,' Piercey said. 'Unfortunately, I expect they're searching the direct route down to Cape Alexandra. No one knows we're heading for the Søsters except us.'

He saw the quick flash of guilt in Legge-Jenkins' tired eyes. The insignificant distances they had covered daily had not helped his confidence. He had overlooked the one thing that Piercey knew they dared never overlook – the weather. They had made the steep zigzag from Prins Haakon Sø up to the ice sheet with the engine of Greeno's Weasel knocking ominously and the air already full of danger as the wind, screaming down out of the peaks of Mount Priam, drove into their flank like a ghostly cavalry charge. The world, which had earlier been so still, had suddenly become one of howling chaos, for up there on the exposed slopes they had felt the full force of the gale and the trailers had swung viciously on their runners so that the stems of the Weasels had been hauled sideways and the tracks had spun wildly on the polished ice. There had been frozen water channels and new soft snow that had provided unexpected hazards that had to be crossed at a snail's pace, and finally one of the trailers had slammed over on its side in a puff of snow which was whipped away at once into the rising drift. The tangle of split tarpaulins and broken rope had stopped them dead in their tracks and, with the worsening weather, there had been no option but to pitch tents, held up for two days of wretched cold when their sleeping bags were wet with condensation and the inside of their frail canvas shelter had been lined with cobwebs of hoar frost.

When they had set off again, the absence of snow, which had been blown by the gale from the polished ice, had added greatly to their difficulties and damaged the runners of the trailers; and it had taken them three days of constant effort and frustrating delay to cover only a few miles. Then on the fourth day, it had begun to blow once more, bringing the snow again so that they had had to camp and sit in the rattling tents listening to the howl of the blizzard outside.

The going had improved after they had lightened their loads, but they had not dared to outrun the struggling dog teams which were marking the route ahead with bamboo poles and hacking with ice axes at the hummocks that were likely to impede the trailers. And the constant halts as they had overrun the dog-drivers, the stops to cool off the engines, the need to change bogey wheels or tracks or rescue sledges, were producing a mounting sense of fury in them all; and every exasperating repair had darkened their faces with impatience as they had discovered their rations were beginning to grow short. And, as the odds had mounted, Legge-Jenkins had seemed to fade, like a long-distance runner who had spent himself too soon. He was obviously having second thoughts already about the wisdom of detouring to the Søsters, and was beginning to wonder now just how much accusation there was in the looks they all kept giving him.

'There are too many of us,' he was saying, and Piercey detected the unease in his voice again. 'Do you think we made the wrong decision when we decided to come here? I know you didn't agree.'

Piercey shrugged. 'If we meet Fife at Cape Alexandra, then we didn't,' he said. 'If we don't – '

Legge-Jenkins looked up quickly, faintly alarmed.

'Do you think we might not?'

'I'm accepting that possibility.'

Legge-Jenkins sat silently for a second, his face empty; he seemed querulous and uncertain. 'My hand doesn't help,' he said. 'I just hope it doesn't become so bad I have to turn everything over to you.'

Piercey studied him cautiously, making no comment. As fast as Doree's hands improved, Legge-Jenkins' seemed to deteriorate. It was something which had its roots not so much in their injuries as in the difference of their characters, as though Legge-Jenkins felt the need of a visible sign for them all of his inability to deal with the enormous responsibility which had been thrust upon him, and was using his injury as a means of explaining away his failure.

'It's the cold,' he said. 'It's not being able to wear gloves properly. And it doesn't seem fair to ask people to do what I can't do myself.'

It was clear he was preparing the ground ahead of himself, letting Piercey know in advance that he would like to shuffle off his responsibilities.

'If I begin to feel I'm a drag on the party,' he went on, 'I shan't hesitate to turn over the show to you.'

Piercey said nothing, and Legge-Jenkins turned away, as though he preferred to be alone with his uncertainty, as though he knew Piercey was growing tired of his complaints. O'Day's fruitless struggle with the transmitters, the constant changing and re-changing of condensers that seemed to get them nowhere, weighed more heavily on his shoulders than on anyone else's, and his depression grew more marked with every exhausting day. Most of the others, Piercey had noticed, even Ivey and the normally morose Hellyer, had managed to remain optimistic, and it was only now, when the dark brown crags of the Søster Nunataks had failed to appear, that Legge-Jenkins' uncertainty had started to spread to them all.

'Adams must have been mad,' he was saying slowly in a low voice. 'Bringing all the amateurs and leaving all the best men with Tom Fife. Look at Hannen and Jessup and Smeed and Erskine, and the Dane, Benediktsson.'

'After what we've done since we left Prins Haakon Sø,' Piercey observed, 'nobody here's an amateur any longer.'

Legge-Jenkins gave him a quick, fretful look and, bending over the expedition diary as though it were a crystal ball that would advise him of their next move, he studied it for a moment and then began to write in it, holding the pencil awkwardly in his injured hand. He made no attempt to prevent Piercey seeing what he'd written, in fact, he almost seemed to hold the book as though he wished Piercey to read it, as though he felt it might explain his problems.

'*Number Three Weasel has proved a great handicap –*' Piercey could see the words quite plainly, and the despair in them didn't surprise him much ' *– and we have been delayed days by the weather and this useless lump of machinery. Without it, we might have managed to find the Søster Nunataks long since. Now it seems we never shall.*'

Piercey frowned. Legge-Jenkins seemed to have abandoned himself completely to his fears. There seemed no longer to be any hope in him and the one thing they needed most of all now was faith in their ability to do what they had set out to do.

'*There are now only four of us uninjured,*' he had continued. '*Four of us have burns of varying degrees of severity, as already noted, and two others, Greeno and Pink, are now reported suffering from injuries caused by sledging. We ought probably to have built a man-hauling sledge as I suggested before we left, so that we could bring more much-needed equipment with us, and we must consider now if we are able to carry out the plans we originally made –*'

He looked up as he saw Piercey watching him and, as though he knew Piercey had read what he'd written, as though he felt it needed some explanation, he spoke quickly.
'Well, it's no good having any false hopes, is it?' he said.

The snow stopped at last and the wind died. The clouds disappeared and the temperature fell again, and the sky was filled with a host of stars all many times brighter and more remote than Piercey ever remembered in more southerly hemispheres – frozen, austere, and astonishingly brilliant.

They managed to fix their position at last, and when they struck camp the following morning they were all feeling more optimistic in spite of the abandoned Weasel and trailers that had already drifted up and would soon disappear from sight. Only Legge-Jenkins remained inconsolable at the loss.

They moved off, with the dog teams – more important than ever now – going ahead under Legge-Jenkins. Ivey and Greeno were inside the Weasel cabin with Hellyer; and Pink, Doree and Piercey clung to the lurching trailers, staring backwards at their own tracks stretching away behind them to the shapes of the abandoned vehicles that slowly diminished as they receded into the vast plain of snow and ice.

They made good progress during the morning and the halt at midday was a more cheerful affair. The sun was out in spite of the cold when they stopped for a mug of tea and a bar of chocolate, and Piercey went to where Ivey was sitting on the ground on a strip of canvas and a bedroll they had unpacked for him.

Ivey looked up at him and managed a smile.

'How do you feel?' Piercey asked.

'The sun helps.' Ivey gestured at the dog teams squatting in the snow, their tongues lolling, their restless tails waving slowly as Pink moved among them, checking the traces. 'It's nice to see the dogs,' he said. 'Though they look a bit tired to me.'

'Never mind the dogs. What about you?'

'I could be warmer,' Ivey admitted. 'It's being unable to move much, I suppose. But I'll be all right. It's going to be colder than this, after all, isn't it?'

'What about your feet?'

·'I can't feel 'em much.' Ivey looked up at Piercey. 'Is that a bad thing, Doc?'

Piercey knew that it was indeed a bad thing. It could indicate that the frostbite, which was already showing signs of appearing on the tips of Ivey's toes in ominous patches of hard yellow-white flesh, was spreading.

He managed to smile, however. 'No,' he said. 'It's not necessarily a bad thing.'

Ivey looked up at him seriously. 'You'll not try to kid me, Doc, will you?' he asked. 'I'm not afraid.'

'I'll not kid you.'

Ivey looked serious again. 'We're in a bit of a mess, aren't we?' he said.

'We'll be all right when we get to the Søsters.'

'Legge-Jenkins said we were lost.'

'Not as lost as all that.'

Ivey grinned. 'Only *fairly* lost?' he said.

'That's about the picture.'

'Any chance of us having to winter here, Doc?'

'Good God, why should there be?' Piercey said. 'Fife'll be waiting for us. If we don't reach Cape Alexandra on time, he'll land the Weasels at Scoresby Sund and push north to establish a camp. He'll pick us up somehow from there by air, I expect. Don't worry.'

'I'm not worried. At least, not if you're not.'

'Well, I'm not.'

Ivey grinned. 'OK,' he said. 'Then I'm not either.'

During the afternoon, the wind started again, whipping up the drift at once. Its return depressed them all immediately. They had spent so much time battling against it since they had left Camp Adams.

Within an hour, it had slowed them down to a crawl as the drift cut visibility, and it was then that Doree, travelling with Piercey and always inquisitive, always investigating everything that caught his interest, noticed that the rivets on the runners of the leading trailer had torn away, and he started to bellow to Hellyer to stop.

'This bloody aluminium,' Hellyer grumbled, trudging back to inspect the damage. 'No resistance to low temperature fatigue.'

Unfortunately, the drill for enlarging the holes had been left behind somewhere in the snow and they had to use the spike of an ice axe. In the freezing wind, it was a tedious clumsy process round the upturned trailer and, as Hellyer's never-certain temper wore thin, altercations kept breaking out between him and O'Day over the loss of the drill.

'You were using it last,' Hellyer stormed, blinking the snow from his eyelashes. 'For that lousy carve-up you call a transmitter. I expect you put it down somewhere and didn't pick it up.'

It was too late to move on again by the time they had finished the repairs and they decided to set up camp for the night, raising the tents in the lee of the Weasel. They were all a little deflated again by now, all of them exhausted by the new battle against the wind and snow.

'Know how far we came this afternoon?' Legge-Jenkins asked Piercey as they crouched in the lee of the Weasel.

'Not very far,' Piercey said slowly.

'Nine miles,' Legge-Jenkins said. 'Nine miles. That'll never get us to Cape Alexandra before the ice comes in. At this rate, we'll still be struggling round here in the middle of winter. Once O'Day gets his transmitter going, we'll have to arrange a rendezvous and get them to take us out by air. It'll mean abandoning everything, of course.'

Piercey shrugged, worried by the growing conviction that Legge-Jenkins' despairing statements were a bad influence on them all.

As he turned away, he saw Doree watching him in the gloom, his eyes peering anxiously through the drift from under the furred hood of his parka as he lashed down the tarpaulin over one of the trailers.

'The poor man's Ed. Hillary doesn't seem to give much for our chances,' Doree said calmly.

The contemptuous description reflected the attitude of all of them to Legge-Jenkins' unhappy posturings.

'It's nothing,' Piercey pointed out. 'It's just his manner.'

Doree nodded. 'Exactly,' he said.

Piercey didn't reply. Lying in his sleeping bag the previous night he had wondered several times if it might not be a good idea to take into his confidence those of the party he could rely on to be cheerful – Doree, perhaps, Pink, Sergeant Greeno – but now he decided against the move. Doree's words showed too much the disgust he felt; and, besides, Piercey had a feeling that his bland innocence whenever the subject of the IRMAS was brought up might well become more pronounced. He had already managed to annoy Hellyer with it and there was far too much service-civilian rivalry already. The conditions under which they were living tended to make men confide in each other and he had no wish for Hellyer to be given the opportunity to complain.

Doree was watching him as he turned over his plans in his mind.

'Hellyer's formed a splinter group,' he said abruptly, as though able to divine what Piercey was thinking. 'Hellyer agin everybody else.'

'Hellyer was *always* against everybody else,' Piercey said. 'That's nothing new.'

Doree bent over the tarpaulin, his back against the streaming drift. 'He says we ought to have dumped IRMA.'

'Hellyer talks too much,' Piercey said shortly, trying to discourage the conversation.

Doree paused for a moment, then he looked at Piercey again.

'Pinky says the dogs are losin' weight,' he said in deliberate matter-of-fact tones. 'He says a pound of pemmican and biscuit isn't enough for them on the work they're doin' at the moment. He says we should have brought what was left of the maize meal and dog food with us.'

'We couldn't carry everything,' Piercey retorted. For a moment, he found Doree's comments irritating, and he had to remind himself sharply that this was something he must not allow himself to do. 'I checked everybody's lists,' he went on more calmly, 'and what we left behind we left behind in full agreement with everybody else.'

'Yes.' Doree shrugged. 'All the same, though, it makes you think, doesn't it, Doc, when you consider how far we are from England, Home and Beauty.' He paused, his eyes on Piercey's face. 'What's your view, Doc? You're the expert. Are we goin' to make it?'

Piercey looked sharply at him and for the first time he saw a flicker of anxiety on Doree's face, and he was glad he hadn't turned angrily on him for his observations.

'We'll make it,' he said.

Doree nodded. 'Pity about the compass,' he said. 'I'd never have recommended these RAF types for this job. Too unsteady by a long way.' He grinned. '*I'm* an RAF type.'

Piercey managed a smile and, as Doree turned back to his work, he moved away gratefully.

Pink and Greeno were erecting one of the tents, their figures blurred by the snow and the fading light, and they glanced at him as he approached, their eyes full of doubt, so that he moved past them quickly because he didn't want to have to answer any more questions. They all seemed to be turning towards him for reassurance now.

He was in a troubled mood as he climbed into his tent, where Ivey was already inside his sleeping bag. Largely out of a sense of loyalty, he had accepted Legge-Jenkins' decisions, feeling that dispute would only accentuate the splits which were already developing in the party, but he saw now that there was no room for finer sentiments any longer. Someone had to be tough and show toughness. Even in his decisions, Legge-Jenkins had wavered and the time had come when someone with sufficient experience and strength of character had to impose his will firmly on the others for the safety of the whole party.

It wasn't a happy conclusion to reach but Piercey felt it was inescapable and that he must accept the problems of the situation for the sake of them all.

He spent a restless night, troubled as much by Legge-Jenkins' behaviour as by their inability to find the Søster Nunataks and the dump there that they so badly needed, and he had hardly dropped off into a fitful chilled sleep, it seemed, when it was morning and he was being awakened by O'Day's high cracked voice shouting outside. For a second or two, he moved irritably inside his sleeping bag, feeling suddenly old and resentful at the thought that he must face the cold. But the sleeping bag was soggy and damp and O'Day's voice was urgent. He had been working over the damaged transmitter half the night, and for a moment Piercey thought he must have got it working after all, even without the spares he needed.

Cold and damp and stiff with sleeplessness, he climbed out of the tent into the snow where East and Clark were standing, their faces turned towards the west, and O'Day gestured wildly at him, and broke into a long-legged dance.

'The Søsters,' he said. 'Look, Doc! *Voilà! Ecco!* The Søsters!' and it was only then that Piercey noticed the black unfriendly crags through the drifting snow that crossed their vision like a swirling white mist. The sight of them made him want to burst out laughing with joy and relief.

Doree had appeared now, and Hellyer, and Piercey returned to the tent where Ivey lay. He noticed that the youngster's eyes were bright and feverish and that the livid skin on his face along the edge of the bandages was beginning to crinkle and turn brown.

He pushed aside the worry that he felt at once and forced a smile.

'The Søsters, Ivey,' he said gaily. 'We can see the Søsters! We were camped on the doorstep all the time. We're halfway home now. Come and have a look at them. They're a sight for sore eyes.'

He helped the boy out of the tent and sat him in the snow, his lashless eyes moist as he stared towards the craggy peaks in the distance.

O'Day was walking round with his hands clasped over his head like a boxer by this time. 'God will provide,' he was crowing. 'My old Ma always said not to worry, God would provide. Three dits, four dits, two dits, dah, Søster Nunataks, rah rah rah!'

They were all watching him, grinning, then Piercey, noticing that Legge-Jenkins was busy with the logbook, pulled himself together sharply.

'Get the Weasel warmed up, Hellyer,' he said briskly. 'Let's get hold of those spares. The sooner we start transmitting the better. And let's have the sledges ready. There's a lot to do.'

The sharp whine of the starter seemed loud in the stillness, then the engine roared to life and Hellyer cheered and began to drive round in bottom gear for a while to flex the frozen rubber of the track.

They were all suddenly more cheerful and there was a lot of noise over breakfast, everybody talking at once.

'We'll have a celebration tonight,' Piercey suggested.

'Whose birthday is it?'

'Nobody's. It's just a good idea to make one day different from all the rest occasionally.'

To give O'Day more time and to allow Pink and Greeno and Ivey more rest, they decided not to strike camp and the Weasel went off with empty trailers towards the Nunataks, followed by the dogs with empty sledges, and during the day they ferried rations and equipment and the precious radio spares.

O'Day pounced on them at once. 'Soon be finished now,' he said. 'Papa'll soon have Baby's guts in and then we'll be dit-dahing all over the atmosphere, clogging up everybody's earholes with sound.'

In addition to the spares and food, the dump yielded more of the precious antifreeze mixture for the Weasel and even Hellyer, his fingers broken and bleeding from the constant repairs, was happy.

'We can run from here to Thule now if we want,' he crowed, patting the vehicle as he climbed down for the last time. 'We can get to Cape Alexandra easy with a few days of good weaseling. Surely to God Fife can get something in to us there somehow.'

They were all exhausted by the time they had finished but the party that night managed to be cheerful, in spite of being split up between the three tents. Piercey allowed them all rum and there was a lot of shouting and laughter.

The next morning they found that a sharp fall in temperature during the night had formed a thin crust over the powdery snow and, to avoid all the miserable manhandling of the sledges, all the tedious packing and re-packing when the top-heavy equipment threw them over, they decided to carry as much of the loose gear as they could on the trailers and to load Doree's IRMAS on the sledges to give them more stability. Optimism had suddenly returned to the party and there was a holiday atmosphere among them now in spite of the cold and the sweeping drift. They all looked forward to putting the area of the Søsters behind them. They had seemed like symbols of bad luck and now that they had picked up the precious dump and could turn south and east, they all felt light-hearted and hopeful of reaching Cape Alexandra before it was too late.

'I'll be glad to get out of this bloody area,' Hellyer said, voicing the feelings of them all. 'Perhaps now we can look forward to a bit of steady weather and no wind.'

'You'll be lucky,' Pink said. 'This whole coast's a katabatic area. The wind just drains off the ice cap and goes on blowing. It never stops. It feeds on itself. Once it starts, it just goes on without mercy.'

Because of the certainty of crevasses ahead of them, the first of the dog teams under Legge-Jenkins moved off early to lay a route, and the rest of them were packing the last of the equipment into the trailers when O'Day shouted from his canvas shelter.

'Hold it!' he said. 'I've got the transmitter working!'

They all crowded round as he pounded happily on the morse key, his face radiant as he looked up at them.

'We're off,' he crowed. 'Somewhere south of here, Jessup's leaping up from his set at this very moment, his head throbbing and his eardrums shattered.'

'For Christ's sake,' Hellyer said. 'Come out of the clouds for a bit, man. Is it going?'

O'Day grinned. 'Well,' he admitted. 'If he gets his earhole close to the headset and everybody talks in whispers, he might just possibly pick me up. We're a bit near to the Nunataks here and it's a dead area. We'll be better off when we've moved away a bit.' He grinned at them. 'At least though,' he said, 'there's life in the old body again. Give us a position, somebody. We're home and dry.'

They were all in high spirits as they started off again, and by midday they had reached the edge of the glacier that flowed out into Fraser Bay, and Piercey could see the humping on the surface that indicated crevasses. Legge-Jenkins had wisely taken a wide swing to the south towards Cape Alexandra to avoid the worst of them but they still had to move cautiously, watching carefully for the flagged bamboo poles in the drift.

What might not be dangerous to the dog teams could still be dangerous to the heavy Weasel.

Nevertheless, they seemed to be making good time and, though they had to stop for bogey-wheel breakage, Hellyer had organised the technique of repair so well by this time the halt lasted only a quarter of an hour.

The surface seemed to have improved as they set off once more, and they were moving fast, with Piercey listening to Hellyer's chatter and watching the snow ahead of them where Doree was prodding in the distance with his steel-tipped pole for crevasses. For the first time, he felt reasonably safe again. They had plenty of fuel once more and the spares they needed and more than enough rations now. It seemed that they had surmounted the worst of their obstacles.

He was just feeling warm with a sense of security when the Weasel lurched suddenly, and immediately all thoughts of safety vanished at Hellyer's shout of alarm. He heard the engine race and saw everything go dark, and at once, even through the confusion as the vehicle slewed round violently, flinging him forward in his safety strap with a shower of loose tools about his head, he knew that they had broken through a hidden snow bridge over a crevasse and were God alone knew how far down in the ice.

t w o

Even as the Weasel came to rest, there was another crash above Piercey's head that shook the whole vehicle and the sound of splintering wood and breaking glass. For a moment, as the noise increased in the darkness, he was certain that the walls of the crevasse had caved in on top of them, scaling them in an icy tomb.

Then something hit him behind the shoulders, knocking the breath out of him, and what felt like the edge of a crate fell on his fingers with numbing pain. He hunched his shoulders as other loose articles came flying past, as though he were in the centre of an unended pile of a giant child's enormous bricks, and he heard more glass break, then the high-pitched whining roar as the engine ran away, followed by silence.

As the noise stopped, he lifted his head cautiously, only to find a jerrican of petrol was jamming him in his seat, forcing him forward against the safety belt. He turned slowly and reached behind him, shoving at it, working with difficulty because it was impossible to get at it properly and he daren't yet release the safety belt. After a while, he felt it give, and the pressure on his shoulders stopped, then he heard the crash as the jerrican fell away out of sight.

Lifting his head, he looked around him. Through the window he could see the ice walls disappearing below him, the blue transparence merging with a dense ultramarine beneath the Weasel that continued downwards deeper and deeper into utter blackness. The thought of the depth below them made him catch his breath, and he looked upwards, to where the smooth ice lifted away towards the day, and thankfully, he realised they were not trapped. Above his head he could see the hole through which they had broken and what looked like the square bulk of one of the trailers obscuring the light. It was freezing cold and there was a strong smell of petrol around him and a steady dripping sound somewhere in the shadows, and he could hear the click-click-click of a wire sparking.

'Hellyer,' he called softly, hardly daring to hope for an answer. 'Hellyer, are you all right?'

There was a low moan somewhere beneath him, then he felt Hellyer stir.

'Yeh,' Hellyer's voice was slurred. 'Yeah, I'm all right.'

'Then, for God's sake, switch off the petrol before the whole lot goes up.'

He felt Hellyer stir again and fumble around in the semi-darkness. Then his voice came up to him once more, strained and thin.

'Off,' it said. 'Petrol's off.'

'Ivey.' Piercey put his hand out cautiously, feeling for something that might be solid. 'How about you?'

'I think I'm all right.' Ivey's voice was muffled and breathless as though he were in pain. 'The end of the cab's been smashed in and I'm wedged. But I'm all right – I think.'

'Good.' Piercey realised he was trembling a little from reaction and he knew that his hand was unsteady as he groped about him.

'What happened?' Ivey asked.

'Snow bridge collapsed. We're in a crevasse. About thirty feet down, I imagine.'

'Christ' – Hellyer's voice was awed and slow – 'it's a big bastard. You could put a bus in here easy.'

'I think we'd better try to get out,' Piercey said, trying to keep his voice calm. 'In case it goes any further. Can you see if the trailers came in too, Ivey? I think they did.'

'Looks like it,' Ivey said. 'I think they landed on the roof. It's stove in.'

Piercey found a torch and flashed it round them at the scarred ice walls. The Weasel appeared to be jammed longways on in the crevasse and the roof was bowed down near the centre of the windscreen where the trailers had landed on top of it. A lot of the luggage from them had smashed into the cabin and passed through the shattered windscreen.

'Thank God we had safety belts on,' Piercey said. 'How about you, Ivey, did you get thrown about?'

'A bit. But I'm all right.'

'Well, don't try to move. I'll get out and look around.'

Squirming clear of the debris that filled the cabin, Piercey found he was able to reach the window and open it. There was something outside, jamming it. He gave it a push, and felt it give way and fall, and heard the tinkling of icicles dropping out of sight after it. Then, as though the point of balance had shifted, the Weasel gave a lurch sideways and settled into a new position, and for a second, Piercey's heart was in his mouth as he waited for a further drop. Above the clatter of tools falling, he heard Ivey draw in his breath and the long-drawn-out slithering noise as something slipped off the roof and disappeared out of sight, carrying with it the snow and the rattling lumps of ice they had brought down with them from the lip of the crevasse.

For a second or two, as the Weasel settled again, there was silence, then Piercey let out his breath in a great gasp.

'All right, Ivey?' he asked.

'I'm all right.' Ivey's voice was thin and small, as though he couldn't trust himself to speak.

'Hellyer?'

'For Christ's sake, get me out of here!'

After a while, when it seemed that the Weasel was securely wedged again, Piercey began to climb through the cabin window onto the roof, and as he stared upwards at the blue-green smoothness of the ice walls, a head appeared in the hole thirty feet above him, and they heard Doree's voice.

'You all right down there?'

'So far.' Piercey called back. 'What about Greeno and Pink? They were on the trailer.'

'They're here,' Doree shouted. 'They jumped clear. Pink's laid himself out and Greeno's twisted his ankle again, but I think they're all right.'

'What about the others?'

'They're on their way back. I can see O'Day coming now with East and the dogs. I expect the others'll come when we don't turn up.'

A rope appeared and with numb fingers Piercey tied a double bowline in it, then he clambered back into the cabin and helped Hellyer onto the roof.

'Hang on, Ivey,' he said. 'I'll be back in there, in a moment, and free you.'

'I'm all right,' Ivey said. 'Don't worry about me.'

Hellyer's nose seemed to be badly cut and there was blood on his face but he seemed to have recovered a little and his voice was thin and sharp with rage.

'That useless service bastard, Doree,' he was snarling. 'They're all the same. What with hyphens and dropped 'g's' this blasted expedition's too bloody upper crust to be true.'

'If I were you,' Piercey said, 'I'd save my energy for making sure I got out of here. In case it interests you, this place has probably got no bottom.'

He picked up one of the chunks of ice they had broken off in their passage into the crevasse and threw it down into the darkness.

'Listen!'

There was no sound as the ice disappeared and Hellyer looked at Piercey, his face taut and strained.

'I didn't hear it hit bottom,' he said.

'Neither did I. I thought I might.'

Hellyer was silent as Piercey helped him into the looped rope, and as he was pulled upwards, Piercey climbed back into the twisted cabin to Ivey. It was obvious enough that they'd never salvage the Weasel, and his heart was sick inside him as he realised what it meant.

Ivey was jammed in a corner under all the equipment that had come through the roof, and Piercey lifted it carefully from him, stacking it safely out of the way.

'I'm sorry I can't be quicker,' he apologised. 'But I daren't throw this stuff out of the window. We might need it – especially now. We'll have to think about it before we let it go. We'll have to haul some of it up first even, to give me some elbow room to free you. Can you manage to hang on a little longer?'

'Will she go any further down, Doc?' Ivey sounded like a small boy suddenly.

'My God, I hope not.'

It was an hour before they could free the injured boy enough for him to be hauled to safety. Every single item in the cabin and on the roof had to be roped up and pulled to the surface first and Piercey had to resist the temptation to send the assorted boxes and packages out of sight into the depths.

After a while, he heard Legge-Jenkins' voice above him, nervous and concerned, then O'Day came down on the end of the rope to help. They lifted Ivey into the bowline and secured him with a safety belt from the cabin, and only then would Piercey allow himself to be hauled up to safety, too.

As they pulled him over the lip of the crevasse, he sprawled in the snow for a moment without moving, his mind able for the first time to grasp at the depths of that fantastic blue-black chasm beneath the Weasel and the full horror of what they had escaped. He had heard of dogs disappearing into crevasses without ever being heard to strike bottom, without even a whimper escaping them, had read of Mawson's companion vanishing without trace with his whole team, and he sat up slowly, sickened and numb at the thought.

He felt shaken and cold and was grateful when Doree bent over him and offered him a mug containing brandy.

'I took the liberty of breaking out the emergency kit, Doc.' he said. 'The occasion seemed to call for it.'

Hellyer and Ivey were still sitting in the snow a few yards away, Hellyer's face smeared with blood from his cut nose. Like Piercey, they seemed dazed and shocked at the thought of what they had escaped. Then Hellyer lifted a mittened hand to his face, moving it slowly with a dazed expression as though he might be concussed.

As Piercey stared at them, Legge-Jenkins came across to him from the lip of the crevasse.

'How much have we lost?' he demanded in a high, nervous tone.

'Most of what we had,' Piercey said in a flat voice.

He saw Legge-Jenkins flinch, as though he'd been struck, then Hellyer suddenly sniffed and, turning to him, Piercey was surprised to see tears of fury and frustration in his eyes.

'After all that bloody work,' he was saying softly. 'After all that bloody work I did.' He held out his hands and Piercey could see where the burns had cracked open in the cold as he had removed his gloves to make the incessant repairs the Weasels had needed. 'Look,' he said. 'Look at my hands. All that! All that lousy work and now they're gone! Both of 'em!'

They all stared at him in silence for a moment, then Doree moved forward with the brandy.

'Cheer up, old chum,' he said gently, and Hellyer whirled on him fiercely.

'Cheer up?' he snapped. 'Christ, half our kit's down that bloody hole, but your lousy IRMAS are still safe on the sledges. We could have afforded to lose *them*.'

'Never mind' – Doree's voice was unruffled – 'they'll be comin' in soon with helicopters. The chopper boys'll have us out in no time. O'Day'll get a message off.'

'I don't think so.' O'Day's head had appeared over the lip of the crevasse. He looked sick and wretched.

'The transmitter's gone,' he said.

They were all silent at once, staring at O'Day's strained face, taut and pale and with no sign of his normal slap-happy cheerfulness.

'Gone?' Legge-Jenkins said.

O'Day pulled himself over the edge and sat down in the snow.

'I had a look,' he said. 'I can't see it. And I think we've lost all the spares we got from the Søsters, too.'

The whole complexion of things had changed in a second. Somehow, to Piercey, it seemed to be something they didn't deserve. After their struggle to get to the Nunataks, a needless cruelty had been inflicted on them.

No one spoke much as they worked to salvage their belongings, though Piercey knew that each man was fighting individually to console his awful disappointment. Without the things they had obviously lost, without the Weasels, the repaired transmitter, the food that had disappeared into the depths of the crevasse, their chances of getting to the coast – let alone as far south as Cape Alexandra – had suddenly become extremely slender.

It took them three days to salvage the last of the equipment from the lost Weasel. There was obviously no chance of rescuing the vehicle itself and they didn't even bother to consider it.

Legge-Jenkins seemed to be stupefied with shock as he stared at the pathetic little pile of equipment they had brought up, and all he could find to say was, 'Something's got to be left behind, Piercey. Something's got to be left behind.'

The sense of guilt, the certainty that he was responsible for all the disasters that had come on them was clear in his face.

The incessant freezing drift that had plagued them ever since they had neared the area of the Nunataks hampered the work of salvage. It was hard to see what they might still save with the snow steadily obscuring everything in the crevasse and covering all that they rescued. Standing on the smashed roof of the Weasel, they sent up packages and crates on the rope, poking cautiously with the crevasse pole at half-obscured shadows in the snow to make sure they were only drifts and broken ice and not something that might make all the difference between life and death to them.

On the fourth night, the wind started up again and the snow began to pile up round the tents in huge drifts, forcing in the sides until Piercey felt he was suffering from the nightmare of being in a diminishing room where the sides gradually drew in on him. One of the tents had been lost and O'Day, Greeno, Doree and Legge-Jenkins had to share a rough shelter they had rigged from the sledges and Doree's IRMA crates and the tarpaulins from the trailers; while Piercey shared one of the tents with his patients, Ivey and Pink; and East, Clark and Hellyer shared the other. To allow all the civilians to be together had seemed to Piercey to encourage a situation that could breed trouble with Hellyer in his present frame of mind, but Legge-Jenkins had wearily insisted that it would be all right and for the time being Piercey had let it go.

As the tent grew smaller and colder, they drew closer together, lying half on top of one another, and in the end Piercey dressed and went outside.

Doree was outside, too, knocking the snow from the sagging canvas roof of the shelter, and he crossed through the murk and put his mouth to Piercey's ear.

'Autumn,' he shouted over the noise of the wind. 'Season of mists and mellow fruitfulness.'

'How's Legge-Jenkins?' Piercey shouted.

'Like an undertaker who's lost his corpse,' Doree bawled back. 'Scrawlin' in those damned little books of his, addin' up figures with a face that's enough to make a sow litter. What's up with him, Doc?'

'I think he feels an enormous sense of inadequacy,' Piercey said.

Doree stared at him. 'I expect you're right,' he said. 'But I wish he'd pull his bloody finger out a bit, all the same.'

As he waved and disappeared into the shelter, Piercey stared after him for a second, then he knocked the snow from the tent and for the rest of the night they huddled wretchedly together for warmth, listening to the slap and rattle of the canvas in the wind that beat and dragged at it and set their cigarette smoke eddying and swirling and swaying.

The following morning they dug their way to the surface with their plates. The others were outside already, standing near the crevasse, shivering, their faces pinched with cold, their heads enveloped in their own frozen breath. They looked weary, as though they'd all passed a sleepless night, a group of sunken-eyed ghosts with frosted half-grown beards, all of them exhausted with too much thinking. They had already been too long on the trail and the need for a fixed camp was growing urgent. As Piercey appeared, Doree crossed to him and helped him to drag Ivey into the open air. Then Legge-Jenkins, who was pawing fretfully through their scattered belongings, looked up.

'What are we going to do?' he asked immediately.

The fatal hesitancy had returned to his manner and Piercey answered firmly, certain in his own mind what they ought to attempt.

'There can be no question of aiming for Cape Alexandra now,' he said. 'We've got to get to Fraser Bay as fast as we can and go to ground in that hut of Rollo Fraser's. There's still a chance we can be airlifted out, but if not, ten of us can't live in two small sledging tents for the winter.'

He saw the others staring at him, their faces expressionless, and he knew his blunt news had shocked them. Yet somehow they seemed reassured by his firm statement of the facts, as though they sensed that there was no question of wavering in his mind.

He forced a smile. 'There's nothing to worry about,' he said boldly. 'We can do it. We can find food in Fraser Bay. There are bound to be seals and penguins. What about the guns?'

'We lost the shotgun,' Greeno said. 'We've still got the rifle but not a lot of ammunition.'

'We've always got the dogs.'

Piercey saw them glance at each other as he spoke and he knew what the thought meant to them. Killing the dogs for food was an upsetting idea that seemed to be swollen by the loss of the Weasel to a catastrophe, and as he saw the outraged shock on their faces, he felt he ought to amplify what he'd said.

'We've got to face facts,' he said, almost as though he were addressing them as leader and not merely expressing an opinion. 'We've got to do everything we can to survive. It won't be easy but it can be done, if we take the necessary precautions and don't let ourselves get the wind up.'

Legge-Jenkins began to fiddle with his notebooks. Already he seemed to have lost stature, as though he were merely hanging on to Piercey's decisions now instead of making his own.

'There were always too many of us,' he muttered half to himself 'I always said there were too many.'

Hellyer heard him and swung round quickly, his face white and bleak, all his old dislike and contempt bursting out of him in a torrent. 'OK,' he said bitterly. 'You'd better shoot one or two of us off then, hadn't you? Why not try one of those secret weapons of Doree's?'

Doree turned to him, like the rest of them suddenly tired of Hellyer's snarling.

'Cheese it, old boy, for Christ's sake,' he begged.

Hellyer stepped back defensively, staring round at them. 'Why not?' he asked. 'Point one at Hellyer, the Bolshie. Pull the trigger and Ban-the-Bomb Bill's gone up in a puff of smoke.'

'You'll go up with a smack on the jaw if you don't dry up,' Greeno growled. 'I'm sick of your bloody whining.'

'You service blokes don't half stick together,' Hellyer jeered. 'It's like being in a club.'

Piercey pushed them apart. Hellyer's mutiny, he knew, was chiefly the unreasoning, exhausted protest of a tired body and frustrated spirit. They were all at breaking point, suddenly weary to the marrow of their bones.

'Stop quarrelling!' he snapped. 'All of you!' He stared at them, feeling a little like a schoolmaster with a set of quarrelsome pupils. 'We've got more to do than that. Let's see what we've got left and what we can get rid of.'

The group began to split up, turning away in a slow tired shuffling movement, their heads bent against the drift, then Hellyer's voice stopped them dead.

'There's one thing we can get rid of,' he said with a bitter satisfaction. 'We can get rid of those blasted secret weapons.'

'You'd help us all, Hellyer,' Piercey said sharply, 'if you'd just hold your tongue for a bit.'

Hellyer subsided at last and they spread their belongings in the snow, laying out the instruments and books and clothing in silence except when the raw edges of their tempers broke through in sullen exchanges that occurred chiefly between Hellyer and Sergeant Greeno. Then Pink brewed a large can of tea and they stood around in a half-circle drinking it and staring moodily at their pathetic belongings, cringing from the brush of the snow and the ice particles that rustled against their clothing on the moaning wind.

'Is that all?' Legge-Jenkins was staring at the pile with a broken expression, his mug of tea sagging limply in his hand. 'Surely there's more than that.'

'There's nothing left down there now except drums of fuel and antifreeze,' O'Day said. 'And *they* aren't much use to us now.'

'Are you sure?'

'I've just come up. There's nothing left worth fetching up.'

'I'll go down myself tomorrow,' Legge-Jenkins said as though he didn't believe him.

'I must have been a hundred feet down, man,' O'Day said, the irritation in his voice barely concealed. He gestured at the drift that was dusting their eyebrows and beards and sticking to their clothes. 'It's over the Weasel now and if it keeps up like this there'll be nothing to see by tomorrow.'

'Yes.' Legge-Jenkins nodded vaguely, his head twisted against the wind. 'Of course. I understand.' He seemed unable to make up his mind what to do. 'We must think a little,' he said. 'What have we lost?'

'Well, the butagas stove's gone for a start, and the smoke-pots. Even if they get an aircraft over us now, they'll never see us. We've lost the only sound Nineteen and all the heavy stuff. Most of the food and ropes, the axes, the shovels, the trail flags, the cooking utensils – '

'Never mind what we've lost,' Piercey interrupted sharply, feeling the list was growing to depressing lengths. 'What have we *saved*?'

'We've still got the two dud Nineteens,' O'Day said. 'I might still make something out of 'em. It'll take some time but I'll have a go. We've still got an aerial and four twelve-volt batteries, but keeping 'em warm's going to be alpha priority one-A if we want to keep any power in 'em.'

'Go on.'

'Two tents, two Primus stoves, the rifle, the dog pemmican, the rum, a tarpaulin, two lanterns, two ice axes – '

They listened until O'Day had finished, then Legge-Jenkins turned to Piercey, his eyes haggard.

'Well, that's that,' he said. 'We're finished.'

There was a flicker of fear on the tired faces round him, a reflection of the mounting pessimism they were all beginning to feel. To Piercey it seemed that for the first time since they had lost the Weasel, they were beginning to grasp how utterly desperate their situation had become, how insignificant they were against the forces they faced. In spite of the strength they had mustered and the courage they had shown, their defences were utterly inadequate and they were powerless against events, minute in that vast desert of snow and ice around them. The realisation was frightening and humiliating.

He forced the thought from his mind abruptly and interrupted roughly. In spite of the biting cold and the weariness and the bruises he could feel on his shoulders where the jerrican of petrol had hit him, he still believed firmly in himself. There was no room in his mind for defeat and the very admission that failure was a possibility was a step in the wrong direction, he felt, a retreat before the implacable enemy of the ice cap.

'Nonsense,' he said briskly. 'Of course we're not finished.'

He saw Legge-Jenkins' eyes flicker with resentment as he brushed aside his opinion, but it seemed important just then, with the catastrophe of the loss of the Weasel still fresh in their minds, to make it clear to everyone that there was no feeling of defeat in *his* mind, at least.

'We still have enough rations to reach the coast if we cut them down a little,' he said. 'We've still got two Primuses and two tents. We've got the dogs. We're still mobile.'

'We lost most of the food and the medical supplies,' Legge-Jenkins said.

Piercey saw Ivey's eyes on him, full of the need for reassurance. The boy was sitting in the snow holding his mug of tea awkwardly in both hands, and he wished to God Legge-Jenkins would shut up.

'We've lost the shovels and the wireless spares – ' Legge-Jenkins ran a hand over his face and paused, consulting his notebook, while the others watched him silently, their faces white with exhaustion.

'We ought to have built man-hauling sledges before we left Camp Adams,' he went on nervously. The thought seemed to trouble him. 'We might have carried more if we'd done that. I always said we should have.'

'They'd slow us down,' Piercey said sharply. 'We'd try to take too much and we've got to travel fast. The sun'll be gone soon and we ought to be at Fraser Bay before we lose it. We've got to leave behind what we don't need. In my experience, it's always the men who prepare for every possible contingency who have to give up. The ones who travel light and fast make it. We must concentrate on clothing and food.'

There were a few nods, as though his direct lead encouraged them.

'We've got to keep the dogs going at least until they get us to Fraser Bay,' he continued. 'Ivey's got to be carried.'

'I bet Fife was at Fraser Bay while we were mucking about round the Søsters,' East said bitterly, and Clark joined in quickly.

'The whole expedition was cock-eyed from the start,' he said. 'Wrong sledges. Poor stoves. Look at that time when we went to the Søsters with Adams and couldn't cook.'

Clark was normally a quiet youngster, absorbed with his rock specimens and only opening his mouth for one of the long-winded stories he enjoyed, and his outburst showed that his irritation over the mistakes had been rankling for a long time. Piercey guessed that his fears of too much talking in the tent at night had been well-founded. Obviously Hellyer had not been silent.

Hellyer stepped forward now, a small cocksure figure, obviously keen to take advantage of the shift of enthusiasm.

'I'd like to know' – he spoke with noisy aggressiveness, gesturing with his mug of tea – 'what's going to happen to Doree's IRMAS. We've not had any decision about them yet, and – '

'Shut up, Hellyer,' Piercey snapped. 'And listen to me.'

His tone seemed to startle Hellyer, and for a second he stood with his mouth open as though about to protest, staring at Piercey with bright, angry eyes. Piercey stared back at him, his expression hostile. The time had come to shut Hellyer up for the safety of them all. If their courage and resource were not enough now they would die, and would deserve to. Life had been reduced to the old elemental struggle for survival and it was up to them to accept the challenge, not fight among themselves.

'I think' – Hellyer spoke slowly, then he stopped and his eyes fell before Piercey's stare, and Piercey saw the others were all watching carefully to see who backed down first.

'I think' – Hellyer's eyes flickered round the others and again he paused, then his angry glance seemed to melt before Piercey's stony stare, and he stepped back a pace.

'OK,' he said. 'I'm listening.'

Piercey drew a deep breath. He knew the responsibility was all his now. In that moment, it seemed, Legge-Jenkins had faded into the background and the momentary rebellion from the others had been quelled as it had to be quelled if they were to survive.

He gazed round at the whiskered faces and hollow eyes. It was time to announce some sort of decision about the future. He had spent the last three nights talking over with Pink the carrying capacity of the sledges and he had made up his mind already what they ought to do. Legge-Jenkins was absorbed with his charts and notebooks and seemed quite willing to let him make any arrangements he wished.

At least, Piercey decided, the decision was a simple enough one to make. They had no records or equipment left to worry about. They were all at the bottom of the crevasse. There was only themselves now. They had nothing to lose but their lives.

The snow had started again, fine dry frozen flakes that filled the folds of their clothes, and the sight of it made Piercey feel cold, and old and tired with a sense of futility. They were struggling against an enemy that would never let up, he knew, and he felt in that moment something of what Legge-Jenkins had been going through. Then he saw the others staring at him, waiting for him to speak, and he forced the feeling away again quickly.

'We'll have to carry as much as we can on our backs,' he said, and he noticed that no one, not even Legge-Jenkins, interrupted him. 'I suggest we start by jettisoning everything except what's absolutely essential. I've been thinking this over in the night, and I feel that each man should be allowed to keep the clothes on his back, two pairs of mittens, six pairs of socks, a spare pair of boots, his sleeping bag, his tobacco, and two pounds of personal gear. Agreed?'

There was a chorus of assent and Piercey began to fish in his pockets.

'I suggest we start with what we have on our persons,' he said.

He brought out a gold cigarette case his wife had given him before they were married and turned it over in his hand. It was an article he valued, more from sentiment than anything else. It had his initials on it and he'd had it a long time.

As he stared at it, he tried to remember his wife's face but, overcome with tiredness, he found it more difficult than he had imagined. He began to wonder how long it would be before he saw her again and, thinking of it, he was caught by an awful sense of loneliness at the knowledge that he had to face six months of winter before he could even hope for rescue.

He saw the others watching him, their eyes curious, and he tried to set the value of the cigarette case against its importance as a symbol. Then, with a gesture, he tossed it onto the snow.

'That's gold, Doc,' Doree said quietly.

'If I don't survive to carry it home,' Piercey pointed out, 'it won't matter much, will it?'

Still watched by the others, he emptied his pockets of everything he could find, even the few coins he had with him, then he took out the prayer book he'd brought from Camp Adams.

'I think, from now on, praying'll have to be by guesswork,' he said.

He ruffled the pages and tossed the book down in the snow and watched the flakes fall on it, fine and dry, and start to cover it immediately. Within twenty minutes there would be no sign of it, no indication that it had ever existed.

Around him, the others were also emptying their pockets, and it seemed to Piercey that he had already taken over from Legge-Jenkins.

'That seems to be it,' he said.

They were all silent now and returned to their tea, and Piercey thought that even Hellyer had been sufficiently impressed to be silent. But as Piercey turned away he spoke in a growl.

'Can we make a ceremony of dumping the IRMAS now?' he asked. 'Sing a hymn of praise or something.'

Piercey saw several heads jerk up, as though Hellyer's words were alien to their mood, then Doree turned on him with a smouldering look, stirred out of his unruffled good humour at last by Hellyer's nagging.

'Oh, for Christ's sake, man,' he snapped. 'Dry up about the bloody things.'

'There speaks the High Priest of Sudden Death,' Hellyer jeered.

'The High Priest of Sudden Death'll be more than glad to give the High Priest of Bloody Awkwardness a punch up the bracket if he doesn't stow it.'

Hellyer laughed in Doree's face and in a moment they had turned on each other. Immediately, the tension spread to the others, and East and Sergeant Greeno, taking sides at once, were involved in a sulphurous exchange of insults. Then East shoved Greeno, and Greeno shoved him back, and East stumbled against Ivey, who was sitting on the snow watching them, knocking the mug of tea from his clumsy hands.

East recoiled at once and they all stared silently at the brown stain on the snow.

'Now look what you've done,' East growled, suddenly embarrassed and ashamed of himself. 'Knocked the kid's tea over!'

They had all paused for breath and suddenly it was all over. Ivey was staring at his empty mug, the snow plastered on his parka and on the fur round his hood, and they could see his lashless scarred eyes were full of tears. For a second, they all stared at each other, weary, frustrated, bitterly disappointed men, all of them suddenly a little frightened. Ivey was still staring at the patch of stained snow where his tea had disappeared and he seemed on the point of weeping.

Then Sergeant Greeno, the fine flakes sticking to his beard like dust, stepped forward and, picking up the injured man's mug, poured some of his own tea into it. As he handed it back to Ivey, East took it from him and added more from his own mug, then Doree, and finally, sullenly, Hellyer.

Nobody said anything and Piercey was conscious of a new feeling that they had all suddenly become aware of how much they depended on each other.

'I think we'd better try to push on,' he said quietly, and they nodded and turned away in the fading daylight and thickening drift.

three

The journey to the coast was a grim affair of desperate men and weakening dogs. Their rations were now so sparse that Piercey had had to cut their daily intake of food to the minimum and every scrap of equipment that could be carried on a man's back was slung around their shoulders to make room for Ivey on the sledge. At the end of the first day of struggling through the wind towards the east, they were all too weak and tired to care much what happened.

The business of halting for the night was long and complicated now. They had only two small tents and a rough canvas shelter they managed to construct from skis and sledges and the salvaged tarpaulins, and the normal simple swift routine of pitching camp had to be forgotten. There were only two stoves and not much paraffin, and the cooking had to be done in the shelter, where they could eat in some measure of warmth. But it was a laborious business to raise the stiff canvas, even when the wind wasn't trying to snatch it from their hands, and it was difficult for a cold and hungry man to hang on to his temper.

Then, as if their worries weren't enough, they began to notice that the condition of the dogs was falling off, and they were still fifty miles from the coast when the first of them collapsed.

It got to its feet with difficulty, pulled for an hour or so more, then stumbled and fell again, staring up at them with its handsome, imploring eyes.

'It's had it, Doc,' Pink said.

They got the dog on its feet after a while, and let it walk with a loose trace in the hope that it would recover, but an hour later it fell once more and this time they knew it would never rise again.

Pink's face was drawn and unhappy and Piercey could see the despair in his eyes. Ever since they had first acquired the dogs in Scoresby months before on the journey north, they had been Pink's special responsibility and it had become a standing joke that he and Jessup could talk dog language and preferred the company of the teams to that of everyone else.

'It didn't look ill – ' he said hesitantly, blinking to keep the drift from settling on his eyelashes as he looked at Piercey.

'What about the others?' Piercey asked.

Pink shrugged. 'There'll be more soon,' he said. 'I don't know when, but there will.'

Piercey nodded grimly. 'They've got to get us to Fraser Bay,' he said. 'Even if we have to drive them into the ground. You'd better pick out the best and kill the others for food. At least, then, we can have *one* strong team.'

He saw the small flicker of alarm in Pink's eyes as he stooped over the dying dog and fondled its ears. The other men had gathered round now, their faces drawn and exhausted, their moustaches and beards covered with frost, waiting to see what Pink would say. Piercey's words had brought a sense of shock to them all. The huskies were vicious, surly brutes with each other but they had always regarded their drivers with affection, and the news that they were to be shot seemed to herald the beginning of a catastrophe.

Pink was silent for a while before replying, then he straightened up and nodded.

'All right, Doc,' he said. 'If that's what you think.'

He turned away and he and Doree picked out the strongest animals, then, with everybody watching silently, they harnessed up the weaker team and drove them slowly over the ice towards a fold in the land. Still watching, they saw Pink unharness the first dog and lead it, its tail wagging, a little distance over the snow to where Doree was waiting. As the first shot rang out, they all turned away, as though they had been motivated by the same impulse.

During the night, the wind got up again, shaking and rattling the tents, but there were no complaints suddenly. They were all silent and morose and absorbed with their own thoughts. The killing of the dogs seemed to be the first dangerous step into a greater unknown.

They reached Fraser Bay in a freezing mist that was as bleak and forbidding as the barren black cliffs around them.

Fraser's old hut, a small stone erection with a collapsed wall, looked like some bleak crofter's dwelling, lacking even elementary comfort and devoid of all colour, warmth and hope. Around them, apart from the heavy breathing of the exhausted dogs, it was as still as death.

Heavy with the feeling of defeat, they stared wretchedly at the tumbled walls and broken roof of the hut and the snow and ice which filled the interior. The journey had taken out of them more than they had realised. They were all weak and dizzy with hunger, and they were still two hundred miles away from the nearest of the trappers' huts that dotted the east coast north of Scoresby Sund.

For a while, they moved about with slow, tired steps, dumb with disappointment and misery, knowing they would have to build the biggest part of the hut up again, then East, poking among the rocks and the scattered remnants of forty-year-old boxes and barrels, noticed a rough cairn standing on a small bluff. There was a piece of wood attached to it, and he snatched it off, and started digging frantically, dragging away the stones that formed the pile.

He stood up after a while, the snow plastered to his clothes, opening a sealed tin with his knife, and as they crowded round him, he held out a torn sheet of paper that had obviously been wrenched from a notebook.

'They've been here,' he said in a low furious voice that was choked with disappointment. 'They've been here already!'

There were tears in his eyes as he swung round on Legge-Jenkins and flourished the torn paper in his face.

'Look,' he said. 'It's signed by Tom Fife and Jessup. They got the Weasels up to Cape Alexandra. They even got to Camp Adams. They were here while we were arsing about round the Søsters. If we hadn't gone there, we'd have met them.'

An argument broke out at once, loud and full of recriminations which were chiefly the last protest of exhausted men pushed to the limit of their physical endurance, then as Legge-Jenkins backed away, weakly trying to defend himself, Piercey pushed among them, thrusting them aside with angry gestures.

'Shut up, you damn fools,' he snapped. 'What good does blame do? They've gone and we're on our own. Why waste your energy fighting about it? There's enough to do without that.'

They calmed down at once as they realised the truth of what he said, and the group broke up in silence. As they turned their backs on Legge-Jenkins, sullen and bitter, deflated after all their hopes and sick with a depression that was half the result of hunger, Piercey saw Legge-Jenkins' eyes, sunken in a haggard face, grow dull with hurt. The movement away from him, instinctive and innocent as it had been, had been like a finger pointing at him for his guilt, his pig-headedness, his weakness, and his utter failure to hold them together in a unified body.

As they ate their meal in the shelter in silence, Piercey could see their faces were drawn with weariness and pinched with cold, and he decided to let them disappear into the tents to get some sleep before starting work. But a new blizzard blew up shortly after midnight, screaming down off the black mountains around them and shaking and rattling the tents until they felt they would be swept up and blown out over the frozen sea.

Their sleep was fitful at best, and Piercey was the first to emerge the following morning, the others following in ones and twos, cursing the drift and boots that were so frozen they could only lace them up after an hour of walking round in them. After a sparse breakfast, they began to explore their surroundings, staring over the empty bay towards the gaunt cliffs to the south that were veined with snow along their northern and eastern slopes. It was a wild inhospitable place with little to recommend it beyond the remains of the hut which stood in the shelter of the cliffs on the rocky shelf of land. Beyond it, nearer to the sea, there was a bluff of loose pebbles and small stones, that obscured the beach and the view of the bay so that they seemed to be shut inside a bleak prison from which they could not even see the daylight.

'God, what a place!' Doree's comment echoed the thoughts of them all.

The weather seemed to be improving a little, however, and their first task was clearly to re-erect as much of the broken-down hut as they could. Without asking Legge-Jenkins' advice, Piercey sent Clark and East back to where they had shot the dogs, with instructions to bring back the dumped equipment and the frozen bodies of the dead animals; then he sent Greeno and Doree down to the bay with the rifle to kill as many seals as possible. They would need blubber and meat and a stove of some sort with which to cook and keep O'Day's batteries warm. Not much pemmican had been saved from the crevasse, and with their equipment had gone all but a little of their tea and coffee and flour.

Working in the streaming drift, the rest of them set to work freeing as many of the frozen stones as possible with an ice axe and rebuilding what they could of the hut. No one was excused except Ivey who still lay inside his sleeping bag, his face growing thinner, his expression inconsolable at the thought he was a drag on them all.

'Isn't there *anything* I can do, Doc?' he begged.

'Just keep yourself as fit as possible,' Piercey said. 'Don't worry, we'll find you jobs now we've got a base again.'

'I don't enjoy just waiting, Doc.'

Ivey's eyes were full of appeal and Piercey, longing to give the boy some hope, had to force himself to take the realistic attitude that sprang from his belief that sympathy would only weaken Ivey's resolve.

'We've got a long time to go until Tom Fife arrives,' he said. 'It's going to need a lot of patience – from you, most of all.'

'I'd feel better if I could do something, Doc.'

Piercey knelt beside the boy, trying to imbue him with some of his own fierce determination to survive.

'Look, son,' he said. 'There are many kinds of courage and sometimes just waiting's one of them. It's up to you. Can you do it?'

Ivey stared up at him silently for a moment, then he nodded.

'Sure,' he said. 'I can do it, Doc.'

four

Across the scimitar curve of Axel Helberg Bay, the squat silver cylinders of the whaling station at Helbergfjördur stood out brightly against the bleak barrenness of the mountain behind. Over the gothic structure of steel pinnacles, Fife could see the thousands of tiny white specks that were the terns and kittiwakes and great black-backed gulls battling for the offal that floated offshore and the garbage that lay among the moored ships.

The thumping of the hired boat's engine carried across the silent water and came back in a curious double thud through the tangy air from the chocolate-cake mountains that provided a sombre background to the muted colours of the town. The bow wave had spread out in a wide arrowhead of ripples behind them until it washed the rocky shore of Stakness where the teeming guillemots and puffins set up their clamour. Jessup, Smeed and Erskine were standing on the collapsing jetty of the old whaling station as the boat drew away, disappointment, monotony and frustration etched on all their faces, their shoulders sagging as much as the roofs and walls of the dilapidated buildings they had taken over as a base.

There was a brooding feeling of helplessness hanging over Fife as he watched the naked concrete buildings of Helbergfjördur draw nearer. Without speaking, he offered his tobacco pouch to Hannen who sat at the tiller, depressed like Fife by the sense of failure that lay over all of them.

They had been back in Axel Helberg Bay some time now, fretting under the inactivity and bitterly conscious that ten of their companions were marooned beyond the pack ice out of reach of any kind of help. The responsibility rested heavily on Fife's shoulders, and he had lain awake at night worrying over it. In his heart of hearts, he knew perfectly well that he wasn't to blame, but as Adams' deputy, the responsibility still remained his.

Things often went wrong with expeditions and the skill of the men who took part in them lay in their ability to make do with what was left, but with the accumulating knowledge of years that was passed on from one expedition to another major disasters were few. Everything that was experienced was written down and absorbed by those who followed and modern exploration was a matter of science not chance. Men were occasionally lost, of course, killed in falls, in flying accidents, like Gino Watkins in kayaks, or like Mawson's companion, Innis, in crevasses, but since Nobile's airship journey he couldn't remember anything of the present magnitude. Certainly one man was dead and now, perhaps, ten more had followed him. It was a heavy load to lay on a man's shoulders in peace time.

They had limped back into Axel Helberg Bay, listening to the clanging of the loose plates that hung from the *Brancard* and sickened by the desperate quality of the ship's distress as the seas ran against them and the waves mounted and steepened over the wound.

There had been an overpowering feeling of relief as they had seen the light on Helberg Hjelmen, the sharp-peaked mountain above the bay. Now, they had thought, now we can get a new ship and move back up north ready for the first sign of spring. There had been trawlers off the coast, a few of them British, and they had stared at them with hatred, feeling that with their stupid political quarrel they were responsible entirely for obstructing the last faint chance of

135

rescue that year. The air had been full of the clatter of chattering skippers, their broad northern accents filling wheelhouse and radio cabin with their complaints at the growing bitterness of the trawler war, and their joy at the Government's decision to add destroyers to the frigates which were already keeping watch over them, their elation and triumph coming through all the gabble of gale warnings and time signals and weather reports and the unctuous disembodied tones of the BBC. They had put in a radio request for dry-docking facilities and for tugs to stand by to assist them in, but when they had dropped anchor in Axel Helberg Bay, there had been no interest in them from the shore whatsoever, and it was not until the evening that a tug had appeared on the scene, the skipper casually explaining to the fuming Schak that something must have gone wrong with their message. It was nothing to do with him, he had said, nothing at all. The wireless station had just failed to pass the message on.

'Well, take us to Sjøgren's wharf,' Schak had said, 'and for God's sake, look slippy. There's a dry dock waiting for us, and it's urgent.'

But in Sjøgren's shipyard, it appeared, no dry dock was available after all and they had been obliged to lie behind a trot of Icelandic trawlers – those damn trawlers again! – until the mistake was sorted out.

Accompanied by Fife, Captain Schak had stormed ashore, watched by surly Icelanders working on the docks and among the trawlers and on the lorries laden with fish, the bright orange tops of their thigh boots gaudy among the drab background.

'Mistake,' Schak had said bitterly, indicating the dry dock which was empty of everything but ropes and baulks of timber and hoses, all laid ready for an incoming ship. 'A guy doesn't make two mistakes of this sort in one day.'

There had been little satisfaction, however, from the old man who sat behind the old-fashioned roll-topped desk inside the office.

'We can promise nothing,' he had insisted. 'Nothing at all. Whoever promised you the dry dock made a mistake.'

'It's empty,' Fife had pointed out. 'Why can't we go straight in?'

'Because there is a trawler to go in this afternoon. It is all arranged.'

The old man had avoided their eyes, scratching doodles with a biro on the pad on his desk and they had stormed angrily out of the office and hired a taxi – not without difficulty – and driven immediately to the unceremonious seafront at Reykjavik.

'We can charter a ship,' Fife said.

'You asked the Committee?' Schak asked laconically.

'I'll get the ship first,' Fife said. 'And ask afterwards.'

But there were no ships available, they were told, and when they asked the chances of getting the *Brancard* into a dry dock the story was the same as at Helbergfjördur. A ship was due to go in. A government vessel was in urgent need of repair, something that couldn't be turned down because of future contracts and the ship's importance in the growing fishing war.

In the end, in desperation, they had called on the British ambassador, but he had indicated his helplessness with a shrug.

'I'm up against a blank wall,' he had said. 'There's nothing I can do – and there won't be until this dispute is settled.'

'Trawlers,' Schak had said bitterly as they had found themselves on the pavement once more, shoulders hunched against the biting Arctic wind. 'Trawlers! A goddam lousy son-of-a-bitching fishing gang. That's what's done it.'

They had left the bare concrete blocks of the city, baffled, frustrated and despairing, Schak to go back to his ship and wait for mail and the hope of an improvement in relations with the Icelanders, Fife to join the members of the expedition at Stakness across the bay, to try to carry on working with the single station that was now left open on the East Coast of Greenland, to reorganise for the spring and the attempt that still had to be made to find the rest of Adams' party.

The Americans had given up their search at last and the Danish Sledge Patrol, pushing as far north as they dared from Danmarkshavn, enduring God alone knew what cold as they struggled up the line of trappers' huts to the north, had finally had to pull back, beaten.

'There is no one there,' they had announced. 'There is no sign of anyone having been there, and the wireless is dead.'

Fife had cabled London, demanding assistance in the shape of a ship from England or Canada or Norway and extra Weasels, but no one had been prepared to make a decision without calling a meeting of the Committee and the following day the answer had arrived. *'Ship impossible. Make repairs on spot.'*

This had been followed by another cable, requesting information about the American aid from Thule. *'Please assess dollar value,'* it had insisted desperately, and they knew then that someone had heard of all the attempts that had been made by air to find Adams and was growing worried at the cost.

After that there had been a whole flood of messages from Sir Willard Mortimer that had revealed his embarrassment at being concerned with an expedition centred on Iceland at a time when Icelandic relations were, to say the least, difficult.

'Insist care Icelandic relations,' they had said in various forms. *'Delicate situation Commons-wise.'*

Fife had thrown them all away without bothering to reply. All his efforts to contact Admiral Lutyens in London had come to nothing. His cables remained unanswered and

Mortimer's secretary, in answer to a cautious inquiry as to his whereabouts, had announced that he was believed to be in Paris. With the cable had come another request demanding caution in dealing with the Icelanders and, then, after another infuriating flurry of demands and counter-demands that had driven Fife almost demented with their demonstration of Mortimer's love of memos, there had at last been a long message promising two extra Weasels – no more – and a lengthy set of instructions on where to put them ashore.

Fife had retorted at once with an insistence that two vehicles were not enough, but Mortimer's reply had been a bleak reminder to him of the mounting costs of the expedition which had already far exceeded the original estimate, and then, apart from staccato telegrams to know what was being done, nothing beyond the cables which had arrived from the relatives of the missing men, and the bags of mail which had remained unclaimed in the headquarters hut at Stakness as mute reminders of their failure.

Hannen cut the engine and, as the boat glided into the landing stage among the movable cranes, the crowded quays and the chandlers' shops, Fife stared round him with a morose face and angry eyes. As the boat bumped alongside, he jumped ashore quickly, impatient to get on with something.

'I'm going to see Schak,' he said quickly. 'Perhaps he's found someone who'll do the repairs.'

'It's too late, now, Tom,' Hannen reminded him gently. 'We'll never get up even to Cape Alexandra now. Only Angmagssalik's left open.'

'There's next spring,' Fife said stubbornly. 'We shall be going next spring.'

Hannen didn't argue. It was difficult suddenly, with Fife's lonely obsession with his responsibilities, to reason with him.

'Will you be long?' he asked.

'Not if Schak's found a ship or someone to repair the *Brancard*. If he hasn't, I shall probably be all day.'

Fife turned and stalked off. His temper for some time had not been easy to deal with, he knew. Normally taciturn, he had not been able to stop his silences growing to brooding, with unexpected outbursts against the Icelanders, the villagers of Stakness, or Mortimer, or even Hannen himself or Jessup, for failing to make the radio contact with the missing men he so desperately needed. He was well aware of the way he was riding roughshod over everybody around him but he was sleeping badly, fretted with too much worry. Fortunately Hannen and the others had understood and shrugged off all his anger.

He didn't look back as he left the boat, stalking with hunched shoulders across the railway lines and over the swing bridge, stepping over the coiled hawsers and old fenders where the rats ran riot near the trawlers, among the baulks of timber and the stacked oil drums and fish boxes and the fragments of dismantled ships – the winches and the anchors and the ventilators. His nostrils were full of the smell of brine and fuel oil and tar and paint and dusty rope.

The *Brancard*, he noticed disgustedly, was still lying behind her trot of trawlers, still against the wharfside, the gaping wound in her flank untouched, her decks bare of workmen. Over the stern a man was just emptying a bucket of water and the cook was stringing a line of washing near the galley door.

Schak was on board waiting for him, chewing a cigar and, dressed in a short leather coat and long-peaked cap, looking, like most transatlantic captains, as though he were just going off on a fishing expedition.

'Well?' Fife asked straight away.

'Nobody. I've tried 'em all. My goddam ear aches with telephoning.'

'Surely *somebody'll* take the *Brancard*.'

Schak shook his head.

'Perhaps *I* can persuade 'em.'

Schak shrugged. 'If I can't, you can't,' he said shortly.

'I can try.'

Schak pulled a face. 'Tom, this isn't like taking two dog teams up to look for Adams. I guess that was a pretty risky thing to do when you think about it. Maybe they don't realise yet in London just how risky. But I do. *I* wouldn't have gone, not at this time of the year. But doing that and getting the *Brancard* repaired are two different things entirely.'

Fife's face was sullen, his black eyebrows down over his flinty eyes.

'I've tried 'em all, I promise you,' Schak assured him. 'They're just not playing.'

He turned away and picked up a batch of letters and newspapers.

'Yesterday's,' he said. 'Came in on this morning's *Icelandair*. I picked them up with our own stuff.' He gestured at the newspaper Fife was opening and indicated the headlines.

'I see Mortimer's let it out,' he said. 'All that cable talk about keeping the expedition affairs within the expedition don't seem to have counted for much.'

Fife nodded. The front page was neatly divided into three parts, it seemed, with three main stories surrounded by photographs and irrelevant minor parts.

'Russia and Iceland well represented,' Schak commented. 'Iceland threatening action over the trawlers and talking of pushing the limit out to fifteen miles in reprisal for the destroyers. And Europe blowing nice and hot again, with the Yanks threatening over Russian fallout on the Norwegian border. Adams would have enjoyed sharing the front page with that lot.'

Adams' face, aloof and handsome, stared at them from the centre of the sheet. Below it there was a picture of his wife, and further down still, Sir Willard Mortimer, leaving his office, rolled umbrella, bowler hat and everything, together with the interview he had given the press – guarded as befitted the politician, indignant as befitted the father-in-law, informative as befitted the chairman of the expedition's committee.

'Whatever my personal feelings may be,' he had announced, *'we shall not pause for one instant in our efforts to find the lost men. Names will be given as soon as we are certain of them.'*

He saw his own name among the type.

'You're in charge of the rescue operations, I see,' Schak pointed out dryly.

'I wish to God there were some operations to be in charge of,' Fife said.

He tossed the papers aside and flipped through the letters that had arrived. There was one he noticed from Gibb, the man who had been flown home with a broken leg. As they had expected, he had reported his arrival to London by letter and Sir Willard Mortimer, full of unctuous concern, as chairman of the committee, had promptly flown north to talk to him, and his inquiries after his son-in-law's health had produced an uneasiness in Gibb which had immediately made him suspicious.

Gibb was full of apologies and explanations. He had tried hard, he said, to avoid letting the secret out but as Mortimer's questions had grown more direct, it had been impossible, without telling outright lies, to avoid letting him know what had happened.

Fife flipped the letter thoughtfully with his thumb, then he slipped it to the back of the pile and glanced through the inevitable circulars that followed every expedition around, the personal bills he never seemed able to pay and always did, the letters from all his relatives who considered it their duty to write him lengthy dull epistles because he was a long way from home. He was on the point of stuffing them all into his pocket, when he noticed a handwriting and a postmark that were unfamiliar and he opened the envelope curiously.

To his surprise it was from Rachel Piercey, and he remembered gloomily that he had not had the courage to answer her last inquiries.

It was a calm letter, lacking all the hysterical appeals of Mortimer's cables and the businesslike bustle of the newspaper reports.

'Please tell me,' she ended. *'Is my father with Commander Adams' party? I have the impression that he was and, as I have not heard anything from him, I can only conclude that he must be. I'd be very grateful for a straight answer. Please tell me what has happened to my father.'*

Fife shoved the letter into his pocket with a rough gesture that hid an uncomfortable feeling of guilt. I'll answer it later, he decided. I'll get down to it when I get back, and make a decent job of it. The fact that she had managed to stir him more than he realised when he'd first met her hadn't made it easier to write to her. To have to tell her the blunt facts of what had happened and make the bald statement that her father was missing, probably dead, had been harder than he'd expected, and he'd kept putting it off until he felt he could manage to make a reasonable job of it. He knew he had to do it some time but he also knew he hadn't the courage to state bluntly that Piercey was dead when he might not be, or even that he might well be alive when he wasn't honestly sure that he was.

'Let's go and see old Sjøgren again,' he said gruffly.

They climbed down the gangway and crossed the dock area, followed by the surly glances of the Icelanders. The fishing dispute, blowing up overnight, it seemed, from a series of isolated incidents into a serious clash of wills between governments, had soured all their relationships with them.

Over the door of old Sjøgren's office was the motto, *'Starfid er Mann's Bedste Blessur'* – Work is Man's best Blessing – but there wasn't much satisfaction from the dour old Norseman sitting inside.

'I can promise nothing,' he insisted again. 'Nothing at all. Besides' – he gestured with his pipe – 'there is the whole of the winter and spring.'

'This isn't a five-minute job,' Schak said angrily. 'This is going to take weeks. My goddam ship's got a hole in her side you could drive a coast-to-coast bus through.'

'I will do it,' the old man said placidly. 'But not yet. When I am able.'

'See here,' Schak said slowly. 'I've been in here dozens of times for one thing or another and you've never been difficult before. We were hit by a trawler – '

The old man looked up quickly, his blue eyes keen. 'A British trawler,' he pointed out.

'Ah!' Schak drew back a step, big and burly and threatening, but the old man didn't drop his gaze. 'Now I guess we've got it in a nutshell at last. It's this goddam trawler upset, isn't it, that's behind everything. We're not going to get the dock at all, are we?'

The old man's eyes dropped to his blotter and a shadow crossed his face. 'Our trawlermen are saying that you were trying to put your ship between the British trawler and the gunboat that was trying to arrest her.'

Schak exploded. 'There wasn't a gunboat within a hundred miles!' he snapped.

'The story is that the Englishmen were running from inside the twelve-mile limit and the gunboat was trying to stop them.'

'Goddam it' – Schak chewed fiercely at his cigar – 'how in hell could we have been near the limit? We were nor'-east of Scoresby Sund. You know damn well I wouldn't get myself involved in an international dispute that doesn't concern me, anyway. I've got more sense.'

The old man moved uneasily. 'What I feel and what I know,' he said slowly, 'have nothing to do with it. That is the story and it is firmly believed.'

'Some guys would believe any crap.'

The old man behind the desk was unmoved, his face placid before Schak's anger. 'I am not a trawler owner,' he said. 'I have never been a trawler owner. I have always worked in a shipyard. But my customers are *all* trawlermen – Icelandic trawlermen – and just at this moment they do not like English ships.'

'We've nothing to do with the goddam trawlers,' Schak said.

'We are a proud people,' the old man went on, refusing to be rushed. 'This country was first settled by the Vikings in the ninth century and we do not take easily to other nations trying to impose their will on us. We are an independent republic, owing allegiance to no one.'

'For the love of God, Mr Sjøgren, don't preach politics at us. We know all that.'

Suddenly the old man's stiff manner melted and he looked at them unhappily. 'My customers,' he claimed, 'say the breeding grounds round Iceland are being fished out. They say that the twelve-mile limit is essential to maintain the industry – and we depend on fishing for our economy. They maintain your trawlers are poaching when they come inside that limit. They are afraid of your trawlers because they feel they will take their livelihood away. And because they're afraid, they're angry and will believe whatever they want to believe.'

'Mr Sjøgren – '

The old man held up his hand again as Fife stepped forward. 'They would not like me to put right your ship,' he said. 'I might lose customers if I did – regular customers who are my own countrymen. I can't afford to do that. My workmen are Icelanders, too, and I cannot force them to do this work.'

'All right, Mr Sjøgren,' Fife said. 'So we're not going to get the *Brancard* repaired. Then, for God's sake, use your influence to help us charter a ship. We only want to land Weasels to search for these lost men.'

The old man looked sideways at him. 'On whose authority are you chartering, Mr Fife?' he asked.

'On mine.'

The old man shrugged. 'Mr Fife, it's already common knowledge that your committee has turned down your appeal for a ship from England or Canada or Norway. How can you expect anyone to offer you anything on those terms? *You* can't pay. Besides' – he shrugged again – 'with the winter already approaching, it would seem there is plenty of time for you to sort it out with your committee. Nothing will get up there now until spring.'

'When the ice goes back,' Fife said, 'we'll only have a few weeks. We can't afford to take any chances on not being ready – not after they've spent a winter up there. We've *got* to be ready. If we get the ship, I'll get my committee to back me up.'

'There are months yet, Mr Fife.'

'There's one less than when we arrived,' Fife reminded him sharply.

The old man regarded him, his blue eyes unhappy. 'Very well,' he said at length. 'Suppose I find you a ship. Suppose you could go and search for them now – this minute? Where would you look? Where would you go? There has been no sign of them. They're dead, Mr Fife. It's obvious they must be dead.'

'I'm not accepting that they're dead,' Fife said. 'It may be simply that they can't maintain wireless contact.'

'The papers say their hut was burned down. No one can live up there in winter.'

'They can go to ground. They still had two tracked vehicles. They were equipped with spare transmitters and they must have taken them away with them because we found none up there. Surely your damned customers don't begrudge help to men who may be in desperate need of it.'

The old man sat in silence for a while, drawing lines and circles on his blotter.

'British ships can still run into Reykjavik or Helbergfjördur for shelter from a gale' – he spoke slowly and distinctly – 'there is a cemetery behind the town which shows how many times they have done so. They have brought their sick and injured to our hospitals and buried their dead in our soil, and they can still do so – '

'But they don't,' Schak interrupted angrily. 'Not now because they known damn well if they do, they'll be arrested and accused of fishing inside your goddam twelve-mile limit. And they know perfectly well that if they *are* accused, they haven't a cat in hell's chance of disproving it. It's their word against an Icelandic gunboat skipper's and everybody knows what the court will say – even *you* know that.'

The old man nodded and it was impossible not to be impressed by his calm acceptance of the facts.

'That is so,' he said. 'But this is politics, and politics, whether they are ours or yours, are seldom sensible or fair. If there were a certainty that these friends of yours are alive, something would be done. We are human here in Iceland and we're noted for our hospitality, but since these men have so obviously disappeared, are so obviously dead – '

147

'They're not dead,' Fife snapped.

'Mr Fife' – the old man's voice was a protest – 'it is now almost two months since their radio was heard. What are we to believe? They *must* be dead.'

'One of the weather stations got a signal from them.'

'Long after they are assumed to have left their base, Mr Fife. And nothing has been heard since. Nothing.'

'I still believe they're alive.'

Old Sjøgren gave a despairing gesture, as though he found Fife's insistence difficult to bear.

'Mr Fife, their signal was weak and indistinct. It was impossible to make out any message. What can that possibly indicate? It was garbled and unreadable and there was no position and no names.'

'Their transmitter may have been damaged. They could repair it.'

'In two months, it should *already* be repaired.'

The stubborn, shut-down look had appeared on Fife's face and the old man shook his head. 'I have every sympathy with you, Mr Fife, but with things as they are I could never persuade my men that there was an emergency. Find your missing party and then it will be different.'

'I can't find them without a ship.'

'Then pick up a signal from them. You'll not be without a ship for long then. Pick up a signal and you'll find you have all the ships you need. Until then, I cannot persuade either my workmen or my customers to believe there is any need for them to relax their feelings about your country and your ship or the decisions they have made.'

Fife made an angry gesture and the old man looked up at him.

'You know my own feelings, Mr Fife,' he said with dignity. 'At my age, all one wishes to do is live in peace with the rest of the world. But I am unable to do a thing for you while the trawler dispute continues between Britain and Iceland.'

Outside, Schak flung his cigar to the ground and screwed it out with his heel.

'What a goddam thing to happen,' he said. 'I bet Fuchs and Hillary never had to worry about this sort of thing.'

Hannen was waiting in the boat when Fife returned to the jetty. He climbed aboard and sat in the stern in silence as Hannen started the engine and headed away from the shore.

'We got nowhere,' Fife said eventually. 'They just don't want to know.'

'I was afraid of that,' Hannen said.

He bent over the engine, pretending to be occupied with it, knowing Fife didn't want to talk, and Fife understood the gesture and was grateful for it. Somehow, staring across the dark water at the brown hills behind Stakness, he didn't look forward to returning. The hostility there was almost as strong as the hostility in Helbergfjördur. Most of the old people who still lived there had sons or brothers or cousins who were fishermen, and their anger at the trawler dispute showed itself constantly in small incidents – the tendency to hold up mail and the difficulty of getting fresh milk and eggs, which had forced them to hire a small boat to make a regular trip to Helbergfjördur across the bay where the big stores were less influenced by the problems of the trawlermen. It was like living in an enemy country with everyone hostile to them and resentful of their presence there.

Neither of them spoke as the boat trudged noisily across the bay. There hadn't been much to say for a long time now.

As they bumped against the broken jetty at Stakness, Fife rose to his feet, waiting as Hannen made fast, then he walked slowly up the gravel path with him to the hut where Jessup had built his radio shack.

The Yorkshireman was crouched over his dials and he looked up as Fife entered. For a second, he stared at the expression on Fife's face, then at Hannen who followed him in, then in answer to Fife's unspoken question, he shook his head.

'Nothing?' Fife asked.

'Only mush.'

He reached across the table and, moving the papers about, picked up a pile of cable forms.

'Here,' he said. 'For you. Relatives and so on.'

Fife nodded and Jessup picked up another pile of cablegrams.

'Some from the Big Wheel himself here,' he said, holding them out.

'Mortimer?'

Jessup nodded and Fife gestured angrily. 'Throw 'em away,' he said. 'I'm not interested in Mortimer.'

Jessup still held out the forms. 'Better read 'em, Skip,' he said. 'He's on the warpath.'

'I'm not interested in what Mortimer thinks of me.'

'I am,' Jessup said. 'We all are.'

Fife stared at him for a second, then he nodded.

'Sorry, Jesse,' he said. 'And thanks.'

He flipped through the buff forms slowly. They were all the same – demands from Sir Willard Mortimer. '*Where is Adams?*' '*Demand know why Adams not rescued.*' Then later, obviously after Fife's report had circulated in London – '*Demand know circumstances Adams' death. Concern expressed in Commons. Consider bad publicity harmful to expedition and committee. Imperative Government know more. Inform immediately measures being taken rescue Adams' party.*'

The terse phrases seemed to grow louder and more hysterical as the message advanced and Fife shoved the cable form in his pocket, half-read, with a gesture of anger.

'I wish the old fool would get off my back,' he said.

'He was Adams' father-in-law,' Hannen pointed out gently. 'It could be that he's interested.'

Fife looked up at him, accepting the rebuke. 'Yes, I suppose so,' he admitted. 'It could be. I expect he's got the same feelings that everyone else's got. But I wish he'd keep 'em separate from his politics. It's harder to believe him when you feel he's being a politician at the same time as a father-in-law.'

He paused, then he turned to Jessup again.

'Look, Jess,' he said, 'that weather station that picked up their signal – '

Jessup hunched his shoulders. 'There's nothing, Skip,' he growled stubbornly. 'You know the story as well as I do now. It's weeks since they picked up that signal and it was mostly static, anyway. They got nothing that was worthwhile. No position. No names. Just G3ZBD and a few numbers. And what's the good of a call sign and nothing else?'

'They were probably trying to send a position.'

'Well, nobody got it. They only knew who they were because they'd heard 'em sending met. reports to London. Besides' – Jessup gestured – 'the man wasn't even interested at the time. He didn't even know then that they were missing.'

Fife nodded and Jessup turned heavily back to his set.

'I've not stopped listening,' he said over his shoulder. 'I keep working all the hams. I'm trying to keep them at it all the time, but I think they're all losing interest a bit now. They can't keep a round-the-clock watch for ever and you can't expect them to be very enthusiastic when they pick nothing up.'

'No. Of course not.' Fife shook his head.

He stared out of the window, his eyes sombre. The water of Axel Helberg Bay was flat and steely-looking and reflected the high peak of Helberg Hjelmen and the silvery tanks of the whaling station as though it were a mirror. His thoughts crowded in on him, harsh and full of questions that he couldn't answer, and after a while he turned and went out, walking down the gravel path to where the old jetty ran out into the water.

Hannen, his eyes compassionate, stood watching him through the window, a lonely figure on the sagging timbers, then he noticed Jessup staring at him.

'Working up a temper for tonight, poor old sod,' Jessup said. 'That temper of his is beginning to get him down. He'll end up like Eric Pinney – going to South Georgia with a crate or two of whisky to spend the winter alone and having to be lifted two months ahead of schedule because it's all gone.'

Hannen nodded, and Jessup fished underneath a pile of papers and produced another cablegram which he handed slowly to Hannen.

'This one came too,' he said. 'I hadn't the heart to give it to him with the others. Not when I saw his face. You'll have to do it.'

Hannen glanced at the cablegram then his brows came down, and he glanced quickly at Jessup.

'You'll *have* to tell him some time,' Jessup said.

Hannen nodded and went outside. Fife was still alone, still staring at the water and, as he heard Hannen coming up behind him, he turned and saw the form in his hand.

'Hello, Pat,' he said flatly. 'That about the Weasels?'

Hannen's face was serious and Fife frowned.

'What's wrong?' he demanded quickly. 'Are the bastards pulling the economy excuse again? Aren't they sending them after all?'

Hannen shook his head. 'There'll be no Weasels now, Tom.'

Fife frowned again, suddenly knowing that Hannen's presence was connected somehow with disaster.

'No Weasels?' he said. 'Why not?'

Hannen held out the buff slip. 'Jess's just given it to me,' he said.

Fife took the cable form and stared at it. The message was simple and to the point.

'*Weasels held pending inquiry*,' it said in terse cablese. '*Deputy Fife return London. Report Mortimer immediately.*'

As he lifted his eyes, Hannen was watching him.

'It's the chopper, Tom,' he said. 'You've got to go home.'

five

England was grey and misty with the smoky look of approaching winter when Fife landed at London airport. The lights at the other side of the runway were blurred with the flurries of rain that kept drifting across the fields, and the sound of distant lorries on the road to the west came on the gusty wind as he climbed into the airport bus. It didn't look very different from the airport in Iceland which he'd left only a few hours before in a flaying northern rain. There was the same featureless expanse, the same blustery air, the same modern utilitarian building blocks with their overheated saloons where the tourists would be buying souvenirs and eating bacon and eggs and drinking coffee.

As he entered the stuffy lounge, a man whose face seemed familiar came up to him and asked if he could speak to him for a moment. Fife nodded and was led to one side, then he realised that the other had a microphone in his hand and that there were television cameras around him.

'This sort of thing could happen to any party wintering near the Pole,' he said in answer to the probing questions that set his mind floundering as he was caught unawares.

'But ten men are missing, Mr Fife.' The interviewer's voice sounded accusing. 'Ten of them! That's a lot!'

'They'll be found,' Fife said stubbornly.

'But they've been missing a long time now. Has everything been done that *can* be done to find them?'

'Of course.'

'Then why was so much time allowed to elapse before anyone went in search?'

Fife grew wary as he became aware of the dangerous trend of the questions and his answers to the rest of them were monosyllabic. Realising he was not going to commit himself, they let him go at last and, conscious of press cameras levelled at him and with the flashbulbs going off in his eyes, he fled thankfully towards the exit, glad to get away from all the curious eyes that rested on him.

It was raining steadily by the time he reached the city where he deposited his luggage at the air terminal and took a taxi at once round to the headquarters of the British East-West Greenland Expedition near the docks.

There were a couple of reporters sitting in a car outside who had obviously been tipped off from the airport, but he brushed them aside and pushed his way in without answering any questions. The office was empty except for an old woman with a cigarette drooping from her lip who was pushing disinterestedly at a broom.

'There's nobody here,' she said, in a flat unconcerned voice. 'They've all gone.'

'Where can I get hold of someone?'

'I dunno. I expect they're all at home. It's late.'

For a while, Fife debated ringing up Adams' wife, then he decided that just at that moment he felt he couldn't face her questions. He was tired and needed a good sleep, and in the end he decided to return the following day.

He picked up a taxi outside and, collecting his bags, returned to the minute flat in North London where he'd lived since the death of his wife. Feeling stifled by its small rooms after the tangy air and open spaces of Iceland, he telephoned his mother in the north of England. She sounded pleased to hear his voice, but was obviously puzzled that he was back so much ahead of schedule. She'd read what had happened to the expedition and, even through her relief that her son was safe, he could hear her anxiety.

'They're saying you ought to have found them, Tom,' she said. 'They're saying it's your fault that things went wrong and that you ought to have got to them before it was too late.'

'Of course they are,' he pointed out bitterly. 'There's only me left to blame.'

He had no sooner put down the instrument when it rang again and he found himself talking to one of the London dailies.

'Mr Fife, we're trying to find out what happened up there,' they told him, and his face went dark at once.

'I'm sorry,' he said. 'I can't make any comment at this stage.'

'But Mr Fife – '

He slammed the receiver down, in a growing temper, and went outside to buy an evening paper. The Adams story was still on the front page, he noticed, alongside the Parliamentary indignation at the trawler dispute which had become involved in the disaster.

Someone had managed to introduce it into the debate in the House, he saw, demanding to know why one of the frigates from Iceland couldn't race up to Camp Adams in place of the damaged *Brancard*. '*Our ships must be allowed to fish in their lawful waters, without let or hindrance by any country, and by the same token British subjects in faraway places must be able to rely on the long arm of the British government to offer to them in their distress the same measure of help.*'

The sheer fatuousness of the remarks made Fife squirm.

By the following morning, the rain had stopped and he pushed among the Londoners struggling to get to work, feeling as if he were in an antheap, with all the ants disturbed and hysterical around him. In the morning papers, he saw that the Adams story was being linked now with the uproar in the Commons over the dispute on the Norwegian border, and he realised with a start that someone in the Opposition had got to know about Doree's rockets and had thrown them into the melting pot of politics with an accusation that they were weapons and should never have been allowed to jeopardise Britain's position by being sent to a neutral country. His own face was there, stark among the headlines, startled-looking as he had been photographed passing through the airport lounge, and his own words, brief and guilty-sounding as they were quoted out of context. There was an interview with Adams' widow too. '*I had a feeling that something like this would happen. Something must have gone wrong. My husband was a most experienced explorer,*' and the newspaper comment. '*Commander Adams' deputy is bound to come in for criticism for the delay in inaugurating a rescue.*'

The accusations were beginning to fly already, it seemed, and fingers were beginning to point at Fife.

Feeling low in spirits, he called at the laboratory where he'd worked in case there'd been any messages for him from Lutyens, and he was immediately aware of the sidelong glances everyone kept giving him. They were obviously startled to see him back and clearly thought it was a sign of disgrace.

The atmosphere of the place suffocated him and he left as soon as he could and took a taxi to the river.

The fallen leaves were matted damply together and plastered to the pavement, and the sign outside the headquarters office was shining with moisture. *British East-West Greenland Expedition*, it said. It had an exciting sound, he thought, and it had excited him when he'd first heard of it. But it had been conceived in confusion and executed in chaos, and its disastrous end somehow, now, seemed the only logical result to all the mistakes that had been made.

There were one or two harassed girls inside the office, their faces worried as though their own fortunes had been caught up in the failure of the expedition, and a few obvious relatives asking questions. He could see open files on the desks among the empty teacups and a few lists, and photographs of Adams and Mortimer and the group on the crowded decks of the *Brancard* taken when she had departed from London on the voyage north.

They were all there – Adams himself, between Mortimer and his wife, Legge-Jenkins, Hellyer, Doree and Greeno, and young Ivey. O'Day. East. Clark. Pink. And Piercey. Fife saw his own features next to the doctor's and the grave face of Piercey's daughter.

He turned away, his ears full of the clatter of feminine voices, all of them a little anxious now, and slightly fretful and strained. No one seemed to recognise him and he reflected bitterly how much less was known of him and Hannen and Jessup and all the others than was known of Mortimer. If Mortimer had walked in, he decided, wearing his white collar and soft hands like badges of office, they'd all have noticed him and sprung to attention.

He was just deciding he was being unnecessarily cynical when he found himself staring at Rachael Piercey – almost as though she'd stepped out of the photograph he'd just been looking at. She was dressed in a heavy mackintosh with a soft blue felt hat pulled round her face so that only wisps of fair hair showed against her cheeks. She was talking over the top of a desk to a girl with a flour-white face who wore a patterned dress that looked as though it were made of chintz. In spite of her anxiety, she still seemed calmer than the other girl, who was fiddling all the time with a cup that held the dried remains of the previous day's tea.

Instinctively, Fife stepped back and pushed his way round by a different route to the inner office. Just then, he felt, he hadn't the courage to face her – or anyone else, for that matter.

At the desk, a harassed middle-aged woman was sitting, and behind her there was a photograph of Adams himself in naval uniform. She looked up as Fife entered and from the blank look in her eyes he saw again he hadn't been recognised. Then suddenly, she looked startled and jumped up.

'Mr Fife,' she said, realising at last who he was. 'What are you doing here?'

'I arrived last night,' Fife said. 'I flew in yesterday.'

'Yes, of course. I remember now. A cable was sent on Sir Willard's instructions. He's been expecting you. Shall I contact his office?'

'No,' Fife shook his head. 'Not now. I need a little more time.'

He had no desire to face Mortimer until he had spoken to someone more experienced and with less axes to grind.

'How about Admiral Lutyens?' he asked. 'Where can I get in touch with him?'

She looked blank. 'I don't know. Sir Willard's been trying to contact him for some time – ever since we got your first message.' Her eyes filled with tears. 'Oh, Mr Fife,' she mourned. 'Isn't it awful? Whatever's happened?'

Fife shook his head. 'I don't know,' he admitted. 'I wish I did. What about Admiral Lutyens?'

She seemed bewildered. 'He seems to have vanished,' she said. 'We can't get any sense from his home. Sir Willard's been trying to summon the committee to discuss what's happened. He said he'd heard in the House of Commons that the Government had called him in over this business of the Russian fallout on Norway. He's a bit of an expert, you know.'

She picked up a newspaper and thrust it at him. 'They're trying to say now we were armed, Mr Fife,' she went on indignantly. 'They're saying we had weapons and had no interest in geology.'

'Look' – Fife pushed the paper aside, suddenly spurred by the news into a greater need to find Lutyens – 'I must contact the Admiral.'

'Won't Sir Willard do?' She gave a little fluttering gesture. 'Mr Fife,' she said, 'it's been awful here the last two days. We've even had anonymous messages accusing us of jeopardising the trawlermen's position with Iceland. There's been nothing but telephone calls. The newspapers won't leave us alone. I've run out of things to say to them. And now it's the relatives and all the firms involved. They're out there now, some of them. I hardly dare put my head out. I don't suppose you could – ?'

She stopped, looking at him appealingly, but he shook his head. 'No,' he said. 'Not now. I must get hold of Admiral Lutyens.'

The need to speak to someone with experience had become urgent. Only out of Lutyens did he feel he could get any sense. With Mortimer, he felt the whole thing would dissolve into acrimonious confusion, with side issues of politics and business. Old Lutyens, with his leathery face, his years of dealing with men of action and his own vast experience of polar exploration, could be relied upon to come straight to the point, to find out what could be done and, if he agreed, to support Fife to the bitter end.

He took Lutyens' address and left his own on a scrap of paper.

'If he should turn up, please ring me immediately,' he begged.

Eventually, he knew, he would have to face Mortimer and Adams' wife, even Rachael Piercey and a few other of the relatives he had met, but it was more urgent first – more urgent even than sympathy or reassurance – to set things moving before the issue was confused with international politics and bad publicity, with questions in the House, the Prime Minister's concern, the indignation of the backers – all the things that would spring at once to Mortimer's teeming mind.

As he descended the stairs, he saw the newspapermen outside on the pavement again and he slipped out of the back door instead and took a taxi. Back at his flat, he spent a good hour on the telephone trying to contact Lutyens – at his club, his office, his home. But at every one of them, the replies to his inquiries were guarded, and his impression was that what the woman at headquarters had said about him being called in by the Government over the Russian incident might well be true.

For a while, he sat debating how to approach Mortimer. There seemed to be no alternative now. He was still the paid servant of the expedition and its nominal leader and his instructions to report to the Committee were clear. Sooner or later he'd have to face it.

During the morning, the telephone rang several times, each one a newspaper inquiry, but he refused to answer any questions and his temper was growing slowly worse when the doorbell rang.

He jumped towards it, scowling, thinking for a moment that they'd come in person to see him, then he saw it was Rachel Piercey standing in the corridor, still wearing the mackintosh and blue felt hat.

Her eyes were cold and he remembered again how beautiful he'd thought them when he'd first met her.

'Come in,' he said, holding the door open. 'I'll get some coffee.'

She shook her head, pale-faced and taut with anger, and he was horribly aware of how he'd avoided answering her letters and had dodged her that morning. Obviously she'd seen him and managed to get his address.

'A drink then?' he suggested, her silence making him uneasy.

She shook her head again, her eyes flashing. 'No thanks,' she said sharply. 'I don't want coffee. I don't want anything. I just want the truth.'

She sat down unwillingly and Fife stood by the window, studying his fingers and wondering how to start.

'Why didn't you wait for me?' she said, her face stony. 'You must have seen me.'

'I'm sorry,' Fife said. 'I should have.'

'You might have remembered how long I've been waiting,' she said bitterly.

Yes, he thought. He might.

'I'm sorry,' he said again.

'Why didn't you answer my cables?' she demanded. 'I sent at least two, and a letter.'

'Look,' he said desperately. 'I know how you feel but I was pretty busy.'

'All that time?'

'Well' – there was really no excuse, he knew, but he felt he deserved a little mercy – 'look,' he said, 'I was thinking of other things.'

'Not with much success, it seems,' she said coldly.

Her contempt sparked off his own uncertain temper.

'I tried to find them,' he snapped.

'You didn't manage it.'

'That's what they're all saying now,' Fife growled.

'What can you expect?' she burst out.

Fife's face darkened. 'I tried to get up to them,' he said sharply. 'I don't suppose it means much to you, any more than it means much to the Press, or all the other relatives, or to Sir Willard Mortimer and the Committee, but I wouldn't like to make that journey again.'

The anger went from her face suddenly and she managed an apology, a blush colouring her cheeks. 'I didn't know about this,' she said quietly. 'There's been nothing in the papers about any attempt to get to them.'

'No.' Fife shook his head, his anger subsiding just as quickly as hers. 'They haven't got around to that yet. They probably won't now. It's not news, I suppose, that we only just made it ourselves.'

'Please tell me,' she said quietly. 'I'd like to know.'

He sat on the edge of his chair, still ill at ease, and tried to describe the journey they'd made up to Camp Adams, to give her some idea of the cold and the discomfort and the abysmal sense of failure they'd felt when they'd found they'd arrived too late.

When he'd finished, she sat quietly for a moment, her fingers interlaced, then she looked up.

'I'm sorry,' she said. 'I didn't understand.'

Fife shrugged, tongue-tied now that his anger was gone.

'I'm sorry about your mother,' he said lamely.

She made a movement with her shoulders, as though she preferred not to think about it, and he went on clumsily.

'I know what's it like,' he said. 'My wife died five years ago when I was in South Georgia. By the time they got me out it was too late.'

She said nothing, and for a moment they were warmed with the comfort of shared sorrow.

'Could it have been prevented?' she asked at length.

Fife hesitated, wondering how much he might have stood in the way of disaster. 'It might,' he said. 'I might have been even more rude to Adams than I was – but I suspect, that if I had, he'd have left me behind in England anyway. As it was, he didn't take me with him up to the East Coast Camp.'

He was silent, for a moment, still a little troubled, wondering if perhaps he might have done more, then he looked up, made uneasy by the way she sat motionless, watching him, waiting for him to continue.

'I wish we could have reached your father,' he went on slowly. 'We tried. We tried very hard. All of us.'

'Yes,' she said, calm again now. 'I'm sure you did.'

She looked down, fiddling with her handbag, then when she raised her eyes again, they were steady and frank and friendly at last.

'Is it true the expedition was armed?' she said.

He shook his head. 'No,' he said. 'No, of course not. That's a lot of damn parliamentary nonsense. It's those met. rockets of Doree's they're talking about. They were perfectly innocuous, as far as I know. It's just that there was too much secrecy about them. If everybody had been given the facts, all this rubbish could never have been brought up.'

She was silent for a moment, then she looked up quickly. 'Is it true there was a signal from them?' she asked. 'The papers said there was.'

Fife nodded. 'Yes. There was a signal.'

'Didn't it tell you anything?'

Fife hesitated, suddenly aware of how little it *had* told them. He could see all his own questions to Jessup forming in her mind and, as he thought about it, he couldn't honestly find much to comfort her. All his insistence in Iceland that Adams' party were alive, that their transmitter had merely failed, and that with courage and a little faith they could all be rescued, seemed to wither away inside him now as he realised that there really was nothing – nothing at all.

'No,' he said, admitting it also to himself now for the first time. 'No, it told us nothing. It was weak and garbled and almost all that was decipherable was the call sign. The weather station which picked it up probably wouldn't even have noticed it but for the fact that they'd heard them before transmitting to London.'

'Were there no names?'

All his own questions were being thrown back at him now, he noticed. He shook his head. 'I only wish to God there had been,' he said. 'They were never heard again.'

'What does that mean?'

He shrugged. 'It might mean nothing or it might mean everything.'

'I see.' She paused, her fingers moving uncertainly over her handbag again, then she looked up at him with steady eyes. 'Please be honest with me,' she said. 'I'm not afraid. I was at first when my mother died but that's over now. Is my father alive?'

Fife shook his head, suddenly unable to feel the optimism he had felt before. 'I hope so,' he said.

'Do you think so?'

'*I* do,' Fife said firmly. 'I always will till we find them dead.'

'But you really know nothing at all – where they are, how they are, whether in fact, they *are* alive?'

Fife shook his head again. 'No,' he said miserably. 'I don't know. I honestly don't know.'

It wasn't a very happy interview but she managed to make him feel better and a little less of an outcast. Now that they had sunk their differences, he was at ease with her. She had the ability, rare with people who knew Fife, to make him talk, and at least, she seemed to understand. She accepted his offer of coffee in the end, and they sat talking quietly over it.

'Why didn't you wait for me at headquarters this morning?' she asked at last, not rebuking him any more, but merely curious. 'Didn't you see me?'

'Yes,' Fife admitted. 'I saw you all right. But I just hadn't the courage to wait for you. I just couldn't face you just then. I didn't want to talk about it.'

'I'm sorry I insisted. Do you mind now?'

'No, it doesn't matter now,' he said. 'It was simply that I had nothing to tell you and I hadn't the guts to say so. I've got all this to put into letters, too,' he pointed out. 'To every one of the relatives and parents. It won't be easy.'

She paused, stirring her coffee. 'Why are you back in England?' she asked.

'I was recalled.'

'Oh!' she looked faintly disappointed. 'I thought perhaps you'd come back with some plan – some idea of what could be done.'

'I had a plan of sorts,' he admitted. 'It didn't amount to much. It was mostly based on hope and the feeling – just the feeling, you understand, no more – that they were all right. But I can't do anything about it without help here in England. That's why I was laying low. That's really why I kept out of your way this morning, I suppose. I don't want to be found by the wrong people.'

'Wrong people?'

'Sir Willard Mortimer. He's Adams' father-in-law. He's got influence but not much experience. I wouldn't want things to go wrong. I must get back up there with a new ship.'

She paused for a moment before her next question.

'What do you think of their chances?' she asked.

'Your father has plenty of experience...' he pointed out, unable to go further.

He was finding her much more easy to talk to than he had expected, so that he wondered now why he had dodged the issue of answering her letters. She seemed calm and unlikely to throw any of the feminine tricks that he'd been afraid of. Like many men of action, he was not at his best in the presence of women, chiefly because his experience of them was not great, and he was surprised now to find how simple it was.

'What about the others?' she asked. 'Had *they* experience?'

'Apart from your father and Legge-Jenkins,' he admitted, 'they're all first-timers, but Doree and Ivey are both climbers and they all know how to look after themselves. They were chosen with that in mind.'

She paused again. 'I got the impression,' she said slowly as though she were feeling her way and didn't wish to say anything that might offend, 'that Mr Legge-Jenkins was going along to work a laboratory rather than to lead a party. And I believe, from my father's letters, that *he* thought the same.'

He was surprised at her perception and by the information that Piercey had been so forthright with her. But, at least, he thought, it meant it was easier to say the things that were in his mind. If Piercey had considered her able to face such facts, he didn't have to clothe what he had to say in soft words.

'Legge-Jenkins had experience,' he said, 'he'd spent a winter up there before. He's an experienced dog driver.'

'Does that make him a leader?'

She was disturbingly blunt and her eyes were searching as they stared into his. He had to admit that it didn't, but he hesitated to say so in so many words.

'Experience *always* counts,' he said.

She paused, studying her fingers, then she looked up at him again with those steady eyes of hers. 'My father always thought you should have been in the party going up to Prins Haakon Sø,' she said. 'It was clear from his letters from Stakness that he thought you *would* be going, and that you'd be Commander Adams' deputy there.'

Fife said nothing and she went on in forthright tones.

'Why *weren't* you with Commander Adams' party?' she asked. 'You and Mr Hannen and those others – Jessup and Smeed and Erskine? And the man from the Danish Geodetic Institute. My father told me about them.'

He studied his hands for a moment. Obviously, Piercey had had few secrets from this girl.

'Adams and I had a few basic differences,' he said. 'Perhaps he felt it would be wiser if I weren't with his party. It might have been difficult to have people with differing ideas living so closely together.'

'What about the others? Mr Hannen and Jessup and Smeed – '

'They agreed with me.'

'Were there so many who disagreed with Adams?' She sounded surprised.

He nodded. 'Yes,' he admitted quietly. 'There were.'

'Why?'

He hesitated for a moment before answering, then he decided that since she knew so much already not much harm could be done by telling her the truth.

'Several of us felt that the expedition was hurriedly organised, and badly conceived,' he said. 'We felt that not enough time had been spent considering all the possibilities – and that there was too much acceptance of wrong material and equipment.'

'And this' – she looked at him frankly – 'is why Adams is dead and the rest of them are missing?'

He looked at her equally frankly. 'That's my opinion,' he said.

They spent the rest of the morning talking quietly together and, to Fife, still tensed with the need to find Lutyens, it had the effect of calming him down a little. Rachel Piercey had a frank manner and she obviously knew a great deal about him. She had clearly discussed him with her father and had noticed far more about him than he'd realised during their first brief meetings at Piercey's home.

They were still sitting over the coffee when the telephone rang, and as Fife had half-expected, it was Sir Willard Mortimer. He sounded angry.

'Why didn't you get in touch with me at once as I requested?' he demanded.

'I reported to headquarters as soon as I arrived,' Fife pointed out, feeling almost that he was talking to Adams himself. This was how all their conversations had gone – Adams arrogant and demanding, Fife irritated by the suggestion that he was not behaving competently or intelligently.

'The cable said you were to contact *me*.' Mortimer's voice was sharp with annoyance.

'My instructions come from the expedition committee, Sir Willard,' Fife said. 'I've been twice to committee headquarters.'

There was a silence for a moment, and Fife was reminded of how Adams, too, had had a habit of pausing for a second after he had come up against the incontrovertible fact that people could disagree with him and still be right.

When Mortimer went on, his tones were more conciliatory.

'I'd be glad if you could come round here immediately,' he said, 'and talk this thing over.'

'Of course,' Fife said. 'What about Mrs Adams? Will she be there? I feel I ought to see her too.'

'I think you can leave my daughter to me, Fife,' Mortimer said. 'Naturally, she's still very upset and she doesn't wish to see anyone. Any information you have for her you can give to me and I'll pass it on. I'll look forward to seeing you within the hour.'

As Fife put down the instrument, Rachel Piercey began to pull on her gloves.

'Mortimer?' she asked at once and he nodded.

In desperation, they spent the next few minutes trying once more to contact Lutyens by phone, but in the end Fife put the instrument down with a sigh.

'It looks as though Mortimer's going to run the show after all,' he said.

They walked to the door together and, on the pavement, she turned round to him.

'Would it help if I came with you?' she asked, impulsively.

'I wish it could.'

'After all, I'm anxious to know, too, what's going to happen.'

Fife managed a wry smile. 'Mortimer won't give anything away,' he pointed out. 'Not till he's thought a lot about it. He's too much of a politician. Besides, he might even think I was trying to hide behind you. Thank you all the same, but I'll sort it out on my own.'

'Shall I wait?'

'Knowing Mortimer, you might be waiting all evening.'

She nodded and he signalled to a cruising taxi for her, then, as it pulled up in front of them, he became suddenly aware of loneliness. There was no one in London he cared to see and certainly no one he could confide in. His parents were in the north, he had no wife and not many friends. He'd always seemed too busy to make friends and, with his interest chiefly in fieldwork, he'd never even got to know well the men he'd worked with in the laboratory, who'd always regarded him as a little mad, anyway, for preferring exploration to comfort and security and the high salaries he could certainly have demanded if he'd stayed at home.

'Suppose we had a meal together,' he blurted out, thinking of their parallel desolation. 'Then I could pass everything on. This evening, if you're still in town.'

She smiled. 'I am,' she said. 'I'd got an hotel. You know how difficult it is getting to Orford. I wasn't looking forward to the evening.'

'Perhaps it would help us both if we shared it. Besides, I expect I shall lose my temper with Mortimer, and I might be glad of company afterwards.'

He helped her into the taxi and caught a bus to Mortimer's office in Park Lane. There were one or two photographers on the pavement outside who jumped forward as they recognised him, but he was too quick for them and slipped inside before they could waylay him.

He was shown into a waiting room filled with deep armchairs and expensive magazines and tasteful pictures, and in spite of his errand he was kept waiting for twenty minutes, before a girl whose face and figure were as smooth as everything else in the office opened the door for him.

'Sir Willard will see you now, Mr Fife,' she said.

Mortimer was standing by the window as Fife was shown in, a big pale man with little left of the brilliant young scientist he had once been. He was in a dark suit and, with his white collar and cuffs and the well-cut, curling grey hair above his ears, seemed the epitome of a successful city man; and curiously once more Fife was reminded of Adams. Mortimer had the same suave good looks, the same self-assurance of background and money, the same certainty in his behaviour that made Fife's indifferent clothes and untidy hair seem clumsy and oafish.

He made no attempt to shake hands and Fife wondered if a little of Adams' dislike had been transplanted in him through letters or reports.

'Give Mr Fife a drink, Anne,' he said to the girl. 'I think I'll have one also. The usual.'

He sat back at his desk with a brandy and soda in his hand and stared for some time at Fife before he spoke, as though he were torn between indignation, natural sorrow and anger.

'This is a damn bad business, Fife,' he said at last in his harsh voice. 'Those confounded newspapers have been on the telephone all morning. They're camped outside now.'

'I've seen them.'

'I hope you didn't tell them anything.'

'No.'

'Good. Pity they caught you at the airport. It looked damn bad. I saw it on the news.'

Mortimer rose and walked to the window again, restless and troubled.

'What happened?' he demanded.

'It was all in my report, Sir Willard. There isn't much more I can add.'

Mortimer gestured impatiently. 'Yes, yes,' he said. 'I know. I read the report. But isn't there anything else? Isn't there anything else we can tell my daughter?' He whirled, the strain bursting out of him at last. 'Good God,' he said. 'The whole damned base! What happened, man? There've been fires up there before. Why didn't they deal with it?'

Because Adams hadn't taken the trouble to make sure of all his emergency arrangements before he had set off on his local journeys, Fife wanted to say. Because he had been preparing his surveys before Fife had left with the ship, before the base was even complete. If anything were responsible for the disaster, Fife knew, it was haste.

He looked up, trying to put his feelings into words without being offensive or hurtful.

'Perhaps everything hadn't been done in the way of precautions,' he said slowly.

Mortimer turned round sharply, his eyebrows raised, hostile at once in spite of Fife's caution. 'What are you suggesting, Fife? I advise you to watch what you say. There'll be an inquiry over this, you know. The Press'll force one.'

His manner irritated Fife, and his face darkened as his ever-ready temper boiled up.

'I'd be glad of an inquiry, Sir Willard,' he snapped. 'Any time the Committee considers one should be held.'

'There'll be blame, Fife. Someone's got to accept the blame.'

'I'd still be glad of an inquiry.'

'What do you mean? Are you going to make accusations or something?' Mortimer's face had grown hard and wary and he looked more than ever the successful businessman-politician.

'There were many things that were wrong,' Fife said sharply. 'I mentioned them in my report.'

'Much better if you'd reported them to Commander Adams.'

'I did that, too. Many times.'

Mortimer stared at Fife, his eyes hostile, sizing him up, Fife noticed, with the same arrogance he had met in Adams so that he wondered if this were something that had drawn the two men together.

'There seems to have been some slackness somewhere,' he said. 'Emergency-wise. Where were *you* when it happened?'

'I was on my way up to the East Camp, working on the instructions already laid down by Commander Adams.'

'Oh!' Mortimer seemed a little disconcerted. 'Even so, there still seems to have been some slackness somewhere in the arrangements. Something like that. Surely to God something could have been done? Why didn't we fly in, for instance?'

'We had no aircraft.'

'But the Americans, man, the Americans – '

'Sir Willard' – Fife spoke in measured tones in an attempt to get through to him – 'we don't know even now where they are. And Greenland's two thousand miles long and a thousand miles wide.'

Mortimer seemed a little disconcerted. 'It seems to me there's been some neglect,' he said, trying a new tack, and Fife felt like one of his clerks being hauled over the coals for some misdemeanour. '*Why* don't we know where they are?'

'Because they didn't turn up at Cape Alexandra. We were there, as arranged. We stayed some time. We went to Fraser Bay. There was no sign of them.'

'In the name of God, why didn't they stay where they were? They could have been airlifted, then.'

'Their instructions were to get to Cape Alexandra.'

Mortimer's eyes were hot and angry. 'All these plans and emergency arrangements,' he said. 'Obviously no one gave them much thought. It would seem to me' – Mortimer's voice was fat and pontifical as though he were addressing a board meeting – 'that they ought to have stayed where they were. Who decided on all this nonsense? Legge-Jenkins?'

'It was suggested by the Ministry when Doree's rockets were included among our equipment. In fact, it was virtually laid down as a condition of financial support. Commander Adams agreed to it.' Fife gave him a glance of bitter satisfaction. 'Commander Adams,' he said. 'And you, Sir Mortimer.'

Mortimer's head jerked round. 'Are you accusing me – ?' he began.

'I've read the minutes,' Fife said calmly. 'I've read the instructions. They were the only clear instructions we ever had. They were signed.'

Mortimer's pale face flushed and Fife guessed that, involved with all the other multifarious schemes that occupied his time, he had probably never read the papers to which he'd set his name.

He was hurrying past the subject now, anxious to avoid questioning. 'This man, Legge-Jenkins,' he said. 'Who is he? Some damned bluestocking from a council school? How did he come to be in charge of the party?'

'Commander Adams chose him.'

Mortimer turned to the window, ignoring the reply. He was silent for a moment, then he turned slowly. 'There'll be trouble over all this,' he said sullenly. 'The Minister was asking me yesterday in the House what had happened. There are bound to be questions – especially with the Air Ministry involved over those darn rockets. The backbenchers are restive about it, and the Opposition's in full cry. It's embarrassing, Fife, especially with things as they are in Iceland and the Opposition throwing out this damn stupid accusation about weapons. The FO's going to be involved before we know where we are. The Party's getting restless. They want facts and when they get 'em they're not going to like 'em. The situation's damn dangerous.'

'It needn't have been,' Fife said stiffly, determined not to let Mortimer shuffle the responsibility on to him.

Mortimer stopped dead in his tirade and his face flushed. 'Are you suggesting that the plans were bad or something?' he demanded.

Fife paused and drew a deep breath. This was it, he thought. This was the sixty-four thousand dollar question. 'Yes,' he said. 'If you insist, I am.'

Mortimer seemed to calm down abruptly, as though he felt the need to proceed more warily, as though Fife's firmness, the certainty implicit in his words, shouted a warning to him.

'Are you prepared to make that statement in front of the rest of the committee?' he asked slowly.

Fife nodded. 'Yes, I am,' he said.

Mortimer paused. 'You'd better be careful, Fife,' he said. 'I hope you're sure of your facts.'

He sat down at his desk and began to move papers with brisk gestures, and Fife knew he was seeking a means to close the interview to enable him to sit back and think of his next move.

'I had hoped we might work together, committee-wise, to save a little credit,' he said. 'Particularly as the Press seem determined to tear us all to pieces. But you're obviously hostile, Fife. It's my impression, in fact, that you've been hostile from the very beginning. Yours is hardly the attitude of a deputy leader. A deputy leader's job's to support his leader – '

'I'm quite aware of what my duties were,' Fife snapped.

'I begin to wonder,' Mortimer retorted. 'Especially with this fiasco on us. I suppose you've seen the papers. It might be of interest to you to know that the PM himself's been on to me. Questions about those damned rockets are going to embarrass a lot of people.'

He drummed with his fingers on the desk for a moment. 'I think under the circumstances,' he said, 'that we'd better conclude this interview. Nothing much good seems to be coming out of it. There'll have to be an inquiry, of course, to decide where the blame lies. As chairman, I'll have to set that on foot at once.'

Fife leaned forward quickly. The danger he had feared was beginning to take shape. Mortimer was making the disaster into a boardroom affair, and the last thing in the world he wanted just then was one of his interminable committees.

'Look, Sir Willard,' he said. 'We don't need an inquiry just now.'

'Oh!' Sir Mortimer's expression seemed to lift, almost as though his hostility increased. 'A moment ago you were welcoming one.'

'Surely it's more important just now to produce another ship – to mount a search party.'

Mortimer snorted. 'Do you realise how much that will cost, young man? We can't spend that kind of money without the committee's agreeing to it. We've already overspent. We budgeted for seventy-five thousand pounds and it ran to eighty before we even moved from England. It's gone well over that now. It's all got to be found.'

'Sir Willard – '

Mortimer crossed to the window and stared out, still talking, his businessman's instinct grasping at familiar straws.

You realise the *Brancard's* still under charter to us?' he said over his shoulder. 'She's costing money all the time she's laid up, up there – and she's going to cost a damn sight more with this fishing dispute. They're not going to let us get off lightly with that annoying them.'

He turned round and faced Fife. 'It's all very well talking glibly of rescue parties,' he said sharply. 'It would mean mounting a completely new expedition. Another ten thousand pounds, at the very least.'

Suddenly, sickeningly, Fife had the impression that to Mortimer the disaster had become just another item of finance in his busy world.

'We'd have to have a meeting of the committee,' he was saying. 'And I'm not sure I can persuade them.'

'*I'd* like to try, Sir Willard.'

Mortimer brushed the suggestion aside with a scornful gesture. 'There'll have to be a general meeting,' he said. 'Our financial backers are entitled to know what's happened and what's being done. We'll have to get all the interested parties together and hold an impartial inquiry into what went wrong.'

'That might take weeks!'

'Naturally,' Mortimer stiffened. 'These are busy men, Fife. They're concerned in national and international affairs, and it isn't easy to arrange a date that's suitable to them all. They may even be out of the country like Admiral Lutyens, for instance. We don't know where he is and, according to the rules, we can't proceed without him.'

'Is it so essential to stick to the rules?'

'This thing has to be done properly.'

Fife felt his face going red. Watching Mortimer, knowing even of his sorrow over Adams' death, he still found he could feel nothing but dislike for him.

'It seems much more important to hurry the preparations for a rescue,' he said, hanging on to his temper with difficulty.

'Hurry?' Mortimer's face wore the same placid expression Fife had seen on old Sjøgren's. 'With winter on us? We can't make any move until the spring.'

'Sir Willard,' Fife urged. 'We should be ready. You must know that a signal was picked up.'

Mortimer gestured and Fife realised once more just how little his one thread of hope meant.

'I saw it in the paper,' Mortimer said coldly. 'Faint, obscure, unreadable and meaning nothing. It was never repeated, Fife. Never. Not even a hint of it. It doesn't seem to me that there's any need to hurry.'

Fife's eyes were angry, and Mortimer pushed a copy of *The Times* at him, jabbing an impatient finger at a paragraph at the bottom of the page. '*It is now accepted,*' it read, '*that in view of the absence of any radio contact, the remaining men of Commander Adams' party must be assumed dead.*'

'That, Fife,' Mortimer said. 'That's what I mean. What else can we assume but that they've all perished?'

He used the word with a sort of dramatic enjoyment, almost as though he were rolling it round on his tongue, and Fife had a strange impression that he was addressing not him but the House of Commons. It was the sort of word politicians liked to use to make an event sound more important.

He was on the point of protesting again when the office intercom buzzer went. Mortimer pressed the switch and spoke at once.

'I don't wish to be interrupted,' he snapped immediately.

'Sir Willard' – it was the voice of the smooth secretary that came over the loudspeaker and she sounded ruffled for once – 'it's the national Press.'

'I've nothing for them. Tell them I'm giving no telephone interviews.'

'It's not on the telephone, Sir Willard. They're here in person. They insist on seeing you about the new developments.'

'What new developments?'

'They want your views on some Russian statement they've got.'

'I'm dealing with the British East-West Greenland Expedition at the moment.'

'They say it's about the expedition, Sir Willard.'

Mortimer stared at Fife for a long second, then he bent to the microphone again.

'What is it they've got?' he asked.

'It seems the Russians have picked up this news the Opposition had – about the rockets. They're saying now we were a military expedition.'

Mortimer considered for a moment, not taking his eyes off Fife, then he bent to the microphone again.

'I'll see them in a moment,' he said. 'Come in, in five minutes' time, and we'll get something ready for them. Tell them they'll have to wait until then. I'm not talking off the cuff. And find out what they've got and bring it in with you.'

He pressed the switch and looked at Fife. 'Well,' he said, almost as though he were accusing him of treachery. 'It's public property now. It's become a political issue now. An international issue even. There'll *have* to be an inquiry now. The public will want to know.'

six

By evening the story of the Adams' expedition was flung into the news again with a wholly unexpected outburst from the Russian delegate to UNO, and the new developments were splashed across the front pages of all the late night finals.

There was a man selling them on the corner by the Soho restaurant where Fife helped Rachel Piercey from the taxi, and they read the story together as they waited for their meal to arrive.

The Russians had pounced on the accusations which had been made in the Commons, as a retort to the Western objections against their atomic tests at Novaya Zemlya, and their version, full of claims that the Danes and Norwegians were in league to form an Anglo-Scandinavian bloc against them, was a blind lashing-out against world opinion.

'Five out of the eleven men who comprised the Adams party,' they pointed out, *'were experts drawn from the three British services – led by a Naval commander, and armed, with American collusion, with the latest secret weapons.'*

The story ended with a statement from Sir Willard Mortimer, obviously made just after Fife had left his office, in which he disclaimed all knowledge of any weapons. *'I can promise the country,'* he ended, *'that there was nothing in the equipment carried by the expedition that was anything more than standard geophysical equipment. I can only imagine that the Russians have got hold of the wrong end of the stick as usual and have assumed that the meteorological rockets and launcher which were taken north for testing by a qualified RAF scientist were something highly secret and dangerous.'*

Fife laid down the paper, nauseated, and looked across the table at Rachel.

'It's politics now,' he said. 'That means nobody'll do a damn thing in case it's wrong and all the issues'll be confused and nobody will say what he thinks or what he means in case it doesn't conform to party policy or in case his constituents don't agree.' He looked tired suddenly. 'And finally there's this,' he added, jabbing his finger at a paragraph at the bottom of the story. ' *"There is a growing criticism about the methods of the rescuers and the delay that took place before a rescue was set on foot."* That's me. They've decided I'm guilty before we've even had the trial.'

She looked serious. 'What are you going to do?' she asked.

'There's only Lutyens now,' he said. 'He's the only one who can help me. There's nobody else whose voice carries sufficient authority to overrule Mortimer if he tries to push the blame my way.'

The following day, on her suggestion, the two of them took Piercey's car and drove to Lutyens' home in Sussex, but the house was empty except for one old woman who was acting as caretaker.

'The admiral's not at home,' she insisted. 'You could try his son, of course. He's in Bath.'

Fife glanced at Rachel and she nodded at once. 'Let's go to Bath,' she suggested.

Lutyens' son was a Naval captain with a sharp, intelligent face that reminded Fife vividly of his father, but he didn't hold out much hope for them.

'My father's in North Norway,' he admitted. 'The Admiralty sent him. He'll be there some months, I suspect.'

They drove back to London in darkness, both of them silent and thoughtful, and the next morning, even before Fife was dressed, the telephone in his flat rang and a cable from Hannen was passed to him. The words, stark in cablese, showed that the political uproar had already reached Stakness.

'Rumours expedition to be withdrawn,' they said. *'Please confirm.'*

Fife telephoned a reply, trying to reassure Hannen when he didn't feel particularly reassured himself. Once politics invaded their territory, he knew, anything could happen. Nothing would be sacred and nothing and nobody would be important enough to stop the march of events. Helpless in London, aware of the storm that was beginning to gather round his head, Fife felt vaguely like a traitor who had started all the destructive forces of gossip, discussion and Press inquiry which were already gathering to break down everything they were still trying to do.

The evening papers were busy with the story again that night. *'Is it true that the Adams' expedition was armed?'* someone had asked in the House and the Under-Secretary to the Air Ministry had had to make a strenuous denial.

'Greenland observations,' he had pointed out, 'have the greatest impertinence in the making of forecasts of Atlantic and polar weather, which it need hardly be said, is of tremendous urgency in these days of flying. The secret rockets which were with the expedition were of importance not only to Britain but also to international weather stations.'

'Then, in Heaven's name' – the words had been flung back immediately, it seemed – 'let us try to rescue these men with their secret apparatus before someone else gets there first.'

The reply, cautious to the point of vagueness, had been that as the Expedition Committee itself was about to hold an inquiry into the matter, it was felt wiser to wait so that effort could be concentrated and not diffused.

'It has never been the policy of the government,' Fife read, 'to interfere in the affairs of private organisations. The British East-West Greenland Expedition is well capable of looking after its own business, and no doubt they will demand assistance if they think it could be of any use.'

Nobody seemed prepared to commit themselves to anything and, to Fife, with the whole business dissolving from an urgent, important, even desperate matter into a national parish pump affair, the last sentence seemed ominously indicative of the impression that was rapidly gaining ground everywhere. Adams' men were dead, it seemed to say quite clearly, and their equipment lost. There was no point in creating a crisis over something which could not be altered. There seemed no point in hurrying to provide a rescue when there was nothing and no one to rescue.

During the following days, Fife wrote letters to the relatives of all the missing men, trying to sound encouraging when he had no facts to offer that might give any hope. Then he visited his home in the north and spent a weekend with his family that was thoroughly depressing for them all, because they knew the neighbours were talking and that the Press was making veiled accusations about him.

'You should talk to them, Tom,' his mother said unhappily.

He shook his head stubbornly. 'The less I talk at the moment, the better,' he insisted. 'Every word I say is probably going to be thrown back at me later.'

On his return south, he became occupied with a new and more detailed report for Mortimer, and had several meetings with the various men and firms who had supported the expedition – the Cozzens Trust, the petrol organisations, the radio manufacturers, Kinglake, the editor of the *Recorder*, which had given its backing and used its columns for publicity.

He was even asked to call at the Air Ministry where he was shown into an unlabelled room to be interviewed about Doree's rockets by a man whose name he was never told.

'We regard those rockets so highly,' he was told, 'we're quite prepared to put the whole of our facilities at your disposal to fly out these men.'

'We've got to find them first,' Fife said between his teeth, feeling he was beating his head against a brick wall. 'We've got to find them before there's any airlifting done.'

It was an unhappy period of uncertainty for him, with his bank account dwindling rapidly as he travelled about the country trying to persuade someone to give him permission to return to Stakness. He was still officially being paid by the Expedition Committee, but like the rest of them, he had accepted a merely nominal salary. He had needed only the slightest of reasons to join in what after all was chiefly an adventure and he had never needed excuses, scientific, financial, or otherwise, for getting away from his laboratory.

Unfortunately, he had done it so often he had never been able to save much and he could now see his savings vanishing like dust before a wind as he took trains and taxis and used hotels in his efforts to whip up enthusiasm for a rescue. It was something he had always had to do before the start of any venture and he had always found it distasteful trying to persuade people to put their hands into their pockets and stump up. But, where normally he had found at least a polite interest, now nobody took the trouble even to listen to him. Most of the people he called on seemed to prefer not to get involved in what was rapidly becoming a political dispute, and those who *were* willing to see him seemed to be interested in him only as someone they had seen on television who was achieving a certain amount of notoriety in the Press. His appeals to Mortimer never had the slightest hope of bringing results.

Mortimer's whole attitude now, in fact, was that it would be better for them all if the whole thing were forgotten and the remainder of the expedition recalled, and Fife began to wonder even if he had had second thoughts about the inquiry. His own part in the organisation of the expedition had not been small, and with the hostile reactions in the Press and in the House of Commons, it seemed he was beginning to be afraid of what might come out. In spite of a new cautious friendliness which, Fife suspected, was merely the good politician busy changing step and avoiding enemies, he was rigid and uncooperative.

'I can't see any further use for the remainder of the expedition remaining up there,' he said bluntly, giving Fife the honest eager-beaver look he kept for awkward constituents. 'There seems, in fact, little sense now in hanging on to the base at Stakness, especially now that it's become an embarrassment to everybody, with the fishing dispute.'

Fife felt vaguely as though he were being driven backwards into a boardroom and defeated there. 'While the rest of the expedition remains up there,' he said, 'they're the nucleus of a relief expedition. If you once disperse them, it'll take months to bring them together again.'

'Oh, come, Fife!' Mortimer's friendly expression slipped a little in face of Fife's stubbornness. 'Relief expedition? What for? We have to face facts. We've heard nothing from them since that last wretched signal, and even that was uncertain.'

'They're all right,' Fife insisted. 'I feel it.'

'That's not much to raise support with,' Mortimer commented coldly. 'And we can't afford to make fools of ourselves again. This whole affair's been difficult for the Government to a degree. Just when the country didn't wish to be involved, here we are, accused – however wrongly – of setting up a military expedition. And, just when we wish to take a stand against Iceland, we find they are in effect responsible for the maintenance of what is being suggested is a British base. I know we'd planned for two winters there, but, under the circumstances, I think we'd be wiser to settle for one.'

'There hasn't been *any* wintering party up there at all yet,' Fife said sharply. 'Except Sampson's, and that's useless without a camp in the east.'

'Then if it's useless,' Mortimer said, leaping at the excuse at once, 'isn't that all the more reason why everyone should be withdrawn?'

His mind seemed to be made up and, in desperation, Fife sought out Rachel Piercey at her home in Orford and dragged her round to see Kinglake, the editor of the *Recorder*, in an appeal for help.

'My dear chap' – Kinglake was surprisingly willing to see them but unable to offer much in the way of comfort – 'I don't run the committee. It's nothing to do with me.'

He moved to the window, looking down into the street, a heavily built man with a handsome plethoric countenance and slow movements that spoke of confidence in his own capabilities at judging either a man or a situation.

'I only wish it were,' he went on. 'It so happens that Lutyens is an old friend of mine and we came to the conclusion long since that Adams ought to have been used in an organising capacity at base and the leading left to you.'

Fife's jaw dropped and Kinglake smiled. 'It can do no harm for you to know that now,' he said. 'It might even help, under the circumstances. Unfortunately, however, I wasn't on the committee and Lutyens had to work alone and nothing came of it.'

He paused, still standing by the window. 'If these men were rescued,' he went on slowly, 'it would be the story of the year and the man who found them would be the explorer of the year. But' – he swung round on his heel – 'I don't think they're *going* to be rescued and, because of that, I advise you to keep well out of it, Fife. A second failure would do you no good.'

Fife looked up at him, his face angry and puzzled, and Kinglake crossed to his desk and picked up a long galley proof 'Look at this,' he said. 'It might interest you.'

'Last paragraph,' he added as Fife's eyes flickered over the article. 'That's the one that concerns you.'

Fife's eyes dropped to the bottom of the proof. There was no need to read. The words seemed to leap out at him. *'Are we certain,'* they said, *'that the Adams' party hasn't been abandoned too hastily by the man they should have been able to rely on?'*

Fife's eyes lifted to Kinglake's face and Kinglake shrugged and replaced the galley proof on his desk.

'I killed it,' he said.

'Thanks.'

'Apart from the chance of it landing us in a libel action with you, it seemed to be jumping the gun a bit. All the same' – Kinglake made one of his slow gestures – 'it gives you an idea what the Great British Public is beginning to think, doesn't it?'

Fife nodded. 'I know where the blame'll land in the end,' he said. 'Adams is dead – '

' – and death has a habit of erasing mistakes,' Kinglake ended for him. 'Nobody's ever thought much of Scott as a man who made mistakes.'

'That only leaves me.'

'Exactly. But what did you expect? Surely not rewards?'

'No.' Fife's head went down in a stubborn gesture. 'Just some sort of attempt to back me in a rescue. But they're not even thinking about that. Mortimer's just out to dodge any criticism that's coming.'

'Naturally. His name's being bandied round the lobbies just now for a job in the Government.'

'I hope for the sake of the country that he never gets it,' Fife said bitterly.

Kinglake smiled. 'I think you need have no fear,' he said. 'The PM's got more sense than that. Mortimer hasn't got the common touch. I'm told he interviews his constituents as though they were looking for a job. His idea of politics is to keep out of trouble and appear in *"Sayings of the Week"* in the Sunday newspapers.'

He moved to the window again and stared down into the street, his heavy features brooding. For a long time neither of them spoke and, listening to the hum of machinery below somewhere in the bowels of the building, Fife got the impression that the whole point of the interview was being lost.

'There are only a few weeks in summer when you can get a ship up there,' he said slowly. 'If we're not ready when the pack breaks up, we may be too late.'

'I realise that,' Kinglake said.

Fife paused and went on thoughtfully. 'And in the meantime my head's on the block.'

Kinglake shrugged. 'We sank a lot of money into this expedition,' he said. 'If I sank any more, *my* head would be on the block, too. I can't help you.' He paused and, putting his hands in his pockets, stared at the carpet. 'However,' he went on, 'I'll make you a promise. Bring me a sign that they're alive – just a sign, a signal from their transmitter or something like that – a signal that really means something – and I'll back you all the way. I can't do any more.'

'That's what they told me in Iceland.'

'Without that signal, you can close the files, Fife. It's finished.'

It seemed almost as though Rachel had to lead Fife into the street, where he stood with his hands in his pockets, staring round him at the lights and the bustle of people and traffic. For a moment or two he was silent then he looked at her and gave a jagged laugh.

'Close the files,' he said wonderingly. 'Finished. Well, that was blunt enough. I suppose I thought it might come to this in the end. I just didn't expect it so soon, that's all.'

seven

As the days slipped by, Fife was horrified to realise just how many were disappearing in nothing but talk.

In spite of Mortimer's disapproval and Kinglake's inability to help, he continued with his crusade to raise a new expedition, but with every day that passed it grew more difficult. Not only did no one see the point of one, but the drama of the disaster had been lost now in all the other uproars that filled the columns of the daily Press. The expedition and the fate that had overtaken its members were being slowly forgotten, and in the end Fife was forced by lack of money to find a job – a temporary one he could drop at a moment's notice if necessary – hating every minute of it, loathing London, resenting every day that occupied his time.

A court of inquiry into the disabling of the *Brancard* by the *Lady Harding* was called for and he was interviewed by the representative of a northern trawler-owners' association asking if he would appear as a witness when the time came. The conversation only served to depress him further and, as usual instinctively, it seemed – he fled for consolation to Orford and Rachel Piercey, burning to tell her of the indignation he felt. With her quiet enigmatic face, she seemed to be the only real ally he possessed. Throughout the whole wretched period, her understanding had been the one thing he had been able to rely on. She was always ready to listen to him sympathetically as he poured out his flood of angry uncertainties, always willing to be harried along the fringes of his fury, to feel what he was feeling, to appreciate his frustration and misery.

There was a curious atmosphere growing up between them. They had been drawn together by a common disaster, and in the increasing storm that was blowing up around his ears he leaned heavily on her for her commonsense. She never failed to be ready with coffee or a drink or a meal, never complaining at this temper which simmered constantly like a pot on a fire, checking his anger with intelligence that was never so spontaneous or combustible as his was, her calmer spirit quieting the tempests that shook him to his depths.

Inevitably, it seemed, she was waiting for him, opening the door to him almost before he had arrived, as though she'd been watching for him and had run to meet him.

'They'll fly Schak down for the inquiry,' he said furiously, when she'd installed him in front of the fire and put a whisky in his hand. 'Then not only will we have to find a ship, but we'll also have to find a captain for it.'

His frustration came out of him in a final angry outburst as he swallowed the whisky at a gulp. 'Everybody's just *assuming* that they're dead,' he said bitterly, 'and that there's no need to hurry because there's nobody to find. In fact, I'm damned if I don't think it's becoming just a bad political deal to have them found.'

'Tom, you can't mean that!' The idea seemed one of the wilder suggestions that Fife had thrown out, the sort of thing she was learning to ignore, knowing it sprang from his hot temper and quick indignation and hatred of artificiality.

'No,' he admitted more calmly. 'I don't suppose I do. But I think Mortimer's worried now. I think he's beginning to suspect that neither Adams nor his own reputation's going to come out of all this unscathed. I think he's beginning to realise at last that what I said, what we all said, is right after all – that the whole affair *was* flung together too quickly.' He gave her a wry smile. 'I think perhaps he feels now that it might not be politically expedient to produce any rescued diaries or records.'

'Surely, Tom, he's not refusing to help?'

'No. No. I'd never accuse him of that. But he's got it firmly fixed in his mind now that they're dead and he's beginning to feel that the less said the better. He's all set to withdraw everybody in fact. He even wants to get the Americans to fetch Sampson's party in.'

He paused as she sat quietly opposite him, waiting for his anger to burn itself out.

'That would have been the lousiest, most humiliating thing he could have done,' he said bitterly. 'It would have looked as though Sampson had made a hash of *his* part of the programme, too.'

'What happened?'

'I think in the end I got him to agree to leave it to Sampson, if any decision was reached to withdraw everybody.'

'Tom.' She looked anxious. 'How are *you* going to come out of all this?'

Fife managed a wry smile. 'I shall spend the rest of my life working overtime to pay off all my debts,' he said. 'I've just about had it. Even if they want me to go back to Stakness, I'll soon not be able to afford to.'

'I didn't mean that,' she said quietly. 'I was thinking about blame.'

He gave a harsh laugh. 'You've seen the papers,' he said. 'Adams is dead, and mine's the only other name they know.'

'But they can't do that to you, Tom!'

'They can. They will. Mortimer's written it all off. Time's going by and it doesn't matter so much now that his daughter's lost her husband. I think the marriage was only jogging along on one cylinder for a long time, anyway. And now that everybody's accepted that they're all dead, he's determined that the blame's not going to be laid at *his* door.'

The Russian accusations had died a natural death. They had had no foundation in fact, as everyone had known from the start, and had been merely an arguing point in a greater controversy; but the trawler war showed no signs of dying and the Icelandic government, concerned at being involved, however obliquely, in a vague international wrangle and anxious to hit back at the source of her humiliation in what she called 'gunboat diplomacy', began to object to having on her territory the base of the disputed expedition and its representatives.

The Opposition in the House of Commons had not let rest the news that the remains of the expedition were still at Stakness, and Fife began to hear hints that Mortimer, pressed by members of his own party for action to relieve them of the embarrassment, was putting pressure on the committee to wind up the affairs of the organisation. The Press added its weight, too, but paradoxically, now that what had been expected for some time was being openly suggested, nobody seemed anxious to be the first to make the move which would announce to the relatives of the missing men that all hope had been abandoned.

Autumn vanished in a succession of smoky fogs, and the frosts followed, starring with ice the puddles in the parks and petrifying the mud along the fringes of the paths. Newspapermen still pestered Fife occasionally but he was learning to live with them, and for the most part, they had accepted that they were going to get nothing from him, and he went to his work every day, uninspired and unexcited, bored by his duties and by his colleagues, his interest caught only by the Press comments that started up like a lot of disturbed hares every time someone unwisely introduced the subject of the expedition in the House of Commons or made some demand for action.

He saw Rachel Piercey from time to time, going out to Orford when he felt low in spirits, meeting her in London once and taking her to dinner and even dancing, stumbling clumsily round the floor with her, envying all the carefree young Londoners about him who were so obviously enjoying themselves, and apologetic about his capabilities as a dancer.

'I think I must be the worst quickstepper in the world,' he admitted.

'Not quite,' she smiled. 'But almost.'

He knew he had no right to demand so much of her time, but she seemed content to be there when he wanted her around, yet never bothering him when he forgot her in some flurry of excitement that he felt might result in something being done.

Their relationship was easy, undemanding and calm, and she rarely nowadays referred to her father. But, he noticed suddenly she also never refused him when he asked to see her, and that when she met him her eyes lit up and there was a new happiness in her face; and he began to wonder if perhaps he ought not to keep out of her way for a while before he got himself involved, because he suspected that her emotions had become concerned with more than just the disappearance of her father.

Then, towards the end of the year, just when he was beginning to hope that the newspapers had forgotten him, an unconfirmed report in the morning papers announced that the Russians were offering to fit out a relief expedition to find the missing men, and immediately the whole vexed question leapt into flame again and all the shelved responsibility began to sit uncomfortably on unwilling shoulders once more.

Names were bandied about as the nucleus of a rescue team, and famous men who had been on the successful transantarctic expedition were said to have been approached. Noticeably, Fife's name was not mentioned but all the old angry questions were asked again as the causes and results of the disaster were brought out once more.

In a fury, he went to see Kinglake.

'My dear chap' – Kinglake waved a hand gently – 'I don't tell my reporters what to write.'

'They're suggesting I'm not fit to lead this damned rescue,' Fife snapped.

Kinglake shrugged. 'That's the way it goes, Fife. Once stir up public opinion, and you're a dead duck. It might be arms for Germany, the Fascists, the Communists, or just the persecution of an old lady over her pet dog, but once the wind starts blowing, it's an unforgiving one and it can be a violent one, as you might discover if this thing ever gets to a court of inquiry. It doesn't even always bear any relation to the facts. It just feeds on itself and goes on blowing and it never stops until it's swept everything away. It's brought down governments and swept more than one king off his throne.'

What he said was true and there seemed to be no answer to it.

Kinglake stood by the desk looking at Fife, his expression sympathetic but unhelpful. 'Nobody knows how it starts, Fife,' he said, 'or what'll rouse it. We try occasionally to get it going over something we consider important – neglect, stupidity, dishonesty, those sort of things – but the Great British Public stubbornly refuses to be moved. And then, suddenly, when you're least expecting it, a gale starts blowing about something else entirely and a lot of things are swept away. The public's already made its decision about you. It's nothing to do with us.'

During the next few days, with the muddy puddle of blame stirred up again, Fife was bombarded by telephone calls from the newspapers once more and by frantic appeals from Mortimer.

'We must get this search party going, Fife,' he said earnestly. 'We must accept the Air Ministry's offer of aeroplanes.'

'We can't find them with aeroplanes,' Fife snapped. 'There's only one way to do that, and that's to go in on foot and look.'

'Very well, have it your own way. But we really mustn't let the Russians get there first.'

It was obvious that Mortimer's waning hopes of gaining anything from the affair had taken a deeper plunge with the latest news and the faint chance of salvaging something had led him to stir the pot once more to see what it contained.

'Does it matter *who* gets there first?' Fife said angrily. 'So long as *someone* gets there.'

'It's a matter of national pride,' Mortimer answered stiffly. 'It's essential that we organise a relief party.'

'We already *have* a relief party,' Fife snorted. 'It's up there in Stakness sitting on its behind doing nothing because it hasn't a ship to put it ashore.'

For a brief instant, it began to look as though something would be done at last, but two days later the Russians announced that they had no intention whatsoever of organising a search for Adams' lost party and never had had. '*If the capitalist nations of the West,*' they stated with categoric firmness, '*choose to land on the Greenland ice-cap parties which, in spite of denials, can only be military expeditions, they can hardly expect Soviet help to rescue them. Let them rescue them themselves.*'

It was a cold-blooded statement but to Fife it seemed no more cold-blooded than the immediate fading of interest that was shown elsewhere.

Press concern vanished at once and the telephone calls from Sir Willard Mortimer stopped abruptly.

Then out of the blue came the announcement that the British East-West Greenland expedition was to be withdrawn. A letter, typed on thick white notepaper with the expedition's letterhead, dropped on Fife's breakfast table, with the news that his services would no longer be required.

'Owing to the failure to carry out the programme intended,' it stated, *'and the death of Commander Adams and the assumed deaths of the rest of his party, it has been decided with the greatest of reluctance to wind up the expedition.'*

There was a statement in the morning papers, together with an interview with Sir Willard Mortimer and a photograph of him taken with his daughter, Adams' widow, at his country house.

'I have lost a son-in-law,' he had said with becoming dignity, 'but this isn't what has led me to persuade the Board to withdraw the expedition. It seems that little can now be salvaged from what we tried to do and it would be foolish to throw good money after bad. The men in Iceland will return by sea, and the Americans have agreed to send a party in to the West Camp to rescue Lieutenant Sampson's men.'

Fife finished his breakfast in a rapidly rising temper and was waiting outside Mortimer's office long before the staff had arrived to unlock the doors. He had to fume through a solid hour before a few leisurely girls appeared, and yet another hour before Mortimer himself arrived and he was shown in.

'You're wasting your time, Fife,' Mortimer said at once. 'There's nothing we can do. Too many things have happened.'

'Too many things – ?'

'Good God, man.' Mortimer looked at him as though he were a little mad. 'You've got to be realistic. We can't get support for a relief expedition.'

'We haven't tried very hard.'

Mortimer gestured irritably. 'Fife, this uproar over the Russian fallout could cause a war if it weren't handled properly. Millions could die. Do you think people in authority can be bothered with ten men who may be dead already?'

Fife glared, then he forced himself to control his feelings. 'All right,' he said, 'I understand that. But recalling Sampson's party like this –'

'The committee had no alternative.'

'You might have left them a bit of dignity,' Fife snapped. 'The statement in the paper said they were being "rescued".'

'A mere slip of the tongue.'

'What's everybody going to think when they come trailing behind a lot of Yanks?'

Mortimer frowned, growing angry at Fife's persistence.

'There was no alternative,' he said again, sitting down behind his desk. 'It was decided that the whole business was best wound up as quickly as possible.'

'Who decided?' Fife demanded. 'You? I shall have plenty to say about this when the committee arranges its damned inquiry.'

Mortimer began to fish in a drawer for pens and blotters, his eyes veiled. 'It's just possible now,' he said calmly, 'that there may not be an inquiry.'

Fife stared. 'No inquiry?'

'I think we might save a little dignity and a few reputations by doing nothing.'

'Reputations? Whose reputations?'

Mortimer looked at him placidly. '*You* won't come out of this affair very well, Fife. Surely you must be aware of that.'

'I'm *well* aware of it,' Fife grated. 'But there are a few others who aren't going to escape blame either.'

He knew he was only lashing out blindly, but he was itching to dislodge the smooth certainty of security on Mortimer's face.

Mortimer, however, remained unmoved. 'I think we'd be much wiser to leave well alone,' he said. 'It only adds to the cost and it couldn't help much anyway. My son-in-law's dead and it seems to me that no further good can come of delving into this unhappy affair any more.'

Fife had sunk back into his chair, staring fascinatedly at Mortimer. It was almost as though he could see the tortuous working of his brain. He had clearly come to the conclusion that those high hopes of reward he had had might now even result in derision and he was ready to go to any lengths to avoid it.

'Of course,' Mortimer went on smoothly. 'I realise you have been considerably inconvenienced by this whole affair, that you must even have lost money by all the delay. I'd like to try to put this right, and I know you have only a temporary job at the moment.'

'Go on,' Fife said slowly, guessing somehow what was coming.

'We have room in Western Chemicals, one of our subsidiaries, for a man of your skill, Fife. A top man, of course. The salary would more than satisfy you, I'm sure.'

'Are you trying to bribe me to keep my mouth shut?' Fife said furiously, and at last, with a surge of triumph, he saw the placid look disappear from Mortimer's face.

'What are you suggesting, Fife?' he demanded, his neck going red.

'I'm not interested in your damned company,' Fife snapped, his temper overriding his common sense. 'I wouldn't be seen dead working for you.'

Mortimer's pale eyes grew cold and deadly. 'You might wish eventually that you'd accepted,' he pointed out icily. 'There aren't many jobs that would satisfy a man with your qualifications, Fife, and you might find it difficult to unearth someone who'll consider you acceptable.'

There was an implied threat in the words and Fife knew his insulting rejection of Mortimer's offer had gained him an enemy far more deadly than any earlier refusal to agree with him could ever have done. He knew Mortimer's power was sufficient for him to stand in his way if he wished, and the very knowledge that he had probably jeopardised his whole future drove him on furiously, goaded as much by a sense of a headlong tumbling to disaster as by the veiled suggestion that he could be bought.

'I'm not interested in being accepted just now,' he said. 'I'm interested only in getting those men back to safety and, if that's not possible, then in seeing that the blame's put squarely where it should be put. I'm damned if I'm going to see any of *them* blamed, that's for sure, and I'll be ready whenever the inquiry wants me.'

Mortimer had recovered his equanimity now. 'There will be no inquiry,' he said firmly.

Fife was on his feet at once, his face dark with rage. 'Won't there?' he said. 'I'll damn well see there is!'

For once, Rachel was not enthusiastic about what he had done, and her mood transmitted itself to Fife in a feeling of depression. All the way to Orford, through the frost-blackened countryside and the sad emptiness of the trees, he had been suffering from a sense of having burned his boats behind him, and to find that Rachel, of all people, couldn't agree with him, destroyed every last glimmer of the pleasure he had felt at insulting Mortimer.

'Does it matter any more about an inquiry?' she asked quietly. 'Does it matter who's right? Does it matter whether it's us or them? Does anything matter any more? Aren't we all trying too hard, Tom?'

'Maybe,' he agreed. 'But it's all grown so damned impersonal. Because there's an international crisis, no one's interested in the suffering of a few individuals. It isn't sense any longer trying to find them because there are only *ten* of them. If there were ten thousand it'd be different.'

There were tears in her eyes as she tried to make him see he was destroying himself, that his obsessive belief in rescue, which sprang up again and again, undaunted, at every new glimmering of hope, was turning everyone against him. She had long since given up trying to fight against the slow changes in her emotions. In spite of his clumsiness, his awkwardness, and the perpetual naive rebellion that rejected even the people who were fond of him, she knew she had lost.

She was watching him with unhappy eyes, longing to touch him, to comfort him in his perplexity, but he seemed not to notice her.

'He was trying to bribe me to make me keep my mouth shut,' he said hotly. She said nothing and he went on defensively, as though he knew he was wrong.

'We'll get nothing if we just sit down under it all,' he said.

'We haven't got much by standing up to him, have we, Tom?' she pointed out. 'My father's still missing and it looks very much now as though he's dead.'

He stared at her, shocked, and she hurried on before he could interrupt.

'Tom, there's no money coming into this house. No one's paying me now and I can't go on living here indefinitely. I've got to sell up and get a job or something.'

Her words stopped him dead. In his obsession with his own troubles, he had forgotten the effect of the disaster on her.

She looked up at him, backgrounded by the old house he'd come to regard as a haven of refuge when his anger grew too much for him, cool and calm but troubled by the absence of any future. She'd never failed him when he'd fled to her for support, always been there when he'd needed her, offering him the atmosphere of a house that had been inhabited by a happy loving family, listening solemnly to him so that, even through his wretchedness, he had glowed with the feeling that he was important to her at least when he felt an outcast with everyone else.

He felt guiltily responsible for her, as though everything that had happened were his fault.

'What'll you do?' he asked slowly.

'Get a hospital post. Something like that. It shouldn't be difficult.'

'No. No, it shouldn't.' He felt desperately that he ought to do something for her, as though she had been caught up in his own personal landslide and carried away, too.

'Rachel,' he begged, 'don't sell up. Not yet. Something will turn up.'

'After all this time?' She looked unhappily at him. 'I can't go on hoping for ever, Tom. I'm not one of those people who have the sort of faith that can go on thriving when common sense says there's no point in it.'

'Rachel, please!' Fife felt a little like that incurable optimist, Mr Micawber. Something would turn up. Something would turn up. With nothing to indicate that there was any hope, it seemed a poor sort of promise to offer anyone.

He was less certain, less sure of himself, when he went on.

'Look, Rachel,' he said. 'Let's go on trying just a little longer. Let's force this damned inquiry on Mortimer. Let's make him do something. It's only Mortimer who's persuaded the committee to vote against a rescue.'

'Tom,' she said wearily, 'we haven't the money to fight Mortimer. You'll never make them change their minds now.'

'We might make them agree to half a dozen men being left up there – officially to tidy everything up, to hand Stakness back to whoever it belongs to. Surely to God we can make it spin out to the spring. After all, since this damn fishing dispute started, nobody up there's ever shown much inclination to get on with things where we are concerned. There'd be a few experienced men on hand then, like Hannen and Jessup and Smeed.'

'Tom, dear,' she said gently. 'Will they want to stay? Will they all have the same faith you've got. They're not making any money while they're there. There's not much financial reward from exploration. You know that, and some of them may not be drawing any other salary. And if they've got ambition – or fiancées, or families – they might prefer to come home.'

Fife felt deflated. What she said was only too correct.

'They'll have to come home, Tom,' she said. 'Even if they feel the way you do. Now the expedition's declared ended, there's nothing to keep them there.'

'There are a few of them' – Fife was grasping at straws now, he knew – 'a few madmen like Jessup and Smeed who'd stay just for the devil of it. Hannen would stay.'

She looked at him tenderly, her eyes full of compassion and pity for him.

'You won't be there, Tom.'

He shook his head. 'No, not me, Rachel,' he agreed quietly, almost fatalistically, as though he'd accepted that whatever was done now could never intimately concern him again. 'Not now. They'd never send me back. Never.'

'Is it important to you?'

'I suppose so,' Fife admitted. 'If there'd been no such thing as exploration, I'd probably have invented it. But now it's finished. Nobody will want to be associated with failure.

Nobody will invite me any more. At the very least, they're going to say, "He's unlucky. Look at the Adams' expedition!" '

She touched his hand. 'What will you do?' she asked.

'I don't know.' He shrugged. 'I've got to do *something*. This job I've got isn't much to write home about and I'm broke. I'm as broke as I can be. I've spent all I possessed – which was never very much, God knows – trying to persuade everybody to raise a relief. I might find a university job, of course, or one of the petroleum companies might even offer me something, though I doubt it. They were involved in this damned affair, too. I know this, though' – his brows came down – 'whatever turns up or doesn't turn up, I'll never accept Mortimer's offer. I'll never be one of *his* bought officials.'

PART THREE

Darkness

o n e

Suddenly there were no more quarrels. The excitement, the desperate work had passed now, and their ordeal by patience had begun, and as they became absorbed with the necessity to make the ancient, ice-bound hut in Fraser Bay fit to live in, they were all too busy with their duties to have the time to consider their wretchedness or their past disputes, and they drew instinctively together with the need to depend on each other.

Piercey had felt no compunction at usurping the leadership of the party. He had no wish for reward or credit, simply an animal desire to survive. He had faith in his own experience and, since Legge-Jenkins clearly hadn't any in his, he had taken over naturally and instinctively. In conditions such as they were having to endure now, they had all found their own level, and if it hadn't been Piercey who had been thrown to the top, it would have been some other aggressive spirit, he knew, someone else with the will to live, someone like Doree whose burned hands had recovered almost miraculously, or even Hellyer with his hostile single-mindedness.

The sun had finally disappeared soon after they arrived and they had all stood outside the hut to watch it go. The day had been clear and still for once, and the southern horizon had been a vast expanse of orange which, as the sun sank, had changed slowly to a green shimmer. This, in turn, had merged with the blue of the sky high above the horizon where the stars were already beginning to sparkle. The northern arch of the heavens had been dark, however, right down to the horizon, grim and menacing like a black vault as the last shafts of light had sped across the ice and then were gone, and they had felt horribly alone and abandoned in the desolation. The shadows had vanished, the colours had faded and the peaks of the Fraser Mountains had stood faint and black in the distance. Even the ice had looked grey and hazy suddenly, so that distances had merged into each other in the half-light.

For a moment, no one had said anything, then Hellyer's voice had broken the silence.

'That's it, then,' he had said. 'Ring up the corporation, somebody, and tell 'em it's time to put the street lamps on.'

Doree had laughed and Piercey had blessed the touch of humour which had come so unexpectedly from Hellyer's bleak and uncompromising character to prevent what might have been a saddening event from depressing them too much.

He had not allowed them time to consider just what the disappearance of the sun would mean to them all. Soon they would be in polar darkness, and there was nothing in all the world more desolate than the northern night. It was a return to the ice age with no warmth, no life, and no movement, and the very thought of it under their present conditions was enough to still the blood in their veins.

For several days as the shadows drew deeper, he drove them hard to stop them thinking. Obsessed with his own hurt despair, Legge-Jenkins' thoughts seemed turned inwards to his own failure and, whether he had chosen it so or not, Piercey had no option but to direct operations. In everything they did, Legge-Jenkins remained somehow just outside, never quite giving his full attention to what was happening, never quite sharing the fragmentary moments when someone managed to raise their spirits with a laugh or the feeling that their hardships had drawn them closer together. There were many occasions when Piercey, feeling he needed a sense of achievement, had stood back so that he might regain control of events, but he seemed indifferent, and in the end, he accepted the pointlessness of trying and concentrated on setting their house in order before total night came, searching the old hut for anything that might be of use to them. There was no food, as he had half-hoped there might be, preserved in tins and protected by the ice over the years, but outside there was an ancient blubber stove that Hellyer cleaned up, a broken sledge, boxes and warped barrels and a few scraps of planking that had come from a boat bottom. In addition, they unearthed a thermometer, a magnifying glass, a few old pencils, a tin of salt, and other scraps of apparently useless equipment such as tweezers, skewers, bottles, and enamel dishes which they cleaned up and hoarded against emergencies.

But there was not much that made their condition any better. Their helplessness was almost complete. There was little they could do for themselves except hope that spring would bring Fife from Stakness.

'It'll be all right,' Piercey kept telling them all as they crouched in the hut. 'We shall be all right now.'

He tried hard to be confident. Any other attitude would have been foolish, he told himself. It would have been the equivalent of admitting there was no hope. They were pinning their faith now not on immediate rescue, which had been their aim until the loss of the second Weasel, but on Fife's getting the *Brancard* through to them as soon as the winter ice broke up. To expect him to fail would have been ridiculous. They couldn't even consider it. *Fife would be back for them*. Every man of them had confidence in Fife – more perhaps, Piercey thought sombrely, than there had ever been in Adams. Even now he'd be in Axel Helberg Bay fitting out ready for the spring, well aware of their plight by the very absence of radio contact. The thought helped them all in their duties.

More to stop them brooding than anything else, Piercey had written out a long list of trivial jobs which had to be done every day for the sake of their meagre comfort, and they were all busy in one way or another. Hellyer, with no machinery to look after, had devoted himself to making the blubber stove fit to work so that Doree and Greeno could use the primus in their forays after food, while O'Day occupied himself with the damaged transmitters and the others with repairing or cooking, or building a food store.

Gradually, the rough shelter grew. They built up the walls as well as they could, and rigged a roof with skis and planking and pieces of sledge, then they lashed across it with ropes the tarpaulins they'd salvaged from the Weasel. It was dark and ugly and cramped, but at least it was solid and when the drift had covered it and frozen hard, it would even keep out the wind.

As each small task was completed, Piercey began to feel more confident. Only the state of their rations worried him now, for Greeno and Doree had been able to bring in little in the way of game and he had hoped to lay in a stock of seal meat before the polar night stopped all hunting.

'There aren't any seal, Doc,' Doree said, his eyes staring out of his exhausted face as he sat with Greeno over their evening meal of stew. 'We arrived too late. They must have moved south after the sun.'

'There'll be others,' Piercey said firmly. 'They don't all go. I'll try tomorrow with Hellyer.'

The following day, however, they were marooned in the hut by the weather. The wind returned, unforgiving, heartless and unrelenting, whirling the draughts around them and eddying the smoke about their heads, never letting up for an instant, it seemed, in its battle to force their surrender. After a while, the snow began to creep through the thousand tiny openings between the rocks that formed the crude walls and they had to tear up rags and pieces of old clothing to tuck into the chinks. And when, to save their precious primus for emergencies, they tried cooking on Hellyer's old blubber stove, the gale, relentless, malevolent and wrathful, filled the hut with thick black clouds of greasy puther that drove them outside into the cold, half-choked, their eyes streaming with tears.

'I'll make the bloody thing work,' Hellyer growled fiercely. 'I've never been licked by anything yet.'

It did Piercey good to see the determination in his mouth as he bent his blunt features over the rickety chimney he began to construct. Suddenly Hellyer had become an ally, transformed, it seemed, by the unrepenting wind, to a bulwark of reliability. If anyone survived here, he thought, it would be Hellyer. He had the aggressive, awkward stubbornness to overcome things that went ninety per cent of the way towards survival. In some like Doree, it showed in a quiet determination; in Hellyer it appeared as a rough, blaspheming viciousness that refused to be silenced.

Now that he no longer had to work on freezing recalcitrant machinery, his hands, like Doree's, had begun to improve. Greeno's ankle and Pink's ribs seemed to be better too and Piercey began to hope that they would soon be able to do their full share of work.

The light grew steadily weaker and there was only a sunrise glow now above the mountains in the middle of every day, which grew perceptibly less with every twenty-four hours. Soon, even on clear days, it would not be discernible at all. Then they would all discover what spiritual resources they had. The Arctic night accentuated a man's faults and unstable men found it frightening. Even in clear weather when there was starlight or moonlight reflected by the gleaming countryside, and the distant mountains were sharply outlined in black against the frosty white, they would need all their reserves of courage.

For, although they had all recovered a little with rest, there was no doubt that they were starting off at a tremendous disadvantage. The desperate slog to the coast and the work they had done on arrival had drained them of strength and energy and now, with the weather growing steadily worse and the temperature still falling, the cold imposed an extra tax on their endurance. The drift came like a continuous white sandstorm which nothing could prevent penetrating into their shelter. During the day, all their efforts went towards mere existence, and at night they huddled together, wretched with cold and the damp that came from the melting ice in the ancient cracks of the hut.

For, in spite of all their efforts, there wasn't much in the way of comfort for them in the cheerless little den they had built, with its yellow flicker of light that was even further diminished by the black rock of the walls. They stacked the bedrolls round the sides during the day so that their crude cooking apparatus could occupy the centre, and any movement had to be round or over every obstruction. What they could, they thrust through the makeshift beams of the roof to get it off the floor, so that their heads were constantly among hanging clothes or wet socks that obscured what fitful light there was, and their backs were against the ice-bound walls that dripped, whenever there were enough of them inside to raise the temperature, in steady drops to the puddled floor.

As the tides and the incessant winds worked in the bay, they could hear the movement of the pack ice shifting relentlessly under some invisible and titanic power. The whole surface of the sea, as far as their eyes could reach from the bluff, was a chaotic jigsaw puzzle, and on the brief occasions when the wind dropped they could distinctly hear the sound of the tormented floes – the grunting and the whining, the bumping and the rattling, the shrieks like ships' whistles, the rumbles that came like waves breaking on an iron-bound shore or the muffled rolling of drums, or the curious sad sighings like thousands of human beings in pain.

Doree and Greeno shot a seal at last, then another, but they were only small and there was still not enough meat or blubber to carry them through the winter, and they went off again, in the waning daytime glow, to camp down by the coast, waiting and watching and searching while the periods when there was enough light to hunt by grew shorter and shorter.

When the wind got up, the drift grew worse and the air became so charged with particles of ice and snow that the work of building shelter walls round the entrance to the hut was slowed down to a standstill.

Nobody spoke much as they struggled on in the occasional periods when they could work outside the hut, but Piercey could see how their virtual imprisonment was affecting them all. To Hellyer, it was clearly a challenge, a vicious enemy that had to be beaten back with equal viciousness. To Legge-Jenkins it was just another unbearable burden on his back.

For some time now, he had been growing more morose, eating little and nagged at by failure, until his health began to worry Piercey more even than Ivey's. There was something about him that was not normal, as though his mental agitation were sapping his physical strength.

Then, on the day when they were staring through icy eyelashes towards the bluff in the hope of seeing Doree and Greeno returning up the slope, Piercey noticed that Legge-Jenkins was groping around slowly as they worked in the streaming drift, his gestures clumsy and uncertain, almost like a character in a slow-motion film, feeling his way about like a blind man, his stiff, winglike arm held out beside him, getting in the way of everyone else and reducing Hellyer to a seething cauldron of fury.

'Doc,' he begged. 'For the love of God, tell him to go and look after Ivey or something! He's only in the way.'

As Piercey crossed to Legge-Jenkins and took his arm, he saw his eyebrows and beard were covered with ice and that more of it was spreading across his face so that he was finding it difficult to breathe.

'I'm sorry, Piercey,' he said faintly. 'I'm letting you down.'

He was obviously exhausted and Piercey called at once to Hellyer and the others and they led him back to the hut and helped him into his sleeping bag.

'I'm sorry,' he kept saying. 'I'm sorry.'

He was repeating the words over and over again like an incantation, as though trying to make them all understand how he felt about his failure, then Hellyer touched his shoulder clumsily in a gesture that was oddly moving.

'That's all right,' he said. 'Nothing to worry about. You'll be OK now.'

As the others turned back to their various duties, Piercey sat down on his bedroll, exhausted by the wind and the cold that so consistently sapped their energies, and fished out some of his precious tobacco. To make his pleasure last longer, he had taken to smoking just one pipe a day now, and he found the effort of resisting the temptation to smoke more helped to steady his nerves. He lit his pipe and sat in silence for a moment, watching the others through the blue whorls eddying in the draughts that still managed to find their way into the hut. Then Hellyer, who was sitting alongside him trying to make a blubber lamp from a tin to save their precious paraffin, lifted his eyes towards his face.

'Worried, Doc?' he asked quietly.

Piercey nodded, his expression not changing.

'What about? L-J?'

'And Doree. He's overdue.'

'Doree's all right,' Hellyer said. 'He knows what goes on around him.'

Piercey looked up quickly and Hellyer gestured awkwardly and went on in a low voice.

'Look, Doc,' he said. 'I'm sorry about all that bitching I did over Doree's IRMAS, only – well, there seemed to be so bloody much that was wrong, and I' – he paused and glanced across the squalid little hut to where Legge-Jenkins was lying – 'well, I never honestly thought *he could cope*. Did you?'

Piercey paused, then he answered truthfully. 'No,' he said bluntly. 'I didn't.'

The time for false loyalty was past now. Legge-Jenkins *couldn't* cope. There was something in his make-up which had given way under responsibility. For some time, he had done little else but write in the log and weakly – as though he were trying to recover the reins of control – organise jobs for the others who took no notice at all and went instead to Piercey. After today, nailed down to his conscience by a second failure, Piercey had a feeling he'd do even less.

For a moment, with Hellyer silent and thoughtful beside him, he sat watching the others in the yellow light of the paraffin lamp that threw up the crowded interior of the chilly little hut with a stark truthfulness that was depressing. Ivey was talking from his sleeping bag to O'Day who was crouched over the box where he kept the transmitters and the few scattered spares they had managed to save. Most of his tools had gone with the Weasel and before he could do much he had to make new ones, and he was busily filing down one of the skewers they had found in the hut into a screwdriver of sorts.

Pink was repairing harness for his beloved dogs, and Clark was telling some long-winded funny story to East.

' – this chap had this bird, you see, called a Rary – '

'What the hell's a Rary?' East's voice sounded irritated already.

'It's a sort of bird. Just a bird – '

He saw Legge-Jenkins' eyes on him and then a hand move in a weak signal to him to draw nearer, and putting the pipe into his pocket, he shuffled, stoop-backed, across the cramped hut and sat down again alongside Legge-Jenkins, who looked up at him with a weary expression, as though all the strength had suddenly gone from him.

'I think you'd better take this over, Piercey,' he said listlessly, shoving the expedition diary over to him.

Piercey looked down at the gaunt, intelligent, despairing face, and Legge-Jenkins gestured weakly, trying to explain.

'I find it difficult to write much any more,' he said. 'I think we must all be getting weaker. I find I can't even read my own writing now.'

Piercey flicked the pages over. Legge-Jenkins' writing seemed normal enough, allowing for his injured hand, and he suspected his failure as a leader had grown in his imagination until he had begun to feel there was little he *could* do well.

'Besides' – Legge-Jenkins' face twisted – 'I think they're all against me a bit.'

'Rather the opposite, I think,' Piercey said. 'Especially now.'

Legge-Jenkins shook his head. 'They are,' he insisted. 'Healthy men don't want an invalid in charge of them.'

'You're not an invalid, L-J. You're low in spirits, of course. We all are. I think you should eat more.'

Legge-Jenkins gestured awkwardly with his burned hand. 'I can't face it, Piercey,' he said. 'Not any more. Things just haven't gone right for me.' He looked up at Piercey apologetically. 'I know Adams only chose me as Deputy to spite Tom Fife. Did you know that?'

Piercey nodded and Legge-Jenkins stared at him for a moment before continuing.

'It put a responsibility on me I didn't feel able...' he stopped, as though he hesitated to lay bare his unhappiness and went on more slowly. 'It seemed to make the responsibility greater, Piercey. And then everything seemed to go wrong. I feel now that I'm nothing but a dead weight on the party.' He pushed the diary again at Piercey. 'Here, take it,' he said. 'I shan't be difficult. You're fit and well, and perhaps you'll do better than I did.' He sighed. 'The others seem to take notice of you, anyway. Whatever you suggest, I shall accept. Please regard me as an ordinary member of the party from now on.'

Piercey stared at him for a moment, then he took the log-book. Legge-Jenkins had always seemed to regard it as a symbol of his position, and accepting it seemed to complete the business of taking over from him which had been going on gradually for some time now.

'Very well,' he said.

Legge-Jenkins seemed to have expected him to plead with him a little, to make a show of begging him to carry on, for he looked startled at Piercey's blunt agreement. For a second, he went on staring at Piercey, his expression pained, then he turned and moved down inside his sleeping bag, and Piercey was certain there were tears in his eyes.

For some time, he sat staring at the logbook in his hands, then he opened it slowly and read Legge-Jenkins' last entry.

'*... we are all very low in spirits now,*' he had written, '*and the party is held back by a great many injuries. We have had to shoot one of the dog teams and there seems to be a dearth of seals on the shore. The weather has become bitter suddenly and the sun has disappeared...*'

The whole impression was one of lack of spirit and hopelessness, and Piercey looked up, feeling faintly depressed. Clark was just finishing his story and East's face showed he was already sick of it.

' – and as this chap backed the lorry up to the cliff and tipped out this bird, guess what he said.'

'Well, go on. What did he say?'

Clark grinned. 'It's a long way to tip a Rary,' he said triumphantly.

East stared at him contemptuously. 'I must say,' he commented coldly, 'they give degrees to some weird types these days. It's being a geologist that does it, I expect – messing about all day with little bits of stone. It must atrophy the intellect in the end.'

His spirited disgust cheered Piercey strangely. Somehow, they didn't seem to have lost all hope.

As he moved back to his seat, Hellyer watched him from where he crouched over the tin he was trying to flatten.

'Has he packed it in, Doc?' he asked quietly. 'L-J, I mean.'

Piercey nodded. 'He's turned over the leadership of the party to me,' he said.

'I didn't mean that, Doc,' Hellyer said. 'I meant, has he just packed it in – has he just stopped trying?'

Piercey studied him for a moment, then he nodded. 'Yes,' he said. 'I think perhaps he has.'

'Thought he would in the end,' Hellyer commented.

He was silent for a moment, staring round at the other men in the hut, all of them absorbed with their tasks, even Ivey holding the files while O'Day worked, and then at Legge-Jenkins who was lying staring at the wall.

'Some people are like that though, aren't they, Doc?' he said compassionately. 'They just *don't* cope.'

Piercey nodded and Hellyer went on slowly. 'I reckon Adams was playing a pretty dangerous game with us all, don't you? Picking L-J as his deputy up here instead of Tom Fife.'

Piercey shrugged, 'It might have turned out differently.'

'Would *you* have picked him, Doc?'

Piercey smiled at Hellyer's bluntness. 'No,' he admitted. 'I wouldn't.'

Hellyer grinned at the confidence, and it seemed to break down yet another barrier between them. 'Thought you wouldn't' he announced cheerfully.

He was silent for a moment, busy over the tin he was working on, then he looked up again. 'How about Ivey, Doc?' he asked. 'How's he?'

Piercey's expression changed. 'He worries me,' he said. 'I don't want to think of gangrene, but I must.'

Hellyer looked uneasy. 'Makes you think, doesn't it? In spite of wireless and the petrol engine and the atom bomb, it doesn't take much to reduce a bloke to the lowest common denominator.'

Piercey was silent, letting him talk.

'Look at us,' Hellyer went on. 'Cooking with blubber, eating blubber – Doc, for God's sake, can you wash with blubber? You can do almost everything else with it, it seems.'

He paused, staring at his hands, then he raised his eyes to Piercey's and smiled warmly.

'I'm glad you're in charge, Doc,' he said simply, 'It's best that way – for all of us. We all feel better about it.'

He turned back to his work and Piercey knew that all the hostility in him had gone now that Legge-Jenkins was dependent on his skill and courage.

He sat for a while, listening to the wind coming down out of the mountains, vengeful, vicious and implacable, and the thought that he had to live with it for a matter of months in this squalid hovel took the heart out of him for a moment and made him wonder if he'd got the sort of moral courage he thought he had. Then he sighed and, searching his clothes for a pencil, he began to write in the diary, his own square hand firm underneath Legge-Jenkins' neat scrawl.

He set the date down and underscored it heavily, then his hand began to move across the page, moving faster as he became absorbed in his task.

'Took over leadership of the party today,' he wrote. 'Legge-Jenkins, whose hand has been troubling him for some time, complains that he can no longer write and that the pain is such that he finds it difficult to move about. I feel certain he could recover if he allowed himself to do so.'

He paused, then continued. 'Morale is good otherwise. O'Day has hopes of making a complete transmitter out of the two damaged Nineteens and Hellyer is a tower of strength. Even Ivey tries to help. We are dry and hope to have a better ration when Doree and Greeno return. Injuries generally are improving though Ivey still causes concern. Arguments have suddenly become non-existent in the need to pull together.'

He paused, feeling somehow that even his own optimism was still not sufficient to offset Legge-Jenkins' gloom.

'Spirits are high,' he wrote firmly in conclusion, 'and we have no doubts whatsoever that we shall survive the winter without trouble.'

He looked at it, satisfied, then he signed it and fished for his pipe again.

t w o

What Piercey had written in the diary wasn't strictly true.

They all still hoped. If they lost hope, they wouldn't have taken the trouble to perform the trivial duties that were necessary to keep them alive. Doree and Greeno wouldn't have searched so painstakingly for food, Hellyer would never have bothered to make a blubber lamp to save paraffin, and O'Day wouldn't have crouched so long in the poor light over his transmitters.

But, as time passed, a feeling of apprehension began to spread through them all. With the exception of Legge-Jenkins, they were all making a sincere effort to be cheerful, but there wasn't very much to be cheerful about, and the monotony, now that they were no longer on the move, was getting on all their nerves a little. The wind took its toll in small outbreaks of temper as the interior of the hut grew more squalid and they grew weary of climbing over each other every time they wished to move. Clark's stories began to irritate suddenly and even Hellyer's efforts to increase their comfort with lamps and patent draught excluders infuriated them with the noise he made. He seemed to be perpetually banging at a piece of tin and, fretful with hunger and cold, they turned on him, provoking noisy arguments and bad temper. If they had had even the simplest comfort to shorten the hours, life might have been easier, but they didn't even have a pack of cards between them.

Piercey tried hard to devise ways of passing the time, but without much success. There were duties to attend to but, without equipment, there were never enough and they were all able to spend too much time thinking. And always there was Legge-Jenkins at the back of the hut, silently despairing, all hope, it seemed, long since fled.

Without drugs, there was little Piercey could do to help him, except talk, and he found himself suddenly in the role of a psychiatrist, struggling hopelessly to force out of him some sign of interest in what was going on around him. But with Legge-Jenkins encased in his own despair, it was impossible to break through and Piercey was obliged to watch him sinking deeper and deeper into a self-made darkness that didn't come entirely from hunger.

Hellyer watched his struggles with a puzzled expression. In his extrovert aggressive attitude to life, he found Legge-Jenkins' condition difficult to understand.

'Doc,' he said, 'he isn't as ill as all that, is he?'

Piercey shook his head. 'Physically, no,' he agreed. 'But he's ill all right.'

'What's wrong with him?'

'Several things,' Piercey pointed out. 'Undernourishment for one. There's a marked loss of weight and fatigue. He doesn't eat enough – even of what we've got. But there are other things, of course, too.'

Hellyer's eyes narrowed. 'Other things?' he said. 'What other things?'

Piercey paused for a moment, then he decided Hellyer was tough-minded enough not to be afraid of the implications.

'In simple lay terms,' he said, 'it's a form of fear neurosis. I imagine it's the sort of thing that happens to children when they don't want to go to school or face examinations, the sort of thing that makes a man say he's got a cold when there's a job at the office he doesn't want to do. He didn't feel he could cope with the responsibility, and this is a defence and an explanation at the same time. I think it started even before we left Prins Haakon Sø because he knew there – even from the moment Adams died and he was in charge – that he couldn't cope. The argument we all had when we first arrived here completed it. Everyone made him feel everything that had happened to us was *his* fault. It made him feel an outcast.'

Hellyer seemed to be struggling to apologise and Piercey hurried on.

'Nobody was to blame,' he pointed out quickly. 'We were all in it and it was a perfectly natural thing to do. But it shut him out, you see, from the rest of us. With anyone else, it wouldn't have mattered. They'd have fought back or even accepted it. But not L-J. He's a clever man, but all this is something that's beyond him – it's his examination, and that burned hand of his is his excuse not to go to school.'

Hellyer stared across the hut. 'Poor sod,' he said gently. He glanced at Legge-Jenkins' silent form, his face puzzled, his eyes narrow with thought again and Piercey was interested to know what he was thinking.

'How do you feel about it, Hellyer?' he asked.

Hellyer turned slowly. 'You mean about him?'

Piercey nodded and Hellyer seemed bewildered.

'Well, I don't know,' he began. He paused, thinking, then: 'God, Doc,' he said, 'I never liked him much – or, rather, I never thought he was the man to be in charge. I suppose that was obvious. But, God, I'd never have wished this on anybody!'

Piercey was watching him with calm eyes. 'I didn't mean that quite,' he said. 'What I meant was, doesn't it make you afraid?'

Hellyer looked up at him quickly. 'Afraid? Well, I suppose so – a bit. But what's the good of getting the wind up?' He paused, thinking, then he went on quickly. 'During the war, my old man, who'd never worked at anything but a lathe all his life, suddenly began to keep chickens in the backyard and grubbed up a forty-yard allotment under a brick wall where there'd never been one before. He didn't know the first thing about chickens or gardening when he started, but he was determined the Jerries weren't going to get *his* family down, whatever happened. This is the same sort of challenge, isn't it?'

Piercey smiled, somehow feeling that Hellyer's reply was just what he might have expected of him. 'I'm glad you're not afraid, Hellyer,' he said. 'God knows, there's plenty we could be afraid of, but somehow, I didn't think *you* would be.'

'Why not?'

Piercey smiled. 'During the war, I had an orderly with me. He was constantly in trouble, always doing extra duties for getting drunk, always punching the corporal, always arguing with the CO. But I found that when trouble came, he was steadiest of the lot – in spite of still wanting to punch everybody in the teeth when he lost his temper.' He smiled again. 'He had the same sort of noisy disapproval of everything that you've got.'

Hellyer pulled a face. 'Christ,' he said. 'See yourself as others see you. I never thought of myself like that.'

Piercey smiled again, suddenly warming to Hellyer. 'It's not always the sweetest natures that inspire the greatest confidence,' he said. 'And it's a good thing to have someone in a place like this who has plenty of confidence. Fear's like a disease. It spreads. Fortunately, however, so does courage.'

The wind died at last, just when they were beginning to think there was no end to its viciousness, and the air became thankfully still. The clouds dispersed and the temperature fell to a fantastic depth so that the dogs were frozen by their fur into their snow shelters and had to be dug out. There were starlit skies for days on end, casting a soft pale light over the forbidding land around them, but the silence, the stillness, the very absence of life had a terrifying effect on them that was curiously more disturbing than the wind. With the stilling of all movement, it seemed as though the whole vast continent had died, sealing them into the icy valley as though they were immured in death itself.

And with the dropping of the wind, Piercey noticed a dropping in spirits, as though the fretful nagging that had kept them on edge had given them something else to think about other than being hungry.

He didn't try to deceive either himself or anyone else. Their life had become a struggle against nature, as fierce and elemental as actual physical combat, from which there would be no escape, for it would be a battle against a tireless enemy with more resources than they possessed themselves. But in addition, and perhaps worse, their life had settled into an arid routine that was nothing more than mere existence.

Strangely, the men who had the most to do seemed to be the fittest. O'Day never appeared to suffer much from anxiety and Doree and Greeno actually seemed to thrive on the dragging journeys they made to the coast with the sledge. And Hellyer, with his aggressive spirit, instead of despairing, was constantly seeking for something to occupy his restless hands.

Already, they all dreamed of food, not simply of *enough* food, but of half-forgotten delicacies such as jam and apple pie and cream, and Doree made them all laugh by pretending to stew his boots or advancing on Ivey with a knife and fork and making out he was a cannibal.

'What I'd give for a kipper,' Hellyer said one day, out of the blue, and whereas once it might have raised a laugh, they all heard him in silence. Hellyer's kipper was a symbol of luxury, of the ability to choose what they wanted instead of the inevitable seal meat they were all beginning to loathe.

In the hope of varying the diet, Piercey also varied the hunting parties, but in the end he wasn't sure that it was a good idea. They invariably came back disappointed and the frustration was worse than the boredom of remaining behind. Even Doree and Greeno came back empty-handed these days.

'The game's gone, Doc,' they said dejectedly. 'There's no sign of it now.'

Piercey said nothing, trying not to show his disappointment but mentally totting up the amount of frozen meat and blubber they had managed to store in the little lean-to they had built behind the hut, the dog pemmican that still remained, the small amounts of cocoa and tea and powdered milk and flour, and the few odd unhelpful things like raisins and candied peel.

He spent many hours talking the situation over with Ivey, whom he had appointed storekeeper, chiefly because he needed in his isolation and immobility to feel useful and because there was little else he could do.

At last, regretfully, they had to kill off the dogs. Although they were a mere pathetic shadow of the animals they had driven down to the bay, Piercey had shied away from destroying them because their death, he knew, would seem to the others the final symbol of defeat. There had already been a few noisy debates on their value as transport as against the amount of food they ate, but the time came at last when it was no longer sense to keep them and there were no longer any voices raised in protest.

His anxieties were making him more touchy than he knew he ought to be, quick to take offence when anyone pulled his leg, and low in spirits with too much thinking. Ivey's feet were showing distinct signs now that the frostbite was turning gangrenous, and Legge-Jenkins seemed simply to have given up trying to live. He lay in his sleeping bag all the time, with his gaunt face to the wall, refusing to eat, with all the signs of starvation growing more marked in a sunken face and dead rubbery skin that had lost all its elasticity. He appeared to have decided that he was no longer of any value to the party and was only waiting for the burden he made on them all to be removed.

He was a depressing sight in the hut as the weather grew worse and the blizzards howled down from the north, and they all grew a little more morose and silent. The absence of the sun was an added depressant, and they were all sinking a little into apathy when Doree and Greeno came back from the soft ice area under the Fraser Glacier with the totally unexpected news that they had killed a seal.

As Pink and Clark dressed and prepared to help drag the carcass up to the hut, Piercey decided it would do them all good to break the monotony by allowing them a feast.

'I think we might allow a little extra sugar,' he said. 'And we might even break out a little of the rum.'

When they had dragged the seal back to the hut and Hellyer had cut an enormous pile of steaks, they brewed a punch of the rum and dropped in some of their raisins and candied peel and a can of pineapple juice which had somehow survived. Piercey permitted himself a solemn little gesture as he raised his mug in a toast to Tom Fife, and they all grew noisy with the first real relaxation they had had in weeks, trying hard not to see the huddled form of Legge-Jenkins, silent in his sleeping bag at the back of the hut, refusing to join in the excitement and the pleasure of eating, his face to the wall, immured in his own despair, and weak now to the point when the baffled Piercey could only rack his brains for something to jolt him out of his self-imposed suffering.

'You know what I'd like,' Hellyer said dreamily, a little hazy with the rum he'd drunk. 'I'd like a hot bath. A great big tub, full of those coloured bath cubes that stink like a whore's boudoir, and lots of steam. And a pile of clean clothes sitting on the stool waiting to be put on when I'd finished.'

'I'd settle for an armchair,' Doree said. 'Nothing special, just a chair. It could have the bottom out and a spring to spike my backside. Anything would do, so long as it wasn't a box or a rock or a bedroll or the ground.'

'I'd like to see a building,' Pink said yearningly. 'A real building, three storeys high. With lights in the shops. Rows and rows of 'em. They always looked so damned warm, and the stuff in the windows always looked so colourful.'

O'Day produced a couple of snapshots. 'There you are,' he said, holding one of them out. 'Have a look at those. There are plenty of shops there. It's Blackpool promenade. That's where I used to go on leave. That's me and my brother, and that one's my old man.'

Doree was studying the cards intently. 'There are women on these cards,' he said sternly to O'Day. 'Women – the one thing we all need a glimpse of most. You ought to be court-martialled, man, and sentenced to be cut into strips and fed to the pigs.'

O'Day was reaching for the cards now. 'I've never seen any women,' he was saying, his face puzzled.

'What's that?' Doree's grimy finger rested on an infinitesimal dot in the background behind the portrait of O'Day. '*That's* a woman.'

'Christ, you can hardly see her!'

'We've got a magnifying glass, haven't we? We found one.'

Hellyer produced the glass, and they all began studying the photographs by the shaky light of the blubber lamps.

'He's right, you know,' O'Day said eagerly. 'They *are* women! Damned if there aren't a couple here in bathing costumes. With real legs and arms and sex-appeal strength nine plus plus.'

'Here' – Hellyer fished among his clothes and pulled out a couple of photographs of his own – 'let's see if *I've* got some. I've carried these damn things around with me for years and never noticed what's on 'em.'

In a moment, they were all at it, staring through the magnifying glass, then Greeno produced a walking picture of himself taken by a pavement photographer in Piccadilly. 'God' – Hellyer gave a shout of astonishment – 'look at all those people! Hundreds of 'em! It makes you go giddy just to look at 'em!'

Just when they were all at their noisiest, laughing and giving names to the minute figures and attributing to them fantastic names and ribald habits, with Piercey finding a new faith in the resourcefulness of man and his indefatigable ability to hold back despair, they suddenly noticed that Ivey wasn't laughing with them.

They turned, their laughter dying quickly, and saw he was staring into the shadows at the back of the hut, a small thin-faced figure with matted hair sitting up in his sleeping bag, his feverish eyes directed beyond the reach of their poor light.

He spoke quietly as they became silent, his voice cutting across their fading good humour like a knife.

'Doc,' he said, and the urgency in his voice silenced them all at once. 'Doc, I think there's something wrong with L-J.'

Legge-Jenkins had climbed half out of his sleeping bag and now lay sprawled across it, his eyes closed, his mouth working as he muttered to himself.

'What's he saying?' Doree demanded as they crowded round him.

'I don't know. I can't hear.' Piercey pushed them back and reached for the lamp.

'What's wrong with him?' Hellyer asked.

Piercey looked up angrily. 'What do you think?' he said shortly, angry with himself and obsessed by a sense of failure, though there was nothing and never had been anything he could have done for Legge-Jenkins. 'Anxiety,' he said. 'Depression. Malnutrition. Half a dozen things. His heart's a mere flutter, that's all.'

'But, Doc, he was never as bad as Ivey,' East pointed out. 'Why should he just fade out like this?'

'Oh, for God's sake,' Piercey said angrily. 'For a thousand and one reasons we'll probably never know. It would need a psychiatrist to tell us.' He straightened up, feeling tired and depressed and suddenly old.

'Only he knows what's wrong with him,' he said. 'And I'm not sure that even *he's* certain. I think he's just lost the will to live.'

They all became silent, their eyes uneasy at his words, and the drab little hut was full of foreboding.

'Will he ever get over it?' Hellyer asked at last in a low voice.

'Possibly. Possibly not. Personally, I imagine he'll not move from there much now.'

Hellyer's jaw had dropped. 'You mean, you think he's dying, Doc?' he asked.

Piercey paused before answering. There was so much that could happen to change their circumstances, but little he could see that could improve them. And he had a feeling that Legge-Jenkins had never had the kind of courage that would let him wait in a hopeless darkness for what would inevitably seem empty months of despair, fortified by an unshaken belief that in the end all would come right. There had been a marked weakening in his resistance from the very beginning, not merely physically but mentally and morally, and Piercey knew now that he had passed the point of no return.

He nodded, his face set. 'Unless they pick us up first,' he said.

'Christ!'

They looked at Piercey, a stunned look on all their faces, as though death were something that hadn't crossed their minds before, then they turned away to their own sleeping bags, the supper forgotten, the merriment gone. The inference behind Piercey's words was clear. If Legge-Jenkins could die, then so could they all.

three

Christmas arrived, a strange Christmas which they tried to celebrate with a little watered rum and a few extra rations and a false hilarity that suddenly fell flat so that they retired early to their sleeping bags, their minds uncomfortably full of thought.

Then the New Year came and, as the days trudged past, Piercey found his chief task once more was in keeping up their spirits. Now that the weather had shut down, they had to spend the days huddled together in the dirt and slime of the squalid little hut with no hope of getting out, and he instituted a series of lectures to keep their minds occupied. At first, he could find no volunteers and he gave the first one himself, faintly embarrassed because he didn't consider himself a speaker and because what he had to say seemed so trivial in that dark little hole in the ice surrounded by a group of young men whose unshaven faces, long hair and matted beards suggested – quite wrongly, he knew – that they had given up hope. He was surprised, however, to find he held their interest, in spite of the disrespectful comments that were made from time to time, and after that it was easier and they all took part, even Ivey giving a ribald talk on senior naval officers from his sleeping bag that reduced them all to laughter.

But the merriment always had a hollow ring in it with Legge-Jenkins silent at the back of the hut like a ghost at the feast, growing gradually weaker and more skeletal, so that

Piercey was surprised at the way he managed to cling to life when he so obviously wanted to die.

They had all accepted now that he would die and had put it behind them – not from callousness, but because there was no alternative and they had to go on trying, for themselves. As his temperature had fallen lower, they had taken it in turns to share his sleeping bag with him, in the faint hope that their own body heat would raise his, but it was a grim duty none of them liked and didn't bring any improvement, and nobody was surprised when he finally faded out of existence, quietly, like a faint flame that had died through lack of fuel to keep it going.

Piercey straightened up, watching Hellyer drawing the blanket over the dead man's face, aware that the chilled bones of all the men around him suddenly seemed colder.

The following morning, their faces sombre, their minds full of a whole night of thinking, they wrapped the body in a scrap of canvas and put it on the sledge and hauled it to the end of the bluff. Digging with ice-axes, they made a shallow hole in the frozen earth and laid him in it, and Piercey recited as much of the burial service as he could remember, while they all stood around him, leaning against the wind that rolled down out of the mountains, their haggard faces held away from the sting of the driving particles of ice, their filthy clothes blown against their bodies by the gale.

Piercey was still upset by Legge-Jenkins' death. In spite of everything, it had had a final unexpectedness that had taken him unawares. Somehow, even at the very last moment, he had not expected him to go, and he felt cheated by the event.

This is how they had buried Adams, he thought uneasily as they stood on the bluff, with the frozen earth broken at their feet and the rocks already collected and piled around the shallow grave for the building of a cairn. Doree and Greeno leaned on the ice axes and Hellyer was standing with a crude wooden cross in his hand, waiting to plant it over the body. This is how it had all started, but, somehow, this time, there was something more ominous about it. This wasn't the end of the beginning, as Adams' funeral had been. This seemed to be the beginning of the end.

When Piercey had finished speaking, they replaced the sparse earth on top of the body and erected the cross on which Hellyer had written the dead man's name and the date and piled the rocks around it in a blunt cairn, then they all turned back towards the hut, moving slowly without speaking.

As they shuffled back to where Ivey waited, eight silent figures with stooping shoulders bent against the weather, Piercey paused and stood alone for a moment, deep in thought, then he noticed that Hellyer was waiting just down the slope for him, his face gaunt, his clothes plastered with the driving snow.

'One,' he said laconically as Piercey approached.

'One?' Piercey stared at him, not understanding.

'Ten little nigger boys going out to dine, one under-ate himself, then there were nine.'

Piercey turned away irritably and began to walk back towards the hut, but Hellyer fell into step alongside him.

'Why did he die, Doc?' he asked. 'He shouldn't have, surely? In spite of what you told me.'

Piercey shook his head. 'No,' he said. 'He shouldn't have.'

It was a question of courage, he thought, and Legge-Jenkins had just not possessed the cold-blooded resolution that would let him sit down in the dark without hope and wait.

They were all subdued for a while. Legge-Jenkins' death had made them all reassess their position and the reserves of endurance they possessed. His failure to live seemed to make more problematic the ability of them all to survive. The rebellion of their stomachs against the unrelieved and insufficient diet grew greater and there was suddenly too much to think about, too many small things to frustrate them, too many things to irritate them that had grown to enormous proportions.

They were all surprisingly weak – the digging of the shallow grave and the collecting of the few rocks for the cairn had showed them just how weak they were – and they all had small unhealed and painful sores on the ends of their noses where the tears that the howling wind had put in their eyes had run and frozen into icicles which had pulled off a tiny strip of skin as they had removed them. The white marks of frostbite were on their faces and they were all exhausted by the lack of room to stretch and the wearying filthiness of the blubber smoke which filled the hut and blackened their faces and hands and penetrated everything.

Perhaps it was the height of the bleak crags that towered around them like prison walls that made their isolation so complete. The landscape about the hut was as gaunt and desolate now as a lunar valley, with great snow-bound rocks alternating with the unreal architecture of the ice and the fringes of frozen stalactites that hung from everything like hair. In the absence of equipment, their only territory was the strip of shore nearest to the hut and the bluff of land from which they could see over the bay, and their only exercise was to walk on this brief stretch whenever the weather permitted, obsessed by the sight of the mountains looming through the mist and the distant snowstorms.

Perhaps it was the implied threat that the mountains seemed to make that encouraged Piercey to write a report on their circumstances – a long and detailed account on any scrap of paper he could beg or borrow from anyone who still had some. At the back of his mind was the feeling that if they should fail to survive, it could be found on their bodies – as Scott's diary had been found – and that it should lay the blame for the disaster squarely where it ought to lie.

He had it all down – the bad planning, the slow deliberations of the various sponsoring authorities and the delays due to transport problems which Adams had skated over far too hurriedly; the decisions to manage without what had not turned up; the reliance on outsiders to perform the tasks that Adams hadn't had time for himself; the acceptance of agreements that ought to have been thrown out; and Legge-Jenkins' final foolish plans that had brought them to this God-forsaken spot and their present unbearable hardships. Well aware of how blame could be placed on the shoulders of the innocent, the one thing Piercey wanted was to see that people like Tom Fife and Hannen should not be accused. Of them all, only Fife had had the honesty and forthrightness to protest.

When he thought of what might happen afterwards, Piercey found himself wondering about his wife and how she would feel. Inevitably, she must know now of the disaster that had overtaken them and he only hoped she still possessed the same courage she had always shown when he had disappeared off the face of the earth before. It grew harder, he found as the days rolled by, to remember what she looked like, and he noticed himself making a conscious effort to recall the sound of her voice and the expressions he'd grown so used to seeing on her face. Then, as his thoughts of home and his hopes of rescue became confused, he found himself thinking of Fife and his daughter, Rachel. Somehow, they had seemed to go together and there had even been a time when he had hoped they might find they had common interests. But nothing had come of it and Piercey, already reaching the age when he felt he would like to see his own future taking shape through his child, had felt more disappointment than he had been willing to admit. Too many things, it seemed, had been left unfinished or unresolved.

Nobody spoke of rescue now. They all kept their own counsel, none of them knowing what the others were thinking and none of them daring to say what they were thinking themselves, so that morale varied according to the weather.

Small things became important and there were many times when Piercey had to talk to them like a Dutch uncle, and he was glad then of his extra years that made them accept what he had to say as if it came from an older relation instead of from a carping comrade. It seemed a perfectly natural move to institute weekly prayers which, if they did nothing else, established Sunday as a different day and helped to mark off the slow roll of time, and Piercey found himself searching in his mind for what remained there of the Book of Common Prayer.

They were all sick of trying to kill time now, and the evenings were mostly desultory talk. The lectures had fallen through as they had run out of subjects and found it increasingly difficult to concentrate on consecutive thought. Women were rarely mentioned except with feelings of nostalgia, and Legge-Jenkins never. It was as though they dared not think about him for fear of what it might do to their courage.

'Doc' – the inevitable question came a dozen times a week – 'do you think they'll have given up hope now?'

'Tom Fife won't forget us,' Piercey kept saying, stubbornly, clinging to the only certain immovable thing in all his uneasy thoughts. 'And besides, the transmitter's almost ready now.'

O'Day looked up. 'The range's going to be bloody limited,' he pointed out bluntly. 'These batteries are on their last legs.'

Nobody said anything. O'Day's transmitter was the only thing that gave them hope now.

As the turn of the year brought longer periods of visibility in the glow the returning sun threw over the horizon, Doree and Greeno started again to go out in search of game. They had taken the sledge to pieces and built a new one they could haul on their own, and they began once more to make their journeys along the coast whenever the weather allowed, making longer and longer reaches to the south across the mouth of the Fraser Glacier, bringing back an occasional Arctic fox or a ptarmigan or a petrel, but never enough, for the seal had not yet returned and the journeys were taking out of them more than they realised. Only the worried Piercey could see the slow deterioration of their strength in their sluggish movements and the fretful tempers they sometimes showed as they had constantly to repair the rapidly disintegrating sledge. And under the snout of the glacier, he knew, there could be thin ice – even with the air temperature thirty degrees below zero – that might well throw up an emergency which a half-starved man wouldn't have the strength to deal with.

'But we might find game there, Doc,' Doree protested. 'It's the first place the seals'll come to when they come back.'

'There'll be moving water there,' Piercey warned. 'And soft ice.'

'I know.' Doree was wearily fatalistic. 'We could feel it weavin' under us when we crossed it. But we might get a seal there, Doc. We might just. Besides' – he shrugged – 'somebody's got to take risks. Somebody's got to chance his arm now and again, or we'll *all* get the chopper.'

Piercey didn't argue after that, because Doree was right.

Somebody *did* have to chance his arm for the sake of them all.

When O'Day announced that he had the transmitter ready at last, it was as though a weight had been lifted off Piercey's shoulders.

Doree and Greeno were about to leave for one of their forays to the mouth of the glacier and he decided to make it

238

an occasion for a celebration, and allowed them all a ration of rum.

'Here's to the transmitter,' he said, lifting his mug.

'Don't put *too much* faith in it,' O'Day warned. 'I'm just hoping we've still got enough power to bounce a signal to someone who's listening. That's all.'

'It'd *better* be good,' Doree pointed out. 'We're running out of ammunition.'

O'Day shrugged. 'The key's like a pump-handle,' he said, 'and it's got no choke, and these goddamned mountains have got enough metal content in 'em to stop anything.'

Doree moved to the door and glanced up at the sky. 'Don't forget us, Doc,' he said as he picked up the rifle. 'If anyone hears the signal and flies a chopper in to fetch you out, just remember to send a runner down to the bay for us before you go.'

They all went outside to watch them leave, then O'Day turned back towards the hut, his face suddenly grave and tense with the responsibility that lay on his shoulders. 'I'll tune up on the meter and get something off before the power fades,' he said. 'Once the batteries are gone, the set's useless. We've just got to hope it reaches somebody and that he's got his earhole jammed to the speaker.'

They all helped to raise an aerial between the hut and the rickety mast he had erected, but it took longer than they had expected and the weather had begun to deteriorate by the time they had finished, the inevitable wind starting again and lifting the snow in little spirals off the rocks.

Then O'Day lit one of the rare cigarettes he allowed himself these days and they all sat down as he made himself comfortable. 'Big occasion this,' he commented. 'Tell me if the aerial melts.'

'For God's sake, get on with it,' Hellyer said, almost bursting with impatience.

They watched eagerly as O'Day began to pound at his home-made key.

'It's a pity I can't describe you lot,' he said as he worked, and feeble grins spread across their dirty bearded faces, not of triumph or even of joy but just of relief that the set was working at last.

O'Day continued to pump the key for several minutes then he switched off and began to disconnect the batteries with a precise care that indicated just how precious they were.

'Is that all?' Hellyer's face fell.

'There's tomorrow,' O'Day reminded him. 'And tomorrow and tomorrow and tomorrow, creeping on its petty pace from day to day. I'm going to send in short stretches, while ever the batteries hold out. More chance of being picked up that way.'

Hellyer nodded, blankly uncomprehending, and O'Day cocked his thumb towards the entrance of the hut. They could hear the wind rattling against the outside now and the clatter of the aerial lead against the stones.

'I'll go and disconnect that lot,' he said, 'before it's blown down. I wouldn't want to lose it.'

As he went outside, the drift came in, in a cloud, and covered the floor in the entrance, but they were still smiling, still feeling warmed with new hope, when O'Day dived back inside the hut, shouting.

'It's Doree and Greeno,' he said, his voice cracked with excitement. 'They're back already.'

'They've been damn quick,' Hellyer said, scrambling after him. 'They must have got something.'

They all pushed outside, half-expecting to see the sledge returning up the slope, but there seemed to be nothing but the whirling whiteness of thickening drift, and Piercey straightened up, squinting towards the coast, wondering if O'Day could have been mistaken. Then he saw two small figures which seemed to be clinging together in the distance and struggling over the end of the bluff, and O'Day stumbling across the broken surface towards them.

'Where the hell's the sledge?' Pink shouted in alarm.

They all started to run, bending against the wind and the blinding drift and, as he panted after the others, Piercey could see that Doree was carrying Greeno on his back, and that they were staggering from side to side as though they were drunk.

Even as they reached them, they fell in a heap in the snow, then Doree pushed himself up.

'For God's sake,' he panted, 'get him into the hut before it's too late.'

Then Piercey saw that Greeno's garments were frozen like armour plate and heard the crackle and the tinkle of the icicles that fell from him as O'Day and East hauled him on to his feet. There was blood round his mouth where two of his front teeth had been knocked out and the tears were welling up out of his eyes and rolling down his cheeks to freeze hard in the tangle of his beard.

The skin of his cheeks was pallid under the dirt and his eyelids were inflamed and half-frozen together by tears.

'I'm all right,' he kept muttering. 'I'm all right. Just keep me moving, that's all.'

As O'Day and East began to half-carry, half-drag him towards the hut, Pink and Piercey grabbed hold of the gasping Doree and set off after them.

'The bloody ice gave way under the glacier,' he panted. 'He went in. I set off back with him straight away before he froze.'

They were struggling into the hut now, Doree heavy in their arms, and as he sank on to a bedroll panting, O'Day and East were already stripping Greeno's frozen garments from him while Hellyer tore at his own clothes.

Quickly they re-dressed the half-conscious man in Hellyer's dry clothes and got him into a sleeping bag while

Hellyer pulled on whatever odds and ends he could find. Greeno's hands and face and feet were already showing the ominous waxy patches of frostbite and, as they set to work to massage them, Ivey reached out of his sleeping bag and struggled to start the Primus.

'Why didn't you put the tent up, man?' Hellyer demanded. 'Why didn't you get him inside it and in his bag?'

Doree sat on the floor, his head hanging between his knees, his matted hair over his face.

'The tent's gone,' he muttered. 'Everything's gone. The tent, the Primus, the sleeping bags, the food, the rifle. They were all on the sledge and when the ice gave they all went through.'

'Everything?' Piercey's voice was very quiet.

'Everything.' Doree raised agonised apologetic eyes in a dirty exhausted face. 'I only had time to drag Greeno out. I had no time to do anything else.' He seemed to shudder then, managing to stagger to his feet, he crossed to where East was wiping away the congealing blood from Greeno's mouth.

'The sledge handle came up and hit him in the face,' he said slowly. 'We were just hauling it round when the right side went down. Then he was in the water. I was still on firm ice, and I managed to grab him and stopped him sinking.' He looked miserably at Piercey. 'I'm sorry, Doc,' he said. 'I tried. But I couldn't even get him out at first. I just hadn't the strength. He was so damned heavy with the water in his clothes. I just had to lie there, hanging on to him and watching the sledge go down.'

They were all silent as Piercey got to his feet, the weight of responsibility hanging heavily round his neck again. Fate was dealing them some underhand blows, and in one stroke they seemed to have lost everything they most needed to survive.

He drew a deep breath and looked round the squalid little hut, prison-like in the barren cheerlessness that seemed such a symbol of their plight, a huddled, cramped little space jammed with their sleeping bags and home-made stoves and the fragments of equipment they had managed to salvage. Then he turned to O'Day who was crouched in the corner near the Primus with Ivey, his long legs twisted under him, and indicated the precious transmitter on its box.

'I hope to God somebody hears your signals,' he said.

four

The official inquiry into the failure of the British East-West Greenland Expedition was fixed for Monday, April 4th, and the note informing Fife of the decision was handed to him at his laboratory.

As he finished reading the arid words that held out neither comfort nor hope, he screwed the sheet of paper up and crossed to the window, his hands in his pockets, his empty pipe jammed into his mouth.

For a while, he stared over the roofs of the city, his mind busy, then he stripped off his overall and reached for his hat. His two assistants stared at each other for a second, then shrugged as the door slammed behind him. Outside, he caught a bus to the station and bought a ticket to Orford.

The weather was blustery and he was startled as he settled back in his seat to realise he was wet through and that everyone else around him wore mackintoshes and carried umbrellas. The rain was lashing at the carriage window as the train pulled out, beating down out of the low Surrey hills, but Fife, absorbed with his thoughts, hardly noticed it.

He had been back at work for some time now, driven by debts to earn some money, a lonely figure regarded with sidelong glances by his colleagues; aware of the whispers around him and the awkward silences that matched his own taciturnity, going about his business doggedly, still obsessed by the need to organise a rescue, still harried by the publicity that seemed to follow him everywhere he went.

The only concession he had been able to wring from the reluctant committee was that four men were to remain at Stakness until the summer, with instructions to return to Camp Adams when the ice melted, to salvage whatever equipment could be saved from the wreckage, to search for records and reports of what might have happened, and to make sure that Adams' body was decently interred and a cross erected over it.

Hannen had agreed to remain in charge, and with him were Jessup, Smeed and Erskine. All the other members of the expedition, seeing no future in failure, had accepted their passage home and were awaiting the ship from Thule that was bringing Sampson's party from the West Coast.

Huddled in the corner of the compartment, chewing on an empty pipe, Fife found he could hardly blame them. They had their careers to think about and, since there was nothing more they could do, they might just as well return home to their families and to their jobs.

With Fife it was different. Although he was back at work, he was still haunted by the belief, in spite of all the evidence to the contrary, that Adams' party were alive somewhere. But nobody believed him and he had even been politely asked by Mortimer to stop annoying him. He still went on, however, begging time off from his job to pester everyone who might conceivably be of help – everyone who had sunk money in the expedition, even Adams' widow, a cold-eyed woman busy with the trivialities of her life and already occupied with other interests.

She had had no time for Fife, and the businessmen who had given practical and monetary help, the trusts which had provided cheques, even Kinglake at the *Recorder* office, had been unable to take a different view from Mortimer's – that it was foolish to throw good money after bad. Everybody seemed only too anxious now to forget the disastrous expedition and all the embarrassment it had caused.

The uproar in the Commons had died down now but echoes of the disaster still had a habit of popping up at embarrassing moments, as little disclosures kept leaking out in the Press. There had been a few red faces on both sides of the House over the absence of any move towards a relief expedition and somebody, caught up by emotion and too much to drink, had shouted 'What about Adams?' at the government candidate at a by-election.

It was becoming clearer every day that mistakes had been made, an the general feeling was that blame should be directed somewhere for the disaster. It was even being said now that pressure was being put on the expedition committee to get the inquiry over and done with, if only to establish that Adams' men were dead and beyond help and to stop the sniping for good and all.

And since it had been decided that someone must finally accept responsibility, no one seemed keen to be associated with Fife. No one had said outright that the blame could be laid at his door, but the gale of public opinion had stirred up too much feeling, and it was obvious that everyone had decided it should be. His face had been in the papers too often, his name too often associated with the failure.

All the triumph he had felt at having forced the inquiry on Mortimer had left him long since. It had taken too long, had occupied too many journeys and used up too much of his money, and had started up too many hares of controversy, with all the newspapers chasing them to see what they contained. And when he thought about it now, without the first flush of bitterness that had driven him to insist on it, he knew perfectly well that whoever came badly out of the inquiry, it wouldn't be Sir Willard Mortimer.

It was still raining hard when he arrived at Orford and he was on the point of taking one of the taxis that waited in the forecourt of the station when he recalled the distance to

Piercey's house and just how little money he had with him, and he decided instead to take the bus and waited for twenty minutes at the bus stop in the rain.

His mind was bleak with defeat and he was running for comfort to the only place he knew he could expect it. The house at Orford had become almost like a home to him and he seemed to flee there at every fresh outburst against him in the papers. Then he remembered what Rachel had said about getting a job and he realised that soon even that would be closed and there'd be nobody there when he felt he wanted to pour out his indignation.

The thought seemed to knock the bottom out of his world. The knowledge that she wouldn't be there, calm, sure, watching him with those beautiful steady eyes of hers, seemed to drain the grey world of daylight for a moment, and he knew he couldn't possibly let her get beyond his reach, couldn't possibly let her vanish to a point where he couldn't fly to her whenever he needed her.

He sat up abruptly, a sudden startling idea occurring to him. Why, you damned fool, he thought excitedly, you're in love with her!

He smiled abruptly as the realisation came to him, as unromantically as possible on top of a bus, and the elation surged through him so devastatingly that he forgot where he was and missed his stop.

He clattered down the stairs a hundred yards past the end of the lane that led to Piercey's house and jumped off the bus as it went round the corner, blushing at the indignant conductor's anger, to stand in the rain, his eyes bright, not noticing the weather, and wondering how he could tell her what he had discovered so unexpectedly.

She was in love with him, too. He was certain of that and had been for some time, and the realisation came as something of a surprise when he thought about it. It had never occurred to him before that there was another woman who could love him the way his wife had. They had been undergraduates together and had drifted happily and instinctively from friendship into love and finally into marriage, and he had considered himself lucky to have found someone understanding and willing to shield him from his own quick temper. He had humbly never expected he could be as lucky twice in his life.

He was on the point of starting down the lane, elated, as certain of his future as he was of day following night and eager to tell Rachel of his feelings, when he stopped dead, his feet in a puddle, remembering the letter he carried in his pocket and suddenly sick with misery that this new knowledge of what he wanted out of life had arrived when his future was at its bleakest and he had nothing to offer in return. With the ground falling away beneath his feet, he could hardly ask any girl to go on waiting for him, could hardly ask her to go on being patient until his fortunes changed. In his stiff, prideful way, it never occurred to him that she might be willing to.

Rachel opened the door to his knock and her face showed her pleasure immediately at seeing him. Then her expression changed to one of bewilderment at his soaked clothes, and she pulled him inside quickly.

'You're soaked,' she said. 'Why on earth didn't you bring a coat?'

'I forgot,' he said dully.

'Then why not take a taxi?'

He looked a little shamefaced. 'I couldn't afford it, Rachel,' he admitted. 'I just can't afford luxuries like taxis any longer. I caught the bus and walked the rest of the way.'

His unhappiness was obvious and she took his hand and pulled him into the hall.

'I'll make some coffee,' she said quickly. 'Or would you rather have a drink?'

'I'll settle for a drink,' he said, and she pushed him into the lounge and stirred the fire into flame.

'I was just working on some problems of my father's,' she said as she sat down opposite him, watching him steam gloomily in front of the blaze. 'It's material he was working on when he left.'

'It's not easy,' she went on. 'It reminds me too much of him and it's not easy to push that aside. The house's a bit lonely these days.'

She paused and looked up at him. 'Tom,' she said slowly. 'I've got a job.'

For the second time in ten minutes, the ground seemed to fall away under his feet. The thought that Orford would be closed now unnerved him more than he had expected.

He forced himself to sound interested. 'Where, Rachel?' he asked.

'Alderly. It's a hospital near Birmingham. I start next week.' She spoke calmly but she seemed a little uncertain, as though she weren't sure she'd done the right thing.

'That's a long way away,' he said.

'Does that matter, Tom?' She spoke quietly but her voice was a little unsteady, begging him to understand what she was trying to say.

She was suddenly on his conscience and he longed to tell her what was in his mind, but the knowledge of how little he possessed and of the bleak prospects for the future that were implicit in the letter in his pocket, checked the words on his lips and he managed only a brief mutter of sympathy, feeling cruel, an incessant guilty ache in his mind that falsified all other emotion.

She seemed to make an effort to be cheerful. 'But I'm taking your advice, Tom,' she went on. 'I'm not selling the house. Not just yet. I shall keep it going – for a bit longer anyway.'

Fife had put his drink aside and she went on with a quick nervous glance at his face that betrayed her feelings.

'I hope I'll still see you occasionally,' she said, and he nodded.

'I'll come up there,' he suggested. 'We'll make a weekend of it some time. I'll get in touch with you.'

It sounded like a dismissal. I'll get in touch with you. The sort of thing everybody always said when they were backing out of an affair. But he felt he daren't offer more – not just then.

'I'm glad you understand,' she said in a flat voice. 'I felt I had to do something. I'm getting used to it all now.'

Fife stirred restlessly. His emotions seemed to be topsy-turvy suddenly. He had got off the bus at the end of the lane full of happiness, then things had seemed to go wrong and he felt now as though he had let her down.

'Rachel,' he said, suddenly uneasy at her words, as though she were slipping from his grasp already, 'we mustn't just "*get used to it*". It's tantamount to accepting what they all say.'

She didn't reply and Fife took the crumpled letter from his pocket with the black heading, *British East-West Greenland Expedition*, and passed it across to her.

'They've fixed the inquiry,' he said.

She gave him a warm look, realising immediately what was behind his apparent indifference.

'Is that why you came here?' she asked.

He nodded, feeling they were on their old safe footing again instead of balancing on the edge of an abyss, surer of himself and of her as they got back to the normal warm relationship that had always existed between them and was as natural, had he only known it, to being in love as the torment of delight and despair that he usually associated with it.

'Yes,' he said. 'I thought of you, of course, as usual.'

Her eyes glowed, grateful to him, even if only for the fact that he needed her.

'April fourth,' he said. 'Sir Henry Orlesi's going to conduct it. Mortimer's delayed it as long as possible, jerrymandering and throwing up every excuse he could, but it's come in the end.'

'Do you think they'll agree to sending a relief expedition?'

He paused for a moment, his eyes suddenly unhappy, then he shook his head.

'I think they just want to forget the whole affair,' he said. 'They're still arresting British trawlers off the coast of Iceland and British destroyers are still patrolling the boxes to see that they don't. Nobody wants to be reminded just now that we're in any debt to the Icelandic government.'

She reached across and put her hand on his. 'Surely, Tom,' she said, 'out of all these interested people, there must be *someone* who won't think like Mortimer.'

'God, it's to be hoped so. It's all I've thought of for weeks, all I've been waiting for. Whatever comes out of it, whether they allow us a relief expedition or not, we mustn't let them get away with it. Otherwise exploration's right back where it was in the days before Scott. Men who want to lead expeditions must have the right qualifications of patience and temperament, not just enough money or influence like Adams.'

'Perhaps the *Recorder* would whip up support,' she said. 'Kinglake always seemed to be on your side. Perhaps he'll suggest you lead a relief.'

He shook his head. 'Not me,' he said. 'If they send anyone it won't be me. Too much has been said about me. They'd never dare. Besides, it'll be harder still once this starts. Mortimer's got Alastair Doughty to represent him and Sir Thomas Halcrow for Adams' widow. The two best in the country. Money no object. There's only one hope. We've found out where Lutyens is and there's a chance we can contact him. I've been in touch with the Admiralty. If we can get him home I'll be all right.'

She studied her fingers for a moment before she replied. 'Have you got anyone to represent *you*, Tom?' she asked. He looked blank and she knew it had never crossed his mind.

'You'll need someone,' she urged, but his face became grim and dogged and she wanted to weep at the loneliness in it.

'I'll manage on my own,' he said.

'Tom, you can't. These people will tie you in knots. They're going to try, you know.'

'I'll manage.'

His stubbornness upset her. He looked suddenly like a defiant schoolboy.

'It wouldn't be much good,' he said slowly with a smile. 'I couldn't afford anybody, anyway.'

'Tom, if it's money you need – '

'No!' The bleak prideful expression came back again and she knew it was a waste of time trying to persuade him.

'I'll fight them my own way,' he said. 'If I make mistakes, OK, I make mistakes. Perhaps it'll look better even – as though I'm not a slick customer trying to hide behind a lawyer like Mortimer.'

She stared at him, her eyes suspiciously moist, knowing she could never make him change his mind. 'All right, Tom,' she agreed. 'I expect you know best. What would you like me to do?'

He looked uncertain and a little desperate, and she knew he had no plan of any sort.

'I'd just like *all* the relatives to be there,' he said. 'If only to prove to them that these men who were with Adams had families, wives, parents, sons, daughters like you, and that we owe them a duty. Besides' – he ended lamely – 'I'd just like you to be there, that's all.'

Again, she felt touched at the way he said it and sad at his loneliness.

'I'm not very good at weeping,' she pointed out.

He took her hand in his. 'I don't want tears, Rachel,' he said. 'I – well, I suppose I shall make a fool of myself, and I'd just like you around to see I don't. I feel a bit alone at the moment, and I need a little moral support.'

Her fingers tightened on his and she smiled. 'I'll be there,' she said.

five

He was waiting at the station for her when she arrived from Birmingham on the morning the inquiry opened, still a little guilty, still aware that what he'd intended to say to her that day at Orford somehow hadn't managed to get itself said. He'd slept badly, excited at seeing her again after so long, turning over his hopes and fears in his mind until all chance of rest had vanished.

She seemed untouched by his pangs of conscience, however, apparently unaware of his feelings. She took his hand quickly and they walked together towards the underground, and his uneasy conscience grew more uncomfortable as he noticed that she talked about everything except the job she'd got and the fact that they were now at opposite ends of the country.

The inquiry was being held in a Methodist Church Hall near the docks and close to the offices of the Expedition which had now been closed down and stood empty, the blank windows like blind eyes to Fife as he passed them.

They could smell the salty whiff of the river and hear the bustle and clank of lorries and cranes round the ships as they reached the hall. Groups of men stood on corners, ships' crews waiting to be paid off and hanging around till opening time when they would fly like homing pigeons for the nearby bars. They were staring curiously at the taxis outside the hall discharging their passengers, pale city men in dark suits who were obviously lawyers. Fife eyed them hostilely as they passed him and went inside; and, glancing at him, Rachel saw that his face was stony.

'*They*'ll never understand what I'm trying to say,' he pointed out bitterly. 'Thank God I've heard from Lutyens. He's in Norway still but he's promised to fly home.'

He seemed uncertain and fidgety, in spite of the hope implicit in the message from Lutyens, as though he were beginning to wish now that he'd got someone to represent him after all. Seeing all the lawyers arriving seemed to have unnerved him a little.

There were a few reporters and photographers on the pavement outside the hall, and they saw a BBC television van just along the street. As they approached the door, they heard the cameras begin to click, then a thin-faced little woman with an insane expression stepped in front of Fife.

'Murderer,' she shouted. 'Murderer!'

Rachel saw him flinch and back away, almost as though he hadn't the will to defend himself, and as she pulled him inside quickly, his face was flushed and his eyes looked desperate.

'That's what they think of me,' he said. 'And it hasn't even started yet.'

She wanted to weep at the unhappiness in his face.

'Tom,' she said, 'I wish you had someone to represent you.'

'So do I, now,' he admitted.

'Is it too late?'

Fife made a small boy's gesture of defiance with his shoulders. 'I'm not worried,' he said, though she knew he was. 'I can deal with that lot. I know what I'm talking about. I was there.'

She had no confidence in the amount of weight it would carry but she held her tongue, not wishing to unsettle him more. He was obviously no longer sure that the evidence he could offer would make them believe him, no longer sure that experience of the Arctic would count more than experience of the courtroom.

There were ominous signs inside that Sir Willard Mortimer was gathering his reserves about him, and Fife recognised the smooth, pale-faced girl who was his secretary talking to a group of black-coated men who looked like lawyers. She had a sheaf of papers in her hand which she was handing out.

'That's Doughty,' he said, indicating the tall, thin-faced man beside her. 'The best you can buy. Mortimer's making sure his retreat's well covered.'

Rachel stared anxiously at him for a second, then she pulled him to one side. He was still staring with dogged hostility at the group round Mortimer's secretary and he resisted the pull of her hand.

'Look, Tom,' she said. 'This isn't the way to go into this thing. You're against it. You're against *them* – all of them. You can't afford to be. You've got to get them on your side. And being cynical about it will never do it.'

She was staring at him earnestly and his eyes fell as he felt ashamed of himself for his anger. He patted her hand gently.

'I'm sorry,' he said. 'You're dead right, of course. As a matter of fact, Rachel, I think I'm scared stiff of all these damned lawyers. They're after me and I know it.'

The corridor was crowded now but there seemed to be no one whom Fife knew.

'I don't see many allies,' he said nervously. 'Why aren't Sampson and the West party here? They should have been home long since. I hope to God I'm not going to be the only witness for the defence.'

After a while, the door was opened and they went through into the hall. Two long tables had been set out in a T.

As they entered, he saw the members of the management committee sitting to one side and, in the centre of them, Sir Willard Mortimer. He looked tense but confident, his mouth a tight line, his eyes sharp and cautious, and Fife guessed that if there were to be any accusations bandied about, he would already have thought of them and would have his answers ready.

Adams' widow was sitting at the other end of the row of chairs, with a man who looked as though he might be her brother but, remembering what he'd heard of her, Fife wondered briefly if he were just a new boyfriend. She was impeccably dressed, the only indication of mourning a black hat and gloves. Though he knew she knew him well she stared at him unseeingly as he passed her and he felt a new sick feeling in his stomach at the thought that she would never have agreed to be present if Mortimer hadn't convinced her that there was no chance of Adams being blamed for the disaster. Alongside Mortimer was an empty chair which Fife assumed was the seat set aside for Admiral Lutyens, who seemed to be the only member of the committee who was absent.

The dark-suited men were taking their places now along the table which formed the upright of the T, digging into their briefcases and fiddling with papers. The chairs down each side of the room, which had been placed ready for relatives and witnesses, were almost empty.

Fife sat to one side with Rachel, taut and ill at ease, his big hands square on his knees, clumsy-looking in his tweed suit and heavy brogues. The atmosphere was very informal, though in spite of the absence of wigs and gowns, he was impressed by the sense of being in a court of law. The empty chair at the base of the T-shaped tables was for the witness stand, and though there was no dock for a defendant, he knew perfectly well by the time the inquiry was over there would be an accused and he had an uneasy feeling that his name would be Thomas MacReady Fife.

'That's Halcrow,' he whispered, pointing out the plump pale man leaning back in his chair at the lawyers' table to talk to Adams' widow. 'With him and Doughty against me, I'm going to have a rough passage. They say Mortimer's good on boardroom procedure, so he'll be in his element, too. I'm beginning to wish now I hadn't pressed so damned hard for Hannen and Jessup and the others to stay at Stakness. I could have relied on them. They'd had plenty of experience and it would have been a help. I'm going to need help.'

The movement of papers stopped abruptly and they all stood up as Sir Henry Orlesi entered and took his place in the centre of the top table, a small man with black darting eyes that showed his Italian ancestry, and a thin withered face full of wisdom.

He picked up a sheaf of papers and began to read slowly.

'Gentlemen,' he said. 'I have agreed to conduct this inquiry in the interests of the British East-West Greenland Expedition. The committee of the expedition has every right to hold an inquiry and, indeed, is very wise to do so in view of the disaster that has overtaken the men it landed on the coast of Greenland last year. It has nothing to do with the Board of Trade Inquiry, which is to be held eventually into the collision between the Expedition's ship, *Brancard*, and the British Motor Trawler, *Lady Harding*. The details of that unfortunate mishap will be dealt with in another court.'

As he paused, there was a shuffling of feet and someone started to cough, then Orlesi was speaking again.

This is an interim board,' he said, 'convened by the interested parties because of a growing public demand for facts, to inquire into the disaster at Prins Haakon Lake, to decide on what should be done towards salvaging something from that disaster, and to apportion, if possible, the blame for what happened.'

He paused to draw breath and there was more rattling of papers and another bout of coughing.

'However' – Orlesi was speaking again – 'though this inquiry is private and personal, we shall do our best to conduct it as nearly as possible in a formal manner. I shall ask no one to swear on oath, and nobody will be subpoenaed to say more than he or she desires. Nevertheless' – he paused and stared around – 'it should be obvious to you all that it will be in the best interests of everyone if witnesses will be as helpful as they can.

'Unfortunately' – Orlesi paused again, as though he were almost enjoying the dramatic effect of his words – 'we have this morning heard that Lieutenant Sampson and the other members of the expedition who should have been here today – I'll not read their names at this stage – that they can't be present owing to the fact that the ship which was bringing – them south has been held up by storms on the West Coast of Greenland.'

There was a little shuffle, and Fife felt his throat contract, and he sensed rather than felt Rachel's hand slip into his.

'However' – the dry voice continued – 'since so many people have journeyed here today, we propose to go as far as we can and then adjourn until the rest of the witnesses arrive. I take it that no one has any objections?'

Several of the lawyers shook their heads and Sir Thomas Halcrow stood up to say that he felt, in view of the widow's anxiety to know what happened, that they should proceed as far as they could. Orlesi nodded and stared round the room.

Rachel glanced at Fife but he seemed to have been stricken dumb.

'I'm on my own, Rachel,' he murmured. 'If I didn't know the weather up there, I'd have thought Mortimer had arranged it.'

'You should object, Tom,' she urged him in a whisper, but he was too late and Orlesi was already continuing.

'We have a duty to the relatives and dependants of the missing men,' he was saying, 'as well as to those who are living. We have to attempt to assess where the blame lies. For blame there must be. The expedition which set off from these very docks in such high hopes almost a year ago ended in complete disaster. Its leader is dead and the men who were with him, wintering at Prins Haakon Sø, are missing. An attempt was made to find them but, beyond the grave of Commander Adams and the remains of their burnt-out hut, nothing was discovered. We have to assess now what went wrong and if all possible effort was made to get to them before it was too late.'

Fife was fidgeting restlessly in his seat. Somehow, in Orlesi's last sentence there was an ominous edge of accusation.

'The expedition,' Orlesi was continuing, 'was conceived by Commander Edward Hyams Adams, DSO, Royal Navy, with offices near here in St Asaph Street. Articles of Association were drawn up and the expedition and all its workings was a legal entity. Its purpose was to make a geologic survey of the area round Prins Haakon Sø and to the north, and with it went experts to make seismic, gravity, glaciological and meteorological research and surveys. Other members of the party were to do other work which I'll not set forth at the moment. I also propose to take as read the names of the interested parties because so many people and so many firms assisted in the finance and the work of preparation...'

'I wish to God they'd get on with it,' Fife said nervously.

'We also include in the points to be considered,' Orlesi went on, 'the possibility of organising and equipping a rescue expedition. At least, shall I say that this was the original intention when this inquiry was first mooted, but as nothing has been heard of the missing men for several months, we can only assume that this part of the inquiry unfortunately will not now be necessary.'

Fife half-started to his feet, but Rachel's hand on his wrist pulled him down again. He glanced at her, flushed and angry, but said nothing and sat in angry silence as Orlesi continued to outline the expedition's aims, its construction, and its organisation.

The flat, apparently uninterested voice seemed to go on all morning and before they knew what had happened, they were adjourning for lunch.

When they reached the street, the groups of seafaring men had vanished into the pubs, and the taxis had gone and, with the rain that had started and the blustery weather, the place had a deserted look about it.

The first editions of the evening papers were already out and there was a picture on the front page of witnesses arriving. Fife, snapped as he recoiled from the woman who had confronted him in the entrance, looked huddled, shifty and full of guilt, and the story was full of veiled suggestions of failure and omission.

'It's getting all twisted out of shape,' he growled as he stuffed the paper into his pocket. 'It was to have been an inquiry into the possibility of rescue originally, but now all they seem concerned with is blame.'

They ate in a small room at the back of a public house, amid the bustle of waitresses and the chatter of businessmen from the office premises around.

' "We have to assess what went wrong and if all possible effort was made to get to them before it was too late." ' Fife choked as he quoted Orlesi's words. 'He makes it sound as though no one tried.'

After the lunch recess, the inquiry began calling witnesses, and Sir Willard Mortimer moved into the seat at the base of the T-shaped table. He was quiet and self-assured, with all the urbanity of an expert witness, a man who had given evidence before dozens of inquiries and sat on dozens of committees. He looked comfortably at Doughty as he rose to question him and, led gently through his evidence, outlined all the methods of organisation, giving it as his firm opinion that little more could have been done to ensure the safety and survival through the winter of the men at Camp Adams.

'They had ample food and medical supplies,' he insisted. 'I remember I took a hand in checking them myself. I even loaned my office staff to help. From that point of view there was nothing wrong.'

'What about equipment, Sir Willard?' Doughty asked. 'Have you anything you can tell us about that? Fire-fighting equipment, for instance? Transport?'

'I went through the lists myself,' Mortimer said smoothly. 'There were nearly twice the number of fire-fighting appliances available that there are in the workshops of Western Chemicals, a subsidiary of the Mortimer Group, where the danger of fire is very much greater. I felt there were more than enough and so did my – and so did Commander Adams.'

He paused before he mentioned the name and there was a murmur of sympathy. When he went on again Doughty's tones were gentler.

'I'm sure we all sympathise with you in the loss of your son-in-law, Sir Willard,' he said. 'Now what about equipment?'

Mortimer fiddled with the spectacles he held across his knee. 'It was all given by reputable firms or bought from reputable sources.' he said.

'What about radio equipment?'

'Supplied by the Army. There was an Army sergeant with Commander Adams' party, a Marconi-trained man with Lieutenant Sampson's party, and an ex-Merchant Navy operator with the coastal survey party on the relief ship. There was a good communications system and experts to work it.'

The grey weather brought evening too soon and the stuffy room grew stale, and they were all glad when Orlesi decided to adjourn until the following day.

The next morning, with the newspapers full of the story, the weather had turned to rain and the heavy, wind-borne drops were lashing at the windows. Fife greeted Rachel with a sombre face and handed her the newspaper, his finger on a paragraph at the bottom of the front page.

'*British Admiral Injured*,' she read, and her eyes flew at once to his face.

'Lutyens,' he said. 'A car crash. On his way to the airport. I don't know what happened or how he is, but he won't be here. That's for sure. I've been in touch with his son.'

The paragraph was only short and described Lutyens as 'attached to the British Embassy'. It was a mere ripple in the day's events and there were no details beyond the fact that he was in hospital, but it was enough to depress them both.

And the questions, when the enquiry continued, as though they'd been touched a little by the spite in the weather, were more probing.

'Sir Mortimer,' Doughty asked. 'We've heard about the equipment and the transport and the communications. But what about the men who made up the expedition? What were *they* like?'

Mortimer gestured vaguely. 'The usual types,' he said. 'University men, most of them. A few service personnel who'd been granted extended leave or who'd been seconded.'

Doughty paused. 'Do you think,' he asked, 'that, as has been suggested in the Press and other quarters, there were *too many* servicemen?'

'No. Not really. There were twenty-six men in the party, eleven in Commander Adams' group, five in Lieutenant Sampson's group, and nine with the group at Stakness.'

'These last under the leadership of – er – ' Doughty looked at his papers – 'under the leadership of Thomas MacReady Fife?'

'That's right.' Mortimer nodded. 'The fact that most of the servicemen happened to be with Commander Adams himself was probably sheer chance. Perhaps because he was a serviceman himself, he preferred it that way, because he was used to it.'

The questions went on all day, with Mortimer answering them all confidently.

'Sir Willard' – Doughty was bringing his long examination to a close now – 'do you feel everything has been done to find these men?'

Mortimer hesitated. 'I can't say,' he said. 'I have no experience of that. Inevitably, the size of the continent of Greenland has had its effect. It is two thousand miles long and a thousand miles wide. It was late in the season – '

'Not *too* late!' Fife's words were heard all round the courtroom and Orlesi looked over his spectacles at him.

'I'll be glad, Mr Fife,' he said, 'if you would confine your remarks to your evidence which will come very soon. Sir Willard has been most helpful and I'm sure interruptions of this sort can't possibly be of any assistance.'

Fife seemed to be on the point of getting to his feet and Rachel grabbed his hand in hers again and held it tight so that he couldn't rise.

Adams' widow followed Mortimer to the chair at the bottom of the table. She was treated gently but suddenly in Sir Thomas Halcrow's questioning there was a barb.

'Mrs Adams,' he asked, 'in your husband's letters, did you ever detect any suggestion of dissension between the two lots of them – the servicemen and the civilians?'

She shook her head. 'None whatsoever,' she said. 'Not between the groups.'

Halcrow looked sideways at her over his spectacles. 'Not between the groups,' he repeated. 'Am I to understand then that, although there was no dissension between these two groups, there *was* dissension somewhere?'

Mrs Adams nodded. 'I believe so,' she said. 'Over policy, I believe.'

'Between whom?'

'Between my husband and Mr Fife.'

'Were you ever a witness to any incident that resulted from this dissension over policy?'

'Once or twice.'

'You were involved?'

'I was a spectator. I knew Mr Fife disagreed very strongly with my husband over policy. I heard them arguing on more than one occasion.'

'And did it continue after they left England?'

'I believe so. From then, of course, all I knew of it was from the letters I received from my husband from Iceland and the things he let fall before they left.'

'Did he feel that dissension was a good thing in an affair of this kind?'

'No. He always said that disagreement was a good thing because it led to a tightening up of things which might be wrong, but this seemed to be a major disagreement over policy and it worried him.'

'Did it continue?'

'The impression I have was that it did.'

'Yet in spite of disagreement, your husband did not give way?'

'He was the leader.'

'I see.' Halcrow paused. 'It would be my impression,' he continued, 'that if anyone disagreed so firmly with policy, it would perhaps have been wise for him to resign. Did your husband feel this?'

'He didn't say.'

'What was *your* opinion? After all, you must have had wide knowledge of the affairs of the expedition.'

'I would say it *would* have been wise.'

'But your husband didn't insist?'

'He probably felt it was due to inexperience or nerves or merely the strain of getting off.'

'Inexperience! Nerves!' Rachel felt Fife stir and mutter uneasily and she clung fiercely to his hand.

'Did tempers get a little frayed at times?' Halcrow was asking.

'Inevitably, when things didn't turn up. My husband decided that once they were under way it would pass.'

'Thank you, Mrs Adams.'

Adams' widow was followed by an unnamed expert from the Air Ministry who gave a guarded description of Doree's rockets. In view of the international situation, he said, it was felt that it was a good thing to test them as quickly as possible in conditions of extreme cold.

No one asked for any enlargement on the statement and he was allowed to go, still unnamed and enigmatic.

A representative of the Thomas Cozzens Charitable Trust which had supplied funds followed, and representatives of the Committee who stated that they had been satisfied with Adams' qualifications to lead the expedition, and that he had convinced them that his arrangements had been effective and his skill sufficient. They all affirmed that the question of a relief expedition had been considered at length but that it had been decided, in view of the fact that nothing had been heard of the missing party, that it would have been pointless to waste time and money – especially in view of the fact that men had been left at Stakness to investigate Camp Adams as soon as the warmer weather permitted.

There was an air of expectancy as the last witness left the stand, and Orlesi picked up his papers and adjusted his spectacles again.

'We have now covered all possible angles of the organisation and welfare of the expedition,' he said. 'We now come to the subject of the disaster. Since, unhappily, we have no one here and are not likely now to have anyone here who is able to tell us exactly what happened, we must leave this for the moment and come to the attempt that was made to rescue Commander Adams' party. During this, we shall doubtless discover a little of what must have occurred at Camp Adams and be able to conjecture what happened to the survivors of the fire there. However, owing to the lateness of the hour and the obvious sense in not breaking into this important evidence, we shall not call on Mr Fife until tomorrow morning.'

Fife was in an angry mood as he escorted Rachel to the station to catch the train to Orford.

'They've got it all so cut and dried,' he said savagely. 'It's all so simple when they set it out in words like that. But that's all they are – words, words without any meaning. It's nothing like it really was.'

She watched him anxiously, as they approached the ticket barrier, then she burst out impulsively.

'Tom,' she said. 'Come home with me. Come and have a meal. The house's still there at Orford and it'll do it good to have a fire in the grate. I'm going. I must. Why don't you?'

He knew she was as lonely and desperate as he was himself, and the vague disquiet in his heart grew louder.

'You don't want *me*,' he said. 'Not in the mood I'm in at the moment. Much better if I stay in town and get quietly drunk on my own.'

They were avoiding each other's eyes and she looked a little pathetic suddenly.

'I know how you feel, Tom,' she pointed out. 'There aren't many people on your side, are there? But I'm a little alone, too, and it would be better for both of us than sitting all evening on our own thinking. You could catch the last train back.'

He accepted reluctantly in the end, caught by a thousand fearful uncertainties. The plea in her eyes worried him but he felt he was no company for anyone just then. In his heart he was afraid of facing Doughty the following morning, afraid that he'd lose his temper and allow them to make him say things he shouldn't, and worst of all afraid of making Rachel unhappy.

'As a matter of fact,' he said flatly. 'I'd been thinking about sitting in that damned flat of mine on my own, and it made me go cold all over. I much prefer Orford. I always did. You know that.'

She accepted his willingness gratefully and without questions, and they rode in the train sitting close together, saying very little and pretending to read through the storm that was beginning to blow up again in the evening papers, both of them faintly oppressed, Rachel by Fife's blindness and Fife by the feeling that he had no right to be there.

They stopped at the pub outside the station and had a drink, and when they reached Piercey's home, they lit a huge fire and, removing the dust covers from the furniture, prepared a meal out of tins they'd bought in the village and opened a bottle of wine, both of them still quiet. She had obviously grown used to doing things for herself and the knowledge that she had learned to live alone upset Fife and he tried to be more enthusiastic.

'I'm sorry I've been such a boor lately,' he said shyly. 'Only everything seems to have gone against me these last few months. Today just finished it off.'

She gave him a grateful look and he went on quickly. 'It was just that old Mortimer seemed so damned unctuous and everybody else so self-righteous. And what the papers are saying is so damned wrong!'

He knew it wasn't just the inquiry that was troubling him just then but he allowed himself to pour out all his anxieties about it, feeling under the circumstances that it was wiser to stick to that.

'What they all said was right enough,' he admitted. 'Everything *was* the best...*of its type!* But it wasn't the *right* type and if we'd had time to test it we could have changed it or put right the things that were wrong. We never used those damned Weasels until it was too late to make modifications, and it was the same with the tents and the sledges and the stoves and the clothing.

'Nobody let us down – nobody but Adams, that is, who was in too big a hurry. And he *was* in a hurry! That was why Polar Research wouldn't come in. They knew he was in a hurry.'

She nodded, almost as though she weren't giving him all her attention for once, and he paused and drew a deep breath. 'I'm not looking forward to tomorrow,' he admitted slowly. 'All the evidence Mortimer and Adams' widow gave – it just wasn't true. They weren't telling lies because there *was* plenty of equipment and there *was* dissension – but it just isn't as they made it seem to be.'

'Tom' – she turned towards him, cutting short his outburst, all the old willingness to accept his worries as her own overcoming her unhappiness – 'they'll know when they hear you that you did what you did only through experience – '

'Or through jealousy,' he reminded her soberly. 'It could sound like that. Or spite. Or half a dozen other things.'

His quick temper surged up again.

'I only wish to God I could have had them up there with us,' he said. 'They wouldn't bother to ask questions then. They make it sound as though I were a troublemaker and sat around doing nothing while Adams was dying, and only made a half-hearted stroll ashore when it was too late. I only wish I could have had Schak here to tell 'em how jumpy he was because the pack was closing in round the ship. I wish they could have seen Jessup lashing into me because he said I'd driven his dogs too hard.'

'Tom – '

'I *had* to drive them hard – *and* Jessup and Smeed and Erskine, too, because the weather was beginning to break and we hadn't much time and I knew we were all scared stiff *we*'d be caught, too.'

He was talking quickly, but under the indignation there was something else, a need to take refuge in words, and she interrupted sharply.

'Tom, please be quiet,' she said.

Fife closed his mouth abruptly and looked at her with angry eyes.

'Tom,' she went on gently. 'I know all this. You've told me. It's those people at the inquiry you have to convince. Not *me* You're preaching to the converted.'

'Yes.' Fife's eyes dropped. 'Yes, of course. I'm sorry.'

He was edgy and unhappy and full of resentment.

'The whole expedition was wrong,' he said more quietly. 'The whole purpose of it became simply the glorification of Edward Hyams Adams. But it was too big for him, and because it was too big it was a sort of spur to that monstrous ego of his. It was all wrong, but because there's no one to say otherwise – no Lutyens who can give some authority to it all – they're believing that Adams was lost through my slowness and nothing else, and that what's left of his party will never be found for the same reason. They're already accepting it.'

'I'm not, Tom.'

She stared hard at him, her eyes entreating pity, but he seemed deliberately to misunderstand what she was trying to say.

'God knows why not,' he said. 'I've got precious little to offer in the way of evidence.'

'I don't need evidence, Tom,' she said quietly. 'I just believe in you. That's all. Don't you see?'

He avoided her eyes which were bright and suspiciously moist. He knew exactly what she was trying to tell him.

'Thank you, Rachel,' he said.

'Tom, you fool,' she said in a low desperate voice. 'It's not thanks I want.'

He stared at her, his eyes suddenly sharp. 'I'd better catch that train,' he said quickly.

'Damn the train!' Her voice was pleading. 'Tom, surely I don't have to spell it out?'

His forbidding expression had gone but there was a lost look on his face. 'No,' he agreed. 'You don't have to spell it out, Rachel. I know. I've known a long time.'

Her eyes were shining now and she was staring at him, probing the depths of his distress, as though she couldn't take her gaze off his face.

'But I've nothing, Rachel,' he said miserably. 'Nothing. Nothing at all. Especially now. No future and not much hope of one.'

She gave a little intake of breath and reached out to him thankfully, almost blindly.

'Tom,' she whispered, her eyes full of tears. 'Don't be so damned proud. It doesn't matter about having nothing. And it's nothing to do with future and hope. It never was and never will be.'

six

Fife went to the inquiry the following day in an eager mood, suddenly feeling that life was better and that there was hope in the air. This new sensation of loving and being loved had about it some of the excitement he might have felt about finding himself setting foot on untrodden ground. It was intoxicating and dangerous and satisfying and, knowing his own temperament, still full of question marks.

It had all been so much easier than he had thought. The things which had been worrying him no longer mattered, in the knowledge that they didn't matter to Rachel either. Alderly and Birmingham no longer seemed very far away. They'd manage somehow, he felt. They'd not lose each other again – not now, no matter what happened. The obstacles that had seemed insurmountable the day before appeared to have dwindled to nothing during the night.

Only the newspapers broke the mood of confidence, and there were a lot of whispers and curious eyes on the station as they caught the train to the city.

There was a crowd outside the door of the Methodist Hall when they arrived and Fife felt Rachel shiver as they climbed the stairs.

'Your hand's like ice,' he said.

She managed a smile. She had been radiant all the way into town but now her face was pale.

'I'm afraid suddenly,' she said.

'Nothing to be scared of.'

272

'I hope you're in a good mood. It's your turn today.'

His brows came down immediately. 'I'm ready for them,' he said grimly.

A little scared look crossed her face. 'Tom, darling, for heaven's sake,' she begged, 'don't look like that. You'll make them hostile at once.'

His expression softened and he squeezed her arm. 'I won't,' he promised. 'They don't worry me. Not now.'

But inside, waiting for him, there was a message from Lutyens' son, which told them that although the admiral was in no danger, he would not be available to give evidence for some weeks.

'That's that,' Fife said.

His brows had come down again when he took his seat before the T-shaped table, and he was nervous and edgy and, because he was uneasy, he was ready to give battle with anyone who rattled him. He knew it was his own reputation that was at stake now, not Adams'. The direction of the inquiry, under the guidance of Doughty, was shifting subtly towards him.

There was a movement round the room as they read out his name and his degrees and qualifications and the list of his previous journeys – South Georgia, Greenland, Graham Land, Jan Mayen Island, Adelie Land. It made an impressive count and there were a few whispers. Fife saw Rachel sitting among the visitors, a small encouraging smile on her lips.

He told his story slowly and with confidence, explaining how he had tried to reach Camp Adams in spite of the weather and why he had not been able to put the Weasel team ashore at Scoresby Sund as he had planned on the return journey. Orlesi's dark face was wise as he finished, and he seemed satisfied with the explanations as he thanked him. There were a few questions from Sir Thomas Halcrow, representing Adams' widow, but they didn't give Fife any difficulty and he began to feel more calm and certain of himself.

Then he saw Doughty rising to his feet, to represent Mortimer, urbane and pale and deadly, and he found himself staring at him as though he were a sworn enemy. There was something about the man that antagonised him immediately, though he couldn't think just what it was.

'I'll not bother to remind you, Mr Fife,' he said, 'that you are not on oath. This is a private inquiry, not a court of law. However, we would all be glad of your assistance and I trust you'll give it. You are not obliged to answer my questions, of course, but, naturally, it would manifestly help us all if you did so.'

There was a veiled accusation of evasion in the words and Fife responded hotly, his brows coming down in a thick dark line over his eyes.

'I'm well aware of that,' he snapped. 'I don't have to be reminded.'

Doughty raised his eyebrows and glanced at Orlesi, almost as though he were begging to be spared the ordeal in front of him. But he said nothing and Fife saw Rachel move unhappily in her seat.

Doughty was ruffling through his papers now, as though seeking his opening question, his handsome face lowered, and Fife knew suddenly what it was about him that antagonised him. He had the same look about him that Mortimer and Adams had, the same self-confident certainty that came with background and money. He even managed to look vaguely like Adams with his thin nose and aristocratic forehead and, as he began to speak, there was the same suggestion of arrogance. All the signs of gentleness that had been there the previous day when he had put questions to Mortimer and Adams' widow had gone now. It was as though they all, even Halcrow, belonged to the same privileged secret society which didn't include Fife, and they were all closing in for the kill.

'Mr Fife, you have a very impressive record, I must admit,' Doughty said. 'Certainly not the background of an amateur.'

His manner irritated Fife and he had a faint feeling that Doughty felt sorry for him, contemptuously unable to understand the unprofitable way of life he'd chosen when, with all his qualifications, he might well have found a more remunerative profession.

'Perhaps you'll go back again, Mr Fife,' he said, 'and tell us in your own words exactly what happened, giving us all the dates and times you can. And this time, if you will, I'd be glad if you'd go *right back to the very beginning*.'

Again, there was that suggestion – unspoken but ably implied – that Fife had not told them everything he knew. Fife frowned and Rachel saw he suddenly had the air of a man who was a little lost in the wilderness of courtroom cunning they were traversing.

Slowly, but without hesitation, he described again how he had learned of the absence of messages from Camp Adams and had decided to seek for himself the reason for the silence. He briefly described the journey north once more, the wait at Cape Alexandra and the dash to Fraser Bay and Camp Adams, his wish to put a party ashore at Scoresby Sund which had been defeated by the collision, the faint message that had been picked up, and his final recall to England.

'Things seem to have gone very often wrong with this expedition, Mr Fife,' Doughty observed placidly when he had finished.

'Things *always* go wrong on expeditions,' Fife said. 'The skill of the explorer lies in making do with things and even improving on them. That's how we find out.'

'But a *great many* things went wrong on this expedition, didn't they, Mr Fife? An incredible number of things? There is a whole party of men missing, Mr Fife' – Doughty's tones were deadly and Fife could see he had taken as much a dislike to Fife as Fife had to him. They obviously would never have agreed under any circumstances, something in the manner of each sparking off an instant dislike in the other, and Fife knew he was going to have a difficult time.

'– Surely *all* these things shouldn't have happened, Mr Fife,' Doughty was saying now. 'I've been reading about Greenland, and it seems to me that it's no longer the fearsome place it used to be. There are whaling and sealing stations there, weather stations and settlements all down the coast – '

'The *west* coast,' Fife interrupted sharply. 'This was the east coast.'

'There are bases even in the north – '

'– supplied by air, not by sea. No ship's every reached Pearyland.'

Doughty paused and nodded slowly.

'Very well, Mr Fife,' he said. 'As you wish, but you do admit that even on the east coast there are a few settlements, and trappers' huts for the men who make their living off the wild life?'

'Not as far north as Camp Adams was sited.'

Doughty paused, staring down at the papers on the desk in front of him. There was a long silence, then he lifted his head abruptly.

'Nevertheless, Mr Fife,' he said, with a new sharpness in his voice, 'Greenland is no longer an unknown area. Aircraft fly over it. Radio transmissions criss-cross it constantly. Men have learned to live there. If things went wrong, perhaps it's because *things weren't done right*. Couldn't that be so?'

'It could be,' Fife said cautiously.

'It seems to me fantastic in these days of the internal combustion engine, air travel, and radio that these men can actually be dead.'

'We don't know they're dead yet,' Fife snapped.

'We don't know they're alive.'

Fife's face went red. 'I came to this inquiry,' he said, 'in the hope of meeting someone who believed they were and was anxious to find them.'

'Some of the others of us,' Doughty replied silkily, 'came to find out how they came to be lost.'

Fife drew a deep breath, trying to hang on to his temper. 'It seems to me,' he said, 'more important first to establish that they *are* lost. All the rest's a waste of time until then. And time's important. It took two years to mount this expedition. Is it too much to assume that it would take two months to mount a rescue?'

Doughty raised his eyebrows. 'Mr Fife,' he pointed out calmly, '*I'm* asking the questions, not you. If these men are still alive – '

'I think they are.'

'Then I'm sure they'll be rescued.'

Doughty's ready acceptance of the facts, his obvious concern only with apportioning the blame and his clear disinterest in anything else, annoyed Fife.

'They won't be rescued,' he said. 'if we're not ready. When the ice breaks up there'll only be a few weeks when we can get a ship up to them – if that. If we're not ready we might be too late. One day might make all the difference.'

Doughty put down his papers with a weary gesture, as though he found Fife's obsession with rescue too much for him. There was a long pause then he slowly picked up the papers again and continued.

'Mr Fife,' he said. 'We all appreciate your concern for these men but, for the moment, let us assume for the purpose of argument, that they're *not* alive. If they were, surely they'd have been found by now.'

Fife was about to explode into anger when he saw Rachel's eyes on him, trying desperately to warn him, and he gripped the arms of his chair, his knuckles white with the effort to be calm.

Doughty seemed to notice his struggle and he went on placidly, his mildness in direct contrast to Fife's bottled-up fury.

'Mr Fife,' he asked, 'why didn't you inform the London headquarters of the expedition at once that Commander Adams' party was lost?'

'Because I was trying to find them,' Fife snapped, all his good resolutions disappearing again at once.

'Several weeks elapsed between the fire and your first message.'

Fife moved restlessly in the chair.

'I was on the west coast,' he said. 'And it wasn't believed at first that Commander Adams' party *was* lost. Base thought simply that their generator had failed and they set a continuous watch, expecting them to come up again. It was quite possible. It happened to me in Adelie Land.'

'Everything seems to have happened to you, Mr Fife!'

Fife glared.

'It's the job of an expedition to look after itself and assess just how important its emergencies are,' he said hotly. 'Not to whine to headquarters for instructions. That's what they did at Stakness. When I returned, we took action at once. We went to see for ourselves, to find out what had happened. I'd still be trying to find out what happened, if I weren't wasting my time here.'

Doughty frowned. 'There's no need to be rude, Mr Fife. We're here to find out what went wrong.'

'*I'm* not,' Fife snapped. 'I'm not half so much concerned with finding fault as with finding Adams' party.'

'Then you must contain your soul in patience a little longer, Mr Fife,' Doughty rapped back. 'We have business to do first.'

Fife glanced round him like a baited bear. He could see Rachel twisting her gloves, her face pale and unhappy, and he tried hard to get a grip on himself again.

Doughty was studying his papers now, then he looked up quickly and shot his question at Fife as though he hoped to upset him a little.

'Mr Fife, why was Mr Legge-Jenkins taken along with Commander Adams as his second in command instead of you? His qualifications were not so high as yours, his experience was not so great. It was originally intended that you should be in the West Coast party. Why should these plans be changed?'

'I was dropped,' Fife said bluntly.

Doughty allowed himself a long experienced pause, so that the word hung on the air like an accusation against Fife. Then, he slowly picked up his papers and nodded.

'I see,' he said. 'You were dropped.' He repeated the word slowly and paused again, then he leaned forward. 'Why were you dropped, Mr Fife?'

The sheer repetition of the word drove it hard home into the minds of everybody in the room. Fife had been dropped. Dropped. There had been no question of resigning, or asking to be left out, or even of someone else being chosen in favour of him. It seemed much simpler than that, the way Doughty said it. He had been dropped, and the inference seemed immediately to be that he had been dropped because he had been found wanting.

The realization shouted a warning to Fife and he tried to speak more cautiously.

'Commander Adams and I didn't agree very well,' he said.

'Ah!' Doughty made the exclamation sound like a condemnation. 'Why not?'

'Because I felt that things weren't being done properly.' As he spoke, Fife saw Mortimer shuffle in his seat and a few heads turn questioningly, but Doughty seemed unmoved.

'Things weren't done properly,' he said. 'I see. What things?'

'The dogs needed practice, the men needed more skiing experience, more radio work with each other. There was not enough Weaseling, and the loading was done incorrectly, so that things wanted urgently were at the bottom instead of at the top. This resulted in the loss of man and dog rations.' Fife paused and drew a deep breath. 'And, in addition,' he ended, 'a lot of the equipment we had just wasn't suitable.'

There was a rustle of papers and some whispering and Fife saw several of the lawyers who were representing the interested firms move restlessly.

Doughty paused. 'Surely,' he said, 'you're not suggesting that some of the firms who supplied material – famous firms, I might add, Mr Fife, firms that have reputations they can't afford to lose – that they supplied inferior equipment?'

Fife shook his head, harassed by Doughty's subtle attack.

'No,' he said. 'I'm not saying that. I'm saying the expedition was rushed and that the equipment, though it was excellent, wasn't the best for the job it had to do. If there'd been more time we could have tested it, made modifications, even got the firms who supplied it to exchange it – which I know very well they would have done.'

'You were in charge of assembling much of this material. Didn't you object?'

'Yes. I was overridden.'

'By whom?'

'By Commander Adams and Sir Willard Mortimer.'

There was a buzz round the room and Fife saw Mortimer stiffen.

Doughty seemed undisturbed. 'You disagreed, in fact, on policy,' he said. 'In a nutshell, is that the case?'

'Yes.'

'In politics, in business, even in the army, when a man disagrees so violently, he resigns in protest. Why didn't you?'

'Because I'm not a politician, or a businessman, or a soldier,' Fife retorted. 'And because I felt I might still put a lot of things right.'

Doughty paused for a moment, fiddling with his papers, then he looked up sharply.

'Are you sure you weren't hoping to undermine Commander Adams' authority and take over the expedition yourself?' he asked sharply.

'Yes, I am sure,' Fife snapped.

'But it is true, isn't it, that there was a feeling on the committee at one time that *you* were the man to lead the expedition?'

'I don't know. I never sat on the committee.'

'You must have heard. You must have known.'

'I did hear something of the sort.'

'And having heard it, couldn't it have put ideas into your mind? You probably would have liked to have led the expedition, Mr Fife. You'd never led one, had you? Perhaps you were anxious to.'

'I was quite willing to act as second in command.'

'You didn't act very loyally, Mr Fife.'

'I objected whenever I felt something was wrong. The expedition was badly conceived, badly organised and dangerous from the start.'

Fife's words tumbled out. He knew his anger, his righteous indignation, his impatience with the whole inquiry showed up badly against the smooth urbanity of Doughty, but he felt he had already gone too far and couldn't retreat.

'I was asked to join a geophysical expedition,' he said, 'but I found it had become a completely different affair with rigid orders about what we must do and must not do under certain conditions. It was an intolerable situation. Decisions can never be made at a distance of thousands of miles, and Flying-Officer Doree's rockets created the ridiculous position of one half of the expedition being secret from the other half.'

Doughty allowed him to finish then he looked up with a half-smile on his face. 'That was quite an outburst, Mr Fife,' he said, completely unruffled.

'It was quite a situation,' Fife snapped back, irritated by his inability to annoy him.

Doughty ruffled his papers. 'Unfortunately, it wasn't in answer to any of my questions,' he said. 'In fact, if I may say so, you're making it very difficult to continue this inquiry, Mr Fife. We're trying our best to conduct it sensibly, and wild statements of this kind are completely out of order. They prevent us from doing anything in a normal, dignified and proper manner.'

It was too much for Fife. His hatred of deceit, his dislike of the way the whole affair was becoming a pleasant boardroom debate, exploded from him in a storm of bitterness.

'Out of order?' he snorted. 'Out of order? If Adams' party dies, then I only hope to God they do their dying in a normal, dignified and proper manner and that they don't disorganise your damned inquiry by having the nerve to be out of order!'

Doughty stared at him, startled out of his calm at last, but he recovered quickly and threw up the sponge, his manner smooth and urbane again at once.

'Mr Chairman,' he said. 'Mr Chairman – '

He seemed to be at a loss for words and, giving a theatrical shrug, sat down, tossing his papers onto the desk in front of him.

The gesture was one of finality, and Orlesi stared at Fife, his brows down, his face grim.

'I understand how you feel, Mr Fife,' he said. 'You have very strong feelings about your comrades' disappearance, but we have a job to do and we're trying to do it. You're not helping. I suggest we adjourn until after lunch and that you use the time in between to collect yourself so that when we start again you can make an effort to be more calm and helpful.'

He left the room and Doughty gave Fife a last disgusted glance and followed with the others.

Fife left the chair slowly, stiffly, and almost stumbled towards Rachel as she came towards him.

'I didn't come out of that very well, did I?' he muttered.

'Oh, Tom' – her eyes were full of tears – 'what happened to you?'

'I lost my temper. I knew I would.'

'But, Tom – '

'It's no good, Rachel,' he said bitterly. 'I can't cope with men like Doughty. He reminds me of Mortimer and Adams. They all come from the same stable, and it's a different one from mine. They rub me raw. Good God,' he burst out, 'the whole inquiry got off on the wrong foot! It's going off at half-cock like the expedition. Doughty's wrenched it all out of shape. What they're trying to do now is not find a way to mount a rescue but whitewash Adams and lay the blame on me.'

She took his arm and led him out, still red with anger, still dull with his own stupidity and angry with his own impatience.

'It's all we seem to be able to do these days,' he was saying. 'Whether it's international, national or just private like this. Fling abuse about and blame, instead of getting together to do something that might help.'

She said nothing and they ate in the little pub round the corner, in the dreary brown room with its old-fashioned sideboard full of thick plates and artificial flowers. Fife was morose and silent through the meal and Rachel watched him unhappily.

'Tom, darling,' she begged, 'you've got to get someone to represent you. It's hopeless without. Mortimer's got Doughty. Mrs Adams has got Halcrow. Every firm and organisation there is represented by someone. You've got nobody.'

He sat in stubborn silence and she persisted, speaking quickly before he could interrupt.

'You must go to a solicitor. You've got to get witnesses. You need witnesses.'

'It's too late now.'

'It isn't too late. Any lawyer who knows his job would have demanded an adjournment long ago. He'd make them wait until Sampson's party arrived or until you could get Hannen and the others flown home. He'd get Schak to tell them about the ice. He'd get the Polar Research people to tell them why they weren't in favour of Adams. He'd insist on waiting until Lutyens could give his opinion, or at least get a deposition from his son to say what he'd said about it all.'

Fife shrugged. 'It's too late, Rachel,' he said wearily. 'Who's bothered about me anyway? Nobody cares the slightest bit where I end up.'

'I do,' she said hotly. 'I'm very much involved now, Tom, and I care very much indeed.'

He squeezed her hand but he still seemed stubborn. 'It's no good, Rachel,' he said. 'If we demand an adjournment at this stage, they'll just think I'm afraid of what's going to come out. It'll look worse than just carrying on as we are.'

There was a certain amount of truth in what he said but she wouldn't let him rest.

'Tom, darling, it's important that you come out of this affair with something left for the future, and the way things are going, you haven't a chance. You've *got* to have legal help.'

'Rachel – '

'No, Tom, listen! I've listened to you – ever since you came back to England – and now you've got to listen to me. I'm not going to let them destroy you. I'm insisting.'

In the end he heard her out but, bearing in mind what he'd said about the effect of an adjournment at that stage, they decided finally to see a solicitor as soon as the inquiry was halted for the missing witnesses.

They walked back hand in hand, neither of them very certain of the future, both silent and busy with their own thoughts, Fife dreading Doughty's attack during the afternoon.

Outside in the corridor, a Post Office messenger was wandering about, questioning people, and as someone pointed towards them, the boy came across.

'Mr Fife?' he asked.

'Yes.'

'Mr Thomas Fife?'

'That's right.'

The boy grinned. 'Blimey, Mr Fife, you don't half take some finding. I've been shown a chap called Rice and another one called Fine. Then they said you were having a bit of grub. I began to think you'd never turn up.'

'What is it?'

The boy handed over the envelope. 'It's not a greetings telegram, that's a fact,' he observed. 'They said it was urgent and that it'd come a long way.'

'A long way?'

'They said it was from some place in Iceland.'

Fife glanced at Rachel, then he was wrenching at the envelope with clumsy fingers and smoothing out the buff sheets inside. The cablegram was from Hannen and it made his heart leap.

'G3ZBD heard transmitting morse SOS Stop Signal faint Stop No further information position or survivors yet Stop

For God's sake inform where can contact you by telephone Stop Why not come take over Stop...'

For a moment, still stupefied from the morning's questioning, he couldn't believe his eyes, then he straightened out the sheets again.

'Rachel,' he exploded. 'Rachel, they've heard from Adams' party!'

He stared at her, his eyes wide, then he swept her into his arms, hugging her unashamedly before everyone's gaze.

She fought him off, tears of happiness in her eyes at this demonstration of the rightness of his beliefs, and reached for the cablegram.

'It's from Hannen,' he said. 'They've heard them transmitting. He says they're – here' – he thrust the message at her – 'here, for God's sake, read it for yourself.'

The messenger boy was staring at him. 'Is it important or something?' he asked.

'You bet your sweet life it is, son,' Fife said excitedly. 'Here' – he fished in his pocket and, finding he had no change, he dragged out his wallet and pulled out a ten shilling note.

'What, the lot, Guv'?'

'I wish I could afford more.'

'Thanks.' The boy glanced at the note and then at the lengthy cablegram and his face looked doubtful. 'You going to send a reply?' he asked.

'Yes. No – not yet. I need to think a bit. I'll attend to it myself.'

'Thanks.' The boy grinned. 'Whatever it is, Mister, I hope it all turns out well.'

As he disappeared, Fife pulled Rachel round a corner of the corridor, out of the curious gaze of people waiting outside the inquiry, and swung her into his arms.

'Oh, Tom!' She put her hands behind his head and pressed her cheek against his, tears of unashamed happiness filling her eyes. 'You're saved. I wouldn't have believed it, but you are.'

He released her quickly and suddenly the gaiety had gone from his manner. 'Rachel,' he said, 'I've got to get up there. If I can get up there I can find them. I know I can. With Hannen and Jessup and Smeed and Erskine, I could find anything.' He paused, his brow troubled. 'But I've got to have help,' he said. 'I've got to have money.'

She glanced in the direction of the corridor where people were beginning to move through the doors to take their seats again.

'Won't *they* provide it? The inquiry? The committee?'

He frowned. 'I suppose so,' he said. 'Eventually. But when? The Committee as such hasn't any money. It existed merely to raise funds for Adams and that's been spent. They can do nothing without a meeting and without the meeting asking help from the Cozzens Trust and all the others. And no individual one of them can raise enough. And that'll take too long. By the time they've finished discussing it in a normal, dignified and proper manner, we shall have lost them again. They'll have gone off the air.'

She could see he was itching to start moving at once.

'I wish to God Lutyens were here,' he said. 'He'd fix something. He'd have me on a plane up there and get a ship from somewhere, and ask questions afterwards.'

'Tom!' Rachel grasped his hand. 'What about Kinglake? Didn't *he* say that if there were some sign of life, the *Recorder* would back you?'

Fife's eyes lit up and he glanced at his watch.

'How long have we got?'

'They start again in half an hour.'

'They'll have to start without me.'

287

He was dragging her towards the street now, and she glanced back nervously, catching the curious stares of the officials and lawyers in the corridor. 'Tom, you can't walk out on them like this.'

'Can't I?' he said. 'Just watch me. I don't have to answer their damn questions. They said so themselves. Come on, let's get a taxi – '

At the offices of the *Recorder*, the frustration of waiting nearly drove Fife crazy.

'Look,' he told the man at the desk who was busily filling in a green form for him. 'This is urgent. It's important. It's the biggest story this newspaper'll ever get.'

The clerk looked up, unperturbed, with aged eyes that seemed to suggest their owner had lived through every big story there had ever been. 'I'll just fill this form in,' he said. 'It'll enable you to go up to the Editor's floor.'

'Do I have to have it?'

'You'll not get far without it, sir.'

Fife almost snatched the paper out of the clerk's hand and dragged Rachel after him towards the ornate staircase that was covered with decorated motifs of front-page headlines.

'Where to, sir?' the lift operator asked.

'Kinglake. The editor!' Fife's furious impatience was making him jig from one foot to the other and Rachel grabbed his hand again.

'Tom, for God's sake, stop it,' she said severely.

'But, they're – '

'Stop it!'

Fife calmed down abruptly and squeezed her hand. 'OK,' he said. 'I'm calm. I'm in control. I'm sorry.'

Kinglake's secretary looked up in surprise as they burst in.

'Have you an appointment?' she said immediately.

'No, I haven't,' Fife said. 'But I don't need one for this.'

'Mr Kinglake's engaged at the moment.'

'Then please disengage him.'

Rachel pushed him aside gently. 'It's urgent and important,' she insisted quietly. 'We must see him. I'm sure you'll not be making a mistake if you interrupt him. Tell him it's Tom Fife and that we've heard from Commander Adams' party.'

She stared at them for a second, then she turned and vanished through a connecting door. As she went in they could hear low voices discussing something.

Fife turned to Rachel and put his hand on hers. 'Thanks,' he said. 'You make a much better job of it than I do.'

Kinglake's secretary came back within a few seconds.

'Mr Kinglake will see you at once,' she said, and Fife almost bounded past her into Kinglake's office.

Several men holding files were just moving out of the room and it was obvious they had interrupted a conference. Kinglake stood up and pushed chairs forward.

'This is unheard of, Fife,' he said cheerfully. 'Interrupting an editor's conference. I don't suppose it's been done since Suez. How's the inquiry going? Are they biting?'

Fife nodded, still fidgeting restlessly.

'Not too deep, I hope,' Kinglake went on. 'They tell me you're not represented. That was very foolish, Fife. Very very foolish. Especially with Mortimer opposite you.'

As he was talking, he was moving to a cupboard on the wall. 'Drink?' he asked. 'No? Have it your own way.'

'Look – '

'A moment, Fife.' Kinglake sat down, ponderous and deep-voiced and sure of himself. 'An editor's never at his best without a desk twelve foot by twelve foot in front of him. It's remarkable how unimpressive we look when we're out of that chair.'

'Look – '

There was a knock on the door and a boy brought a slip of paper in and handed it to Kinglake. 'From the News Editor, sir,' he said. 'He thought you'd want to know.'

Fife was almost frantic with impatience as Kinglake ignored him and began to read the slip.

'Look, Mr Kinglake, for God's sake – '

Kinglake laid the paper down as the boy disappeared, and smiled maliciously. 'Right, Mr Fife,' he said. 'I can see you're dancing about in that chair as though it's red hot. You can go ahead now. I'm ready.'

'They've heard from Adams' party,' Fife exploded with relief.

Kinglake smiled. 'I know,' he said.

'What?' All the excitement drained away from Fife at once. '*You've heard?*'

'There's not much moves faster than the news, Fife.' Kinglake tapped the paper which he'd just been handed. 'Confirmation's just come in. Via *Visir* in Reykjavik.'

'How did – '

'Don't be so naïve, Fife.' Kinglake was clearly enjoying himself. 'Newspapers represent each other so long as they're not in opposition. We have our contact up there and he has his contact in the cable office. It's the same all over the world. The man who despatched Hannen's cable to you made a point of contacting *Visir* too, and our man on *Visir* contacted us. Everybody'll know about it by tomorrow.'

'Will the inquiry have heard?' There was a sickened feeling of disappointment in Fife.

Kinglake smiled. 'Not yet. But they're bound to hear of it soon. We can't hang on to it for long.' He sat back and put his fingers together in the form of a steeple. 'What do you want?' he asked. 'A passage up there?'

Fife almost leapt out of the chair as he leaned forward. 'Yes,' he said at once. 'I want a passage. An air passage.'

'I thought you might. What else do you want?'

'Help. All the help we can get.'

'How long for?'

Fife shrugged, at a loss.

'I don't know,' he said. 'It may be days. It may be weeks. I must get there, though, and I've no money – '

' – and you came to me because we can make our mind up more quickly than your committee.'

'Yes. Just get me there, Mr Kinglake,' Fife pleaded. 'That's all I ask. I've beggared myself trying to persuade people to do what I'm trying to persuade you to do now. Just get me there. I'll do the rest. I'll find a ship somehow, if I have to take out that damned ship we have already with the hole still in its side.'

Kinglake refused to be hurried. 'What do we get in return?' he asked.

Fife gestured impatiently. 'The story. The pictures. Send one of your men with me, if you like. I don't give a damn. You said that if we found them it'd be the biggest story that ever broke. You could send the best man you've got.'

'On a job with no time limit?' Kinglake smiled. 'Come, Mr Fife, we don't work like that. We don't need one of our men, anyway. I saw your report. I think *you* could do it. Can you use a camera? A modern camera?'

'We all can. Cine-cameras, anything you like. We all learned how to use them.'

'How much money will you need?'

'I don't know. I don't know.'

The old feeling of frustrated impatience was beginning to creep over Fife again and he felt Rachel's hand drop on his and steady him.

The gesture wasn't missed by Kinglake, and he nodded.

'Calmer, Fife,' he pleaded. 'Calmer. You're asking me to spend the *Recorder's* money. At least let me do it in my own time. Don't rush me. I don't like to be rushed.'

Fife swallowed. 'I'm sorry,' he said unsteadily. 'But I don't even *know* how much money. It would take time to work it out and even then it might be wrong. We'd need a ship – '

'Why not aircraft?'

'We don't even know where they are yet,' Fife said. 'Only that they're alive. We've got to go in and look for them – on our own two feet. When we've established some sort of contact we could fly them out if necessary. But we've got to find a ship first – anything. I'll hock everything I've got if necessary.'

'Don't be so damned impatient, Fife,' Kinglake said tartly. 'You don't need to hock anything. The *Recorder* never asked anybody to beggar themselves to provide it with news. We have a reputation for being generous to our employees.'

'Employees?'

'You're on the staff, Fife. As of now. You can draw on our account for money. We'll see that there are funds to fit out a ship or whatever it is you people do.'

Fife sensed rather than saw Rachel turning to him, her eyes shining, and he felt her hand tighten on his.

'There's just one thing,' Kinglake went on while he was still trying to stammer out his thanks. 'For God's sake, be reasonable. Don't ask for the *Queen Mary*. I don't want to have to explain away any astronomical figures to the accountants. I'd never get away with it.'

Fife was still staring at him speechlessly and Kinglake gestured cheerfully.

'Go and find them, Fife,' he said. 'We'll give you all the instructions you need about getting your story back to us. We'll take as much as you like to send. Don't worry about the cost. Don't send us pretty descriptions, though. We'll supply those. Just send us the facts. And photographs. Not of places. Of people. You. Anybody else who's taking part. And above all find those men. Or their diaries if they're no longer alive. I beg your pardon, Miss Piercey, for saying that, but I'm trying to be realistic. And send us pictures of you doing it. That's all we ask. If you do that you'll have more than repaid us. After all the fuss that's been stirred up, this could be the biggest story we've had since they shot Gandhi. Now I think you'd better get moving.'

Fife stood up, dazed, as Kinglake rang the bell.

'Take Mr Fife along the corridor,' he said as his secretary appeared. 'He'll want to see the news editor, the photographic manager, accounts department, a few others. He'll tell you, when he recovers his power of speech. And see that there's a seat on tonight's plane to Reykjavik. *Tonight's.* Not tomorrow's. Tonight's. We've got to get him away before anyone else finds him. I don't care who's on it. Turn 'em off if necessary.'

She nodded, gave Fife a quick smile and waited by the door.

Fife was still standing dazed, hardly able to believe his ears, and Kinglake grinned and sat back. 'Just about now,' he said, maliciously, 'the inquiry will have reached a state of complete uproar, wondering where you've got to.' He paused and smiled. 'Just in case they're taking it too calmly,' he said, 'let's start the party with a story, shall we?'

He pressed a button and picked up a telephone. 'Stanley?' he said briefly. 'How's the inquiry on the missing Adams' party going? What's that? The chief witness's missing? I thought he might be. He's up here in my office. Hold everything for a moment, will you? I'll send him down to you when I've finished with him. Then you can give it all you've got. You'd better come up and see me when you've a minute.' He put down the receiver and looked at Fife. 'Well, that's it, Fife,' he said. 'The decision's yours. I hope you know what you're doing.'

'I know what I'm doing,' Fife said grimly.

'I wonder if you do.' Kinglake's face lost its smile. 'If this doesn't come off, you know, you're out – for good.'

Fife tried to shake off the surging feeling of triumph. 'I'm out already,' he said cheerfully. 'I hope they enjoy the discussion they'll have about what they should do with me.'

'You realize that skipping out like this will damn you forever in the eyes of all responsible people? You're finished, Fife, if you fail. Everybody's going to say, "Well, if that's the way he behaves, no wonder he failed to find Adams in time." And, make no mistake, the odds are against you.'

'I'll chance it.'

'If you don't pull it off, you can't expect help from us. Big newspapers can't afford to be associated with failures. You'll be dropped like a hot cake.'

Fife nodded.

'It only seems fair to warn you,' Kinglake said. 'How do you feel about it?'

Fife paused and Rachel's eyes were on him, anguished as she knew the agony he was going through. Then he lifted his head and stared at Kinglake.

'I'm going,' he said.

Kinglake nodded unemotionally. 'I thought you might,' he admitted.

seven

There was a cold wind with a suggestion of rain in it blowing across the runways as Fife stood in front of the airport buildings, watched by the nervous newspaperman whom Kinglake had assigned to watch his movements and prevent him being seen by any of the opposition reporters who were haunting the airport lounges in search of him. The glow of London in the distance lit up the sky to the east and he could see shreds of dark clouds scudding across it from the north. A wireless was playing music softly in the darkness, interrupted from time to time as the announcer's voice summoned passengers for a flight.

Somewhere out of sight, the whine of a jet plane's engines rose to a screech, and he saw the machine cross the dark aerodrome in a moving line of lights and rise quickly into the sky.

In a few short hours, he had progressed from being a man nailed to guilt as if to a cross by his own quick temper to a man full of hope and faith in himself. The difference in his manner was obvious to Rachel as she waited quietly alongside him for the call to the aircraft.

He seemed to sense what she was thinking. 'Try to phone my family,' he said quietly. 'Get hold of my mother, if you can. There are going to be a few unpleasant things in the papers about me tomorrow and it's bound to upset her unless she knows what's going on. Tell her what's happened and tell her, for God's sake, not to say anything.'

'I'll tell her, Tom. I'll go and see her, too.'

'She's always taken it a bit hard every time I disappear into the unknown for months at a time. It's hard for parents who have strange sons who want to spend the best part of their lives in queer places.'

'It's hard for the women who love them, too,' she said in a low voice.

He looked at her quickly and she smiled and squeezed his arm to reassure him. 'But I'm used to it,' she said quickly. 'I'll be all right. I watched my father going off. And I know you want to go, don't you?'

'Yes.' Fife answered immediately. 'Yes, I do. It's not just that I want to see my name in the paper without a lot of veiled abuse after it. It's because it was my job to fetch those people out and that's what I want to do.'

They were silent for a moment, then she spoke again, quietly, her words full of feeling.

'I hope you find my father, Tom,' she said. 'I know that sounds silly because I hope you find them all. What I mean is, I hope it's *you* who actually finds him. I hope it's you who tells him all that's happened – about my mother, about us. Somehow, I think it'll be easier that way. I think you'll understand each other.'

'We always did.'

'Tell him about us – as soon as you can.'

'I'll tell him.'

They were awkward still, certain of each other, but not used either to their own new feelings or the sudden importance of the other, and from time to time, now that they were parting, their conversation died away in a manner that it had never done before.

While they were waiting, they saw Kinglake advancing down the ramp towards them, big and burly and red-faced, the lights glinting on his glasses, followed, as though by a court, by half a dozen other men. He looked vaguely like a tank approaching, and moved with the same solid certainty.

He didn't bother to shake hands, as though it were a triviality that could well be dispensed with.

'I'm glad they managed to get you away from all the other passengers,' he said. 'There are always people in there with cameras. Fix your customs all right?'

Fife nodded.

'Seen the evenings?'

Kinglake thrust a newspaper at them and Fife saw his own face in the centre of the page, and the headline, 'ADAMS INQUIRY MYSTERY. MAIN WITNESS VANISHES AFTER QUESTIONING. WHERE IS FIFE?'

'Yes,' he said. 'I've seen them. They've got plenty to say.'

Kinglake glanced at the paper in his hand. 'There's more inside,' he said. ' "Our special correspondent's" been at it again.' He seemed to be enjoying a private joke against himself and his profession. 'I'm not sure whether he's suggesting just plain wind-up or that you've gone over to the Russians with the secrets of those met. rockets you had. I'm not even sure whether *he's* sure either.' He flipped the paper across his hand. 'They're after you now,' he went on cheerfully. 'They'll never forgive you for bunking off like this or us for helping you. If you don't pull it off, you're a dead duck. By tomorrow, the gale'll be blowing round us both; but while *we* can afford to ignore it, if you fail, it'll blow *you* clean off the face of the earth.'

Fife nodded without speaking and Kinglake glanced again at the paper. ' "Where is Fife?" ' he read aloud. ' "Fife." Everybody knows who "Fife" is now. It's the measure of a good story when you can use a name in a headline without bothering to explain who it is. Some damn fool'll get up in the House tonight, I suppose, after a browse through the evenings, and demand that a few heads roll at MI5. "Where is Fife?" ' He smiled. 'They'll know tomorrow when they see the *Recorder*.'

He paused and glanced round him at the airport before turning back to Fife. 'Got everything you want?' he asked.

Fife shook his head. He had spent the afternoon and evening collecting items of his equipment, trying to make lists in jolting taxis as he hurried from one place to another, but his luggage still looked remarkably thin and he was certain he'd forgotten half of what he'd need. He'd spent two solid hours – hours when he might have been attending to his own needs, or with Rachel, who suddenly couldn't be put aside with ease – under a bright light that was hot enough to make his head ache, listening to a whole wealth of instructions, first from the *Recorder's* news editor and then from the photographic manager, listening to what they wanted, bewildering hours of trying to absorb in a few moments what it had taken them half a lifetime to learn.

There was a thick, typed wad of instructions in his briefcase, about the cable and wireless routes from the north to London and the ways and means there were of getting round delays. His head was still bursting with them. They had taken him to discreet back doors where they could rely on silence, to obtain what equipment he couldn't lay his hands on in time and he was still a little uncertain what he'd bought and what he'd forgotten.

'No,' he said. 'I don't suppose I have got everything. But I can borrow what I need and if necessary I can buy.'

'Don't hesitate,' Kinglake urged. 'We'd all look a bit silly if it fell down through lack of spending. He glanced round at the reporter standing in the group nearby. 'Got all you want?' he asked.

'Yes, sir. I've had a long talk with Mr Fife.'

'Good, good. I've seen that we get a leader on this. How about photographs?'

For a moment, Fife was blinded by the flash units, then Kinglake reached for Rachel.

'Might as well have you in as well,' he said. 'After all, you've got an interest in this affair, too, haven't you? Are you two engaged or something, by the way, because that's quite a story, too.'

He didn't wait for a reply but pulled her forward and the flashbulbs went off again.

Kinglake swung round to Fife as the photographer retreated. 'Don't be afraid to use that cable, Fife,' he said. 'We're going to follow you all the way, and I'd like to have the country biting its nails with anticipation.'

'I just hope I pull it off,' Fife pointed out, suddenly obsessed with a feeling of inadequacy. He knew the north. There was a peculiar devil up there that existed only to humiliate men who thought they'd defeated it.

Kinglake wasn't listening, though, and was talking now to the men who'd come with him.

'Did you cable them to expect him?' he was saying.

'They'll be there with a car.'

'Any snags?'

'Only the fishing dispute.'

Kinglake was obviously not interested. 'Mothers' Union politics,' he commented contemptuously.

'Things are still a little delicate, it seems.'

Kinglake gestured irritably. 'A lot of old ladies squabbling over where to hang the washing. Did you warn them that the agencies aren't in on this? We're paying and we want first service.'

'I stressed that.'

'Good. Have they heard anything more?'

'No, nothing.'

'I hope to God we do hear more,' Fife said softly.

As they talked a hostess appeared, smart and trim in blue. 'We're ready for you now, Mr Fife,' she said. 'If you'll just come this way.'

Kinglake held out his hand.

'I don't know quite what to say to thank you,' Fife said.

Kinglake gestured. 'We invested a lot of money in Adams,' he said bluntly. 'We're risking a little more to make sure we get some return for it. It's business. That's all there is to it.'

'Well, thank you, anyway, for having faith.'

Kinglake shrugged. 'Mine never came within a mile of yours, Fife,' he said. '*I'm* just playing a hunch. That's how we live. If it doesn't come off, it'll sink into obscurity and be forgotten and there'll be nobody here to welcome you back. Nobody. But if it does, we'll scoop the lot and you'll be another Hillary.'

He stepped back and turned away abruptly and began to walk up the ramp towards the lights.

Rachel looked up at Fife, suddenly shy, almost as though she hardly knew him.

'Be careful, Tom,' she said. 'I'll be praying that you bring them back.'

He nodded, and she kissed him, then she, too, turned on her heel and followed Kinglake up the ramp. At the top, she turned and glanced back at him through the glass and raised her hand.

Fife stood for a moment, staring after her, then as she turned away again, he bent to pick up his briefcase and followed the hostess as she walked to the bus.

Hannen was waiting for him in the airport lounge at Reykjavik. He came forward, smiling, and shook hands, then took Fife's bag as they started to walk to the door.

'I hope to God something comes of all this, Pat,' Fife said fervently. 'I've stuck my neck out as far as it'll go.'

Ever since leaving London, he had been assailed by fears. It had seemed so simple in England to recruit help and to tell them he was going to rescue the Adams' party, but considering it on the way, with nothing else to do but think about the flaws in the plan, he had begun to have appalling doubts.

They climbed into the big American Dodge that was waiting for them, and Hannen glanced at him as he sat back. 'We got your cables,' he said. 'The boys are glad to have you back. I've got things moving. I've been in touch with Scoresby and arranged for us to pick up three teams of dogs and sledges. A doctor'll be waiting for us there, too, and there'll be sledging rations. I've arranged fuel for the Weasels – '

'What about the *Brancard*?'

Hannen shook his head. 'There I stuck,' he said. 'Nothing in the world'll induce 'em to hurry while we keep destroyers off the coast. They're hostile. They're more hostile now than they were last year.'

'For God's sake, *Brancard's* not a trawler!'

'She's a British-chartered ship and dislike of Britain has moved up a couple of notches since last year.'

Fife's heart sank. The high hopes with which he had started off seemed to be growing fainter already.

Hannen glanced at him. 'Take it easy, Tom,' he suggested. 'We'll find a ship all right, especially now that someone's prepared to pay cash. Money talks. By the way' – he smiled – 'did you know Mortimer's on to you already?' He held out a wireless message form. 'Jessup handed it to me before I left.'

'Throw it away,' Fife said abruptly. 'I've had enough of Mortimer.'

'You might as well know what's in it first. It says "*Deplore hasty departure. Committee considering action*".'

'They can only sack me,' Fife growled. 'They said so themselves.'

Hannen grinned. 'There's a bit more,' he said. ' "*Feel newspaper take-over intrusive. Report Committee at once. Signature Mortimer, Greenice*".'

'Throw it away,' Fife said again.

'You're not going to report?'

'No.'

'It doesn't impress you?'

'The only thing that would impress me now would be a loud clear signal from O'Day. What did Jessup think of the signal he picked up?'

'He didn't pick up a signal,' Hannen said.

Fife swung round quickly, startled. 'I thought he did,' he said. 'I hope nobody's exaggerating. I'm pretty deeply committed.'

'Listen, Tom,' Hannen said. 'There was no message. One of the local youngsters came in – a ham with a station in Stakness. He's been doing a lot of listening to Jessup, naturally – he couldn't help it – and he knew what was going on. He said he picked up messages between another ham in Labrador and a pal of his in Newfoundland. It's the ham in Labrador who claims to have picked them up. The youngster heard him telling his pal he'd heard Pat O'Day transmitting.'

'Transmitting what? There must have been a message.'

'SOSs and long dashes.'

'Nothing else?'

'No. Jessup's worked it out they must be on one of the Nineteens. They hadn't taken the Fifty-Three with them. You saw that when you were up at Camp Adams. He says they must be on battery power and that their batteries must be low and that O'Day must have already got his position off, when he was picked up, and was just sending the long dashes and SOSs to let somebody get a bearing.'

Fife's optimism had sunk to his shoes again. 'God,' he said. 'I hope we've got more than that!'

'We have,' Hannen said. 'A bit. But not much. We started listening out at once. The youngster who picked up the chap in Labrador arranged a sked straight away and let us know at once. He showed some sense and didn't let the fishing dispute get in his way, thank God! He's arranged to be in touch again at midnight. Jessup's standing by now.'

Fife nodded.

'You'd better talk to the bloke yourself,' Hannen went on. 'We started listening out ourselves at once, of course.'

'Hear anything?'

Hannen shook his head. 'Jess set a round-the-clock watch and warned everybody else to listen out as well. He'll tell you about it. I'd better let him. You know what a touchy devil he is about his own department.'

Jessup was already by his set when they arrived at Stakness, crouching in the shack he had erected in one of the huts, a small brightly lit room with a temperature so high it made them gasp after the sharp air outside. He had his head close to the loudspeaker and his hand on the dials, and he glanced up as they entered, staring at them through the blue whorls of tobacco smoke. He lifted his thumb in greeting then he indicated a tall brown-eyed youngster who was standing shyly by the set.

'Geir Gustafsson,' he said, 'Station TF9XX, Stakness. He lives here and works in Helbergfjördur. Goes over by motorbike. He's the chap who picked up the bloke in Labrador who heard Pat O'Day.'

'It was two nights ago, sir,' the boy said, as Fife turned to him. '*I* was not in contact with him, you understand. Not myself. I tried to make contact but there was too much – too much – '

'Mush,' Jessup interrupted shortly.

The boy nodded and smiled. 'That's right. Too much interference. He was in contact with another amateur in Newfoundland – Station VO1ABD. It seems they were old friends, sir – amateur broadcasting makes for friends, even though we don't often meet – and they were just chatting.'

'Go on,' Fife said. 'What were they saying?'

'He said he'd heard messages from the Adams' party.'

'When?'

'Three days ago – that is, three days before I heard him.'

Fife frowned. 'Why the devil didn't he get in touch with somebody?'

The boy shrugged. 'I am sorry, sir.'

'No, no. It's not your fault. You didn't waste time. Go on.'

'Yes, sir. He was saying the signal was weak and very brief and that he had been unable to contact them in return. They went off the air very quickly, it seems.'

'Have you got his frequency and call sign?'

Jessup held up a slip of paper. 'Here it is, Skip. VO2PXY. I've been trying him for ten minutes.'

'Get him, Jess. Quickly.'

Jessup crouched over the microphone, one hand on the slip of paper, his fingers on the dials. 'Calling VO2PXY. Calling VO2PXY. This is G3ZBD. Come in, VO2PXY.' He turned to Fife. 'He should come up soon, Skipper,' he said. 'He said he'd be listening out.'

They got a brief contact for a moment and heard a nasal Canadian voice, then the static swelled up again and Jessup crouched cursing over the set.

'He keeps getting lost,' he growled. 'The blasted interference's scrubbing him all the time.'

'Go down a little, sir,' the boy alongside him suggested. 'I think he operates on a lower frequency than he says.'

After a lot of interference and the ineffectual fending off of an enthusiast in Goose Bay who insisted on joining in, they eventually picked up the man in Labrador, but the reception was bad and it took long agonising minutes before they made proper contact.

'The band's bloody congested,' Jessup growled, fiddling with the dials. 'He ought to get *us*, though. This transmitter's strong enough to blow everything else off the air.'

It seemed an age before they managed to make contact again and Fife's heart was thumping wildly. After a lot more crouching and cursing, they picked up the Canadian again abruptly, and his voice filled the cabin.

'This is VO2PXY. Please clear the air. I am waiting for Station TF9XX.'

Jessup adjusted the volume control.

'Please carry on VO2PXY. TF9XX is here with me now. You are in the clear and I can read you. Please hang on.' He passed the microphone to Fife. 'Go ahead, Skip,' he said. 'He's all yours.'

The Canadian was apparently still a little startled to find his trivial conversation with his friend in Newfoundland had suddenly become of such importance but he was very helpful and tried to explain exactly what he'd heard.

'I guess it was very little – ' he said apologetically.

'Give us all you've got,' Jessup broke in. 'Did you log it?'

'No' – the nasal Canadian voice came back clearly now over the interference – 'it was mostly static and his signal was pretty weak. I didn't think much about it at first. Not till later when I realised I recognised the guy's "fist".'

'Did he give a position?'

The disembodied voice came over the static, roaring suddenly as Jessup moved a dial.

'No, I guess not. No position.'

'Names?'

There was another infuriating break in the contact as some disconnected music broke in, then the man in Labrador came back. 'Sure is a hot spot on this frequency these days,' he said. 'Gets more congested every week.'

'Listen' – Fife interrupted the chatter – 'did he give any names?'

'Names? What sort of names?'

'Names of people with him. He might have done.'

'No, siree. No names. He was hard to read at first and very weak. He was lost in the interference and difficult to pick out. Half the time I couldn't touch him. I gave him KN – '

'*Go ahead, all other stations keep out*,' Jessup translated.

' – but he just went on with his SOSs and his dashes. Obviously he wasn't receiving me. Guess his receiver's dud or something. His equipment sounded poor all round, in fact. Then he disappeared and I listened out and heard nothing more and I guess I began to wonder if I'd made a mistake. I'd heard so little I thought I was imagining things and I didn't want to make a fool of myself and start anything when I wasn't certain. So I contacted VO1ABD in Newfoundland – he's a buddy of mine. We work each other often. I asked him to keep a watch on the frequency, too. When we didn't hear him again, I thought I must have been hearing things. I reported it, of course, but nothing turned up. I was just talking it over with VO1ABD when I guess I was picked up by TF9XX in Iceland.'

'Did you get a bearing on him?'

'A bearing?' The man in Canada sounded startled. 'I don't have that kind of equipment, brother, and in any case Marconi himself couldn't have got a bearing on that signal.'

Fife was aware of a slow sagging of his spirit as the Canadian gave them his news. He moved restlessly, feeling he was getting nowhere.

'Please listen,' he said carefully. 'You said you got no call sign. How did you know it was the Adams' party?'

'I guess I don't for certain. Not even now.'

Fife glanced at Jessup wearily.

'His signal was weak,' the Canadian was continuing, 'and there was a lot of interference but I'd heard him before – months ago – working London. Weather reports. All sorts of traffic. I'd picked him up several times before they disappeared, R/T as well as W/T. And when he was keying, that operator of theirs had a distinctive "fist". He was good. No trace of swing.'

'Please go on.'

'This time he was sending differently – there was a lot of click as though he'd got a home-made key, and he sounded as though he might be tired or something, but I guess I'd still recognise him ten years from now if I heard him.'

'You can always tell, Skip,' Jessup said quietly. 'A good man can always recognise another by the way he punches the key – and Pat O'Day had a touch of his own. I'd recognise him anywhere, too.'

'Please go on,' Fife said into the microphone. 'You say there was no message?'

'Nope. Nothing. Just the SOS and the dashes and even that was hardly strong enough to come through all the gabble.'

'Why the hell didn't the weather stations pick 'em up?' Fife whispered to Jessup. 'They were nearer.'

'Lots of reasons, Skipper. Greenland's a damn funny place for radio.'

The disembodied Canadian voice was still talking. 'Say,' it asked abruptly, 'is all this important?'

'It might be,' Fife said. 'It might be.'

'Is this the missing party? I heard over CBC some time ago something had gone wrong. That's what made me sit up, I guess.'

'They're the same party,' Fife said.

'Say, what do you know?' The voice sounded pleased. 'Fancy VO2PXY picking them up – after all this time, too!'

'Listen' – Fife interrupted the distant operator's pleasure – 'these men are missing. This is Adams' deputy speaking. We've got to find them. Can you tell us anything else?'

'No. I guess not. There's nothing else to tell.'

'Did you hear them again?'

'No. Never. I listened out on the same frequency but I never heard them.'

'What frequency was it?'

'This one.'

Jessup took the microphone as Fife handed it back to him with a despairing gesture. 'Please keep on listening out, will you, VO2PXY?' he asked. 'It's urgent and important that we contact them again.'

'Sure I'll listen. I'll get all my buddies to listen, too.'

'Let us have anything you pick up. Anything. You understand, VO2PXY? *Anything*.'

'Yeah, I'll do that. Anything else?'

'No. No more. I'll sign off now, but if anything comes up – no matter how unimportant it seems or even if you're not sure – let us know. There'll be a round-the-clock watch here.'

'OK. Will do.'

Fife turned away as Jessup put down the microphone.

'It's precious little,' he said heavily. 'He couldn't even be sure it *was* them.'

'Hang on, Skip,' Jessup said slowly, reaching across the table. 'They were probably conserving power. O'Day's a good operator and he'd do it the best way he could, to get the most out of the set.' He picked up a sheaf of papers. 'Besides, don't blow your top yet, they've been identified all right. We had a couple of bearings passed on to us. Thule got a smell at 'em. They were sending out SOSs and their call sign and a long dash. It was all a bit messy. A lot of static. Never a real bread and butter contact. But they got him and took a bearing of sorts. The line from Thule crosses the coast roughly round here' – he gestured at the map on the wall. 'In north King Frederick VIII Land, up here near Lambert's Land.'

'Go on.'

'Hang on.' Jessup shuffled his papers. 'We got one or two others, too. None of 'em much. That's the worst of this damned area. The people who *ought* to have got 'em never got a whisper, yet they picked 'em up as far away as the weather station on Cumberland Sound. *They* reported a weak signal and got a rough bearing, too. Neither of them could tell whether it was reciprocal or not, of course – the signal was too weak – but, hell, they're not in Franklin or Quebec, are they? The signal could only come from the east coast. And though they were both a bit rough, they cross up here near Cape Fraser.'

It was too late that night to do anything further, but Fife spent half the night composing signals to the Americans in Thule and to all the weather stations in Greenland. Jessup silently handed him the replies when he went into breakfast the next morning.

He was in Helbergfjördur soon after nine-thirty, seeking out the *Brancard*. She was in dry dock at last, he noticed, but although there were a few patches of new red lead about her, she was still shored up, swamped under looping tangles of rope, and not much seemed to have been done.

As he walked towards her along the dock where the gulls whooped and dived over the offal from the trawlers, Schak came towards him, chewing a cigar, his shoulders hunched, obviously in a sulphurous mood as he squinted into the drizzling rain that beat across the water on the sharp Arctic wind.

'You made it then,' he said, without bothering to greet Fife. 'I'm glad you're back. You might be able to budge these obstinate sons-of-bitches. I can't.'

He snatched the cigar from his mouth and as he fell into step with Fife he flung it away so that a gull dropped down to investigate it as it fell sizzling into the water.

'I've tried chartering,' he went on, 'but they're all playing careful. Nobody wants to upset the neighbours by chartering to the British. As for that' – he gestured savagely at the *Brancard* – 'the bloody bill must be sky-high now. We've reached dry dock at last but that's about all. Nobody's hurrying.' He pulled out another cigar and stopped to light it. 'Why the hell don't you tell that bloody government of yours to stop bullying these people with their lousy destroyers. We might get something done then.'

Fife ignored his outburst. 'Let's go and see Sjøgren,' he said.

Schak spat out a fragment of tobacco. 'OK,' he said. 'I quit calling weeks ago, but I'll go along with anything you say.'

The old man in the office with the motto over the door heard them out in silence, then he shrugged.

'There's not much I can do about the *Brancard*,' he said. 'Not now. It's too late.'

'You're goddam right it is,' Schak snarled. 'About five months too late.'

'Look,' Fife said. 'We've got to have a ship. I'll take her up there just as she is, if necessary.'

Schak looked startled. 'Say, hang on,' he said. 'I'm the one who says whether she goes anywhere or not.'

'We've got to have her!'

They were all on edge, Fife with disappointment, Schak with months of frustration.

'They'll have my certificate,' he said, 'if I take a ship out to sea before she's repaired. I *can't* take her out.'

'All right, then,' Fife said. 'I'll find someone else.'

Schak glared and transferred his cigar from one side of his mouth to the other. 'You damn well won't,' he growled. 'Not my ship.'

'If *you* won't – '

'Lay off me, Fife. Who said I won't? I said I *can't*.'

'Look' – Fife was growing desperate – 'we've got the Yanks to fly every day it's clear. They've promised to put out everything they can spare. And they will, if I know the Yanks. We've got every listening station within a thousand miles alerted now. I'm going to get myself put on the coast of Greenland somehow and I'm damned if a damaged ship's going to stop me now.'

Schak scowled. 'Sure,' he said. 'That's fine. I admire your sentiments. But you run into a blow, Mister, and you and me and Hannen and the Weasels and all your goddam dogs'll be at the bottom of the Denmark Strait, and that'll help a lot, won't it? That tub's still got a hole in her side you could drive a bus through.'

They were silent, for a second, both of them driven by the fury of disappointment.

'Just lay off me,' Schak growled at last. 'That's all. And don't start telling me Adams' party'll be in a bad way. I know they'll be in a bad way. *I'd* be in a bad way after a winter up there. But there's nothing I can do. I can't take the goddam ship out – even if she were repaired. She's still under charter to the expedition committee in London.'

'The expedition's wound up.'

'The committee isn't. And I'm answerable to them.'

They were glaring at each other when the old man at the desk, who had been watching them with amused and interested eyes, interrupted mildly.

'There is just one solution,' he said. 'And nobody has bothered to inquire about it yet. Perhaps *we* can find you a ship.'

'What?' They stopped their quarrelling and swung round on him at once.

He smiled, his eyes gentle. 'Under the circumstances,' he said, 'things are now very different.'

'You said' – Schak's big shoulders hunched angrily with suspicion – 'you said you couldn't do anything about it.'

'About the *Brancard*, no. It's too late to do *anything* about that. But I told you months ago that if you received a signal from these men there would be help available.'

'What about the trawler dispute?'

The old man shrugged. 'We still accept your trawlermen in our hospitals. We give them shelter. We salvage their ships. The fact that we also later fine them for being inside our fishing limit is a different matter. Besides, it seems it was a young boy from Stakness who first picked up the information that they were alive.'

Schak and Fife glanced at each other and then back at the old man.

'What have you got?' Fife asked quickly.

'*Pinguin!* She's a very old ship,' the old man said. 'She's an auxiliary barque built in Denmark sixty years ago. She's had her rig altered, of course, but she belongs to a long line of aristocrats.'

'I don't care how old she is if she's available immediately,' Fife said. 'Can she do the job?'

'Her sides are two foot thick.'

'What power's she got?' Schak asked.

'Steam. It's as old as the ship and was only intended for an auxiliary, but although she's slow she's manoeuvrable and strong. Her dignity shows in every line and angle from her bowsprit to the brass lamp over the saloon table.'

'Radio?'

'Ship-to-shore only.'

'That doesn't matter,' Fife said. Jessup can hook up his Fifty-Three.'

'Everything would be done to assist.'

Fife turned to Schak, his eyes suddenly bright. 'What do you think?' he asked.

'She sounds all right.'

'She should be,' the old man said. 'She comes from the same line as *Fram* and *Discovery*. She'll never let you down.'

'I'll take her,' Schak said.

The old man smiled. 'I think not,' he said. 'She is my nephew's and he wouldn't let anyone handle her but himself. But I think I could talk him round. In fact' – the old man smiled – 'when we read in *Visir* this morning about the signals you'd received, we thought about your ship being in dry dock and he looked at me and we decided –'

'When can we have her?'

'She's at Reykjavik now.'

'How soon can we load?'

'She can be round this evening. It requires only a telephone call. You can use my wharf.'

Fife was watching the old man carefully. 'Once, Mr Sjøgren,' he said, 'you told me that your customers wouldn't let you do a thing like this.'

The old man nodded. 'Perhaps they still won't,' he said. 'I haven't asked them.'

'But you're prepared to take a chance?'

'Of course. Now we know they're alive.'

Fife eyed him a moment longer, admiring his courage, then he nodded.

'Mr Sjøgren,' he said. 'Your ship's chartered. It'll be paid for. I'll get it confirmed by cable from London immediately.'

'There'll be an Icelandic crew, of course.'

'Mr Sjøgren, I wouldn't mind if they were Red Indians so long as they can handle her in the ice.'

'I can promise you that.'

'We'll have everything ready by this evening. There are five of us.'

'Six,' Schak corrected him. '*Brancard* doesn't need me.'

Fife nodded and looked at the old man with shining eyes. 'Mr Sjøgren,' he said, 'if this were a proper expedition, I'd co-opt you on to the committee. And your nephew. We're in business again.'

PART FOUR

The Return

o n e

They were all very weak now, in spite of the return of the sun and the faint stirring of hope that had come with its arrival.

They had noticed first a growing brightness in the south that day by day had changed to a distinct glow, then the sky had turned blood-red through the veil of mist that gleamed and glittered in the air, and they had waited in a state bordering on worship for the sun to appear. The frozen sea had been a dull white beneath the grey-blue heavens, then the frost smoke above it had become redder still and suddenly arrows of fire had shot across the land in sparkling splendour towards the darkness that still lay in the north, throwing an orgy of colour over the mountains. They had been watching for hours on the bluff so that they shouldn't miss it, Ivey carried out in his sleeping bag, all of them silent as though at some pagan prayer, and as the blaze had flared up they had gone mad with shouts of joy.

Surely, they had thought, surely now, in spite of the fantastic cold that still remained, they would be found.

But there had been no sign from the south that anyone knew they still existed, and rations were down now to an ounce or two of bacon and pemmican a day, with the rare small bird from the soft-ice area at the end of the glacier.

It had been a disaster losing the rifle, and now that the batteries had lost their power the hope that had rested in O'Day's transmitter had faded too.

There had been an aeroplane once – some time ago now – a big DC54, perhaps from Thule or somewhere like that, which Piercey, alone on the bluff at the time, had seen flying along the shore to the south, so far away its engines were barely audible. He had watched it dwindle to a tiny dot in the sky, his throat aching with a sick disappointment, and disappear in a grey line of cloud beyond Cape Fraser, then he had sat down abruptly on the bluff, startled to find there were tears streaming down his cheeks.

He had never dared to tell the others. He wasn't sure he had the courage to watch their faces. He wasn't even sure now that he had any courage left. They were all rapidly reaching the point when nothing mattered much any more except sleep, which was the only thing that allowed them to forget their hunger.

Hunger, he had noticed with a clinical detachment, had made it harder over the past few weeks to think rationally about things, even to concentrate sufficiently to think at all. The winter had taken more out of them than they had realized. The eternal battle with the wind, the constant struggle to stay upright every time they moved from the hut, the constant sapping of their strength with the cold, these had all made inroads into their reserves of endurance. The implacable enemy was wearing them down slowly.

They couldn't go far from the hut now. Apart from Doree and Hellyer, no one seemed to have any energy left. Even O'Day seemed to be fading rapidly now. His weakness had been held at bay as long as he had had something to do, but now that there was nothing left, he appeared to have lost all interest and Piercey knew he wouldn't improve. Although Ivey could now use in a clumsy way the clawlike hands that would always remain twisted until they could be properly operated on, Piercey had had to remove three of his toes at last and he knew perfectly well he would have to remove more before long. Greeno had been saved only by Doree's dreadful haul up from the foot of the glacier, but his feet were badly frostbitten and Piercey was afraid of them going the same way as Ivey's.

As for himself, Piercey knew his movements had become as slow as an old man's and he was troubled by his growing irritability and restlessness, by the worrying headaches that had started, and by the giddiness that made him sit down from time to time to recover his reeling senses. These were all symptoms of slow starvation, he knew, and he began to watch for the swelling of his ankles and the loss of hair that would confirm them.

Blindly refusing to accept defeat, however, he had taken to watching the sky every day, hoping against hope that O'Day's signals had not been bounced back by the mountains as they all now believed. Fighting off the lethargy that was beginning to creep over them all, he still forced himself out of the hut every morning when the weather allowed, trying to ignore the belief at the back of his mind that hope was dead, stumbling dizzily to the end of the bluff where they had buried Legge-Jenkins and staring over the sea, praying that he'd see a ship there or another aeroplane.

And often, when he stood there, swaying on his unsteady legs, he wished he dared move the grave to some other point where it wasn't such an obvious reminder to them of their plight, for it stood on the end of the bluff, in the one spot where they'd been able to scrape a shallow hollow in the frozen winter soil, stark and bare as some calvary to which they would all come before long.

The blubber had all gone now and they were trying to burn the wood from the old boxes and barrels that they'd dug out of the litter in the snow at the back of the hut, but it created more smoke than flame and more often than not sent them stumbling outside, choking and with streaming eyes. And now that they no longer had any blubber, they no longer had light in the evenings and had to sit in a perpetual darkness that was like being buried alive.

Only Hellyer and Doree had any strength at all now, it seemed, and for the sake of them all, Piercey tried quietly to make sure that they got the pick of the meagre rations. Everything depended on Doree's skill as a hunter now. He was tireless in his efforts to trap game, in a way which convinced Piercey that he felt a sense of guilt at losing the rifle and a need to make up for it. He had invented snares of every kind and even managed to catch an occasional fox, but he was hampered all the time by the need to get close to his quarry and more often than not came back exhausted with the miles he had tramped in search of it.

'Doc,' he admitted, 'I can't get near 'em these days. They're too damn quick for me now.'

He and Hellyer, after their earlier disputes about Doree's rockets, had grown close together in a common unanimity about survival, and were indefatigable in their efforts to construct spears or bows and arrows from the scraps that littered the back of the hut. They slept close to each other, swopped fragments of food, and did all the odd jobs that the others were now too weak to do, prowling along the coast in a stumbling, shambling gait that betrayed their weakness, patiently searching for the terns and plovers that had begun to return.

The hut was filthy now to the point of wretchedness, the whole of the inside black with blubber and woodsmoke. Their clothes were shiny with dirt and grease, and they all looked like scarecrows with their matted hair, long beards and grimy faces and hands.

Piercey's diary was like a medical case-sheet. '*I notice,*' he wrote, '*that, when I listen to my heart, it isn't as strong or as steady as it was. Clark also complains of a fluttering pulse but this has affected us all from time to time. We are all suffering from one sort of stomach complaint or another*

and, generally speaking, hearts are weaker in every case.
There is also a lot of faintness, restlessness and headache,
loss of muscular ability and elasticity of skin. In addition, we
find difficulty in collecting our thoughts now and
concentrating. We look like skeletons, and our boots, worn
through after the winter, are no longer watertight. I tell
everyone constantly that we are only suffering a little from
insufficient nutrition but they all know perfectly well that I
mean "starvation".'

With the certainty of what ailed them all, it was becoming
harder to keep their spirits up, especially on the days when
the weather kept them in the hut and they lay in a coma of
cold and hunger, overcrowded and insanitary, with nothing
to do but think. Once Piercey had caught Ivey making his
will and taken it from him.

'We don't make our wills yet,' he had insisted firmly.
'There's time for that when we get back home.'

Ivey had shrugged. 'It'd be much better if you just let me
die, Doc,' he had said quietly, and Piercey saw that the
willingness to search the dregs of their souls for the last spark
of courage to keep them alive was wearing thin.

Ivey was staring down at the grimy sleeping bag round his
body and legs, and he went on weakly. 'Doc,' he said, 'do
you know how long it is since I last did anything useful?'

Piercey knew perfectly well how long it was. There was
not much else to do now but count the days and he knew
almost to a minute how long it was since the fire had crippled
Ivey.

'Two hundred and ninety-five days,' Ivey said and his
voice sounded desperate suddenly. 'And apart from odd
occasions, I've spent most of that time in this and dependent
on everybody else.'

'You've been a great help,' Piercey said, forcing himself to
sound cheerful.

But there were two great tears in Ivey's eyes and they rolled slowly down his cheeks and into his beard.

'You can't kid me, Doc,' he said.

They were silent for a moment, then Ivey seemed to get control of himself again.

'Do you think they'll find us soon, Doc?' he asked.

'No doubt about it.'

'There's no chance that they could miss us, or forget us, or assume we're dead, is there? I don't think I could face another winter, Doc.'

Piercey didn't reply. There would be no second winter for most of them, if help didn't come soon. They were in the paradoxical position now that, when summer came, there would be game around them, yet without a gun they would be too weak to take advantage of the fact. Some of them, perhaps, would live through another winter but by then the party would inevitably be smaller.

It seemed fantastic to Piercey that there was so little they could do for themselves in a world that was so fully equipped to help them. Even with his own fierce determination to survive, he wasn't sure any longer that he could face another season of ice – naked, glassy and grim – without any of the meagre comforts they needed to make life bearable.

Staring round at the others, he often found himself wondering which of them would die first. Ivey, he suspected, then Greeno, then perhaps O'Day, whose eyes seemed a little wild these days. He put himself, Hellyer and Doree as the last survivors, in that order, with Doree's amazing endurance carrying him on to the bitter end in a paralysing horror of utter loneliness. Then he pulled himself up sharp, realising the drift of his thoughts, and began a new, faintly hysterical searching for something that would produce a new emotion beyond the despair they all felt in their private thoughts.

At the end of April, there was a warm spell that melted a lot of the snow and exposed some of the rotting skins at the back of the hut which they hopefully turned over in search of the scraps of meat adhering to them. The ice along the shore became soft and began to retreat and an enormous frozen cathedral fell off the end of the glacier into the sea with a roar, flinging great blocks of ice through the air in ton weights and sending a vast tidal wave racing up the shore. A few shy purple flowers began to thrust themselves up and clumps of tiny white blossoms appeared in the crevices among the rocks. Plover began to be seen more often, dapper little black and white birds, and the Arctic tern and the skua, and Doree began to grow desperate as he failed to catch them.

'The ice's moving out,' Hellyer pointed out. 'We should be storing rations now for a move south to meet Fife.'

During the winter months they had often discussed the possibility of a move along the coast when the spring came. It sounded easy the way Doree had put it, but Piercey had rejected the idea, knowing that most of them didn't have the strength now for such a march. They had no portable rations, no portable stove since the end of the paraffin had rendered the last Primus useless, no tent and no rifle. Without them, they couldn't hope to survive such a journey. It was impossible, too, to carry the injured men and Piercey had no intention of leaving them behind.

In desperation, Doree had finally put forward a plan for himself and Hellyer to make a dash south to bring help but Piercey knew that without Doree's strength and Hellyer's aggressive determination the rest of them couldn't survive long enough to be saved. O'Day, Clark, East and Pink never left the hut now and there was no question of Ivey or Greeno moving. And, when he thought about it, he hadn't even much hope that Doree and Hellyer could succeed. In spite of the dregs of energy they still possessed, a march such as they planned would sap their strength in a matter of days. Yet, while it seemed better to stick together and hope, Piercey was troubled by the thought that he had no right to refuse them a chance of life while they still might conceivably produce the strength to reach safety themselves.

They ate the last of the bacon and pemmican towards the end of the month. The wind was lashing the sleet outside into a fury that depressed them all with its reminder of what lay ahead of them as the dipping arc of the season came round towards autumn again. Nobody said much as Ivey handed out the rations and they ate their meagre meal in silence. Their food boxes were all empty now and there was nothing left to drink but hot water, with a little powdered milk used so sparingly it was barely noticeable. Hopefully, Hellyer had tried the experiment of making tea from the saxifrage that had appeared but they couldn't manage to persuade their stomachs to accept it.

'We can try shrimpin',' Doree said slowly after a while.

'Never did like shrimps,' Hellyer said. 'My old man often tried me with 'em at Southend.'

'They're better than nothin'.'

'How're you going to get 'em?'

'Don't know yet. No harm in tryin' though, is there?'

Hellyer looked concerned. 'You try too bloody hard,' he said firmly.

Doree shrugged. 'Somebody's got to keep on tryin',' he said.

The following day, with the exception of Hellyer, Doree and Piercey, they didn't even bother to get out of their sleeping bags. There was no food to look forward to, no blubber to keep the stove going, no serviceable transmitter to keep their spirits up – and it was still cold enough to make them shiver immediately they left the warmth.

In the afternoon, however, the wind died down and the sleet stopped, leaving the smooth rocks of their prison black and shining as polished steel, and Doree went off alone hunting while Piercey and Hellyer experimented a little with trying to stew some of the feeble plants that grew around them. Towards evening, the wind got up again, growing stronger all the time, slapping at the worn canvas roof and driving gritty dirt into the hut. When it grew late, Piercey began to worry. Doree had never been away so long since they had lost the sledge and he began to wonder where he was.

When he didn't return, he decided to go and look for him, and he and Hellyer went down towards the bluff and stared along the shore. The pack had drifted out from the coast now, leaving a narrow channel about a mile wide in the bay. The clouds had rolled back in the rinsed air and the faint outline of snow-covered mountains to the south showed in the clear sky.

They stopped for a moment on the end of the bluff where Hellyer's restless hands had erected a flagstaff topped by the remains of an old red-checked shirt, and as they gazed towards the south, they were both hoping in their hearts that somewhere on the empty expanse they might see a dot or a puff of smoke. But the sea was devoid of movement and they paused, turning their eyes to the sky. Then Hellyer looked at Piercey.

'Doe,' he said unexpectedly. 'What's scurvy?'

The question startled Piercey. 'Scurvy?'

'You know – what these old blokes used to get.'

'Scorbutus,' Piercey explained. 'A dietary disease caused by the absence of vitamin C. They use fruit juices, vegetables and milk to keep it at bay.'

'Have any of us got it? Have I, for instance?'

'You tell *me*,' Piercey said. 'The symptoms are tender, swollen joints, loose teeth, bleeding gums, fits of giddiness and fainting.'

Hellyer gave him a bleak smile. 'Well, *I* haven't got it,' he said. 'Not yet, anyway. I've got damn near everything else, though. Rheumatism, toothache, diarrhoea, constipation, flatulence – my God, Doc, what flatulence I've got! – spavins, duck's disease and housemaid's knee. But not scurvy. Not quite. Can you die of it, Doc?'

'Yes. But we won't. They'll find us first.'

'Yes, sure. Sure they will.' Hellyer paused then went on uneasily. 'There are only a few weeks, Doc, when they can get in.'

'They'll get in. Tom Fife'll get in.'

'If he doesn't, they'll never find us alive. And time's already getting on.'

Piercey looked at him quickly but Hellyer's face was quite composed and devoid of fear.

'Doc,' he said, 'if they don't get in soon, it'll be too late. We shan't be here next year. I don't kid myself that we shall.'

They began to stumble slowly along the coast again in silence. Their situation was desperate and they both knew it, and though they had all adapted themselves to their squalid form of life, fear had become hydra-headed with hunger, uncertainty and doubt. If a rescue party wasn't ready at just the right time, they need have no fears about the following summer. There simply wouldn't be any summer the following year for most of them.

They were growing tired now, and they stopped and stood in silence to gather their strength, then Hellyer began to stare about him anxiously. 'Doc,' he said uneasily. 'There's no sign of Doree.'

They began to move on again, a little faster now, among the rocks and scree, stumbling over the rough surface as they grew more anxious, falling and staggering and losing their tempers with hunger and weariness and a sudden new fear.

'The silly bastard's overdone it,' Hellyer said nervously. 'I told him he would.'

They found Doree on his knees among the rocks, still clutching the club he'd made out of a ski. He was trying to get to his feet and the tears were rolling down his cheeks into his beard. Feebly he gestured in front of him at the body of a small goose.

'I got one,' he said. 'It got away from me, and I had to chase it. I – I don't think I'm quite the bloke I was, Doc.'

It was obvious that he'd expended his last feeble store of energy trying to catch the wounded bird and his great frame had finally given way. More than anyone, he had kept them alive with his hunting, expending everything he possessed on their behalf, until suddenly there was nothing left.

He was breathing heavily and there was a dazed disbelieving look on his face as Piercey felt for his pulse.

'I got giddy,' he said feebly. 'The old ticker's stoppin' and startin' like a grandfather clock with the spring gone. I've had it, Doc, I reckon.'

His heart was fluttering badly and Piercey, holding him against his knee, felt the panic begin to rise.

'You silly old bastard,' Hellyer was saying in a strange unsteady voice. 'You've done too much again. I kept telling you you were doing too much.'

'Have to have a lie-in,' Doree said drowsily. 'Have a good sleep. Be all right after a bit of grub.'

Piercey glanced at Hellyer and saw in his hard eyes a glimpse of the fear that he knew must be obvious in his own face.

'Come on,' he said quickly. 'We've got to get him up to the hut!'

They staggered back with Doree and got him into his sleeping bag, then they stewed the goose until its flesh was soft and pulpy and fed him a little of it.

'All right now, Doc,' Doree said wearily, his eyes closing. 'Be fine again tomorrow.'

Piercey and Hellyer stared at each other in the silent hut, watched by the others.

'Two,' Hellyer said laconically.

Piercey frowned. 'Don't be a damn fool,' he snapped.

Hellyer shrugged. 'I'll do the hunting,' he said in a flat, unemotional voice. 'I'm not as good as Doree but I'll have a go.'

It was almost as though Doree's collapse marked the end of another phase.

During the night, Ivey began to mutter to himself, his voice rising occasionally until it was so loud it woke them all up.

They struck one of their few remaining matches and crowded round him, but he began to sob uncontrollably, pushing them away feebly with his ugly hands, shaking his head from side to side in a weak show of anger.

'What is it, Doc?' Hellyer asked.

Piercey's face was grim. 'The usual,' he said. 'The same as Doree and O'Day and the others. Malnutrition. A weak state of delirium brought on by sickness, immobility and – lack of hope.'

Hellyer said nothing but Piercey knew exactly what was in his mind. Three, he was thinking. Ivey was number three.

They calmed Ivey down and made him comfortable again and returned to their sleeping bags, and Piercey sat for a while, wide awake in the darkness, his mind busy. Outside, the wind had started beating at the hut again and he could hear an empty oil drum clanging as it rolled backwards and forwards against a rock. Suddenly he felt he no longer had the courage to face daylight when it came. The interior of the hut would look as though it had been painted black with the smoke. Their faces would be black. Their hands would be black. Their clothes would be black. It would be like being in the pit of hell.

Ivey was silent now and Piercey guessed he was sleeping again, but he could hear Greeno moving, fidgeting restlessly as though he were in pain.

Four, Piercey thought immediately. Four. Greeno was number four.

t w o

The wind had been blowing from the west for some time, driving the ice off the shore, so that there was a narrow lane of land water through which they had been trying to force the *Pinguin* for days, but it had dropped again now and there was a mist over the sea, silver-grey and cold as the land mass that had brought it down from the Pole. The ship's upper works were touched with a dull film of condensation and every rope and every line was dusted with tiny droplets of moisture.

The fog hung silently over the still sea, smooth and cold, and as the long slow swell came up from astern, the *Pinguin* rolled sedately, curtseying like an old dame, her tall masts creaking and scattering drops of water from the melting hoar frost to the deck.

On the bridge, young Sjøgren, a thickset blond man in a heavy knitted jersey, glanced at the compass, watching the card move. Schak was alongside him, leaning against the binnacle, staring ahead, his face hard.

Fife stood on the bridge, fretting at the slowness of their progress and concentrating on the woolliness ahead, his senses alert, his eyes peering over the Weasels that jammed the deck, his mind listening, his brain and body tense with excitement. Then Hannen appeared alongside him, standing with hunched shoulders, his hands thrust deep into his pockets.

'Temperature's gone down with a bump,' he said. 'The ice isn't far away.'

They had pushed forward blindly since daybreak in an enclosed world of their own, hemmed in by the curtain of fog that cut off everything beyond a quarter of a mile all round, and shut out all sight of the land. Occasionally, a lump of ice, sculptured by the sea into the shape of some weird monster, appeared out of the woolly greyness ahead and glided slowly past, scraping the side of the ship with a scratching noise like the tearing of claws against the steel.

They had left Stakness exhausted from the struggle to get their equipment aboard but full of hope, but almost at once a storm had come screaming down out of the north round Jan Mayen Island, coating the ship with ice and sending them running back to the land for shelter, fuming for three days in the harbour with all the houses around them in muted colours through the driving rain against the chocolate-coloured cliffs. When they had moved off again, they had run into the ice south and east of Scoresby Sund, thick winter ice that had not yet broken up, and had had to turn towards Angmagssalik to wait.

They had used the delay to buy dogs and exercise them in teams instead of waiting until they had fought their way further north, passing the time impatiently, listening to the reports that came through from Scoresby and King Oscar's Fjord, until they received the news that the glaciers were on the move at last and that the surface of the ice was being distorted by the pressure, and splitting.

They had up-anchored at once and moved north again, picking up a Danish doctor and supplies at Scoresby, but they had barely left the shelter of the harbour again when a new patch of bad weather came pounding down the funnel of the Greenland sea, with the sky whitened out with snow and sleet and grey clouds scudding before a wind that had driven the tides across the end of the sound in vast thundering storms which forced them back to the shelter of Liverpool Land for days.

As soon as the gales had decreased, they had pushed on again, but it seemed that even the elements were against them now and as soon as the wind had dropped there had been fog, thick black fog which had coated the upper works of the ship immediately, so that they had had to work with axes to keep them free. Far behind their schedule now and beginning to fear already that they were going to miss the few short weeks of summer, they had pushed on desperately, fearing they would never reach clear water.

'This is the one bloody year of all years when the pack's not going to open,' Jessup had said in a low soured growl of frustration. 'This is the one year when a ship's not going to be able to get through.'

They were growing frantic now. Time was already growing short. They had already been held back too long and the signals they picked up from the weather stations seemed to indicate little likelihood of a general break-up of the ice.

In spite of the elements, however, they had reached the free water round Cape Alexandra at the end of May. The clear blue sea along the coast had seemed a good omen to them but they had run immediately into wide isolated floes drifting south from the pack and they had known that it was just Cape Alexandra playing its tricks, as the winds that curved down off the mountains drove the ice out from the point. Further north there would still be solid ice.

The rudder chain ceased its clanking as the helmsman corrected the yaw that the swell had started and the ship was silent again except for the creak of the rigging and the steady thumping of the ancient engine. The vessel seemed unnaturally quiet and there was a tenseness, a feeling of expectancy in the air.

The pack ice was just ahead of them somewhere in the mist, they knew, and beyond it Fraser Bay.

'There it is!' Fife spoke abruptly, and almost immediately, the lookout in the bows swung round and pointed.

'Ice ahead!'

The deck of the ship became alive at once at the shout and everyone began to swarm out from below, with binoculars in their hands as the mist began to disperse.

The coast was hazy, and difficult at first to distinguish from the frozen sea, then as the fog cleared they began to see range upon range of mountains, rising to a height of five thousand feet. The intense clarity that came from the pure dry air made them seem nearer than they were over the fantastic distortions of the pack ice, their peaks as sharp and bright as if seen through a telescope.

The clang of the engine-room telegraph came from the wheelhouse and, as the steady thump of the engines slowed, the ship's head changed course and she began to move slowly into the shifting pack, carefully skirting the edges of the gigantic snow-covered slabs that drifted together and separated again to the movements of the currents and the wind, like some gigantic uneasy jigsaw.

Young Sjøgren, a sealskin cap on his head, took his stand beside the binnacle as lookouts were posted, all staring at the unbroken line of the ice.

'Soon,' he said to Fife in his halting English. 'Soon we shall be there.'

He gave an order to the helmsman and the ship swung to the east parallel to the edge of the ice, moving just beyond the tightly packed floes that were grinding together under the swell, then he left the bridge and climbed to the crow's nest to look for a lead.

Fife watched him climbing the shrouds, a thickset enigmatic figure who, like his uncle, didn't smile much. There had been an odd feeling aboard in the first few days, for the radio news was still full of the dispute over the Icelandic fishing waters, and on their first hours out from Axel Helberg Bay they had seen the prowling Icelandic gunboats searching for offenders. The air was still jammed with the indignant chatter of British skippers and Fife had thought at first it might lead to hostility on board the *Pinguin*. But there had been no incidents and gradually he had realised that young Sjøgren and his crew had put themselves above the political disputes of their country in the need to get up to the marooned men they were seeking. It was an odd situation, a small community of human beings sinking their national differences in the cause of humanity.

There had been one or two brief skirmishes, chiefly of the aggressive Jessup's making. Jessup was a Yorkshireman from Hull whose family had been in the fishing industry for generations, and it was hard for him to avoid feeling strongly about the dispute. But Fife had got him on one side and threatened him with everything he could think of.

'It's all right for you,' Jessup had said sullenly, 'but I've got cousins on those damned trawlers.'

But he had given way in the end, for which Fife had been thankful, for he knew he couldn't manage without Jessup and he had no idea what he could have done with him if the dispute had flared into real enmity.

Obviously, young Sjøgren had talked to his own crew, too, and in spite of occasional flickerings of anger that broke out from time to time over the mess table, there had been no more quarrels.

'There is no room for discord in an affair of this kind,' he had said to Fife. 'We are here to help, not to accuse. They will still be at it when we return. Our gunboats will still be arresting your trawlers, and your destroyers will still be threatening our gunboats, and our governments will still be exchanging notes.' He smiled. 'And when we return, I shall become an Icelander again, reading my paper and demanding stronger action from my government in this affair which is threatening the economy of my country, and you will become an Englishman, indignant at the way your trawlermen are being driven from their traditional fishing grounds. Things will not change much because a few people have the sense for a short time to realise that the world can carry on without nationalities.'

They entered the ice warily for, although the weather reports were still optimistic, there was still no certainty that the ice would break up at all, this far north.

The lead they tried was a quarter of a mile wide at first but it gradually narrowed and finally a belt of hummocked and thickened ice hemmed them in. Motionless for hours, they took the opportunity to exercise the dogs which had been tethered on the boat deck, wet and miserable in their smelly kennels in the raw weather, and managed to move on again at midnight, trying to gain the open water which could be seen from the masthead. But the heavy hummocked ice persisted and they had to retreat again to the east, working round the difficult area with infuriating care and slowness that drove Fife further into his shell of silence.

The fear of a second failure nagged at him all the time, raw and worrying like a sore heel. He had burned his boats behind him in walking out of the inquiry and nothing could save his reputation now except success. Cables of encouragement kept arriving from Kinglake, isolated signals out of a world they had put behind them, and from time to time Jessup transmitted messages back to the *Recorder*, describing their difficulties and the problems they were facing, but often, as they had moved north, Fife had thought of his future. If he failed – and he knew the chances of success were not high – he could never remain in England. After all that had happened, there wouldn't be anything left for him there, and it would mean starting all over again in Canada or

Australia or America. And on the few occasions when he dared to hope that he would find Adams' party alive, he found himself wondering how he could possibly tell a man in the joy of rescue that his wife was dead and had been for almost a year. It was too much for anyone to absorb in the moment of triumph.

He still believed they *would* succeed, because to think otherwise, after so many months of trying to convince everybody he was right, would have seemed ridiculous. But, when he thought about it soberly, he had to admit there was precious little cause for optimism.

There had been no more radio reports of signals. For a while they had continued to come in, but O'Day's transmissions had grown noticeably weaker; then, abruptly and without explanation, they had stopped. The tenuous link they had established with the missing men had snapped again, and the aircraft that had flown over the Fraser Bay area had reported only bad weather or haze that had cut visibility to nil, or a maze of shadows among the rocks that had precluded seeing anything clearly. The violent air currents among the mountains that hemmed in the bay had reduced low flying to a minimum and, with everyone losing heart now that O'Day's transmitter was obviously silent again, they were moving once more into the blankness of anonymity. Whoever was left in Adams' party seemed to have vanished into thin air.

The next day, they found a fresh lead into the ice and pushed north again, moving cautiously through the small growlers and the floes that had broken off the pack, but this lead closed in, too, and they had to retreat once more.

'This damn country possesses evil spirits,' Fife said bitterly to Hannen. 'They're always there to defeat you just when you think you've beaten it.'

They were silent for a moment, both of them well aware of how short was the period when they dared approach the coast so far north. After those few brief weeks, the chances were that at the least a ship could be beset in the ice for the winter and at the worst a total loss.

'Time's going by, Pat,' Fife said bitterly. 'And we don't have all that much. Let's go and see Jessup.'

Jessup was sitting in the cabin behind the bridge which young Sjøgren had given up for the radio equipment.

He looked up as they appeared, then bent again over the dials, his fingers searching all the time.

'No,' he said as they closed the door behind them. 'I know what you're going to ask me, Skip, and the answer's "no".'

'How long, Jess?' Fife asked quietly. 'How long is it since they were last heard?'

'I don't know,' Jessup said. 'I've lost count of time.' He threw across a bundle of papers clipped together. 'That's the last one from Godhavn. They got a whisper. Since then there's been nothing.'

There was a silence as they all uneasily pondered the amount of time that had elapsed, then Jessup turned round, his red, angry face framed by the headset. 'I'm trying,' he said defensively, as though they were accusing him by their silence of neglect. 'I'm trying all the bloody time. I've never stopped trying. But there's nothing. Maybe conditions are against 'em. Their signals were pretty weak, anyway. Maybe the set's given up the ghost. Maybe' – he paused, then ended brutally – 'maybe they're dead.'

Fife didn't reply and Jessup began to regret his haste.

'I'm sorry, Skip,' he said. 'I'm sorry I said that. But we've got to face it.'

Fife still said nothing, flipping through the messages, looking for some hope that he knew was not there.

'What about the Americans?' he asked finally.

'Nothing.' Jessup ruffled through the clipped papers as Fife handed them back. 'That's their signal,' he said, jabbing with a blunt forefinger. 'They've flown all over the place and seen nothing.'

'Even over Cape Fraser?'

'They say so. But you know what it's like. You have to go down damn low to see anything. I've tried this flying lark more than once up here. And so have you. And you know how little you see. With all the lights and shadows that exist on this damn coast, things are invisible unless you're right on top of them.'

'But they *must* be there. They've got a transmitter. An aircraft would be bound to hear them, however weak they were.'

'*If they're still transmitting,*' Jessup said in a flat voice. 'I don't think they are. I think they've stopped.'

He looked up and saw Fife's face. 'Skip,' he said. 'If they were on batteries, they – ' he stopped and turned back to his set. 'Oh, hell,' he said gruffly. 'It's getting me down thinking about it.'

The search for a lead continued for another two days and, in an effort to overcome his impatience, Fife sent off a few messages to the *Recorder*, and took a few photographs about the ship. But no one had much heart to stand about looking enthusiastic. They were all beset by pessimism, and now that the weak signals from O'Day had ceased, the thought that was in all their minds was that they were too late.

Eventually, they found a lead which carried them north again but it slowly narrowed and the ice closed in on either side once more, blanketing their hopes again as the floes floated, huge and silent, alongside, closing the narrow passage through which they pressed. After a while, the engine ceased its heavy thumping as the ship glided silently towards the ice, and the tall masts lurched as she struck, setting the shrouds humming. Then the engine-room telegraph clanged and the bows lifted slowly as she began to gather way again, the raking stem forcing the ice down beneath her forefoot.

The floe cracked and two great masses of ice stood on their edges until their blue-green undersides rose clear of the water, scraping the ship's side and pulverising the barnacles along the waterline.

They fought their way forward slowly, Sjøgren moving cautiously until the floe was clear of the propeller, then the engine-room telegraph clanged and they began to force their way through a collection of small floes and brash ice until they ran up against another large floe. The engines went full ahead again, the ship lurching and staggering as the bow forced the ice apart into great blocks half an acre in size and six feet thick.

With the breeze freshening off the land, they pushed their way into small lagoons of grey-black sea ringed by a chaotic world of frozen white, towers and pinnacles and jagged teeth brushing past them towards the stern, as they forged ahead. But by evening, with flurries of rain coming down on them out of the north again, they were beset once more and facing the prospect of another retreat south, and Fife was staring towards the north with a desperation born of urgency.

The weather began to grow worse and they all watched silently as the sleet drove across the ship, lashing against the ports and freezing against the shrouds and bridge rails. Above, the clouds in the slate-grey sky were dark and lowering as they marched across the masthead.

They all knew what it meant. They were rapidly approaching the point in the year when they could expect only deterioration in conditions, and from then on the temperature would begin to fall, arcing down into the darkness again when all movement stopped and there was no sign of life.

The following day, with the sleet freezing on their oilskins as it struck them with stinging violence in its flight across the ice, they turned out with picks and crowbars and boathooks and oars, smashing the ice round the ship, putting out ice anchors and hauling with the winch, even trying to make cracks in the huge floes with explosive charges. But the pack had an infuriating elasticity that made their crowbars bounce off it and reduced the effect of Hannen's gelignite, so that Fife was working with an exhausted despair, putting all the energy of his big body into the struggle, until he was gasping and desperate with frustration. And as the wind increased they were in danger once more of being beset, of days of remaining in the same place again.

In desperation they put the dogs and sledges ashore, hoping perhaps they could force a way through to the coast, piling the equipment on the tumbled ice while young Sjøgren manoeuvred backwards and forwards, rotating the ship to keep a large circular pool clear against the pressure of the pack.

His eyes were sombre as he stared at the driving rain from the bridge. 'We shall not get much further north now,' he said. 'Danmarkshavn predicts that there will be no general break-up now.'

'None at all?' Fife's heart sank to his boots and he turned to Schak, who was chewing a cigar behind him, for confirmation.

Schak caught the look in his eyes but he shrugged, his heavy face hard. 'They've only told us what we've been expecting all along,' he said.

Fife stared at Sjøgren haggardly and the Icelander thrust his hands in his pockets and hunched his shoulders.

'We're halfway through the summer now,' he said. 'And it's only a short one. You know that as well as I do. Another week or so and then – '

'And then,' Schak ended for him as he stopped, 'we have to think of the ship, or they'll be sending a relief expedition to save *us*.'

'We've got to take a chance,' Fife said desperately.

'By all the dictates of common sense, we should go no further,' Sjøgren said.

'We *must* go further.'

Sjøgren shrugged and glanced round him at the worried faces and anxious eyes. 'Very well, we shall go further,' he said simply.

It was almost as though their courage appeased the gods. By night-time the ice had started moving again and there were signs of fresh leads opening, and they all had to scramble back on board as it became obvious that the ship was going to be able to move once more. By the following morning, they were excitedly smashing forward to the last belt of ice before they reached clear water.

They could see the details of the coast now, the grey gaunt cliffs and the rocky beaches beyond the troubled steeliness of the water, and they were all of them a little staggered by their unexpected luck. It was almost as though, for the first time in months, the elements were in their favour. The break had come so unexpectedly, it had taken them all unawares and they had had to change their plans rapidly as it became obvious they would not now be relying on the dogs and Weasels after all.

They were free of the pack by midday and into the empty water alongside the coast, moving under the jagged snow-covered peaks of Fraser Land. Fife's eyes were red-rimmed with staring. All day he had been watching the shore, hoping against hope he might see some movement.

They anchored in the deep water south of Cape Fraser that night, and with the sleet storms dying away, they all lined the ship's side, staring towards the brooding mountains, still ice-bound, that rose, tier on tier, towards the north.

The wind was falling but the sky was filling with fresh heavy clouds that looked as though they might be bringing snow, and young Sjøgren's eyes were narrow and calculating as he stared towards the black iron-bound shore.

'There will not be enough water to get round the head,' he pointed out. 'There will be no room to move. This is as far as we can go.'

Fife stared at him for a moment, then he swung round, scanning the grim outlines of the shore where a few dark birds were wheeling, stark against the ashen sky.

'We've got boats,' he said shortly.

Sjøgren eyed him, reluctantly admiring his determination.

'Very well,' he said, nodding. 'We will try the boats. Tomorrow we will put every man ashore we can spare.'

As the boats waited by the side of the ship next morning, they were all silent. Cape Fraser was a gloomy place with black granitic rocks, and in the bay to the south there was no vegetation beyond a little short scrub. It was a sad, grim country shrouded in mist, colourless and dead with a cold, savage beauty that was enough to chill the heart within them all.

'If they've been here all winter,' Jessup said quietly. 'I can only say, God help 'em.'

He had abandoned his radio and sat in the bows alongside Captain Sjøgren. Behind him was the Danish doctor from Scoresby, then Smeed and Schak and Erskine, and finally Hannen who was armed with the cameras and flash units which were strung about him until he looked like a Christmas tree.

Fife sat in the waist of the boat among the Icelandic members of the crew, remembering young Sjøgren's words with a strange clarity.

'And when I return,' he had said. 'I shall become an Icelander again and you will become an Englishman. Things will not change much because a few people have the sense for a short time to realize that the world can carry on without nationalities.'

It was a saddening thought that men who could sink their differences so easily could take them up again just as quickly when the emergency had passed.

They lowered the medical supplies and stretchers and the bundles of blankets from the ship, and Sjøgren signed to the man at the engine to start up. The wind had dropped and the water lay alongside the ship like a sheet of lead. The birds had vanished from the shore and the place looked dead, the silence hanging over them with a suffocating heaviness. The sudden cough of the engine sounded loud in the stillness, echoing back from the black sides of the *Pinguin* and thudding across the water to the shore. Sjøgren nodded to the men at the bow and stern, and they cast off and the boat thumped slowly away from the ship.

'We'll go along the shallows,' Fife said, his voice flat and unemotional, as he made a tremendous effort not to sound either excited or depressed. 'We'll split into groups of two and cover as much of the bay as we can. We might just find some sign of them, some indication of where they are.'

Sjøgren, nodded, his eyes on the shore. 'We will land on the beach beyond the head,' he said. 'The shore slopes gently there.'

They chugged their way along the dark coast and rounded the point in the shadow of the merciless crags, their eyes straining towards the land beyond the beaches. There was no sign of life, neither animal nor bird nor human being. Fraser Bay had a stark emptiness that was frightening.

Hannen hitched the cameras on his shoulders, his eyes held by the snow-veined blackness of the mountains. He was silent like the rest of them, and a little oppressed by the starkness of the scenery.

Nobody spoke as they cleared the headland, with the ice on their right pressing them so close they could feel its reflected chill. The shore had a damp depressing cold about it that reached out to them all. They could see a bluff of rocks and scree above the beach, backgrounded by the mountains, and beyond it, the blue-grey woolliness of fog.

'Fraser's hut's in the valley beyond the bluff,' Fife said.

Again nobody replied, and the boat moved rapidly over the dark water, the cliffs throwing the clatter of the engine back at them like a sounding board, the silence and the clarity picking up every cough and the tinkle of every tiny ripple as though it were amplified.

The rocks, ovoid and round where they had been worn smooth by the working of the glacier, seemed to change position as the boat moved in towards the shore at an angle, the mountains behind sliding into position, it seemed, and opening out to show the slatyness of the sky.

'There's a flag up there!' It was Jessup's voice, harsh, unexpected and excited, as he flung out an arm. 'Somebody's been here!'

Everyone broke into an excited chatter, then Hannen, his camera sweeping the shore, spoke quietly.

'There's a cairn there too,' he said. 'On the bluff. It's got a cross on top.'

'It's not the one we built when we came,' Jessup said gruffly. 'We put up no cross.'

'That looks like a grave, my friend,' Captain Sjøgren said gently, and the excited chatter died away again.

'There may be others,' the Icelander went on. 'Or they may not even have got as far as burial.'

They were staring at the shore now, trying to avoid each other's eyes, each trying to avoid the question they knew was in every face. Then Sjøgren gestured brusquely, and the man at the throttle opened it as wide as it would go and the old engine began to labour as they pushed towards the dark water at the edge of the beach.

A group of small terns appeared unexpectedly and fluttered noisily up with high thin cries as they approached, hanging over the arrowhead of ripples that followed them towards the shore; then a giant petrel swooped down from nowhere across their bows, its hoarse cry like a lament. Their eyes were all raised now to the little bluff above them, to the cairn of stones and the crooked cross that was stark against the empty sky. There was no sign of human life.

'We're too late,' Jessup said heavily. 'We're too bloody late!'

three

Doctor Piercey had spent a fitful night, not sleeping much, his eyes staring into the darkness, his mind busy with ghosts, but he was still the first awake in the morning, writing in the diary before the others were about.

'They must come soon,' he wrote. *'Or we can't survive. Ivey is much weaker suddenly. Doree looks a little better this morning but I'm afraid his long treks in search of food are over. And as Hellyer has not the same skill, there isn't much we can do now except hope and pray.'*

They ate what remained of the goose for breakfast but it had been only a small bird and the meal left them all sick at heart and silent with a still-compulsive craving for food.

When he had finished, Piercey went outside. Hellyer was preparing a sickening stew from bones and skin such as they had had to force down their throats more than once, a glutinous mess that was tasteless and useless as nutrition and only served to fill their empty stomachs momentarily, and the smell of it cooking seemed to make the squalor of the hut more depressing.

Pink looked up as he stumbled awkwardly past. They all knew where he went every day, and Pink's lip curled bitterly.

'You're wasting your time, Doc,' he pointed out. 'They've forgotten us. They forgot us long since, or they'd have been here by now.'

Piercey took no notice, and as he staggered to the end of the bluff where Hellyer had erected their flag, he noticed that the wind had dropped completely and that there was a suggestion of autumn fog in the air.

He glanced up at the ragged-ended scrap of red-checked cloth and beyond it at the sky. The sleet storms of the past few days which had silenced them all with frightening thoughts of an approaching second winter had died out now and, in spite of the grey clouds filling the heavens, the immense silence about him was filled with millions of tiny sounds, as though the earth were settling itself down again for the autumn. Surely, he told himself, trying to rouse a little ray of hope, surely they'd come soon. Surely someone would find them before it was too late!

His legs ridiculously weak, he moved along the top of the bluff, glancing towards the empty sea by Cape Fraser and to the south where the fog was thicker, his mind fiercely rejecting the idea that after all these months of hope he was going to fail.

But there was no sign of the ice breaking up out in the bay. There was just a narrow channel past Cape Fraser that was not big enough to allow a ship to pass, and he knew that the bay beyond would be just the same. To the north, the patch of clear water would be even narrower.

He turned, staring to the south again, his throat dry. They were almost halfway through the short summer already and soon they'd have passed the peak of hope. Already they had accepted that the ice was not going to open as they'd expected and, because of it, the game, with its sure instinct for self-preservation, had not returned in any numbers. Soon the sun would have reached its zenith and would begin to slide down towards the darkness of the winter again, and the chances of obtaining food would grow even slimmer. They must come soon, he said again to himself, and he found he was praying quietly under his breath.

Abruptly, he stopped, faintly ashamed of himself, There was nothing in his nature that rejected prayer, but it seemed like panic at that moment. I mustn't panic, he thought clear-headedly. I mustn't give up. Not now.

He turned as he heard a sudden rhythmic thumping sound in the air, faint and barely audible, almost like the loud beating of his own heart, and he wondered at once what on earth Hellyer was trying to make this time.

For a moment he looked back the way he had come, then the sound seemed to die away again and he stood on the edge of the bluff with trembling knees, wretchedly aware of his weakness. The thumping came again and he swung round, irritable with the instability of a hungry, frightened man.

In the name of God, he thought angrily, what's Hellyer up to now?

There had been times in the past when Hellyer's enthusiasm had become too much even for Piercey. Once it had been a sheet of tin from a flattened ration box which he had considered would make a reflector for their lamp, and once a patent stove that would enable them to get better results from the damp wood they were using, and the patient beat of his crude tools had driven them almost demented with its rhythm.

Piercey stared back towards the hut, his brows down, then suddenly, wildly, it occurred to him that perhaps something had gone wrong and the thumping was somehow connected with disaster. For a moment, his heart fluttered sickeningly at the thought of having to face another crisis, then he turned and began to run in a shambling stagger over the rocks and broken scree.

The slope he was trying to climb was loose and he fell twice, cutting his hands and banging his knee. He knew it was largely due to his weak state that he couldn't keep his balance, but something in the rhythmic thumping had started a panic inside him. It was an unfamiliar sound and all sorts of fears coursed through his mind as he stumbled frantically up the slope, feeling wildly that he no longer had the strength or the courage to withstand another emergency.

Then he caught hold of himself and forced himself to walk. Doctors didn't run, he reminded himself sternly. If there were an emergency that called for skill and knowledge, panic and trembling hands would be of no use to anybody when he arrived.

He slowed down, making himself move slowly and purposefully up the slope, but the short scramble up the rocks had made his legs wobbly and disobedient. His pulse was fluttering, too, he noticed, and he was already in no state to deal with anything that required care.

He forced himself to stop to catch his breath. Then, suddenly, he realised that the thumping he could hear wasn't coming from the hut at all, and he swung round, listening, his eyes suddenly wild, his head on one side, all his senses alert, his heart beating madly.

The sound seemed to have died, though, and he shrugged and began to move up the slope again. His ears were playing him tricks, he told himself, scornfully. Several of them had started to imagine things lately and he decided it was beginning to happen to him, too, now. But, as he listened again, he realized there *was* a thumping sound and that it was too rhythmic to be connected with any hammering of Hellyer's – a faint alien sound such as they hadn't heard for months, so unexpected his brain was refusing even to accept its existence. But he was certain now that it existed and wasn't just a figment of his imagination, and he stopped dead again, listening. For a second, he could only hear the rolling pebbles that moved down the slope away from his clumsy feet, then he heard the thumping again, rhythmic, flat and metallic. It came from the other side of the headland, and suddenly, with staggering certainty, he knew it was a boat of some sort.

He whirled round, staring towards the empty sea, then he began to run in reeling, stumbling steps towards the hut.

Hellyer was sitting in his sleeping bag, still weakly trying to bring his noxious stew to the boil, when Piercey reached the hut. He looked up quickly as he heard the sound of feet outside, quick and urgent, the sound they all dreaded for its implication of disaster.

'Now what?' he said slowly. 'Now what the hell's happened?'

He began to climb out of his sleeping bag but he was still struggling when Piercey was among them, his face haggard, his beard flying, his eyes bright, his mouth open like a fish's as he gasped for breath to blurt out his message.

'They're here,' he managed at last. 'I heard the boat! They're here! They're the other side of Cape Fraser! Tom Fife's come!'

Piercey saw their mouths open and their eyes widen. They stared at each other silently, disbelieving, then, their heads turning quickly, there was an immediate dive for the door. The blankets covering the opening were torn down as they struggled weakly through into the daylight, cursing and gasping, and the pot went flying across the fire, filling the hut with steam. Flinging aside his sleeping bag, Hellyer jumped to his feet, but he bumped into Piercey and they both stumbled and fell, while the others fought their way outside and went weaving and staggering like a lot of ghosts groping for the daylight towards the bluff. Cursing weakly, Hellyer pushed Piercey aside and, grabbing for his boots, stood swaying for a second with them in his hand as though he didn't know what to do with them, then he flung them down and went hopping, skipping and jumping clumsily after the others across the rocks in his stockinged feet.

Piercey clung to the doorway, trying to get his breath back as he dizzily watched them moving away in a wild unsteady line, first Pink, stumbling and staggering and waving his arms, then East, and Clark, and O'Day and the bootless Hellyer, all progressing at little more than a weaving unsteady walk towards the bluff, a wild tottering line of scarecrows. Doree was on his feet now, holding on to the wall and trying to make his way towards the door.

'This I am not going to miss,' he said firmly, his face set.

Greeno was struggling out of his sleeping bag, also, now.

'I'm going too,' he said grimly. 'If I never stand up again, my dogs are going to get me to that damned bluff, Doc.'

He stumbled off after Doree, staggering, and waving his arms, and reeling in great arcs, a scarecrow like the rest, then Piercey, his heart still pounding from his run, saw him fall, pick himself up and continue to move doggedly forward on hands and knees.

Piercey found he could speak now as his rasping breathing eased, and he turned to Ivey who was struggling feebly to free himself from his sleeping bag, emaciated, his clawing hands pushing at the grimy folds, his eyes shining with fever in his smoke-darkened face.

'Fife's come,' he panted. 'They'll be here any minute now, son, to take us off.'

He reached into his sleeping bag and pulled out the log-book and the notes he had kept, determined, if nothing else, that the truth of what they had endured should be known in England. Then, as he turned again towards the door to set off after the others, he saw the appeal in the boy's eyes, and, knowing what he was thinking, he stopped dead in his tracks.

'Come on,' he said. 'I'll carry you.'

Ivey's eyes glowed briefly, then he shook his head. 'You'll never manage it,' he said.

'Won't I? Just watch me.'

Slowly, Ivey heaved himself out of his sleeping bag with his twisted hands, and sat on a box, then Piercey knelt down in front of him.

'Sure you can manage, Doc,' Ivey asked.

'Just hang on. I'll get you there.'

'I'm damned heavy.'

'Not so heavy as you were.'

'I'd make a damn good jockey now.' Ivey's laugh, as he put his arms round Piercey's neck, was weak and a little hysterical.

'And I'd make a damn good horse. Unless you feel like carrying me.'

They both laughed this time, a little breathlessly, then Piercey heaved himself to his feet. He felt his muscles crack and his pulse start to pound. Then lights stabbed before his eyes in a succession of flashes, but he was up and feeling for his first step forward.

'You all right?' Ivey's voice was concerned.

'Not as strong as I was.'

'Better put me down. I'll wait.'

'Don't talk daft.'

'You'll never make it with a bloke on your back.'

'Course I will. Best bloke-carrier in all the world.'

Piercey stood in the doorway, gathering what little strength he had left, one hand on the entrance, swaying slightly, his heart pounding frighteningly. In the distance where the others had vanished, he could see their battered flag limp against the sky, and the rough cairn they had built over the body of Legge-Jenkins, and he was filled with an immense pity for the one of them who had not survived, and a terrible sadness, too, that he had not managed to save him.

Struggling to gather his strength, he glanced round the hut, and he suddenly began to wonder, with a sick horrible doubt in his own senses, if he really *had* heard a boat. The possibility that he hadn't and the dread of seeing the expression on their faces if he were wrong, made him hesitate, then the need to find out for sure grew in him to a shout and he set off towards the bluff in a winding stagger that was almost a run.

As the boat turned towards the shore, Fife saw a wild hairy figure burst over the bluff against the skyline alongside the cairn, stumbling and reeling and waving its arms. Immediately behind it came another figure, staggering like the first, then another, weaving and wavering from side to side, as though in a high wind, its tattered shirt flapping round its thin ribs, and, as the engine was cut and they glided into the shallows, they heard the sound of men's voices, weak against the immense solitude of Fraser Bay.

'There's another,' someone said, and Fife began to count, hardly daring to hope as the figures appeared, clawing their frantic way over the lip of the bluff.

'Three. Four. Five,' Jessup was calling joyously.

Hannen had jumped onto the seat in the stern of the boat with the cine-camera while one of the Icelanders held his legs and they could hear the whirring of the machinery as he directed the lens towards the land.

'I got it,' he was saying triumphantly. 'I got the very first one as he came over the top!'

Another figure appeared, limping and tottering weakly, its arms flailing the air as it groped for balance, then another just behind, moving doggedly forward on hands and knees but happily, blissfully alive.

'Six. Seven'. Jessup intoned.

They waited for more figures to breast the skyline but none came and Fife found his heart sinking. He tried to recognise the men who had appeared but it was impossible with their beards and the grime that covered their faces and hid the colour of their clothes. Then he recognised Pink's slight form and the lanky shape of O'Day.

He sought for Piercey, thinking about Rachel and praying that he was among them, too, but he couldn't see him, and he began to wonder if he was going to have the job, after all, of telling him about his wife.

'That's Pink,' Jessup was shouting as the boat ran forward over the last stretch of water. 'And Pat O'Day!'

'East,' Erskine was singing out, waving his arms wildly.

'Clark, Hellyer. And that's Doree coming down the bluff, and Greeno just behind.'

Pink and Hellyer were in the icy water now, splashing up to their knees as they came towards the boat, their eyes glowing.

'It's Fife,' they were shouting. 'It's Tom Fife,' and Fife felt this throat grow tight with thankfulness that he had finally arrived. They had so clearly been expecting him, and it made all the humiliations he had suffered, all the unhappiness, worthwhile to know that he had not let them down.

They were waist-deep in the icy water now, indifferent to the cold, hanging limply over the thwarts, shaking hands, slapping shoulders and shouting in thin cracked voices.

The grinning Icelanders heaved the boat up on to the shingle, not joining in, just watching, their eyes filled with pride and pleasure as they gazed at the ragged men who were hugging Jessup, Smeed, Erskine and Schak.

'God, where've you been?' they were saying. 'We thought you were never coming.'

'We damn near didn't,' Jessup said. 'The bastards gave you up.'

'What?' Hellyer stood with the water up to his knees, gaunt, hollow-eyed, and filthy, the beard over his ragged shirt matted with grease, the bones of his cheeks standing out in sharp angles in his face. 'Gave us up? We never gave you up. We knew you'd come. We knew you wouldn't forget.'

'Thank Tom Fife,' Jessup was saying. 'But for him, we would have.'

'Did you hear the signals?' O'Day was saying excitedly in a weak voice above the hubbub. 'Did you hear 'em?'

They were squatting on the shingle now, gasping and exhausted by the run and the excitement, and Doree, sitting down halfway from the top of the bluff, was reaching out gaunt arms for the hands that stretched out to him. Greeno was lying on his front just behind him, his head lifted, his dirty face grinning like a nigger minstrel's, then Erskine and Smeed hoisted him to his feet and sat him down the right way up, laughing, the tears running down his cheeks.

For a moment it was pandemonium with the noise and the splashing in and out of the water.

'What was it like?' someone asked and Hellyer looked up, a grin like a half-moon on his haggard face as he enjoyed with calm satisfaction the grisly truth from the distance of safety. 'Bloody awful,' he said feelingly. 'Bloody awful.'

Fife was standing on the shingle, shaking hands mechanically, his eyes still watching the land. The triumph he felt over all the smooth people who had doubted him – Mortimer, Halcrow, Doughty and the others – seemed like ashes in his mouth. He knew he had beaten them all, he knew that Kinglake would stand by his promise to drive the story round the world, but just at that moment, thinking about Rachel, it seemed an empty triumph.

Seven, his brain was telling him. Only seven!

'Where are the others,' he said abruptly, raising his voice to make himself heard above the noise. 'Where's Piercey?'

'Isn't he here?' Hellyer half-turned, and then Fife saw two more figures appear on top of the bluff, one carrying the other. Even as they appeared, the one who was doing the carrying sank slowly to his knees and they remained there, both of them on all fours staring dazedly and unbelievingly down at Fife as he scrambled frantically up the slope.

As he reached the top, the scree rolled away from his feet and he went down on his knees, too, in front of them. Ivey had struggled to a sitting position now, though Piercey was still gasping for breath and struggling to lift his head. Then they all broke into weak foolish grins and Fife climbed to his feet, his arms round Piercey, as the others scrambled up the slope. Piercey hung on to him as he rose, half-stooping, still gasping for breath, tears of relief running down his face into his beard.

'Fife,' he said. 'Tom Fife!'

As they bent over Ivey to lift him up, Piercey stood swaying, his heart filling with thankfulness and the dim awareness that he had won.

He glanced up at the scrap of red-checked shirt above his head. Nobody would bother to pull it down now, he knew, and it would flap there as long as the wind blew, until it was torn to ribbons and disintegrated into fragments of red rotten cloth on the end of a collapsing pole, a symbol of their desperate months of loneliness and isolation.

Then he felt the warmth of Fife's hand in his again and was filled with a flooding happiness at the sight of the hairless faces of the men on the beach and their clean clothes, and an immense pride that they had survived. Slowly, as he got his breath back, he straightened his shoulders and pulled himself upright, his smile full of joy, and weak, humble gratitude.

'You've been a long time,' he said simply.

JOHN HARRIS

CHINA SEAS

In this action-packed adventure, Willie Sarth becomes a survivor. Forced to fight pirates on the East China Seas, wrestle for his life on the South China Seas and cross the Sea of Japan ravaged by typhus, Sarth is determined to come out alive. Dealing with human tragedy, war and revolution, Harris presents a novel which packs an awesome punch.

A FUNNY PLACE TO HOLD A WAR

Ginger Donnelly is on the trail of Nazi saboteurs in Sierra Leone. Whilst taking a midnight paddle in a canoe cajoled from a local fisherman along with a willing woman, Donnelly sees an enormous seaplane thunder across the sky only to crash in a ball of brilliant flame. It seems like an accident... at least until a second plane explodes in a blistering shower along the same flight path.

JOHN HARRIS

LIVE FREE OR DIE!

Charles Walter Scully, cut off from his unit and running on empty, is trapped. It's 1944 and, though the Allied invasion of France has finally begun, for Scully the war isn't going well. That is, until he meets a French boy trying to get home to Paris and so what begins is an incredible hair-raising journey into the heart of the French liberation and one of the most monumental events of the war. Harris portrays wartime France in a vividly overwhelming panorama of scenes intended to enthral and entertain the reader.

THE OLD TRADE OF KILLING

Set against the backdrop of the Western Desert and scene of the Eighth Army battles, Harris presents an exciting adventure where the men who fought together in the Second World War return twenty years later in search of treasure. But twenty years may change a man. Young ideals have been replaced by greed. Comradeship has vanished along with innocence. And treachery and murder make for a breathtaking read.

JOHN HARRIS

THE SEA SHALL NOT HAVE THEM

This is John Harris' classic war novel of espionage in the most extreme of situations. An essential flight from France leaves the crew of RAF *Hudson* missing, and somewhere in the North Sea four men cling to a dinghy, praying for rescue before exposure kills them or the enemy finds them. One man is critically injured; another (a rocket expert) is carrying a briefcase stuffed with vital secrets. As time begins to run out each man yearns to evade capture. This story charts the daring and courage of these men, and the men who rescued them in a breathtaking mission with the most awesome of consequences.

TAKE OR DESTROY!

Lieutenant-Colonel George Hockold must destroy Rommel's vast fuel reserves stored at the port of Qaba if the Eighth Army is to succeed in the Alamein offensive. Time is desperately running out, resources are scant and the commando unit Hockold must lead is a ragtag band of misfits scraped from the dregs of the British Army. They must attack Qaba. The orders...take or destroy.

'One of the finest war novels of the year'
– *Evening News*

TITLES BY JOHN HARRIS AVAILABLE DIRECT
FROM HOUSE OF STRATUS

Quantity		£	$(US)	$(CAN)	€
☐	ARMY OF SHADOWS	6.99	11.50	15.99	11.50
☐	CHINA SEAS	6.99	11.50	15.99	11.50
☐	THE CLAWS OF MERCY	6.99	11.50	15.99	11.50
☐	CORPORAL COTTON'S LITTLE WAR	6.99	11.50	15.99	11.50
☐	THE CROSS OF LAZZARO	6.99	11.50	15.99	11.50
☐	FLAWED BANNER	6.99	11.50	15.99	11.50
☐	THE FOX FROM HIS LAIR	6.99	11.50	15.99	11.50
☐	A FUNNY PLACE TO HOLD A WAR	6.99	11.50	15.99	11.50
☐	GETAWAY	6.99	11.50	15.99	11.50
☐	HARKAWAY'S SIXTH COLUMN	6.99	11.50	15.99	11.50
☐	LIVE FREE OR DIE!	6.99	11.50	15.99	11.50
☐	THE LONELY VOYAGE	6.99	11.50	15.99	11.50
☐	THE MERCENARIES	6.99	11.50	15.99	11.50
☐	NORTH STRIKE	6.99	11.50	15.99	11.50
☐	THE OLD TRADE OF KILLING	6.99	11.50	15.99	11.50

ALL HOUSE OF STRATUS BOOKS ARE AVAILABLE FROM GOOD BOOKSHOPS
OR DIRECT FROM THE PUBLISHER:

Internet: www.houseofstratus.com including author interviews, reviews, features.

Email: sales@houseofstratus.com please quote author, title and credit card details.

TITLES BY JOHN HARRIS AVAILABLE DIRECT
FROM HOUSE OF STRATUS

Quantity		£	$(US)	$(CAN)	€
	PICTURE OF DEFEAT	6.99	11.50	15.99	11.50
	QUICK BOAT MEN	6.99	11.50	15.99	11.50
	RIDE OUT THE STORM	6.99	11.50	15.99	11.50
	RIGHT OF REPLY	6.99	11.50	15.99	11.50
	THE ROAD TO THE COAST	6.99	11.50	15.99	11.50
	THE SEA SHALL NOT HAVE THEM	6.99	11.50	15.99	11.50
	THE SLEEPING MOUNTAIN	6.99	11.50	15.99	11.50
	SO FAR FROM GOD	6.99	11.50	15.99	11.50
	THE SPRING OF MALICE	6.99	11.50	15.99	11.50
	SUNSET AT SHEBA	6.99	11.50	15.99	11.50
	SWORDPOINT	6.99	11.50	15.99	11.50
	TAKE OR DESTROY!	6.99	11.50	15.99	11.50
	THE THIRTY DAYS' WAR	6.99	11.50	15.99	11.50
	UP FOR GRABS	6.99	11.50	15.99	11.50
	VARDY	6.99	11.50	15.99	11.50
	SMILING WILLIE AND THE TIGER	6.99	11.50	15.99	11.50

ALL HOUSE OF STRATUS BOOKS ARE AVAILABLE FROM GOOD BOOKSHOPS
OR DIRECT FROM THE PUBLISHER:

Hotline: UK ONLY: 0800 169 1780, please quote author, title and credit card
details.
INTERNATIONAL: +44 (0) 20 7494 6400, please quote author, title,
and credit card details.

Send to: House of Stratus Sales Department
24c Old Burlington Street
London
W1X 1RL
UK

Please allow for postage costs charged per order plus an amount per book as set out in the tables below:

	£(Sterling)	$(US)	$(CAN)	€(Euros)
Cost per order				
UK	2.00	3.00	4.50	3.30
Europe	3.00	4.50	6.75	5.00
North America	3.00	4.50	6.75	5.00
Rest of World	3.00	4.50	6.75	5.00
Additional cost per book				
UK	0.50	0.75	1.15	0.85
Europe	1.00	1.50	2.30	1.70
North America	2.00	3.00	4.60	3.40
Rest of World	2.50	3.75	5.75	4.25

PLEASE SEND CHEQUE, POSTAL ORDER (STERLING ONLY), EUROCHEQUE, OR INTERNATIONAL MONEY ORDER (PLEASE CIRCLE METHOD OF PAYMENT YOU WISH TO USE)
MAKE PAYABLE TO: STRATUS HOLDINGS plc

Cost of book(s):—————————— Example: 3 x books at £6.99 each: £20.97
Cost of order:—————————— Example: £2.00 (Delivery to UK address)
Additional cost per book:————— Example: 3 x £0.50: £1.50
Order total including postage:——— Example: £24.47

Please tick currency you wish to use and add total amount of order:

☐ £ (Sterling)　☐ $ (US)　☐ $ (CAN)　☐ € (EUROS)

VISA, MASTERCARD, SWITCH, AMEX, SOLO, JCB:

☐☐☐☐☐☐☐☐☐☐☐☐☐☐☐☐☐☐☐☐

Issue number (Switch only):
☐☐☐

Start Date:　　　　　**Expiry Date:**
☐☐/☐☐　　　　　☐☐/☐☐

Signature: _____

NAME: _____

ADDRESS: _____

_____

_____

POSTCODE: _____

Please allow 28 days for delivery.

Prices subject to change without notice.
Please tick box if you do not wish to receive any additional information. ☐

House of Stratus publishes many other titles in this genre; please check our website (**www.houseofstratus.com**) for more details.